GOING DARK

THE LOST PLATOON

Monica McCarty

JOVE
New York

A JOVE BOOK
Published by Berkley
An imprint of Penguin Random House LLC
375 Hudson Street, New York, New York 10014

ISBN 9780399587702

First Printing: September 2017

Printed in the United States of America
1   3   5   7   9   10   8   6   4   2

Cover art: man © Claudio Marinesco; fire © Dmitry Pistrov
Cover design by Rita Frangie
Book design by Laura K. Corless

Praise for Monica McCarty and Her Novels

"McCarty's gift lies in writing strong characters into wildly entertaining and often unexpected scenarios."
—The Washington Post

"A master storyteller . . . McCarty breathes life into her memorable characters as they face dangerous adventures. The fresh plots, infused with romance and passion, are also brimming with history and drama."
—RT Book Reviews

"McCarty creates an enjoyable romance with torrid chemistry, appealing characters, and believable historical situations."
—Publishers Weekly

"McCarty sets up the story well and she creates multifaceted characters. . . . The love scenes are steamy and entertaining."
—Fresh Fiction

"Monica McCarty is a master of blending fact and fiction."
—Romance Junkies

"Strong, intricate plotting and believable characters keep the pages turning." *—Library Journal* (starred review)

"A mixture of passion, history, and great wit to create a tale to captivate your senses! To die for!" *—Addicted to Romance*

"Heart-wrenching . . . made a lasting impression on me."
—Under the Covers Book Blog

"Monica McCarty is an absolutely superior author! Her Highland Guard series has to be one of the absolute best Highland series out there! Fun, fast paced, fact driven, and totally fantastic!" *—Bodice Rippers, Femme Fatales and Fantasy*

"A powerful tale of love, woe, hardship, and the power of true love . . . a must read!" *—My Book Addiction Reviews*

To Veronica,
my Scotland travel partner in crime who helped this story
come to life on our second cruise through the Hebrides.
When is #3 again?

Acknowledgments

When I decided to write a contemporary series after twenty-two historical romances, it would have been a lot more daunting had it not been for the overwhelmingly enthusiastic response of my agent, Annelise Robey, and my new editor at Penguin, Cindy Hwang. Ironically, Cindy was one of the first editors I met when I joined RWA about fifteen years ago. Our paths have crossed many times over those years, and it is so nice to finally have the chance to work together. Thank you both for your confidence, excitement, and support in getting this series off the ground and running. Here's to #2!

I have had an impressive run of covers, but *Going Dark* just might be my favorite to date. A huge thanks to the art department for all the hard work they put into getting this one just right. And thanks to production and my fabulous copy editor for helping me keep the secret of my horrendous spelling, tendency to capitalize everything, and the occasional gerund. I do know the rule—I swear.

I also want to thank the 2016 Kiawah gang—Ally Carter, Sarah MacLean, and Louisa White—for helping me get this proposal written last spring, and for all of your collective wisdom about this crazy business.

Jami Alden read my first book—what became *Highlander Untamed*—about fifteen years ago, and she has been the first reader of every book since then. She knows me, my audience, and my writing style better than anyone, and I wait on the proverbial pins and needles for her always insightful comments and feedback. She can never leave me. Seriously.

Veronica Wolff pulled double duty on this book for me. Not only did she accompany me all the way to Scotland to help this book come to life; she also provided that final last-minute-assurance read to make sure I hit a few things just right.

On the latest Scotland trip, Veronica and I also had a chance to reconnect with the tour guide from our first Scottish adventure way back in 2008, Iain Watson, who came out of tour guide retirement for a special trip around the Highlands. It was my luck that Iain's new job is as an officer with Scotland's Ministry Defense Police, which as it happened became pertinent for this book. A huge thanks to Iain for the fabulous tour and the quick responses to my questions.

And finally, when I put out the word on Facebook asking whether anyone knew someone who might be able to help me with a few SEAL/navy-related questions, PJ chimed right in and offered to contact a friend who put me in touch with Paul R. I could have asked him a million questions, but I restrained myself to about a dozen. If there are mistakes, you can be assured those were ones I didn't ask. And, Paul, I owe you an A's game (or two) the next time you are on this coast.

Prologue

MAY 25, 1800 HOURS

SEALs liked to say the only easy day was yesterday. Well, Brian Murphy wished it could hurry up and get to tomorrow because today fucking sucked.

Another sharp roll of the sea sent him sideways, and he had to fight to hold on to his seat—and his lunch.

Christ, he hated this. Even a hundred feet down, the storm was making itself felt, and it was getting worse. He wasn't sure how much longer he could hold on. One more sudden lurch and the long-fought battle with the contents of his stomach was going to be over. In a big all-over-the-floor kind of way that he would never live down.

Suddenly, a sharp grating sound interrupted the constant hum. Keyed as he was to every little sound, he flinched.

"What was that?" Special Warfare Operator First Class John Donovan said in an anxious voice—which should have been Brian's first clue. "Oh God, we're all going to die!"

The words elicited their intended reaction and Brian paled,

causing Donovan to burst into laughter. He was joined by the
others close enough to have heard him. Basically the entire sub.

Donovan was just fucking with him. Brian relaxed—
marginally.

"You're looking a little nervous, MIT." Donovan hadn't
stopped grinning and his teeth flashed white in the dim, battery-
saving light of the sub as he performed last-minute adjustments
on his mask. "The government won't be too happy if you puke
all over its twenty-million-dollar new baby."

Brian, the newest member of the not officially acknowledged SEAL Team Nine, wiped the cold sweat from his brow
and forced his hands to steady as he made adjustments to his
own mask, but the rapid beat of his heart gave him away.

He *was* nervous. Who the hell wouldn't be? After almost
two and a half years of training, it was finally the real thing,
and he was anxious to prove himself. Which was damned
hard to do when he'd been gritting his teeth to fight off nausea
the entire ride.

Of course his first op had to be in a submersible—in a storm,
no less.

He didn't care if *Proteus II* was the height of American
stealth submersible dual-mode technology with all fourteen
members of the platoon seated in relative comfort—relative
dry comfort, that is, as opposed to previous "wet" submers-
ibles that had required them to be submerged in water for the
ride—he hated subs.

He hated the cramped conditions, the dank, reduced-oxygen
air, the creaking as the pressure of the water closed in around
them—he repressed a shudder—and most of all the feeling of
being locked in a tin (or in this case fiberglass) can. Buried
alive. For fifteen hours. In an Arctic storm.

Hooyah.

But leave it to Donovan to find his weakness. They all had
them. Being a SEAL didn't mean you weren't afraid of anything—it meant you knew how to control the fear and could
still perform at the highest, most elite level under extreme
conditions. He'd been handpicked for this op not because of
his Physical Screening Test scores—some of the highest ever

posted—but because of his fluency in Slavic languages, and he wasn't going to do anything to fuck it up. Sub or no sub. But give him a nice high-altitude-jump infil from a plane any day of the week.

Navy SEALs were supposed to be as at home in the water as they were on land. And he was. A sub wasn't either of them.

But if he didn't want to hear about being the SEAL who was scared of subs for the rest of his career, he'd better get himself under control. MIT was a bad enough code name for someone who'd gone to Caltech. But he was damned sure Donovan could come up with something much worse. He'd heard of one guy who'd thrown up on his first mission, and it had taken him ten years to lose the name "Cookie." As in "toss yours."

"My stomach is hurting," Brian admitted. He knew better than to deny, but he could try to deflect. "No more Mexican food in Norway. Those fish tacos sounded a hell of a lot better than they went down."

As a fellow Californian, Donovan winced in sympathy and shook his head. "It's a siren's call, FNG." Fucking New Guy— his other nickname. Why couldn't it be good ol' Murph? "The promise of a burrito or taco is hard to resist, but you'll learn. Nothing will kill your optimism like Mexican food in Europe. They try, God love 'em, but it's never quite right."

"Jesus Christ, don't get him started on Mexican food," Senior Chief Dean Baylor interjected with a glare directed at Brian. "I'm tired of his constant moaning. You'd think it was all he could eat."

"You might understand if you came from a state where they actually knew how to make it. Ranch beans and cheese sauce?" Donovan shuddered dramatically. "I think I'll be sick here along with FNG."

Actually the fucking new guy wasn't feeling so sick anymore. Brian wondered if that had been Donovan's intention. Lightening the mood seemed to be the role he'd carved out in the fourteen-member platoon. Retiarius Platoon. Named for the gladiators who killed with a net and a trident—the SEAL insignia.

Yet here they were, on their way to undertake one of the most difficult ops any SEAL team had ever attempted—an operation that put the "fuck up and you die" in "no fail"—and they were talking about Mexican food.

"It's queso, asshole," Senior Chief Baylor said. "And Tex-Mex isn't Mexican. It's a Texan improvement."

Brian looked at Donovan in horror, but he wasn't going to be the one to tell the last-person-you-want-to-piss-off senior chief that he was out of his ever-loving mind.

Another voice popped in from farther down the hull. "Those are fighting words where I come from, Tex."

Brian recognized the voice of Michael Ruiz, the third Californian in the fourteen-man platoon, although he might as well have been from another galaxy. The ganglands of South Central LA were light-years away from Pasadena, where Brian had grown up, though their houses were probably no more than twenty miles apart. Brian didn't know whether Ruiz had actually been in a gang, but he looked mean enough and had the ink on his arms to make it likely.

"My Winkler can take on your switchblade anytime, Miggy," the senior chief said.

The rest of the team laughed.

"You guys are a bunch of racist assholes," Ruiz said with a disgusted shake of his head. "Except for you, White," he said to the assistant platoon commander, Lieutenant Charles White III, aka Charles "Not" White.

"Technically I'm half a racist asshole, Miggy. My mom was as white as Hart over there. And I like both Mexican and Tex-Mex."

Only in the locker room atmosphere of the Teams could you get away with needling a Mexican guy for his "switchblade," or calling him Miguel when his name was actually Michael, or nicknaming a black guy—*half* black guy—with the last name of White "Not." But when you trusted that guy with your life on almost a daily basis—and vice versa—race was just one more potential topic to give someone shit about.

Senior Chief Baylor and Ruiz had been best friends for years, but the entire platoon was as tight as brothers. They

were the only family most of them had. That was part of why
they'd been handpicked for Team Nine. Men without families
could deploy on covert ops without anyone asking questions.

Donovan leaned closer to him as if he meant to whisper, but
he intended for the entire sub to hear him. "They're both delusional. I don't know what White's excuse is, but Baylor is from
Texas. They still think they're a separate country down there."

The senior chief just lifted an eyebrow. "This from the guy
from the People's Republic of Berkeley?"

Donovan just beamed that shit-eating grin of his. "Free
love, brother."

Senior Chief Baylor muttered a curse and shook his head.
But Brian thought there might be the barest hint of a smile
hovering around his mouth. It was hard to tell with all the
dive gear. Although Brian suspected it would be hard to tell
even without it.

Dean Baylor epitomized the old navy slang of a sea dog.
In his case, a bulldog. The senior chief was the most experienced man in the platoon and the leader to the enlisted men.
He was a no-nonsense, tough-as-nails veteran sailor in the
old-fashioned sense of the job who always seemed to have
the answer—most of the time before the question had been
asked. Even his unimaginative vanilla "Tex" code name made
sense—no one would dare give him a shitty code name like
Cookie. He was feared, loved, and respected; the men would
follow him anywhere.

"You get too much of that as it is, Dynomite."

Dynomite—not Dynamite. Brian had erroneously assumed Donovan's code name had come from his skill with
explosives. But it actually came from the TV character Kid
Dyn-o-Mite portrayed by Jimmie Walker in *Good Times*.
"Good times" were what Donovan showed women. Apparently lots of them. With the laid-back California surfer boy
thing he had going—Brian had never seen so many ugly-assed
Hawaiian shirts in his life—he probably had them lining up.
But he wasn't a surfer. Donovan had been a star water polo
player at the University of Southern California, recruited by
the SEALs after graduation.

"I told you he was delusional, MIT," Donovan replied. "It isn't possible to get too much. I'm sure they taught you that in one of your physics classes? There has to be some kind of natural law for that. Newton's law of attraction maybe?"

"It's the Law of Universal Gravitation, asshole," the senior chief said. "Isn't that right, Mr. Ivy League?"

Brian nodded but didn't take the bait. He wasn't going to point out that MIT—the school he hadn't even gone to—wasn't in the Ivy League. Instead he nodded and tried not to shudder at the thought of being called Ivy for ten years.

Donovan just smiled and shrugged. "Same difference. It all ends the same way: with me having a good time."

Brian laughed, as did the senior chief. At least he thought the gruff grunt was a laugh.

Unlike the enlisted men in the regular forces, most SEALs were college educated, but Brian was still surprised to have Newton make his way into a conversation. Especially since he knew that the senior chief had only spent a couple of years at a junior college. But Brian had learned early on that the distinction between college-educated SEALs and non-college-educated SEALs was a piece of paper.

"Five minutes to game time, boys. Be ready." The voice of Lieutenant Commander Scott Taylor stopped the ribbing cold.

Brian's sub-related nausea and nervous energy were forgotten as he, like each of the other thirteen men, went into battle mode and began the final preparations for their infil.

The platoon was calm, methodical, and cool. No one watching would ever have guessed the importance of the mission—code name Operation White Night—that they were about to embark on. It looked like just another day at the office. If going to the office could get you killed or start a war if you were caught, that is.

They weren't just going deep behind enemy lines; they were diving right into a political shit storm without a proverbial paddle.

Donovan seemed to read his mind. He smiled as he lifted his regulator to his mouth. "Welcome to the Teams, kid. Now let's go see what that crazy motherfucker is up to. And one more thing." Brian looked up. "Don't fuck up."

That was the plan.

What was the worst thing that could happen? Brian winced. Probably not something he should think about right now.

"Hooyah," Brian said with a nod before putting in his own regulator.

Mother Russia, here we come.

"Take five," Lieutenant Commander Taylor called out.

Brian's lungs were on fire as the platoon came to a stop in the small clearing. He immediately reached for a protein bar as he took a long swig from his hydration bladder. Adrenaline had kept him going for the first ten miles, but combined with the long swim in choppy water, the next five had been a struggle. Mile sixteen and he was still waiting for his second wind.

At least the spring storm that had made their swim something akin to moving through swirling concrete hadn't followed them onto shore. The boggy marshes and melting ice of the Arctic tundra that awaited them at the coast had been bad enough without the addition of precipitation.

He supposed he should be glad it had been a balmy spring day of fifteen rather than the minus-forty it could be in winter. It had warmed up quite a bit from that even as they'd left the reindeer, shrubs, and sickly-looking birch trees of the tundra for the Siberian cedar that surrounded the mountains on the west side of the Polar Urals.

Glancing at his watch, he could see that it was still twenty-five at 2350 hours. By day it might even climb to forty-five. A veritable heat wave in the Komi Republic.

Brian assumed it was just a regular rest stop until he noticed Lieutenant Commander Taylor and the platoon operations officer talking with Ruiz, the lead communicator, aka the radioman or RTO. The terminology might be antiquated—radio telephone operator—but the acronym lived on. The RTO was easily identifiable by the antenna array on his back. The satcom kept him in contact with HQ, and like every other team member he also carried the handheld radio and headset for squad communications. Although each operator on the team had his specialty, unlike many other Special Operations units, SEALs were generalists, not specialists. Each man on the team could step in and do any job if called upon.

The LC didn't look happy. Which wasn't saying much. Lieutenant Commander Taylor hadn't looked happy since he was handed this mission. He'd looked . . . focused. Intense. Determined. As if he'd just been given an impossible task that put his ass on the line. Which pretty much summed it up.

As the platoon commander and officer in charge, he was responsible for the success of the op. And even for the men of Retiarius Platoon, who were called on for the most covert, failure-isn't-an-option missions, a recon op in Siberian Russia wasn't going to be easy.

All they had to do was slip past Russia's sophisticated Arctic Sea defenses of underwater satellites, drones, and robots (check), swim over two miles in the frigid waters of the Barents Sea, and land on a remote coast of Arctic Siberia (the Venetsia region, for which there was a damned good reason no one had ever heard of it) without being detected (another check), hump twenty miles into the Polar Ural Mountains of the Komi Republic (three-quarters check), and locate an old gulag in the inaccessible wilderness that sat images showed might be being used as a secret weapons facility. Then they got to do it all over again on the way back.

And oh yeah, the whole time operate under the watchful eye of their team skipper back at the base in Hawaii, the top brass at Special Warfare Command Center in Coronado, US Special Operations Command in Tampa, Joint Special Operations Command at Fort Bragg, and POTUS—the president of the United States herself.

Thanks to a very powerful and secret new stealth drone that could evade Russia's sophisticated antidrone technology, they were beaming live right now to the Situation Room in the White House just like the op undertaken by their now famous counterpart DEVGRU (aka SEAL Team Six) in their takedown of bin Laden.

If anything went wrong, they were screwed. Not only would they likely be killed, but only a month after an American fighter plane had gone off course during a training mission and been shot down in Russian-controlled airspace, killing two airmen and nearly starting a war, the Russian president had vowed to declare war on the US if there were any more "accidental" incursions. Unlike with the fighter pilots, however, their presence couldn't be explained. No one strayed into this part of Siberia by accident.

Although there were plenty of higher-ups in the government who would only be too happy to go to war with Russia and put Ivanov in his place—including the father of one of the pilots killed who happened to be a four-star general in the Joint Chiefs of Staff—President Cartwright wasn't one of them. After the debacle in Iraq with WMDs—or rather lack thereof—she wasn't going to act without proof. Lots of proof. Which was why they were here.

But even if they did find evidence that Russia was up to something, Brian wasn't convinced that Madam President would have the balls—figuratively speaking—to do anything about it.

For years Dmitri Ivanov had been thumbing his nose at the rest of the world, violating airspace, seas, treaties, and just about everything else with impunity. He was like the coworker at the office party who drank too much and everyone stood around watching nervously, hoping he didn't do something that crossed the line so they'd have to deal with him.

Whether Ivanov would actually go through with his threat of war, Brian didn't know. But he wouldn't put it past the crazy bastard. Russia's economy had been in the shitter for too long, and the people were beginning to rumble.

What strength Russia had was in its military, and Brian suspected there was little Ivanov wouldn't be willing to do to hold on to power and save face. Even if he eventually lost the war, he could cause the US a lot of damage in the meantime.

And if Ivanov really did have some kind of doomsday weapon as intelligence seemed to suggest? He could blow them all back to the Dark Ages and even the game. It was one way to shift the balance of power.

Yes, Lieutenant Commander Taylor had reason to be worried with so much at stake, but so far everything had proceeded as planned. However, if his expression was any indication as he conferred with Ruiz and Lieutenant White, that was about to change.

Word of what was going on spread Brian's way in the form of SO3 Travis Hart. In other words, the only special warfare operator third class other than Brian, and the man who'd been the lowest on the totem pole before he joined. Hart had been the happiest man in the world to see his face.

"We lost Sauron," Hart said in his thick Mississippi accent, referring to the Sentinel stealth drone nicknamed for the powerful eye in the sky from *The Lord of the Rings* trilogy.

Travis was a country boy through and through. He drove a truck, listened to Kenny Chesney, wore nothing but roper boots and Wrangler jeans held up by belts with big, shiny buckles when they weren't on duty, and had probably held a gun before he could walk. He was also the platoon's best sniper.

Hart was about as far from Brian's liberal California upbringing as you could get. Yet there was something instantly likable about his simple "God, Country, Family" beliefs, and he and "Jim Bob" (Travis's code name) had become surprisingly close in the three weeks since Brian joined the team. Nothing brought men closer than shared pain, and being the FNG on the Teams was all about pain in its many unpleasant forms.

Before they left, Brian had been stuck with a bar bill for three hundred and fifty dollars at Hulas, their favorite local hangout in Honolulu. How nine guys—he was the designated driver until the next poor bastard FNG came along—could drink that much in Coors Light, he didn't know.

Coors Light was the beverage of choice for most SEALs. So much so that Brian had heard of a team who'd claimed to be the Coors Light Parachuting Team when questioned in bars about the presence of so many big, fit guys hanging out together. Hell, it was better than Chippendales dancers, which Donovan had claimed once—offering Hart up to the ladies to prove it.

But dancing like a stripper and being stuck with the bar bill was all part of the drill. Hazing—like surviving the infamous BUD/S training course—was how you proved you belonged.

"What happened?" Brian asked.

Problems with technology weren't uncommon with new, top-of-the-line, not-far-from-experimental technology—Team Six wasn't the only team who got to test out the new toys—and drones were prone to losing communications and occasionally crashing. Brian hoped that wasn't the case here or someone was going to lose his ass.

Hart shrugged. "Don't know. Ruiz said it suddenly cut off. They're on the satcom trying to find out what happened, but the connection is crap."

The poor radio connection didn't surprise him. Distance and topography could wreak havoc on even the best communication systems. Even if they weren't in Siberia, the trees and mountains like this could put them in a black hole.

Five minutes turned into ten as Lieutenant Commander Taylor went over to confer with the senior chief. You would think it would be the other way around, but the dynamic between officers and senior enlisted petty officers, who were often grizzled veterans with the most experience, could be tricky. Especially when both men were stubborn, proud, and natural leaders.

The exchange of words didn't take long and Senior Chief Baylor came over to relay what had obviously been decided. "Gather up, boys. We're heading out."

"Going old school, Tex?" Donovan asked.

"Looks like it," the senior chief responded with a quirk of his mouth.

"You don't seem too disappointed by our unexpected complication."

"Not having some recently graduated Ivy League liberal analyst who's never seen the outside of a cubicle second-guess the way I scratch my ass? Damned straight."

The men laughed, but they all knew that despite the freedom from oversight, they also wouldn't have Sauron to alert them to company in the area.

Brian didn't let it bother him. Crap always went wrong on ops. It was the one truism you could count on.

For the next four miles they moved as quickly as their night-vision goggles allowed in the thick brush and dense forest. According to Brian's GPS they were less than a mile away from their target when they stopped again.

He was close enough to Lieutenant Commander Taylor to hear him ask Ruiz, "Anything?"

Ruiz shook his head. "It's a brick out here. Should I try the sat phone?"

The LC shook his head. "Not unless we need to. We don't want to risk doing anything that could give us away."

Although the navy and Naval Special Warfare Command used layers and layers of encryption software, satellite phones—if they could get a signal out here with all the trees and mountains—could be vulnerable.

So no drone and no communications. This was getting better and better. That they were light on comms gear already was due both to the long swim and the hike in difficult terrain where every ounce counted, and to wanting to minimize any signals that might give them away.

But communications or no communications, it wasn't as if command could do anything if there was trouble. There weren't going to be any Blackhawks coming to get them. They were the cavalry.

Lieutenant Commander Taylor nodded as if he'd planned for the setback. He probably had. SEAL commanders had contingencies for contingencies. "Looks like we're on our own. I'm sure some of you are going to be disappointed not to be seeing yourselves replayed over and over on the screen later." He sent a knowing look in Donovan's direction.

"Ah, hell, you mean I trimmed up for nothing?" Donovan said, tugging at the short beard he wore.

"Mix in a mirror next time," Brandon Blake—Donovan's best friend and former BUD/S buddy—interjected. "You look like a caveman."

Long hair and beards (aka "relaxed grooming standards") were a theme for men in special mission units like Team Nine. It helped them blend for clandestine ops.

"Yeah, well, Hollywood and Geico commercials will have to wait," Lieutenant Commander Taylor said dryly. He looked back at the men. "We go in slow and quiet—go dark on comms. Donovan and Blake will do a quick recon, and if it looks clear, we'll proceed as planned. Any questions?"

Silence. They'd all been well briefed. When they reached the camp, they were to break off into two squads. Navy Squad under the command of Lieutenant White would investigate the dilapidated wooden barracks building that had housed the workers sixty-odd years ago, while Gold Squad under the command of Lieutenant Commander Taylor would investigate the heavily fortified concrete command building and attached mess hall, where most of the satellite activity had been detected.

Navy and Gold. The LC had obviously gone to Annapolis.

Brian had assumed that Senior Chief Baylor would go with Lieutenant White, as White was the junior officer, but the senior chief was going with the lieutenant commander—as was Brian. That probably wasn't a coincidence.

But if the senior chief resented having to watch over the FNG, he didn't show it. Although showing emotion wasn't exactly something Senior Chief Baylor seemed to do a lot of. "Stony" was putting it mildly.

The platoon started forward, moving much slower this time and communicating only when necessary by hand gestures. No talking wasn't unusual, but it was rare they didn't use sounds—tics, tweets, or others—to communicate. The LC wasn't taking any chances.

About a half mile from target, they intersected with the

dirt "road" and the rusted train tracks that had once connected
this camp to Vorkuta, the coal-mining town that had been
built around one of Russia's most notorious gulags, Vorkutlag,
and its hundred and thirty-two subcamps.

Overgrown with brush and trees, the muddy surface marked
by deep potholes that were filled with water and enormous
rocks, the road looked as though it hadn't been used since the
camp was abandoned in the '60s. It would have taken a tank
to go through here. But one hadn't. Tree limbs would have
been broken, and there would have been some sign of tracks
in all that mud.

Brian saw the two officers exchange a glance. There was
no other visible road into the camp. They'd thought that when
they got close enough and were able to look under the trees
blocking the sat images, this one would show evidence of
tracks.

Brian hoped to hell this wasn't another Iraq WMD goat
fuck, but the hairs on his arms were buzzing.

Donovan and Blake had gone ahead to scout. They returned as the rest of the platoon reached the outskirts of the
camp and gave the all-clear sign.

Lieutenant Commander Taylor gestured forward with his
hand and then held up two fingers. The two seven-man squads
broke apart. Lieutenant White and the rest of Navy Squad
skirted the camp to the west toward the barracks. Brian followed the lieutenant commander and the senior chief east to
the former command center. In addition to the two leaders
and Brian, Gold Squad consisted of Donovan, Ruiz, Hart, and
Steve "Dolph" Spivak.

Spivak's nickname had been easy to figure out. He was a
beast. *The* physical specimen in a team of guys in top condition, he bore more than a passing resemblance to Dolph Lund-
gren, the actor who'd played the Russian foe of Sylvester Stallone
in the Rocky movies.

Like Brian, Spivak spoke a handful of Slavic languages.
But when Brian had tried to talk to him in Russian, Spivak
turned that icy blue gaze on him and told him—in English—
that when he wanted to practice he'd find his Ukrainian grand-

mother, but in the Teams they spoke "fucking red, white, and blue American."

Roger that. Brian wasn't dumb enough to comment on "American." He knew a setup when he heard one.

Brian's senses flared and locked in that position as they moved toward their entry point. Christ, it was quiet. *Too* quiet. There was an eerie stillness to the air. It was the dead of night, but surely there should be some sound of animals? Birds? Leaves rustling?

The hair at the back of his neck stood on edge. His pulse quickened as he scanned the area in front of him and the shadowy contours of the camp buildings began to take shape.

Even through the lenses of his night-vision goggles, they loomed hauntingly before them like a concrete ghost town, a lifeless, austere relic of bleak Communist Russia. Hundreds of these forced labor camps had sprung up in the Stalin years—four hundred and seventy-six by one count.

God, what must it have been like to be sent here? Jail was bad enough, but being a prisoner in a Siberian gulag took bad to new levels.

Although being imprisoned in Russia probably wasn't something he should think about right now.

Brian noticed Ruiz kneel down and point to a mark in the ground. How the hell had he seen that at night? It looked to be a partial imprint from the heel of a boot. Maybe this wasn't as much of a ghost town as it seemed.

His heart pounded a little harder and the finger on the trigger of his AR-15 grew a little more twitchy.

They stopped at a padlocked gate in the rusty fence that surrounded the place. Spivak, the teams' breacher, came forward and pulled a pair of bolt cutters from his pack. One squeeze and they were in.

It was almost too easy.

Brian was the fifth man through the gate, and he fought the urge to turn back around. There was something about this place that didn't sit right with him. Was it the spirit of the men who'd lived hopeless lives and died here under the brutal yoke of Communist Russia, or was it something else?

They walked in a wide V with Donovan on point, heading across the yard toward the concrete building about fifty yards ahead of them that intel had identified as the former command headquarters.

Brian was staying close to Senior Chief Baylor as he'd been instructed, when the other man suddenly held up his hand and stopped. The men behind them stopped as well, with the lieutenant commander giving the senior chief a look that was easy to read. "What the hell are we stopping for?"

It was serious enough for Senior Chief Baylor to break the silence. In a low voice he said, "I thought I saw something. A flash in the distance." He pointed ahead of them to the south.

The men close enough to hear turned to look in the same direction, but Brian felt a shiver across the back of his neck and looked behind him instead.

Shouldn't the gate have squeaked when they opened it?

He turned around and retraced a few steps, scanning back and forth with his gun as well as his eyes. He released the finger on the trigger long enough to reach out and touch the hinges of the gate. Even with his gloves, he could feel the unmistakable slick of oil.

Someone had been here recently.

What were they missing? If no one had used the road . . .

He looked down at the ground. All those World War II documentaries he'd watched on TV might just have paid off.

He didn't realize the others were watching him. "What is it?" Lieutenant Commander Taylor asked.

"This was a mining camp, right? They would have had tunnels."

Hitler had had miles of them.

The senior chief swore. "I don't like this," he said. "Something doesn't feel right."

For once the lieutenant commander looked inclined to agree with him. He tried to contact the other squad using the radios, but no one responded. He cursed and then said to Miggy, "Try the phone."

While Ruiz tried to make contact with the sat phone, Brian

was surprised to see Lieutenant Commander Taylor pull out what looked to be a small personal sat phone. Brian recalled hearing that the LC had come from big money—one of those old families back east. He guessed so.

The lieutenant commander turned it on and tried to make a call, but it didn't appear to be getting a signal, either. Suddenly he looked at the screen, frowned, and used his thumb to hit a button. Whatever he saw there caused his face to lose color. The intense focus and determination slipped. If a look could say "Oh fuck," his did.

"We need to get out of here. Now."

"What's going on?" the senior chief asked.

"For once just follow a fucking command, Baylor!"

The LC's loss of control seemed to even surprise the senior chief.

"Fuck. Everything's dead," Ruiz said. "We're being barrage-jammed."

Was it precautionary security to hide something going on here or did someone know they were here? Either way it wasn't good. Barrage-jamming was unusual, as it knocked out a broad range of radio signals of everyone in the area.

Lieutenant Commander Taylor didn't seem surprised, but his expression seemed to turn even more grim. Whatever he'd seen on that phone wasn't good.

"I'll go find them," Brian volunteered.

"I'll go with him," the senior chief added.

"No one's going anywhere," Lieutenant Commander Taylor said angrily. "Abort," he shouted for everyone to hear. "Now!"

Senior Chief Baylor rounded on him in disbelief. "What do you mean? We can't just leave them!"

The LC seemed to snap. "It's a trap. We're sitting ducks. It may already be too late, but if I have a chance to save some of my men, I have a responsibility—"

"So do I." Before the other officer could stop him, the senior chief shot off toward the barracks.

Instinctively Brian followed him.

He heard Lieutenant Commander Taylor swear and shout

at them to stop, but they both kept running. He saw the senior chief go wide left, obviously targeting the front of the building, but Brian saw something move in one of the windows toward the rear and went right. It looked like a light of some kind.

He'd almost reached the door when a shout from behind stopped him in his tracks. "Get down!"

He turned to see the senior chief running toward him. "Incoming!"

Laser guidance. That was the light.

"Don't fuck up."

Shit. Too late.

The world exploded in fire. White-hot pain shot up and down his body from head to toe. And then, blissfully, everything went dark.

One

TWO MONTHS LATER

Annie Henderson definitely wasn't in Kansas anymore. Or Louisiana, for that matter. Edge of the world was more like it.

Seated in the guest house pub (or more accurately, the pub with a few rooms above it) in the small seaport village on the Isle of Lewis—at least she thought it was the Isle of Lewis, but it could be Harris, as the two islands were apparently connected—after three flights, including a harrowing, white-knuckled forty-five-minute ride from hell in a plane not much larger than a bathtub, Annie was feeling a long way from home and distinctly out of her comfort zone.

But that was good, right? Doing something important and making a difference couldn't be done from her living room couch by getting upset with what she saw on TV. She had to get out there. *Do* something.

"It will be an adventure," her boyfriend, Julien, had assured her. *"Don't you want to help? Do you want to see more dead dolphins and seabirds covered in oil?"*

The memories brought her up sharp. Of course she didn't.

What she'd seen on the Louisiana shoreline after the BP oil disaster had moved her so deeply it had changed her life. The wide-eyed Tulane freshman who thought she wanted to be a veterinarian had switched her major to environmental science, and after graduating pursued a PhD in marine ecology. When Annie hadn't been studying, most of her free time was devoted to the ongoing cleanup effort and the attempt to return the local habitat to its natural state.

She never wanted to see anything like that happen again. Which was why she was here. Although initially when Julien and his friends announced plans to go to Scotland to join a protest against North Sea Offshore Drilling's exploratory drilling west of the Scottish Hebrides, Annie had refused. Activism wasn't new to her, but it wasn't like her to follow a man she'd known only a short time four thousand miles away from home to a place she'd never heard of before.

But after Julien had shown her pictures of the white-sand beaches of Eriskay, the rocky promontories and seashores of Lewis, and the giant granite rock outposts in the open waters of the North Atlantic such as Rockall and Stac Lee near St Kilda that served as nesting places for fulmars, gannets, and other seabirds, she knew she wouldn't be able to enjoy the vacation she'd planned to visit her mother in Key West. So she'd thrown caution to the wind and joined her new boyfriend and his friends.

Just because so far her "adventure" wasn't exactly what she'd expected didn't mean she should overreact. She hadn't made a mistake in coming. So what if she felt a little bit like Dorothy wondering how the heck she'd gotten here? Scotland wasn't Oz and Jean Paul La Roche wasn't the Wicked Witch of the West—even if right now they both kind of seemed that way.

She supposed she couldn't really blame the Islanders for not holding out the welcome mat to the activists who'd descended en masse to the remote island. Oil brought jobs, and the Islanders considered the drilling a local matter. The activists were outsiders—who were they to interfere? But Annie hadn't expected to feel quite so . . . *conspicuous*. Which was a nicer way of saying "pariah." Her group stuck out even in the height of the summer tourist season. The dour, unsmiling locals had turned to stare at them as they entered the bar, and although they'd eventually turned away, it still felt as if their eyes were on her.

But it wasn't just the locals. The man whom Julien had been so excited for her to meet, his mentor, and the person he spoke of with such reverence she'd half expected the pope to walk in, had been a shock. She didn't know Jean Paul well enough to dislike him, but her first impression of a weasel or a ferret hadn't improved any in the two hours since they were introduced. "Bad vibe" was an understatement.

She also didn't like how he was staring at her. It was as if he was sizing her up for something. Coldly. Mercenarily. In a way that a pimp might size up a prostitute.

It made her uneasy. *He* made her uneasy.

Julien Bernard, the French graduate student who'd swept her off her feet when she met him two months ago, seemed to have picked up on his former teacher's disapproval as well. He seemed to be trying to "sell" her to Jean Paul by singing her praises. If he mentioned her "brilliant" PhD dissertation—which was the last thing she wanted to talk about after just defending it—one more time . . .

On cue, Julien said, "Did Annie tell you about her research—"

Annie looked around for a distraction—any distraction—and her eye caught on the headline of a newspaper left behind by the prior occupants of the wooden booth. "Look at this," she said, holding it up and cutting him off. "The story has made it across the pond." *Did people still say that?* She started to read from the article. "The Lost Platoon. Like Rome's famous lost Ninth Legion, the secret SEAL Team Nine has disappeared into thin air." Annie put the paper back down on the table. Allegedly the navy didn't have a SEAL Team Nine, although suspiciously they acknowledged the existence of every other number from one to ten. "I wonder what happened to them."

"Who cares?" Julien said. He gave her that charming and oh-so-French shrug and raising of the brows that made him look even more like his countryman, the actor Olivier Martinez. She'd always thought Halle Berry's ex was incredibly sexy and could admit that that might have been what initially had caught her eye at the fund-raiser a couple of months ago. But it had been their shared passion for the environment and horror at the devastation wrought on the Louisiana coastline after the disaster that forged the real bond between them.

"You shouldn't read that trash, *ma belle*. It's all lies and gossip."

At least it was entertaining. Which was more than she could say about the independent newspapers and political publications that he and his friends devoured. Annie did enough scholarly reading for her research; she didn't need it for her pleasure reading, too.

Although Julien's European charm and modern-day beatnik intellectualism were what had drawn her to him—she'd never met anyone who seemed to know so much about everything— he could definitely be a cultural snob sometimes.

She couldn't help teasing him a little. "I don't know." She flipped the paper back to the front. "The *Scottish Daily News* looks pretty good to me. And they have lots of pictures that make it so much easier to follow along."

Only Julien realized she wasn't serious. The others at the table looked alternatively appalled and embarrassed—except for Jean Paul. He looked . . . *wicked.*

"I'll get you, my pretty, and your little dog, too!"

Maybe if she tried imagining him with a green face and a pointy hat—he already had the long nose and beady eyes— she would stop thinking about far more nefarious bad guys from Mafia and cartel movies.

No luck. At least a handful of years older than the rest of them, who were all in their mid-twenties, Jean Paul looked like a villain right out of a mob movie, even down to the slicked-back hair, mole, leather jacket, and gold chains.

Men shouldn't wear bracelets. It should be a rule.

As for the others at the booth, she didn't really know any of them that well. She'd met Marie, Claude, and Sergio at Julien's apartment in New Orleans many times before they'd all traveled to Scotland together, but they'd never really welcomed her into their cabal. They weren't rude or unfriendly, just not inclusive. She took it to be a foreign thing, as they were all international graduate students like Julien, who was also a teaching fellow at the University of New Orleans.

Despite her eight years at Tulane, she hadn't held that against him for too long.

Julien smiled and shook his head, reaching for her hand to bring it to his mouth. "Forgive me. I was being a little condescending, wasn't I?"

She gave him a look that said, *You think?*

He laughed and picked up the paper. "Very well. We will discuss these missing soldiers."

"SEALs," she corrected, and then explained at his befuddled expression. "Soldiers are army. In the navy it's sailor, but SEALs are their own breed."

"Well, with any luck your SEALs are at the bottom of the ocean somewhere."

Annie knew that Julien had strong feelings about the US military—some of which she shared—but it wasn't like him to be so bloodthirsty. She frowned, noticing him sharing a look with Jean Paul. Was that it? Was he trying to impress the other man?

"Don't you think that's a little harsh?" she asked him.

Julien would have responded, but Jean Paul spoke first. "Harsh? I'd say it's justice. SEALs are nothing more than hired killers. Just because the government is their employer does not excuse what they do." He gave her a pitying look— as if she were either the most naive woman in the world or the most stupid. "Do not tell me you approve of their methods or the shadow wars that they fight? I thought Julien said you went with him to the recent rally to protest military action in Russia after your fighter pilots were caught spying."

Allegedly spying. Although the "accidentally straying off course" excuse had sounded a little suspect to her as well. The incident had nearly caused war to break out between America and Russia—the situation was still precarious. It was a game of nuclear jeopardy with the two players ready to pounce on the button.

"She did," Julien said, immediately jumping to her defense.

Though she knew the impulse had been well-intentioned, she didn't need Julien or anyone else to speak for her. She wasn't going to let his friend intimidate her. As she didn't have a bucket of water—the thought made one side of her mouth curve—she looked Jean Paul right in his mobster hit man eyes. "Just because I do not want to see us embroiled in another war does not mean I want to see innocent men killed."

Jean Paul smiled with so much condescension she was amazed he wasn't choking on it. Or maybe that was just her wishful thinking.

"I assure you that if there is any truth to that reporter's story, those men are not innocent. What do you think they were doing when they 'disappeared'? If it was legitimate, why would your government keep silent? Perhaps they do not acknowledge these men because doing so would expose their illegal activity?"

He had a point, but that didn't mean that American servicemen should be the ones to pay the price for the government's failures. "I do not like the shadow wars being fought by our Special Forces in many of the hot spots around the world any more than you do, but that's because I don't want to see any more of our servicemen who think they are doing the right thing and are only following orders killed or destroyed by war and a government that has turned them into highly skilled machines who can't adjust to real life when they return. The psychological toll it takes on them is horrible. War is all these men know how to do. Special Forces like SEALs only have it worse."

She didn't realize how passionately—and loudly—she was speaking until she finished and realized that more than just the people at her booth were staring at her.

So much for avoiding the "Loud American" cliché.

She felt the heat of a blush stain her cheeks. Pushing the painful memories of her father away, she filled the uncomfortable silence with a jest. "Anyway, who knows? Maybe Geraldo will have a TV special and get to the bottom of it."

Unfortunately she forgot that her audience was too young

and not American, and her attempt at humor was totally lost in translation.

Her ever-gallant boyfriend tried to help her out. "Geraldo?" He picked up the paper. "But I believe the reporter's name is Brittany Blake."

She shook her head, deciding it wasn't worth explaining the overly hyped TV special on the "secret" vaults of Al Capone that were opened live and contained only a couple of empty bottles. Her father used to joke about it.

In the days when he knew how to laugh.

"It was a bad joke about conspiracy theories," she said. "Forget it."

"Ah!" He laughed belatedly.

"You speak very passionately on the subject," Jean Paul said perceptively.

Oddly he seemed to approve. Not that she cared. Although for Julien's sake she wished she could like his friend. But she didn't. She'd felt as if a black cloud had descended over them since he arrived.

In response Annie gave a Gallic shrug that a French-speaking Belgian such as Jean Paul should understand. It was none of his business. "If you'll excuse me, I think I will find the ladies' room."

Making a quick escape, she heard Julien explain behind her, "WC."

She'd forgotten that Jean Paul hadn't spent much time in America. She'd learned from Julien that "bathroom" and "ladies' room" didn't translate well in Europe.

For a Tuesday night the pub was packed, and Annie had to "excuse me" her way through the crowd of men in front of the bar—there were very few women—as she made her way to the "toilet." Given the number of locals, she assumed it was a favorite hangout. Although from what she'd seen of the town, the Harbour (with a *u*) Bar & Guest House probably didn't have a lot of competition.

She had nearly made it past the long, glossy wooden bar lined with taps of ales and ciders, when the door that she'd been about to go through opened, and she had to step back to avoid being hit. Unfortunately she stumbled over someone's foot and knocked into—nearly onto—a man who was seated at the end of the bar.

Instinctively she reached out to catch herself before she fell on his lap. One of her hands found his leg, and the other . . .

Wasn't gripping rock-hard muscle.

"Oof." The grunt he made gave the location away. Even through the denim of his jeans, she could feel the unmistakable solid bulge of something else. She pulled her hand back as if it—he—were on fire.

Or maybe that was just her. Her cheeks flamed with mortified heat as she hurried to apologize. "I'm so sorry! I tripped and didn't see . . ."

The man looked up from his hunched position over his beer, and the cold, steely blue eyes that met hers from beneath the edge of his faded blue cap cut off her breath like a sharp icy wind.

Her first thought was how the hell had she missed him? Her second was *What did I do?*

He was a big guy. Tall—even with him seated on a stool, she still had to look up to meet his gaze—and broad-shouldered, he wore an oversized sweatshirt and puffy down vest that, had she not felt the evidence to the contrary, she might have thought hid a little extra bulk. But that bulk wasn't fat; it was all muscle.

The guy was built like a tank. Or maybe a prizefighter. Beneath the heavy beard—what was with those anyway?— the face that met hers had the tough, pugnacious masculinity of a Tom Hardy or Channing Tatum. Sexy as hell, but maybe a little too much to handle.

She liked men a little softer. And there was nothing soft about this guy. Not just his body, but the way he was looking at her. It might be the middle of summer, but the iciness emitting from those striking blue eyes made it feel like the dark days of December.

Shiver. She managed not to do that, instead giving him a friendly smile. "I'm sorry again. I hope I didn't hurt you."

Which hardly seemed possible, as he was about twice her size.

She expected an immediate denial, a few assurances that it was nothing, and maybe even a return smile. That was what would have happened in any bar in America. In the South it would have been given with a lazy drawl, a charming twinkle, and no doubt a ma'am or darlin' or two. In New Orleans, it would be "cher" or, as it was pronounced, "sha."

What she got was a shake of the head and a gruff grunt that she assumed was meant to serve as his acknowledgment, before he turned sharply around to hunch back over his beer.

She stood there for a moment, staring at the broad back, hunched shoulders, and straight—maybe a little shaggy—dirty blond hair beneath the faded powder blue cap.

What in the world?

She shook her head at his rudeness. Maybe this was Oz after all.

Two

The chilly exchange the night before was forgotten in the warmth of a sunny new day as Annie made her way from the guest house to the harbor along the sunny waterfront street, walking hand in hand with Julien. Ahead of them she could see the distinctly shaped ferry terminal, which looked a little bit like a sombrero, that Julien told her had once been the site of the original castle in Stornoway. The pretty Victorian stone castle that dominated the opposite side of the harbor had been built a couple of hundred years after the original castle's destruction. When she'd asked about visiting the new castle, the innkeeper told her that Lews, as it was called, wasn't open. On prodding, she'd reluctantly added that it was being converted from use as a college to a cultural center.

Annie couldn't blame the Islanders for their standoffishness—or in the case of the man last night, outright rudeness—but she wasn't used to her friendly overtures being rebuffed. She supposed it was something she would have to grow accustomed to. The activists were clearly unwanted, and the tension with the locals was only going to get worse with what they had planned.

Something big. Something that will make a difference.

Her stomach fluttered a little. The thought of what they were going to do made her even more nervous now that she was actually here. *It will be fine,* she told herself. Greenpeace did it all the time. Even Xena—Lucy Lawless herself—had done it. But climbing aboard a drillship in the middle of the North Atlantic to stage a sit-in had sounded much more exciting—and much less crazy—at home. But Julien was right. To draw media attention, they had to do something big. And sadly dramatic got attention—scientific articles didn't.

If she was suddenly having second thoughts, she pushed them away.

Once they passed the ferry terminal building, another reason the locals were likely to become even more unwelcoming came into view.

She winced at the sight of the Porta Potties, tents, and makeshift banners that filled the parking lot. With the daily influx of activists growing, and guest houses and campgrounds full, the camp was only going to get bigger and even more of an eyesore.

Julien must have been watching her closer than she realized. "Is something wrong, *ma belle*? You are not still upset about last night?"

"I wasn't upset. I just hit the jet-lag wall," she said, repeating the excuse for her unusual quietness she'd given him when they returned to their room. Not wanting to give him another opportunity to ask her impressions of Jean Paul, she motioned to the camp. "You have to admit, it's a bit of an eyesore. We aren't likely to rally the locals to our cause with that marring the chamber of commerce views around here." She looked around at the blue skies, the boats bobbing in the idyllic harbor, and the green-covered hillsides that framed it. "All those tents and banners"—not to mention the toilets—"won't make very pretty postcards."

Especially if the drilling went forward, and this turned into a permanent camp like the one on the Scottish mainland at the nuclear plant of Faslane, which had been there since 1982.

Julien smiled reassuringly, perhaps intuiting that she needed it, and squeezed her hand. "The point is to be noticed, Anne." She didn't usually like her name, which was why she went by

Annie, but if everyone pronounced Anne like Julien, she might change her mind. Instead of the hard *a*, it was soft with the emphasis on the long *n* sound. Ah-nnn. "The more unsightly and disruptive we are, the more they will be unable to ignore us," he added. "That's how it works."

Annie felt silly. She looked up at him apologetically, a lopsided grin turning her mouth. "I know. It's just that"—she shrugged—"I didn't expect this place to be so pretty."

"Which is why we are here. To keep it that way, *oui*?"

He was right. The unsightly camp was much better than oily black water, a coastline of sludge, and dead wildlife. The exploratory drilling set to begin a scant seventy miles west of Lewis, Harris, and the dozens of other islands that made up the archipelago would be devastated by a spill. There were already over seven hundred oil fields in the North Sea east of Britain, but this proposed one to the west in the North Atlantic was too close. And she had the studies to prove it. But no one wanted to listen to her research when they had their own "experts."

"*Oui*," she agreed.

Julien waved to a group of activists he knew as they walked by, still holding her hand with the other. She supposed she should be glad they weren't in such rustic conditions and that Julien had been able to find a guest room. But their time would come. They hoped to stay aboard the ship for at least a week. Long enough to bring attention to the issue.

Buoyed by the beautiful summer day and the relaxing presence of the man beside her, Annie felt her spirits lift. Whatever strange funk she'd been in since arriving, she willed it away. It would be fine. There was nothing different about Julien. He was still the exciting, smart, passionate man who had swept her off her feet. If she thought he'd been acting a little strange last night, she attributed it to her reaction to his friend. It wasn't like her to make instant judgments like that. She vowed to give Jean Paul another chance.

Once beyond the parking lot, they turned onto the dock and moorings that fronted the town center. There were a few sailboats sprinkled in among the fishing boats and trawlers. It presented a charming picture, but on closer inspection she could see that many of them appeared to have seen better days. Chipped paint and rust seemed to be the order of the day.

She wrinkled her nose. "Who are we looking for again?"

"Island Charters." Julien moved his head to the side to get a better look down the dock. "Jean Paul said there should be a hut and someone would be there to meet us."

"I'm surprised Jean Paul didn't come with us." Especially as he was the one to set up the charter that would take them on their "dive" near the exploratory drillship. Not that she was necessarily complaining about his absence.

"He is taking care of other things—there are a lot of details to work out. With your experience, he thought you would be the best person to make sure we have everything we need. I know how, uh, *particular* you are."

Annie took the comment in the teasing spirit of which it was given. Her mouth quirked. He was right. She was very particular about her dive equipment, as he'd discovered the few times they were out together in New Orleans.

But her diving and climbing skills were part of why Julien had been so insistent that she come to Scotland. They needed someone experienced, and according to Julien, the fact that she "looked like a model from that swimsuit magazine" made it even better. The cameras would love her. Annie didn't like being reduced to a "pretty face," but she was sure Julien hadn't meant it the way it sounded. Subtlety could be lost in translation.

"Point taken," she said with a self-deprecating smile. "Now, where is this boat?"

A moment later they were standing in front of the small wooden hut about the size of a phone booth. On the wall beside it was a chalk information board with ISLAND CHARTERS printed across the top and hourly rental information down below with various dive and snorkeling packages.

Docked in front of the hut was one of the most dilapidated-looking boats not resting on its side on a beach that she'd ever seen. With its chipped red hull and white wheelhouse, the MV *Hebridean* appeared to be an old tugboat that had been converted for dive use. "Old" being the operative word. She'd guess vintage early '60s.

She turned to Julien. "I hope that isn't it. If it is, Jean Paul is being robbed. Two thousand pounds for a couple days in that pile of junk?"

She caught a movement out of the side of her eye and spun back toward the boat. A man stood from where he'd been kneeling over the port side of the boat on what appeared to be a metal diver lift.

One glance was enough to figure out what he'd been doing. Her mouth pressed into a tight line as she took in the greasy piece of machinery, still dripping with oil, in his hands. He'd obviously been cleaning it in the water.

She reacted viscerally, prickling with anger that she knew was out of proportion to the offense. But anyone who'd seen what she'd seen over the past eight years would understand. Oil didn't wash away. Eventually it ended up on the bottom of the sea, where its decomposition rate slowed to almost nothing. And cumulatively it killed and destroyed.

She didn't understand how anyone could look at something as beautiful as this water and treat it like a dump. Even before the spill, she'd been conscious of it. She'd never forget the visit to Fisherman's Wharf in San Francisco when she was eight, and she'd seen the seal with a plastic six-pack holder around its neck, cutting into it like a knife. The raw wound, and the knowledge that the seal would never be able to get it off, had made her burst into tears.

It had broken her heart. It still did. She cared too much, her mother said. Maybe. But Annie didn't understand how other people didn't. How they could be so oblivious or ignorant like—

She stopped—and jolted—finally looking up into the familiar steely gaze.

It was him. The rude man from the night before, looking even more unfriendly and imposing in the daylight. He wore the same faded blue cap, but the bulky sweatshirt and vest had been replaced by a grease-stained once white T-shirt with ISLAND CHARTERS silkscreened in red across the chest. It was loose fitting, but unlike last night's clothing, it didn't hide the extremely muscular chest and arms.

The guy was built, all right. Like a longshoreman.

Why she was noticing, she had no idea. Big guys weren't normally her thing. Not since high school, at least. A disastrous date with the captain of the football team had cured her of the primitive appeal. Since then, she'd stuck to intellectuals like Julien, who spent more time in the library developing their brains than in the gym developing their muscles. At five-eleven and a hundred and seventy-five pounds, Julien was tall, but not too tall, and lean without being overly defined. This guy, on the other hand, was at least a few inches over six feet and definitely defined, although "overly" wasn't exactly the word coming to mind.

It took her a moment to realize that she was staring. Good Lord, what was wrong with her?

"Was there something you wanted?" He spoke to her, ignoring Julien.

From the sharpness of his tone, she wondered if he'd picked up on her anger and the reason for it. From his word choice, however, he'd definitely picked up on her staring, and she blushed.

"Yes, I—" She stopped, suddenly realizing something. He didn't have an accent. She frowned. "You're American."

"Canadian," he corrected, as if it wasn't any of her business—which she supposed it wasn't.

But there went the excuse she'd given him for his rudeness. It wasn't because he was a local; it was just him.

Jeez. Weren't Canadians known around the world for being nice? Clearly he hadn't gotten the message.

Julien edged in front of her, apparently taking umbrage at the other man's tone and attitude. He wore an expression she'd never seen before. It brought to mind a medieval nobleman haughtily looking down his nose at one of his serfs as if he were the lowly piss boy. "We've come to pay for the charter arranged by our friend. For Anne Henderson."

Jean Paul had put the charter under her name? Annie supposed it was easier, as she would be the one ensuring that the tanks and diving equipment were up to snuff. Oddly, despite the disreputable appearance of the boat and its captain—if that was who he was—she suspected they were. This guy looked as if he didn't mess around and knew what he was doing. Capable hard-ass came to mind. Grim, capable hard-ass. He looked like a man who hadn't had anything to smile about in a long time. She couldn't tell whether it was sadness or general grumpiness. Maybe a little of both.

The captain gave no indication that he'd noticed Julien's condescension, but something told her little got by those steely eyes.

"Must be some mistake," he said, as if he couldn't care less. Customer service obviously wasn't his strong point. "The boat isn't available."

The lie was so obvious Annie almost laughed. "Yes," she said, her gaze sweeping the empty dock. "I can see how busy you are."

His eyes turned slowly back to hers. There might have been the barest flicker of surprise at her response. Clearly he wasn't used to people challenging him.

"It probably isn't what you are looking for anyway," he said with a long knowing stare.

He'd obviously heard her pile-of-junk comment. A comment that on closer inspection might have been premature. The deck and what she could see of the boat were spotless. The dive equipment and tanks arranged neatly on racks in the center of the deck appeared to be in good condition and looked after by someone who knew what they were doing. There was precision in the way the tanks were ordered and the masks and regulators placed. Even the fins were stuck upright in tight pairs, presumably by size. She'd been on too many boats where everything was just thrown in different plastic bins.

She studied the man before her with new, more appraising eyes.

"What do you mean it isn't available?" Julien demanded angrily. She couldn't recall ever seeing him lose his temper before, but he clearly was about to do so. He, too, must have realized that the guy was lying and refusing to rent to them because of who they were. Julien's dark eyes were narrowed to pinpricks, and his mouth had curved into an ugly sneer. "We had a deal."

"Not with me, you didn't." The man hadn't moved an inch. There was nothing combative in his stance, but the threat was there all the same. *Don't fuck with me.*

Annie picked up on it, even if Julien didn't. She knew that despite the idyllic look of some of these harbors, some hid a booming illegal drug trade. Was Island Charters a cover? And if so, was he the muscle? It wouldn't surprise her; he had dangerous written all over him. Nor would it surprise her that Jean Paul would have hired a less-than-reputable charter company. What they were doing would be much easier without someone asking a lot of questions.

"Come on, Julien. Let's go," she said, pulling him away. "There's obviously been a mistake."

Julien looked as though he was going to argue, but maybe her pleas gave him the excuse to back off without losing face. Although in a contest between the two . . . there wouldn't be one.

Julien slid his arm around her waist and drew her against him protectively. But before they turned around to go, he had to get in one last comment. "Your boss is going to hear about this."

Three

Fucking douche bag.

The man the locals knew as Dan Warren watched the two protesters walk away, glad to see them go. For a minute he thought—maybe even hoped—that the feisty little American whose hand had landed in his lap the night before was going to argue with him. And even though do-gooder, antimilitary, idealistic graduate students weren't exactly high on his list, sexy, dark-haired, green-eyed, full-mouthed *Vampire Diaries* chick look-alikes—with the killer body to go along with the rest—definitely were. He could still feel the heat of her hand on him. The speed of his body's reaction was a painful reminder that he'd neglected certain areas for too long.

The instant attraction had been as surprising as it had been unwelcome—especially after that "machine" comment.

He'd noticed her the moment she walked in. Hell, every straight man in the bar had noticed her. Long, wavy dark hair, big green eyes, flawless suntanned skin, sultry red mouth, and the previously mentioned killer body. Tight ass, long legs, and a good-sized rack—a winning trifecta in his book.

But he'd quickly lost interest when he realized she was with the protest group—and the French guy. Until she'd mentioned that damned article. And her boyfriend and his friends had started in on the "hired killer" crap. He might have appreciated her defense a little more were it not for the "programmed machine too brainwashed—and stupid—to realize what they were doing" angle.

The last thing he wanted to hear was some clueless academic giving his or her point of view on what others did. On what others *died* for, damn it.

But what the hell was she doing with a little turd like that? Dan didn't like the looks of him—*Julien* (talk about a "take my lunch money" name)—and not just because he was French. Although that certainly didn't hurt. He didn't usually rely on stereotypes—unless they happened to fit. Dan was good at sizing up people, and everything about that guy rubbed him the wrong way.

He knew the type too well. Smug and condescending, Julien thought culture and education only existed in smooth-talking, upper-crust circles populated by people who liked to hear themselves talk and thought they were smart because they could quote Kierkegaard or listened to opera.

Dan had learned far more working in the real world. He had no use for passive, pretentious pseudointellectuals who probably couldn't tell north from south on a compass and did nothing for all the freedom they took for granted and let others defend. A jackass like Julien would be the last person Dan would want in his lifeboat when the shit hit the fan, but God knows the little prick would be the first one to knock everyone out of the way to get in.

He wondered what Julien and his buddies were up to. But it wasn't any of his business. And minding his business was exactly what "Dan" was going to do.

Even if it was driving him fucking crazy.

But he was still pissed off. Probably because the douche bag had gotten the last word—and guessed correctly that Dan was taking orders.

Julien was right. The boss wasn't going to be happy.

Which was confirmed a short while later when Malcolm MacDonald yelled down the hatch to the engine room, where Dan was working, for him to come up.

The man the locals referred to as "Old MacDonald"—you

couldn't make this shit up—had spent the better part of his sixty-eight years at sea as a fisherman. It was a tough life, and he wore the hardships of it on his face. Grizzled, about a hundred bills overweight—most of it in his gut—and rarely without a cigarette hanging from his mouth, in between coughing fits that made Dan think Old MacDonald would be buying the farm before he saw the other side of seventy, he conversed in grunts, curses, and glowers. Usually.

"You want to explain why I just got off the phone with an angry customer who said you refused to take them on the charter I told you about?"

Dan shrugged. "The guy was an asshole."

MacDonald exploded. "An asshole who was about to pay two thousand pounds cash for less than two days' work!"

Dan's eyes narrowed. "That's a lot of money. I told you I wouldn't run drugs for you."

It had been his one stipulation. What MacDonald did on his own time to make ends meet, he wouldn't ask. The old guy's less-than-stellar reputation in town had been one of the reasons Dan had sought him out for employment. People engaged in less-than-legal activity tended not to ask too many questions.

MacDonald's gaze narrowed right back at him. "Who said anything about drugs? They want a ride out to the drillship."

"Why?" Dan could think of a handful of reasons—none of which were good.

What was the feisty little American messed up in?

"I didn't ask. And neither should you. Asking questions isn't part of my business—you should know that." The less-than-subtle reference to Dan's own hazy background was well-taken. "They hired us to take four of them and an inflatable on an overnight dive. I hired you to captain the fucking boat, not make decisions. You got that?"

If this job wasn't so good—pretty damned perfect actually—Dan would remind the old buzzard that any scrutiny into Dan's background was likely to provoke scrutiny into MacDonald's own business "enterprises." But deciding not to press him, Dan nodded.

But he nearly reconsidered when MacDonald added, "Then

I will leave it to you to find them and fix it before they hire another company to take their money."

Dan knew exactly what "fix it" meant, and every bone in his body balked at the idea of apologizing to that smug asshole. But if he refused, he had no doubt that MacDonald would fire him. He weighed the likelihood of finding another job as good as this one and swore.

Looked as if it was time for him to eat some shit.

This sucked. Dan stood in front of the door with a brass "2" staring at him. It hadn't been difficult to find out where they were staying. When he hadn't seen them at the protester camp at the port, he'd guessed that they were at the Harbour Bar & Guest House. He'd wager what he had in his pocket— which, as he'd just cashed a check, was about two weeks of work—that *Julien* didn't do roughing it.

He lifted his hand to knock and hesitated. He didn't need this shit. He could find another boat.

If the door hadn't opened, he might have turned around.

The gorgeous brunette nearly ran into him. She gasped and then just stood there, clearly surprised to see him, with her killer mouth parted in a way that made him think of all kinds of really inappropriate things.

"Hi," he said a little more softly—and huskily—than he'd intended.

The simple greeting seemed to take her aback. It was as if she didn't know what to do with it. He supposed that was his fault. He hadn't exactly encouraged conversation in their prior exchanges.

She didn't respond right away. Their eyes met and held—and didn't let go. He felt the buzz of something hot and unwanted. But the physical attraction was there. From the uncomfortable pause, he guessed that she had felt it, too—and didn't like it any better than he did.

"Hi," she finally said.

Christ, her voice was insane. Low and throaty, and sexy as hell. She'd make a killing in phone sex.

The vaguely intimate moment was ruined by the arrival of Julien.

"What are you doing here?" he demanded, stepping in front of his girlfriend. From the frown on her face, Dan took it she didn't appreciate the show of masculine posturing.

Dan kept his expression blank. "I came to tell you there was a misunderstanding. The boat is available for you to charter."

Julien didn't disappoint, proving Dan's ability to size people up quickly and accurately. Unfortunately, although he might be a douche bag, he wasn't a stupid one. He'd quickly figured out that Dan wasn't here of his own volition and was being forced to make amends. And from the slow sneer that crept up his face, it was clear that he wasn't going to make that easy.

"A misunderstanding?" Julien repeated. "There wasn't any misunderstanding. You told us the boat wasn't available and the deal we had with your boss wasn't good with you. So if that's all . . ." He started to shut the door, but Dan held out his hand to stop him.

"That isn't all. I have the paperwork. All I need is a signature, and a fifty percent deposit."

"Don't you have something to say first?" Julien demanded, clearly savoring the prospect of making Dan grovel.

But Dan didn't engage in power plays with little girls—or men who acted like them. "I'm sorry for the confusion."

Julien's satisfied smile was punctuated by a single raised eyebrow. "I'm sure you are. But I'm afraid it's too late. After your unprofessional behavior yesterday"—Dan's jaw clenched at being scolded like a toddler—"we contacted another company."

If Dan needed proof that Julien was lying, his girlfriend's reaction was enough. Up until that point, he'd sensed her watching them both as if it were a Ping-Pong match. But now her gaze stayed on Julien, a frown between her eyes. She seemed about to object, but then slammed her mouth shut as if she'd thought better of it. Oddly Dan appreciated that. The little bastard needed upbraiding, but not publicly.

"Look. Another company isn't necessary. The boat is available if you want it."

Apparently the woman had had enough. She didn't wait for Julien to make another objection. "That will be fine," she said. "We spoke to Mr. MacDonald right before you arrived, and he told us about the, uh . . . confusion. We were just on our way to the dock. He didn't tell us you would be coming in person to apologize. Thank you."

She smiled, and despite the fact that her boyfriend had just been trying to make him look like an idiot, he found himself smiling back.

It had been so long since he'd had anything to smile about. It felt wrong, and he immediately sobered.

"Annie Henderson," she said, holding out her hand.

He took it, unable to ignore how small and soft her fingers felt enfolded in his grip—or the sudden heat that spread through him. "Dan Warren," he said.

She removed her hand from his a little too quickly. The flush on her cheeks told him that she'd noticed the connection, too. She turned to her boyfriend. "This is my, uh, Julien Bernard."

"Her boyfriend," Julien said, sliding his arm around her waist to draw her closer. He might as well have lifted his leg and peed.

That little frown between her eyes deepened. She was looking at Julien as if he were a strange beast that she'd never seen before at a zoo.

It was called territorial male.

Clearly she didn't like it. She shifted away from Julien's hold under the guise of taking the paperwork. "Should we go downstairs and find a table? I have a few questions about the boat and the dive equipment before we finalize everything."

Dan lifted his brow, a little surprised by her businesslike tone. But it was clear she took both very seriously, which he could definitely appreciate, as he did as well.

He nodded. "Shoot."

For the next hour she did exactly that, hitting him with dozens of questions about the equipment: the compressed air and other gas mixes he had available, the backups in place, the water temperature, wind speeds, lights, buoyancy compensation systems—pretty much everything he would have asked in her place.

Maybe even a few he wouldn't have thought of.

After a few minutes of sulking—probably at being ignored—Julien gave up trying to follow the conversation and stuck his nose in his phone.

By the time Annie signed the paperwork and handed Dan the deposit, he was impressed—and not dreading the job as much as he had been. Annie Henderson knew how to dive, and what SEAL—even a supposed-to-be-dead one, he thought grimly—didn't admire that in a woman?

Four

Annie tried not to squirm as Julien interrogated the poor waitress about the wine list. From what she could tell, the restaurant had a broad selection of wines from Chile, Australia, Spain, Italy, California, and even Argentina. But apparently the handful of reds from France weren't up to par.

The first time this had happened at a restaurant, Annie told herself that she was being oversensitive. Wine was obviously important to him, and Julien's worldliness was one of the things that attracted her to him. But right now she just wanted to tell him that he was being an ass. They were in a remote corner of Scotland in a small seafood restaurant, and the waitress was probably eighteen, for goodness' sake. What kind of extensive knowledge about Bordeaux did he expect?

But after their argument earlier, she didn't want to ruin the special evening that he'd arranged to make it up to her.

She didn't like the captain any more than he did, but neither had she liked Julien's attempt to humiliate the other man, forcing him to apologize and then lying about contacting another company. If she'd noticed that captain's confident, no-BS, "don't even try to mess with me" silent strength in the contest between the two men, she didn't mention it. Nor did she think too long about who had so obviously come out ahead in the exchange.

She didn't know what was wrong with Julien, but the mean-spirited, childish behavior had reflected poorly on him. She'd told him so and he'd apologized, but it still bothered her.

The waitress finally gave up and the owner came out to talk to him. After a few apologies, the owner brought out the closest thing they had to a Bordeaux. Apparently it met with Julien's rigorous standards. After going through the long, drawn-out process of tasting it, he nodded his approval. The same process had fascinated her the first time—she'd never gone out with anyone who knew anything about wine—but right now it was just adding to her irritation.

For once she wished he would just order a damned beer.

"Whatever lager you have on tap," the Canadian captain—Dan—had said when the waitress came by to take their order earlier and Julien had asked whether he wanted a glass of their wine. He'd shaken his head. *"Never acquired the taste for it."*

If Julien hadn't disliked him enough already, that had ensured it. He'd smiled superiorly, and she knew he was thinking something along the lines of "peasant."

When the waitress started to pour a glass for her, Annie felt a spark of rebellion. "I think I'll have a glass of the rosé instead."

Too bad they didn't have a white zin, but the rosé was almost as "bad" in Julien's book.

Annie didn't care. She liked blush wines. She would tell him about the time at college she and some of her friends had done the "Tour de *Franzia*," a drinking game played with the boxed "pink" wine, but he'd probably keel over and die of horror.

Instead he only gave a slight frown in her direction, before launching into another long series of questions directed at the waitress about the menu and how everything was prepared. When he started in about his girlfriend being a vegetarian, Annie stopped him. He wasn't going to make her a part of this.

Smiling apologetically at the girl, who by now was looking as though she wanted to cry, she said, "I'll just have the rocket salad to start, and the goat cheese and onion tart. Both sound delicious. Thank you."

The young girl nodded back in gratitude. Annie would make sure to slip her an extra ten pounds the next time she went to the bathroom. Julien wasn't a bad tipper, but whatever he tipped wouldn't be enough for that ordeal.

Eventually he decided on the rabbit starter and the veal entrée—exactly what Annie guessed he would order when she'd first glanced at the menu. He liked cute and fuzzy. Annie couldn't do it. She wasn't a vegetarian for health reasons; she just thought that if you ate meat you should be willing to kill for it.

Her father had taught her that the first—and only—time they went hunting together. His lesson had backfired, however, when the ten-year-old Annie refused to pull the trigger and announced that from that moment on she wouldn't eat meat. Her mother, never much on the hunting bandwagon herself, had thought it was hysterical and told him it was his own fault—Annie hadn't gotten her stubbornness or fierce set of beliefs from her.

The rare happy memory of her childhood was interrupted by Julien, asking her about her wine.

They made small talk throughout the meal, but it wasn't until she was pushing around the remnants of her fresh raspberries and chocolate mousse that Julien ventured beyond the "how is your" or "don't you like your" questions.

"Why are you being like this? I told you I was sorry, and I'm trying to make it up to you."

From his peeved expression, it was clear he thought she was being unreasonable. Was she? He had gone to the trouble of arranging a romantic dinner rather than having a curry with the rest of their group, and the prices were high for his starving-grad-student budget. But an expensive meal wasn't what she wanted. What she'd wanted was an explanation.

"I know, and I appreciate it. But I guess what happened earlier bothered me more than I realized. It wasn't like you."

At least she didn't think it was, but then again, how well did she really know him? Maybe that was what was bothering her most of all. She'd run off to Scotland on a wild adventure with a man she had known for two months, and the reality of that was catching up with her. She wasn't usually impulsive.

He'd been acting different since they arrived. Or had he? Could it be that she was only seeing him clearly now because everything else was different, too? Alone in a way they'd never been before—without her familiar surroundings and other friends around her—what she'd excused as foreign or eccentric was now just rude and . . . *weak*.

The much-hated word resonated in her ears. It had been the worst criticism her father could level on someone, and she'd always reacted against it. Just because not all men wanted to play superhero like him didn't make them weak. And ironically being a superhero had made her father exactly that.

Julien wasn't weak. He was kind and compassionate and thoughtful. He'd always treated her with consideration and respect. He was always a perfect gentleman—even when they made love. He took his time—foreplay was the national sport of France, he liked to jest—always seeing to her pleasure first. She'd never had someone spend so much time kissing her shoulders and arms. If she sometimes wished he would just hurry up, she told herself not to be ridiculous. She was lucky to have someone so considerate and romantic in her life.

She was being unfair to him. And she realized how much when he reached over to take her hand, giving it a gentle squeeze before bringing it to his mouth. "You're right, and I'm sorry. But I was jealous."

"What?" Annie was incredulous. "Of the scruffy captain?"

Julien gave her a searching look from under his indecently long lashes. "I saw the way he looked at you, and I thought you might be attracted to him."

He couldn't be serious. She might have noticed the captain's longshoreman's physique and size—it would be hard not to—but that wasn't what attracted her to a man. Admittedly he had amazingly sharp and piercing eyes, and the part of his face she could see beneath the threadbare cap and heavy beard appeared to be good-looking in that tough-guy fashion that *could* be appealing, but physical appeal wasn't what was important to her.

Or rather, it wasn't usually *all* that was important to her.

"How could you think that? *You* are what I'm attracted to. You are drop-dead gorgeous"—not to mention clean-shaven—"sophisticated, cultured, smart, and the most charming man I have ever met." The captain had about all the charm of a rock. "Not to mention that you care about the same things I do like politics and the environment." She shook her head. "Didn't you see him washing out that oily engine part in the sea? God only knows how many carbon emissions that old guzzler of a boat he captains is giving off. He probably has an old pickup truck or SUV to go along with it. A guy like that?" She shook her head. "I can't imagine anything we'd have to talk about."

"You seemed to talk about diving long enough," Julien pointed out. She bit her lip, realizing he was right. She'd felt bad for excluding him, but it was rare she had the opportunity to talk with someone who knew as much about diving as she did. Julien held her gaze and added, "And I don't think talking was necessarily what he had in mind."

The realization of what he meant made her blush. And for a moment she imagined what it would be like having that big, muscular body on top of her—naked—and that sizable column she'd had her hand wrapped around slowly pushing inside.

No. She immediately knew that he wouldn't be slow. He'd be hard and fast and probably a little rough. Just the way she imagined when she was alone in bed at night.

The wave of heat that passed through her was so powerful, so intense, she almost shuddered.

Maybe Julien was a little more right than she wanted him to be. The physical attraction had been stronger than she wanted to admit. But it didn't mean anything.

She returned the squeeze of his hand with one of her own. She rolled her thumb over his finely boned fingers. He had good hands, even if they were a little soft. But she wasn't Jerry Seinfeld; she wasn't going to get skeeved out by something as silly as "man hands"—or rather, the lack thereof.

The captain's hands had been big and rough with calluses. She frowned, remembering the cuts and burn marks as well. She'd noticed a few marks on one side of his face as well that looked recently healed. Had he been in some kind of accident? Was that why he seemed so grim?

Why was she thinking about this?

She turned back to Julien. "I think you are reading far more into it than there was. I don't think Captain Dan likes me any better than I like him. But none of that matters. The only man I have in my mind is you."

Her words seemed to convince him, and things felt back to normal as they walked back to the room hand in hand. She even felt a slight flutter of excitement when he closed the door behind them and started to kiss her. Until he turned on the light and moved on to her neck to begin the long, drawn-out process of unbuttoning her blouse.

With Julien everything was long and drawn out.

He must have sensed her withdrawal. He lifted his head and looked down at her. "What is it?"

He really was good-looking with that dark hair slumped over his brow, his dark eyes, full lips, and clefted chin. If physical attraction was so important to her—she thought with frustration, recalling her reaction to the captain—why wasn't she into this?

"Nothing," she said. "Don't stop." She tried to move his head down to her breast. She liked the way he circled his tongue on her nipple and sometimes sucked, but apparently it was too soon for that. He began to press slow kisses around her clavicle. Not the clavicle, she nearly groaned. He would be there for an hour.

Impatience rose inside her. She couldn't hold back and blurted, "Do you think we could, um, go a little faster tonight?"

He lifted his head again, his eyes narrowed. She could tell right away that she'd made a mistake. He looked mortally offended. As if she'd just impugned his honor as a lover and a Frenchman. "What do you mean? Do you not like how I make love to you?"

"Of course I do!" she exclaimed vehemently. "It's just that I'm a little tired—"

Wrong thing to say. He released her as if she were a . . . box of pink wine. His expression held the coldness that reminded her of his friend Jean Paul's. "Go to bed, then. But it won't be with me until you figure out whether you want that. All in—isn't that how you Americans say it? But you better figure it out fast. I went out on a branch for you, but there are plenty of others who can take your place."

Limb, not branch. But she didn't correct him. She'd never seen him so angry. But what was he talking about? "Julien, wait!"

But it was too late. He stormed out of the room, slamming the door behind him.

It was after midnight when Annie realized that she was going to have to find Julien and apologize. In addition to being sensitive, he apparently had a stubborn streak. As that was a character trait she understood, she figured it was up to her to make it right—even though she hadn't really done anything wrong.

But she was feeling guilty, suspecting that her less-than-amorous response to Julien might have more to do with her illicit thoughts about Captain Dan than she wanted to admit.

She didn't know what had come over her; she never should have blurted out her request like that. It was easy to see how Julien had taken it the wrong way. She hadn't been rejecting him or criticizing his lovemaking . . . exactly. She'd just wanted a little more "rip off the clothes" and not quite as much "romance."

He'd clearly overreacted—and she didn't appreciate his threat to find another woman to "replace" her if that was what he meant by that strange comment—but guilt propelled her to throw on jeans and a sweatshirt, head down into the still-crowded bar, where Sergio and Marie told her Julien had gone down to the camp with Jean Paul and some of the others, and venture out into the cool, starry night.

She sighed at the fresh brace of air. She could definitely get used to this. She loved how the temperature dropped at night here even in the summer. Because she had only lived in the South—Florida, Georgia, South Carolina and Louisiana—it was a new experience for her. Summer in the South meant hot and humid—day or night. Although at this time of year, Scotland didn't have much night. Even though it was after midnight, the sun had set only a couple of hours ago, and would rise again in about four hours. It never really got that dark in the summer—it was more like perpetual twilight.

Unfortunately, despite the more temperate weather, she hadn't escaped bugs. Instead of annoying mosquitoes, the Isle of Lewis had midges—which might even be worse. The dreaded things had swarmed them on their walk back from the restaurant earlier in the evening.

Conscious of the late hour, and used to big cities, where walking alone at night was never a good idea, Annie hurried down the waterfront street toward the ferry building. She had to go past a bar with a few men standing around smoking outside, but other than stare a little too long for politeness' sake, they didn't bother her. Her confident smile and bold "Hi" had done the trick, making them turn away like startled rabbits. Objects weren't supposed to talk.

Still, her heart was beating a little fast by the time she reached the makeshift campground and started to look around for Julien in the throng of activists. There were probably around a hundred people here now. Her nose wrinkled. From the stench, most of them seemed to enjoy smoking pot. It was a part of activist culture—which definitely leaned toward hippie—but drugs had never been her thing.

Tents filled most of the cement parking lot, but in the center a large area had been left as a communal area for cooking and eating. To one side was a large fire pit—ironically fashioned out of an old oil drum—with blankets, cheap lawn chairs, and a few ratty pieces of upholstered furniture probably recycled from a Dumpster strewn around it.

It took her a while to find Julien. With good reason. He and Jean Paul were off to the side seated opposite each other at a picnic table where the light from the fire didn't quite reach them. But she recognized the shadowy profiles of the two men. What she didn't recognize, however, was the third profile. The third profile that was bent very close to Julien's and belonged to a woman. The three of them appeared to be deep in conversation.

Thick as thieves.

Annie felt her skin prickle. There was something about the intensity of the conversation that made her uneasy. What were they talking about? And who was the blond-haired woman who was practically sitting on Julien's lap?

It couldn't be what Annie was thinking. But there was something intimate about the way they sat together that didn't feel right.

The woman inhaled from a cigarette before tapping the ash into a soda can. Annie didn't miss the three bottles of wine and the half-full glasses that were next to them. They'd obviously been here for some time. To Annie's surprise, the woman passed the cigarette to Julien. He took a long drag before handing it back as if it were the most natural thing in the world.

Since when did he smoke?

Strangely it was the sight of Julien smoking rather than the proximity of and the apparent intimacy with the woman that upset her. He'd told her he didn't smoke. Like her, he'd claimed to have a grandmother who died of lung cancer. Had he lied to her or was there another explanation?

As much as Annie wanted to storm over there and confront him, she forced herself to take a few deep breaths before she made her way around the bonfire.

"Make it happen," she heard the woman say as she approached the table from behind Julien and the woman. "I have faith in your persuasive abilities."

Something about the way she said "persuasive" made Annie's breath catch. Jean Paul, who was opposite her, looked up at the sound.

Clearly her sudden appearance had startled him. His eyes narrowed suspiciously. "Overhear anything interesting, Mademoiselle Henderson?"

She didn't like the way he was looking at her—or his threatening tone. He made it seem as if she were intentionally spying on them. She hadn't intended to overhear anything. It was they who'd been too caught up in their conversation to notice her.

So much for trying to give Julien's teacher another chance. She didn't like him.

But she wasn't going to let him bully her. She gave him an overly cheeky smile. "Not yet, but don't stop on my account. You all seemed enthralled by something." Julien and the woman next to him had turned to stare at her as soon as Jean Paul spoke. Annie turned to the woman, who was older than her long blond hair had suggested. Late thirties or maybe even forty. But whatever number, she was striking, with the ageless beauty afforded by good bone structure. "We haven't met," she said to her. "I'm Annie."

"Sofie," the other woman said, briefly meeting her gaze in the dim light before turning back to Julien. "Your boyfriend has been telling me all about you."

Annie couldn't place the accent, but it definitely wasn't French like Jean Paul's and Julien's. She would guess some part of Scandinavia. Swedish maybe?

"He has?" Annie looked at Julien, who wasn't quite as good at hiding his emotions as the other two. He definitely looked anxious about something.

"What are you doing here?" he asked.

"I came to find you. I was worried. It was getting late." She turned to the other woman, who had lit another cigarette. "How do you all know each other?"

The woman shrugged. "Here and there. It's a small world with what we do." She started to get up. "I should go."

Julien and Jean Paul started to object.

"Don't go on my account," Annie said. "I'm not staying."

She looked hopefully at Julien, but he either hadn't gotten the hint or had chosen to ignore it. Instead he looked relieved that she wasn't going to ruin his night. "Don't wait up for me. Some of the guys are going to sing later, and they asked me to play."

Julien played guitar. Not well, but enough to strum along.

"I can walk you back if you'd like," Jean Paul offered.

Good God, no! Every instinct revolted at the thought.

Annie shook her head—hopefully with less vehemence than she felt. "That's all right. I'll be fine. It's only a few blocks."

Before anyone could argue, she gave a short wave. "See you later." And took off back through the crowded parking lot of partiers.

She had a few offers to stay along the way—"Hey, beautiful, what's the hurry?"—but after extracting her arm from a couple of playful grabs, she was back out on the waterfront street inhaling fresh, un-cannabis-laced air.

Angry, and more than a little hurt by Julien's dismissiveness, she wasn't paying attention to her surroundings. Too late, she realized someone was behind her.

Five

Dan Warren, aka Senior Chief Dean Baylor, needed a drink. Which was exactly why he wasn't going to get one. Having a drunk for a mother had taught him a few things at least.

It was what had kept him from the bottle these past two months after the goat fuck in Russia. Men dying was part of the gig. They all knew that. Dean had had men die on him before. But not like this. Not so many. It wasn't the kind of thing you got over. Process? Accept? Maybe. But get over? Never.

The fact that any of them had walked out of there at all was something of a miracle. They should all be dead. And whoever was responsible for this was going to wish they were. Dean was going to make damned sure of it.

But not from here. Not doing this. And the frustration of having his hands tied was getting to him.

As he walked along the waterfront, leaving the boat tied up on the dock behind him, he knew he'd better find another outlet for his foul mood or he was going to explode.

At 0130 hours his choices were pretty limited. He thought about returning to the dock and going for a swim but didn't want to take the chance that someone would see him, and wonder what the hell he was doing swimming in the ocean in the middle of the night.

Maybe a run? A long hike?

Sex?

He nearly groaned. God, that sounded perfect.

But knowing it wasn't in the cards, he cursed. Great. Now his body was teeming with even more frustration, which wasn't what he needed after another long, fruitless night patrolling the shipping lanes around Scotland looking for . . .

He had no fucking idea.

A needle in the proverbial haystack?

Keyser Söze?

It felt like a little of both. Even if the Russian sub seen in these waters a few months ago was here now, finding it would take something along the lines of a miracle.

Dean's nighttime forays over the past few weeks when the dive boat wasn't being used sure as hell weren't getting him any closer to an answer.

But he had to start somewhere. That his best option was returning to the place of the platoon's last deployment before the op to Russia said a hell of a lot about what he had to go on. Which—other than that the Russians had known they were coming—was squat. But the British government had sought their help in tracking down Russian sub incursions in the waters around Scotland about a month before the mission to Russia, so here he was.

Like a fucking jerk-off.

Literally and figuratively.

The lack of progress in finding out who was responsible for the deaths of his comrades in Retiarius Platoon was eating away at him. Lying low. Disappearing. Standing by. Playing dead. They went against every bone in his body. He wanted to *do* something. And this wild-goose chase wasn't it.

The Russians had been tipped off to their op. But by whom and why? Had it been an accidental leak or had someone set them up?

His fists squeezed. When he found out who was responsible . . .

Unconsciously his thumb rolled over the scarred knuckle of his right hand where a thick fragment of glass had been embedded. It was one of dozens. He'd been a human pincushion, pummeled by fragments of metal, glass, and wood from the explosion. His ballistic FAST helmet, which he didn't usually wear, and SPEAR body armor with the plates that he'd debated not wearing because of the added weight had probably saved his life. He'd been lucky.

But others . . .

Fuck. He swallowed hard, his gut twisting as the familiar image flashed before his eyes. He couldn't stop seeing the kid's— Brian's—shocked expression right before the missile had struck and he'd been engulfed in the fireball of the explosion.

Dean could still feel the blistering heat from the explosion that had sent him flying and turned the camp into a wasteland. Everything had been leveled. Erased. Lieutenant White's squad . . . half the platoon . . . gone in an instant.

There was nothing he could have done to help White and the rest of Navy Squad, but Brian's death was on him. Dean had ignored a direct order and the kid had paid for it.

He owed Brian and the rest of the men who'd been killed an answer. But he sure as hell didn't think he was going to find it in Stornoway chartering scuba divers—and sexy protesters.

"For once just follow a fucking command, Baylor!"

Dean's mouth tightened in a grim line as Lieutenant Commander Taylor's voice came back to him. He would do so, damn it. But he didn't like it.

Digging his hands in his sweatshirt pockets, he headed toward his temporary home. He'd let a room in a flat not far from the port, which required him to pass by the protester camp. From the noise and light coming from that direction, they were apparently still going strong.

He caught a whiff of another familiar memory from his childhood as he walked by. How many times had he returned from school to the skunk smell of weed?

Whenever his mom could afford it.

He wondered if she had any idea that he was dead. He doubted it; he hadn't seen her in years. Not since she'd come looking for money when she found out he'd made the Teams.

The memory still pissed him off.

Dean was about to turn up his street when a woman darted past him. She was so preoccupied with whatever was bothering her that she didn't notice him.

But he noticed her. The sexy brunette had been the focus of too many of his sex-starved thoughts for him not to have recognized that shadowed figure right away.

His thoughts immediately turned to anger. What the hell was she doing out here alone at this time of night?

Granted Stornoway wasn't exactly the mean streets of name-your-favorite American inner city, but it had its share of illegal activity—especially along the waterfront—and it wasn't a place where a young woman should be walking alone in the middle of the night.

He went after her without thinking. Proving his point, she took way too long to realize he was behind her.

He could tell by the way she jumped when she turned around that he'd startled her.

But it didn't last. As soon as she recognized him, her eyes narrowed angrily. "Why are you following me? You scared me!"

"Good. You shouldn't be out here alone—" He stopped suddenly, seeing her expression. She looked about ready to burst into tears. "What's wrong?"

Unconsciously he'd reached for her arm. Why the hell he'd done that he had no clue. He didn't go around touching women without an invitation.

He released her before she could protest. But if she'd noticed the too-personal gesture, she didn't let on.

"Nothing," she replied, her expression too blank.

He held her gaze long enough for her to see that he knew she was lying. It must not be something she did often, because a guilty blush rose to her cheeks.

She was so damned cute. He wanted to . . .

Fuck.

He took a step back.

Go dark. Don't do anything to risk your cover.

He heard the warnings loud and clear. But he couldn't very well let her walk around alone. What if something happened?

"Where's your boyfriend?"

The tightening around her mouth before she responded gave a big hint of what might be bothering her. Trouble in paradise? Now, that was a cryin' shame.

"He's still at camp. He's hanging around for the music. Julien plays guitar."

Dean didn't care if he was Jimmy Hendrix returning from the dead for one last show. "And he let you walk back alone?"

She immediately stiffened, giving him a scathing look. "He didn't *let* me do anything. I make my own decisions."

From the way she said it, it was clear she thought he was some kind of medieval misogynistic pig.

One of those, was she? He should have guessed. That kind of oversensitive feminist crap drove him crazy—not everything was a "microaggression." Being a strong woman didn't mean you could be stupid about personal safety. And all he'd meant was that the douche bag should have cared enough about her safety to insist on accompanying her.

Although admittedly Julien probably wasn't much of a defense.

"Then your decision was a shitty one."

She looked stunned. "You just say whatever you think, don't you? I wasn't asking for your opinion."

"Well, you got it." He gave her a long look, taking in the Tulane sweatshirt, tight jeans that left no room to hide anything, and flip-flops. "And unless you are a black belt jujitsu specialist or trained in self-defense and carrying some kind of weapon, I'm walking you to the guest house."

She looked up at him half outraged and half bemused, as if she couldn't quite believe someone like him actually existed. It was a look he'd been on the receiving end of more than once.

Eventually her mouth twisted with a smile. "How do you know I'm not?"

"Because if you had any secret ninja skills, from the way you were looking at me a few minutes ago, I'd be on my ass right now."

Annie couldn't help it. She laughed.
     The Canadian captain was outrageous and yet oddly charming at the same time.

She had to admit that walking back alone might not have

been her best decision. She'd reacted so defensively only because he'd been blunt enough to call her on it.

If she was tempted to argue with him, the group of men who'd just poured out onto the sidewalk ahead of them made her think again. The pub must have just closed, and by the level of boisterousness and general weaving, they'd been in there awhile. More than one didn't look likely to be scared off by a look-into-the-eyes "hello."

"Alas," she said, turning back to Dan. "No secret ninja skills, but I'm definitely wishing otherwise right about now." She looked him up and down as he'd done her. The flood of warmth that poured through her told her that might not have been a good idea. Despite the bulky sweatshirt and loose jeans, the guy was built. *Built.* She pulled her eyes away before she was caught staring—again—and looked back up at him. "Although something tells me that you wouldn't be so easy to put on your ass even if I were."

He grinned and the effect was startling. It felt as if she'd been struck square in the solar plexus.

He was good-looking. Even with the stupid beard. What would he look like without it?

That probably wasn't something she should be thinking about.

"You might be right," he said. "But let me know if you ever want to try."

Was he flirting with her? It was hard to tell. The words were mildly provocative, but they'd been said matter-of-factly and without any innuendo.

That was him, she realized. Matter-of-fact and without innuendo. What you saw was what you got. He wasn't the type to sugarcoat. He would tell it like it was—or at least how he saw it—whether she liked it or not. She suspected there was quite a lot of my way or the highway with him. She couldn't decide whether he was overbearing or old-fashioned. Probably a little of both.

Still, she might not agree with him—and she guessed she wouldn't on many things—but there was something refreshing about his no-BS straightforwardness.

She supposed she wouldn't lose her feminist card if she went along with it this one time.

When he made an "after you" gesture with his hand, she didn't object and moved to the right enough for him to walk beside her.

She peered up at him from under her lashes, taking the opportunity to observe him. Strong "don't mess with me" jaw, razor-sharp eyes that didn't miss anything, squared "ready to take on the world" shoulders. Confident. Tough. Smart.

But defensive. There was a wall up around him that seemed to warn her not to get too close, and there was that grim shadow that she'd sensed earlier.

What was his story? There was something about him that didn't quite fit, but she couldn't figure out what. He didn't seem the type to be involved in something illegal or disreputable as she'd first assumed. He was too solid and principled. But there was definitely something off about him; something that made her think he was trying to fly under the radar. The beard, the hat, the baggy clothes, the job with the not-quite-on-the-up-and-up charter company.

She probably should just let him walk her back and leave it at that, but curiosity got the better of her. It was a downfall. "How did a Canadian boat captain end up on the Isle of Lewis?"

She thought he might have stiffened slightly, but he answered the question so unhesitatingly that she realized she must have been mistaken. "I visited here once as a kid. I was looking for a change of pace when I saw the job opening posted on the Internet." Seeing her expression, he quirked a smile. She wished he'd stop doing that. She liked it too much. "They do have the Internet here, you know."

She laughed. "I'm not sure I'd call it that. The Wi-Fi at the guest house is painfully *slow*, and my phone seems to work in about a two-block radius." She frowned, wrinkling her nose at something in his voice. The tempo was slow and very deliberate. "Where are you from in Canada? I can't quite make out the accent. It's not French, and I haven't heard one 'eh' yet."

"Vancouver," he said. "What about you?" He glanced meaningfully at her sweatshirt. "From your lack of accent, I'm guessing not New Orleans."

She was surprised that he knew where Tulane was. A lot of Americans didn't even know that.

She shook her head. "I've been in school there for the past eight years, but I was raised in different parts of the South." She guessed his next question. "I was born in Florida, which is why I don't have an accent."

"Eight years?"

She nodded. "I just finished my PhD."

"Congratulations. I think I heard your boyfriend mention that. What field was it in?"

"Marine ecology."

He nodded as if something suddenly made sense. "So that is how you became involved with the protest?"

She shrugged. "Sort of. It was Julien who told me about it." She went on to explain how she had met Julien at a fund-raiser for the BP oil disaster a couple of months ago, and how they'd bonded over the devastation and wanting to make sure something like that never happened again. "But these are mainly his friends. I didn't know many of them before I came."

She didn't know why she'd just made the disclaimer.

Or maybe she did. Maybe the situation with Jean Paul was bothering her more than she wanted to admit. So much so that she didn't want Dan associating her with him.

And what about Julien? Was he bothering her, too?

She knew the answer.

She was tempted to say something more. Tempted to voice her concerns that her boyfriend had been acting strangely, and she was having second thoughts about their plans.

Why she thought she could confide in Dan, she didn't know. But not since her father—in the old days—had she been around someone who gave off that "you can count on me" vibe.

Of course when it mattered, she hadn't been able to count on her father at all.

But she sensed Dan would be a good sounding board. He had to wonder—probably even suspect—what they were planning to do, didn't he?

They'd reached the guest house and stopped. She turned slightly and realized how close they were standing, from the blast of body heat that engulfed her. There wouldn't be any cold winter nights with him. He smelled good. Not like the colognes that Julien wore, but fresh and bracing like the wind on the sea.

Was that where he'd come from? She'd been so startled by his sudden appearance that she hadn't even thought about why he'd been out so late. "Where were you tonight? It's a little late for a charter, isn't it?"

He stepped back, and it was as if that wall she'd imagined before came slamming back down. There was nothing remotely welcoming or inviting about his expression—had there ever been? It was as blank and hard as stone.

"Fishing."

She didn't believe him, but neither was she going to argue with him. His tone left no room for challenge. The conversation was clearly over.

The easygoing conversation we had going? Forget it. We aren't going to be friends.

Got it.

She couldn't explain why it stung. Why his sudden withdrawal upset her so badly. Why she felt even more alone than she had before.

Their eyes met in the semidarkness. She wanted . . .

Nothing.

She barely knew him. She didn't even *like* him. Why would she want to confide in him about anything? "I—" Her voice caught. She shook herself and drew a deep breath. "Thank you for walking me. I'll see you in a couple days."

He nodded, and then seemed to hesitate as if he were grappling with saying more. He turned to leave and even took a few steps before turning back again. "Go home, Miss Henderson. You don't belong here."

Miss Henderson.

The ominous warning dissipated in the cool night air as he disappeared into the shadows.

She was tempted to listen to him.

Six

The three officers rose from the table in their matching khakis, differing only in the number of bars of ribbons on each man's chest, as Colt Wesson entered the room.

Pressed, professional, and polished, the officers' appearance was in stark contrast to Colt's long hair, ten (not five) o'clock shadow, motorcycle jacket, faded jeans, and T-shirt picked up from the pile off the floor. It had been so long since Colt dressed regulation he wasn't sure he remembered how.

Commander Mark Ryan, the skipper of SEAL Team Nine and Colt's onetime platoon commander, spoke first. "You shouldn't be here."

That was true for many reasons, none of which mattered. Colt was going to find out the truth. Whether it would be their way or his was up to them.

He eyed them coolly from behind the mirrored lenses of his glasses. The three men opposite him were Retiarius Platoon's direct chain of command, and among the handful of people who would know what the fuck was going on.

"So arrest me." It was an idle threat. To arrest him, they'd have to acknowledge his existence, and no one wanted to do that. It—*he*—was too dangerous. Which was probably why they'd agreed to this meeting.

Rear Admiral Ronald Morrison, the highest-ranking officer in the room and the man in charge of naval special operations in the United States, frowned at him forbiddingly, which would have scared the shit out of Colt when he was twenty, but at thirty-eight he barely noticed. "I'm going to have the badge of whoever let you through customs."

Colt's mouth curved with rare amusement. "What makes you think I went through customs? Maybe I swam from Mexico? Or Canada? I'm a pretty good swimmer." No one cracked a smile. *Hard-asses.* "I had some time off coming," Colt said with a shrug. "I decided to take it."

Captain Trevor Moore, the commander of Naval Special Warfare Group One, who reported directly to the admiral, had always been a straight shooter. He'd never liked Colt, which only showed his good sense. "Don't be an ass, Colt—or more of an ass than usual. You shouldn't have left wherever the hell it is you've been assigned." Crimea—the latest shit heap. "This has nothing to do with you."

There he was wrong; this had everything to do with him.

The admiral was obviously getting impatient. "Cut the crap, Wesson, and tell us what you want. And take off those damned glasses."

The thin veneer of civility snapped. Colt removed the Oakleys—the only thing that had been hiding his rage—and tossed them down on the table. They skidded halfway down the glass-topped polished cherry veneer that was ubiquitous in military conference rooms. He leaned forward, no longer holding back the hostility and menace. "I want the fucking truth, and I want to know why I had to pick up a paper to find out that my men were missing."

Only Moore didn't seem taken aback. He'd known Colt for too long.

The admiral mumbled something about shutting up that damned reporter, and then said, "They weren't your men. And as Trevor said before, this has nothing to do with you."

As a SEAL, the admiral should know better—even if his

operational time had been minimal. Plenty of officers had years of boots-on-the-ground time—Rear Admiral Ronald Morrison wasn't one of them. He'd spent most of his thirty years at Fort Fumble—aka the Pentagon.

"Bullshit," Colt said. "I trained most of them." Until he'd left three years ago, he'd been the senior enlisted petty officer in Retiarius Platoon. Colt was actually a plankowner, one of the founding members of Nine, recruited for the secret team not long after the disestablishment of Special Delivery Vehicle Team-2 (SDVT-2) and merger into team SDVT-1 in 2008. The two SDVTs had been established specifically for covert water operations in subs. But Team Nine had never been limited to underwater operations—what the guys called "one foot in the water" ops—and they were deployed all over the globe. The old paperwork connection to the SDVT was the reason Team Nine was based in Honolulu and had fourteen men in a platoon rather than the typical sixteen. It was also why Colt was at Coronado and not Fort Bragg. For now, the team was still under Naval Special Warfare Command and not JSOC, which had operational control over other Special Mission Units like DEVGRU, aka the other SEAL team that didn't exist, Team Six. JSOC didn't like it, but that was the way it was for now.

"I want to know what the fuck happened."

The three officers looked at one another. It was the admiral who spoke. "It was a training accident."

Did they think he was an idiot? "Try again, Ron."

The admiral scowled, whether at being caught out or at the lack of protocol in calling him by his first name, Colt didn't know—or care. He didn't report to them. "Our hands are tied. We've been sworn to secrecy. The president doesn't want any of this getting out. And you better than anyone know that even admitting to the existence of Team Nine puts the entire program in jeopardy. We don't need any more scrutiny. There are two platoons at stake."

Most SEAL teams were made up of six platoons, but given the nature of Team Nine, it was much smaller—only Retiarius and Neptune platoons. All SEAL teams were close-knit. Team Nine was family. The only family they had.

"Don't you mean *were* two platoons? From what I can tell, no one from Retiarius has been seen or heard from in months and plenty of people in Honolulu are wondering why their stuff has been cleaned out. So where the fuck are they?"

"KIA," Ryan said, finally admitting what Colt had suspected. When the admiral seemed ready to admonish him, he explained, "He'll find out anyway. And this way he isn't stirring up more trouble."

"He's right, Ron," Moore said distastefully. "Wesson is nothing but trouble."

Good sense, all right.

The admiral thought a moment. He didn't look happy, but he must have agreed. "We don't know exactly what happened, but they were on a recon op in the Komi Republic."

Colt swore. "Russia? What the hell were they doing there?"

Moore answered, "We had actionable intelligence that Ivanov was developing a doomsday device."

Colt was immediately skeptical. Those kinds of rumors were always circulating, but to him they were the arena of science fiction, conspiracy theories, and aliens at Area 51. Hell, the Russian president was probably circulating them himself. "What kind of intelligence?"

"It doesn't matter," the admiral answered. "We lost our drone when they were eight klicks from the target, and not long afterward all our communications went black. Satellites picked up a huge explosion about ninety minutes later in the precise area of the old gulag where they were headed."

Colt thought back. "The explosion that the Russians claimed was a missile test a couple months back?"

The admiral nodded. "It was a missile but not a test. The platoon was discovered and targeted. The devastation was clear. Anyone in the vicinity would have been killed. The sub returned a few days later. Empty."

Colt had heard the navy had developed a new dual-mode sub, enabling it to operate remotely. But he'd bet they never thought they would be using it for something like this.

Hearing confirmation was worse than Colt had expected. He put his head down and dragged his fingers through his hair, trying to get a rein on his emotions. Probably to the surprise of the men at the table, he had them.

When he finally lifted his head and spoke, his voice was raw. "Where are they buried?"

All three officers fidgeted uncomfortably. It took Colt a moment to realize what that meant. It was so improbable—so incomprehensible—he didn't want to believe it. "You didn't bring them back?"

All three of these men were SEALs. They knew just as well as he that SEALs always brought back their own. Always. No SEAL had ever been left behind in combat—dead or alive.

Until now.

"There wouldn't be anything to bring back," Moore said. "We couldn't risk sending in another team. You didn't see those pictures. And the Russians wouldn't leave evidence. Besides, we didn't have a choice. You have to understand, Colt. It is a very precarious situation. There is a lot at stake here. One wrong move and we could be at war."

"And that would be a bad thing?" Colt added. Having spent the past year embedded in Crimea, he knew just how dangerous Ivanov was. Americans underestimated him. They shouldn't. Russia might not be the powerhouse the USSR once was, but its president was a despot with a hunger for power and respect who wanted to see America humbled.

There were other ways of dealing with him, of course. That was why governments had men like Colt. But presidents tended to balk at taking out world leaders—even ones who deserved it. Go figure.

The admiral smiled for the first time. "Maybe not. But it's not for us to decide, and the president isn't as much of a hawk as others in her administration."

Colt knew the admiral was referring to the man who'd been his commander not that long ago. General Murray, now the vice chairman of the Joint Chiefs of Staff and the father of the pilot shot down by the Russians last spring, had been the head of the entire US Special Warfare Command before he was tapped for Washington.

The general was someone else who didn't like Colt—

though his reasons were more personal. Given how close the general was with President Cartwright, Colt was surprised that he hadn't sabotaged Colt's selection in Task Force Tier One—the secret unit within a secret unit of JSOC known to the operators informally as CAD (as in Control Alt Delete). He was probably hoping that Colt would be killed.

It was a good bet.

"So fourteen SEALs are killed on a covert operation, and the president thinks she can sweep it under the rug?" Colt shook his head. "She's nuts."

A story that big couldn't be contained; it would eventually come out.

"What's she supposed to do?" Ryan asked. "Admit an act of war—that we had men in Russia illegally on a military mission for WMDs? That will go over really well after Iraq, especially with no proof and fourteen dead men to show for it."

"Not to mention that it would force Ivanov's hand," Moore said. "He swore to declare war if there was another 'unlawful American incursion in Russian sovereign territory.' You know Russian pride."

"He'd be a fool," Colt said.

"Maybe so," Moore agreed. "But it isn't a chance the president is going to take."

"Not with reelection in a couple years."

No one said anything. They all knew how it worked.

Fucking politics. Colt hated everything about it. Even in the Teams as a senior enlisted petty officer, he hadn't been able to escape it. It was one of the best things about what he did now. Politics didn't play much of a factor in his kind of operations. Neither did the law, for that matter.

"It's bad enough with Blake's supposedly estranged sister coming out of the woodwork and fanning the flames with her 'Lost Platoon' articles, and Ivanov using the stories as an opportunity to poke fun at the US for 'misplacing its soldiers all the time,' when we all know what he did. Privately the general is calling for his balls."

Colt didn't blame him. "Don't you care about finding out what happened?"

"Of course we do," Ryan snapped. "They were our men, too. But as the admiral said, our hands are tied. We've been ordered not to interfere."

But Colt hadn't been. His gaze went to Moore's. Clever bastard. Was that why they'd agreed to this meeting?

"How did the Russians know they were there?" Colt asked.

"We don't know," the admiral answered. "They must have made a mistake."

"No way," Colt said. "Taylor wouldn't fuck up something like this."

"You saying that doesn't have anything to do with the fact that you trained him when he was a junior officer? Or that you were close friends?" Moore asked.

Were. Until his "friend" had fucked Colt's wife. Make that *ex*-wife. "Doesn't make it not true."

Colt stood. It was clear he'd gotten as much out of them as he was going to. The rest was up to him. "Gentlemen," he said, tipping a nonexistent hat and reaching for his glasses.

It was Moore who asked what they were all thinking. "What are you going to do?"

"Get some answers."

He had to make sure they were all dead. He wasn't taking the navy's word for anything. And he knew just where to start, although she wasn't going to like hearing from him.

Seven

Annie didn't stay up waiting for Julien to return. When the door opened about an hour after the captain had left her standing on the doorstep, she was already in bed feigning sleep.

She woke the next morning to the incredible aroma of coffee. Good coffee, not the murky brown water they had downstairs.

Julien had decided to surprise her with breakfast in bed, including a latte and her favorite egg and cheddar croissant. Knowing that he viewed any kind of condiment or adornment to a croissant (or what passed for a croissant outside France) as akin to a defilement, she knew he must be trying to make up for the night before.

It wasn't enough; she needed an explanation.

"I had them put mustard on it," Julien pointed out. "They didn't have that yellow kind you like, so it's English. I hope that's all right."

The fact that he managed to say "yellow" without making a face told her how much he was trying. He didn't think much of her American mustard. Usually it made her laugh, and she teased him about making him eat corn dogs with her at the state fair.

Not today.

She took a few bites and put the sandwich down next to

the latte on the bedside table. Julien had claimed the only chair in the small room, so she'd sat up on the bed to eat. "It's delicious. Thank you."

Before she could say more, he added, "I thought we could go check out that beach you mentioned, and maybe take a packed lunch—"

"We need to talk about last night first."

He drew his hand back through his dark hair, where it fell back across his face exactly as it had been in a perfect slump. "I'm trying to apologize. I was upset, but I shouldn't have stormed out of here like that, and I should have come back with you." His mouth turned in the rueful smile that she loved. "I only played one song. I couldn't concentrate because I was worried about you."

She didn't ease his conscience by telling him that the captain had seen her home, knowing how sensitive Julien already was on that subject.

"You didn't seem too worried," Annie pointed out. "You seemed . . . occupied."

Though she hadn't had an ulterior meaning, Julien assumed she was referring to the woman. "Sofie is an old friend, Anne. You have nothing to worry about."

Strangely she wasn't. Although after what she'd seen, perhaps she should be. "You seemed to know each other well."

He gave one of his nonresponsive shrugs. "I met her through Jean Paul years ago."

There was more he wasn't saying, but she didn't feel like pressing him.

"What's she doing here?" she asked instead.

"The same thing we are."

"What?" Annie sat up straighter. "She's going with us?"

He laughed her off. "*Non, non.* Sofie is here for the protest only. She knows nothing about anything else."

Annie wasn't sure she believed him. "Then what were you talking about when I arrived?"

He frowned. "Why are you questioning me like this? I told you there is nothing for you to worry about. You are acting as if you do not trust me."

She was surprised to realize that she wasn't sure that she did. "Ever since we arrived, you've been acting—I don't know—different somehow."

"What do you mean?"

She shrugged. "Distracted. Anxious. Testier than usual."

His brow wrinkled. "Testier?"

She tried to come up with a translation. "A little moody and irritable. You seem on edge about something."

"Aren't you? We have important plans tomorrow, and I just want to make sure everything goes smoothly."

"Maybe we should wait. Push it back a few days."

The calm, easygoing, conciliatory demeanor showed its first crack. He looked truly upset—almost alarmed. "What are you talking about? We can't push it back. It has to be timed—" He stopped. "It has to be tomorrow. Everything is ready. You aren't thinking of backing out now? It's too late. Jean Paul has it all arranged."

Annie decided that there was no use in holding back any longer. She had to be honest with him. "That's part of the problem. I'm sorry, Julien. I tried, but I don't like your friend. There is something about him." She bit her lip, trying to find the right words. "He makes me nervous."

Julien seemed genuinely wounded. "There is no one I admire more than Jean Paul. He is a great man. You don't know him as I do." Nor did she want to. "Why are you saying this?" he demanded. "Is it because of what he said about your special soldiers?" SEALs. She didn't bother correcting him a second time. "I thought you hated the military."

That wasn't quite true. Her feelings were difficult to sort through. She didn't object to everything they did, just that the costs were sometimes too high. And the way the military chewed up and spat out the men who devoted their lives to it without taking care of them afterward? *That* she did hate.

She'd never told Julien about her father. She didn't talk about him with anyone.

"It isn't that." She hesitated. "Weasely vibes" and "looks as if he could give Tony Soprano a run for his money" weren't the greatest ways to explain. "I don't like how he looks at me."

Julien seemed to understand. He nodded and sat back in the chair, giving her a long look. "He doesn't believe you are committed." The explanation took her aback. "Jean Paul is a man of strong convictions and holds those around him to a similar standard. I have told him that you believe just as strongly as we do and are willing to do what it takes, but . . ."

"But?"

Julien looked apologetic. "He doesn't think we can count on you. He thinks Americans are spoiled and weak. That they are all fluff, no substance, and cannot be counted on. That they are all words and with their nice comfortable lives no longer know how to sacrifice for their beliefs."

Annie didn't consider herself much of a patriot, but she felt a little Stars and Stripes stirring in her now. She bristled defensively. What a gross oversimplification. And she knew about sacrifice. "That is ridiculous."

He shrugged. "Is it?" He looked at her questioningly. "You claim to be committed to stopping North Sea Offshore Drilling from drilling and preventing another disaster like the one in the Gulf. You said you wanted to do something—something big that they couldn't ignore to stop them. But ever since we arrived you have been having second thoughts."

"I didn't say that."

"But it's true."

She didn't deny it. "I just said I didn't like your friend. The thought of spending a week with him confined to one small area of a ship . . ." She stopped, seeing the "I know something you don't" smile spread across his features. "What is it?"

"If that is what is bothering you, you have nothing to worry about. Jean Paul isn't coming with us on the drillship—only on the charter to help coordinate everything. He doesn't dive. It will be me, you, and Claude."

She'd just assumed . . . "He's not?"

Julien shook his head.

Annie felt an enormous sense of relief. The only thing that would have been better was if Julien had said he wasn't going at all.

"So what is it to be, Anne? We can't do it without you. Has

it all been talk? Are you going to back out and let the drillship company win, or are you willing to do what it takes to destroy them?"

If she thought it a strange choice of words, she didn't pay too much attention to it. Julien was often a little off in translation.

Annie knew the time for indecision had passed. She thought of everything she'd done the past eight years to try to make sure nothing like the Gulf BP oil spill ever happened again. All the volunteer work, all the lectures, all the research and writing. She thought of all the times it felt as if she was banging her head against the wall to get anyone to listen to her, let alone care. She thought of the dead birds, turtles, and dolphins cloaked in black sludge. She thought of the beautiful Lewis seashore and knew there was only one decision she could make. "I'm in."

Julien beamed. "I knew I chose wisely! Let's get dressed and go find that beach."

Keep your head down. Do your job. Don't get involved. Dean knew what he had to do, but as he sat on the captain's chair in the wheelhouse, watching Julien and the other two men loading the black metal-trimmed equipment cases from the truck onto the boat, every bone in his body fought against it. The hairs on the back of his neck were on edge, and his spidey senses were going wild. It was the most alive he'd felt in months.

These guys were up to no good.

Once again, he wondered what Annie Henderson had gotten herself mixed up in. Although as she hadn't arrived this morning with the other passengers, he hoped she was having second thoughts since he'd left her at the guest house a couple of nights ago.

He watched Julien and the other young guy—Claude—struggle with another large case as they carried it across the deck.

Fuck it. Dean pushed back from the chair, exited the wheel-

house, and descended the bridge stairs onto the deck. He'd
never stood aside in his life, and he wasn't about to start now.

When the two men emerged from below deck, Dean said,
"I didn't realize there would be so much cargo. What do you
have in there? I thought you were planning to dive."

Julien gave him that superior "carry my man purse, you
peon" look Dean already hated. "We aren't paying you to
think, Mr. Warren."

"Captain," Dean corrected.

"Captain," Julien repeated snidely. "We hired you to drive
the boat, not ask questions."

Dean was about to tell him to go to hell, but a third man
spoke behind him. For someone whose life often depended on
his ability to detect someone sneaking up on him, it was disconcerting as hell. Four weeks of sitting on his ass watching
the waterways for something that didn't exist was catching up
to him.

"It's camera equipment," Jean Paul said with an admonish-
ing look to Julien. "We are planning to make a short film to
aid in our protest against the drillship."

"Is that right?" Dean said. He hadn't thought much of their
ringleader that first night in the bar—and his opinion hadn't
changed. Julien was a douche bag but harmless. This guy?
Not harmless. He was pure thug. "Sounds interesting. I've
done some filming myself," Dean lied. "What kind of cameras
do you use?"

"Is something wrong here?"

Dean turned at the sound of his boss. MacDonald was
standing on the dock with a cigarette hanging out of his mouth
and glaring at him something fierce. Old MacDonald had
better be careful or he was going to burst a blood vessel.

Unfortunately he wasn't alone. Annie stood beside him,
looking a little concerned but otherwise pretty damned incredible. Dean wasn't happy to see her—he didn't want her
involved with these clowns—but he had to admit the view
was stunning.

She had incredible legs—of which he could see every endless inch in her very short cutoff denim shorts. Not that he

was complaining. Short was good with legs like hers. Really good. Long, tanned, and toned worked for him.

She wore a plaid shirt over a white tank top and had it tied at the waist. Her hair was loose around her shoulders, but she had on a pink Red Sox hat—that needed an explanation—and tan leather flip-flops with that little rainbow tag on them. Both the hat and the flip-flops were well-worn.

She looked quintessentially American, as if she had just walked off a beach in Honolulu or San Diego, and something about that hit him. If he were inclined toward sentiment, he would say it was a longing for home.

Shit.

He turned away to look back at his boss. No getting sentimental there.

"Nothing is going on," Jean Paul replied smoothly. "The captain just had a question about our camera equipment."

MacDonald turned Dean's question back on him. "Is that right?"

Dean heard the challenge. He wasn't supposed to be asking questions. MacDonald had told him to mind his own business.

Dean was tempted to tell them *all* to go to hell and walk away. But something stopped him. Something that he didn't want to examine right now. He needed the job, but he knew that wasn't the only reason.

"Aye," he said, adapting MacDonald's verbiage. "Jean Paul was just telling me all about the little movie they are planning to make."

Dean didn't believe for two seconds that they just wanted to get close to the drillship to film something. Those boxes looked way too heavy and big for camera equipment. Ten to one they were planning to board the ship via the fancy inflatable they were bringing along and stage some kind of sit-in like those nutjobs from Greenpeace.

His gaze met Annie's, and he let her know that he didn't buy any of it. But it wasn't his business—nor could he make it his business. If she wanted to get herself thrown in jail, he wasn't going to stop her. She could take care of herself—she'd made that clear, hadn't she?

He was just the taxi. He and the boat would be long gone before any police showed up. They might eventually track the charter company down, but he'd deal with that if he had to. Besides, that would happen whether he captained the boat or MacDonald did. But he suspected the cops wouldn't have much interest in them.

She looked away, her pink cheeks all the admission he needed.

Dean had been so focused on Annie that he hadn't noticed MacDonald carrying a hot pink duffel over his shoulder until he held it out to him. Although how the hell he'd missed that, he didn't know. "Take the lady's bag to the sleeping quarters."

He would have sworn the old buzzard didn't have a gallant bone in his body—especially for Americans whom he thought loud, brash, and demanding—but apparently MacDonald had a weakness for drop-dead gorgeous and sweet.

Dean couldn't blame him.

He reached for the pink monstrosity, thinking it was a damned shame to ruin such a nice bag—it was the one with backpack straps frequently seen on expeditions to Everest and cost a couple of hundred bucks—with such a ridiculous color.

"That's all right. I can carry it," Annie started to say.

But Dean had already grabbed it and was heading downstairs. He opened the door to one of the two small rooms that had been made passenger sleeping quarters when the tug was converted into a dive charter and put it on one of the berths.

He would have left, but Annie was standing in the doorway. To get by her, he'd have to brush up against her, which after the other night he knew was *not* a good idea. He'd been hurting half the night: hot, restless, and guilty. He'd sensed that she was looking for someone to talk to, maybe even someone to confide in, and it wasn't—*couldn't* be—him.

"Nice bag," he said instead.

She looked embarrassed—which, seeing as he was growing really fond of those little blushes, wasn't a good thing. "My mom gave it to me for the trip. She thought the color would be easier to spot in baggage claim."

"She's right about that. Not likely to get stolen, either." He paused and gave it another look—maybe more of a shudder. "Especially by a guy."

She rolled her eyes and laughed. "Does it offend your manly sensibilities? Real men don't get bothered by something as silly as a color."

Dean gave her a long, lazy shake of the head. "Sweetheart, if that's your criterion, then I have to think that you don't know too many real men."

She laughed. "You do a good Texan drawl. All you're missing is the hat, a piece of straw to chew on, and the boots."

Shit. Dean controlled his expression—barely. He'd slipped and he knew it. This girl did something to him. Made him forget his defenses. Made him forget his damned head.

He needed to stay away from her. She was too easy to talk to.

"Customers," he said flatly by way of explanation, and then moved past her. He was so angry with himself that he didn't even need to steel himself when their bodies brushed against each other.

Or so he thought, until every nerve ending in his body seemed to jump into overdrive.

Cool down, old man. He was thirty-three, for fuck's sake, not a horny teenager.

Well, not a teenager, at least.

"Thanks—for the help with the bag," she said, clearly confused by his abruptness.

He nodded, trying not to notice that expression on her face again. It was the same one she'd had when he left her at the guest house a couple of nights ago. *Wounded.* As if his curtness and eagerness to leave had hurt her.

But it couldn't be avoided. He was attracted to her—*too* attracted to her. And worse, he actually kind of liked her.

Which didn't make a damned lick of sense. He had lines that he didn't cross, and bleeding-heart liberals—a protester, for Christ's sake—who probably sat around the campfire wearing Birkenstocks and eating granola while singing "Kumbaya," and burning the flag that he'd spent his life defending were definitely over that line. *Way* the hell over the line.

But politics aside, she was sweet. Young—probably too

young for him—and undoubtedly a little "I can change the world even though I've never been in it" naive, but undeniably sweet. And even if he couldn't get behind her politics, he could admire her passion for her studies and her love of what she was doing.

It had resonated with him the other night. It was how he felt about his job.

Or at least how he used to feel.

He felt the now familiar mule kick in the gut of reality, and his jaw clenched against the memories. It came over him like that sometimes. All those men—his men. His friends. Dead. He didn't want to believe that someone had betrayed them. There had to be another explanation.

The navy had been his life for almost fourteen years. Hell, it had given him a life—a fucking purpose. It had saved him and given him a way out of the future that had been ordained for him. He knew exactly where he'd be without it. In some shit hole, with a shit job, a wife he couldn't stand, kids to take out his anger on, and drinking himself into oblivion every night.

Just like his old man. Wherever the hell he might be.

Dean turned his back on her and headed up the stairs. Before he could get sucked in again.

Eight

What was she doing down here? Clearly Annie had watched too many movies. Who did she think she was, sneaking around like this, superspy? There wasn't anything down here.

The first two cases Annie opened contained exactly what they were supposed to: grappling ladders and other climbing equipment that they would use to board the ship. The third contained camera equipment for them to film.

One more and she was out of here. She pulled one of the newer-looking suitcase-sized cases from the stack and flipped open the lid.

She froze. Her stomach dropped, and most of the blood in her body went to the floor along with it.

The small storage room near the engine room only had a single overhead bulb for light, but it was enough to make out the plastic-wrapped cylinders taped together in bundles of three with duct tape, a yellow-and-black cord wound through them. They looked like packages of cookie dough or breakfast sausage.

That wasn't what they were.

She stared at the contents with a mixture of disbelief and horror. Although she'd never seen explosive devices before, it didn't take an expert to know what she was looking at.

Fear set in, and she quickly closed the lid—as if that would somehow make them go away. Her skin was like ice as she backed out of the room and closed the door.

She was so scared that she couldn't think. God, she was shaking! What were they planning to do? Blow up the drill-ship? Julien must be crazy if he thought she would go along with anything like that.

She returned to her room and lay down on one of the berths, no longer needing to feign sickness as she listened for sounds of the men above. She'd claimed not to be feeling well and left them to their lunch. But she couldn't stay down here forever.

What was she going to do now?

Her thoughts went to one person. The captain was involved with this whether he wanted to be or not. She suspected not.

But this was partially his fault anyway. He was the one who'd made her paranoid with that "what the hell are you involved with?" look he'd given her as they boarded the ship. If he hadn't looked at her that way, she wouldn't have had second thoughts. And if she hadn't been having second thoughts, she wouldn't have gone looking for trouble after she'd overheard Julien and Jean Paul talking a little while ago.

She'd been going through the dive equipment on deck but had gone back into the galley to refill her water bottle, when she heard voices in the adjoining room that served as a mul-tipurpose lounge and dining room.

"Give me a little more time to convince her," Julien had said. "I know she'll come around."

"We don't have any more time," Jean Paul responded. "If you don't convince her, I will."

Annie realized they were talking about her, and then, as now, her blood had run cold. She'd confronted Julien with what she'd heard when he came out to help her later, but he'd claimed Jean Paul had just been worried that she'd back out. He'd been convincing at the moment, but the conversation had replayed over and over in her head so many times she couldn't let it go.

She'd known they were talking about something else, so

while they were eating lunch, she'd decided to look in a few of the cases the captain had been so curious about. But never in her life could she have imagined *this*.

Jean Paul, Julien, and Claude were ecoterrorists, and she'd been stupid enough to get mixed up in whatever it was that they had planned.

Explosives. Good God, people could be killed. Her stomach turned for the God-knew-how-many-eth time.

There was no question: she had to tell the captain. He could radio for help or turn around or help her figure out a way to stop whatever they had planned. It wasn't that she trusted him—though oddly she kind of did—but she didn't have anyone else to turn to and she couldn't very well commandeer the boat herself.

As she stepped out of the sleeping quarters into the narrow hall, the boat swayed, making her painfully conscious of her situation. Every scary movie she'd ever seen that took place on a boat picked that moment to come back to her. She was alone with a horrible secret, miles away from shore, surrounded by a bunch of extremists with explosives. Julien wouldn't hurt her, but she couldn't be as sure of the other two.

Her plan to talk to the captain had one problem: he was in the wheelhouse—where he'd been since leaving her so abruptly after helping her with her bag—which was stacked atop the deck level galley and lounge, accessed by metal ladderlike stairs on the opposite side. Meaning she would have to go out on deck and try to slip around where the three men were eating without being seen.

She didn't even make it all the way up the stairs before Jean Paul cornered her.

Her heart leaped to her throat, but she tried to play it cool. "Hey."

He didn't respond. He was looking down the hall behind her. She turned to see what had caught his attention.

Oh God. She'd left the light on in the storage room, and the telltale glow was visible beneath the door.

Her skin prickled, fear setting all her instincts on edge.

Had he guessed that she'd been snooping, and what she'd discovered?

Mustering every ounce of courage that she could, she turned back around to face him. *Don't be stupid.* She wasn't going to be *that* girl in the movie who gave everything away with her terrified expression.

"Excuse me," she said with an irritated flip of her chin, trying to go around him.

He stepped in front of her, blocking her and clearly trying to intimidate her. He wasn't a big man, but size didn't seem to be limiting his menace any.

"Where are you going?" he asked. "I thought you weren't feeling well."

She looked him straight in the eye, giving no hint to the frantic race of her pulse and beat of her heart. "I thought some fresh air might help."

"I will go with you."

"That isn't necessary. I was going to find Julien."

Jean Paul held her gaze as if he knew she was lying. "You should do that."

He stepped aside. She thought it was to let her pass, but he reached out to grab her arm as she went by. She'd changed earlier into warmer clothes, but even through the down of her coat, his touch repulsed her. He had on the ridiculous leather jacket and smelled of wine and cigarettes and sweat.

"Let go of me," she said in a low, steely voice, which was surprising for how scared she was.

He did as she said with a small smirk. "Do what you are supposed to do, *mademoiselle*, and we won't have any problems."

There was no mistaking the threat. He suspected what she'd seen.

Knowing that the best thing she could do right now was to pretend to be with them, Annie said, "I will do whatever it takes to stop the drilling. Whether you and I have 'problems,' I don't really care."

The fierceness of her reply seemed to surprise him. She

must have been a better actor than she realized, because he
let her go.

Instead of going outside for fresh air, she took a seat beside
Julien in the lounge and tried to act normal—or at least as
normal as she could under the circumstances.

The next couple of hours were torture as she pretended
nothing was wrong while waiting for the chance to talk to the
captain. He came down once to grab coffee and something
to eat while Julien, Claude, and Jean Paul were still heavy
into their post-lunch wine. Annie never drank before she went
diving. Although she had no intention of diving anywhere
with these guys, and could have used something to calm her
nerves, Julien would notice.

She jumped up as soon as the captain came in, and offered
to make him a fresh pot of coffee so she could go into the
galley with him, but he said it wasn't necessary, and she was
forced to sit back down. When he came back out, he seemed
to be doing his best not to look at her, not giving her a chance
for some kind of silent communication. She felt like one of
those hostages taken to the bank to empty their account and
helplessly trying to alert the clueless teller that something was
wrong. He wasn't clueless, more deliberately avoiding. The
darkness and anger had returned.

Dan left a few minutes after he came in, leaving Annie
resigned to the fact that she was going to have to wait to talk
to him until everyone went down to rest. But every time she
tried to steer them downstairs, Julien would say, "Just a minute" and launch back into the current political discussion.

They were talking about renewed problems in Crimea. It
was exactly the type of conversation that would have held her
enthralled a few weeks ago—Julien and his friends' take was
always so different and she liked hearing their perspective—
but that had all changed now that she'd learned he was some
kind of psycho extremist.

She listened closely for something that she might have
missed—something that should have alerted her—but even
with what she knew now, he sounded so reasonable.

She still felt like such a fool. How could she not have realized what was going on? She'd been so blinded by Julien she hadn't seen anything beyond his good looks and charm. He'd seemed so perfect. They cared about the same things, thought the same way . . .

Suddenly the realization hit her. That was probably the point. He'd made himself appealing to her. Oh God—she'd been honeypotted! How completely humiliating. Admittedly she didn't have that much experience with men—she'd had a couple of long-term boyfriends over the years—but she didn't want to think of herself as being so gullible. Or worse, desperate.

Annie didn't think she needed a man to "complete" herself, by any means, but had she unconsciously been worried? She wanted a family. A companion. Children. Here she was, twenty-six years old, finishing up grad school, and she hadn't had a serious date since her last boyfriend . . . two years ago. She winced, realizing how long it had been.

Had it made her a little too eager? Too willing to ignore things that didn't seem quite right?

No, she'd been perfectly happy before Julien came along. There was plenty of time for everything else.

But she couldn't deny that it had been exciting, having someone like Julien romancing her.

Annie had begun to fear that they would never rest as they'd planned when Jean Paul finally stood up. "We should all try to get some sleep. We've a long night ahead of us."

"What time are we due to arrive?" Claude asked.

"Just before dark," Jean Paul said. "Around ten."

In other words she had about six hours.

"We should be in the water no later than two a.m.," Jean Paul added. He looked meaningfully at Julien. "I trust that will give you enough time to make sure everything is ready?"

Julien nodded with an anxious look in her direction. Apparently she was "everything."

After going below, Claude and Jean Paul went into the room on the right; she and Julien went into the one across the hall on the left. As soon as Julien shut the door behind them, he tried to broach the subject. "I need to talk to you about tonight."

It was small comfort that he looked as if he wanted to throw up.

She forced a smile to her face. "Can it wait until after we get some rest? I'm suddenly exhausted."

He heaved a heavy sigh of relief like a man who'd just been given a stay of execution. "We are supposed to meet Jean Paul and Claude at ten, so I'll set the alarm for nine."

"Sounds good."

He thought he would only need one hour to convince her? Did he think her so malleable? She was even more insulted, which under the circumstances was ridiculous. Must be some kind of gallows humor.

Annie was glad for the single berths, as she didn't have to get into bed with him. She doubted her acting abilities would go far enough to prevent her from cringing if he tried to touch her.

Wrapping the wool blanket around her shoulders, she turned toward the wall and curled up to wait.

It didn't take long. The dark, windowless room, the gentle lull of the ship, and the three glasses of wine soon put him in a nap-time coma.

But she forced herself to listen to his steady breathing for nearly an hour before slipping out of bed to go in search of the captain.

Normally Dean liked the time alone at the helm, staring for hours out the window, watching the mesmerizing roll of the ocean that stretched as far as the eye could see.

It was relaxing. Normally. But today there wasn't anywhere to hide from his thoughts, and his daytime fantasies were anything but relaxing. They had his body primed in a way it hadn't been in a long time. Not even the soothing croon of Adele's latest was helping.

When the clouds thickened into gray mist, darkening the skies with a burgeoning storm, it only grew worse. The walls seemed to be closing in on him.

He needed to get some air.

He stood up and reached for the door just as it flew open.

Annie ran straight into his arms. At least it seemed that way at the time. But maybe it was just because he'd been thinking about her for most of the afternoon, and quite a few of those thoughts involved her showing up here, falling into his arms, and christening the wheelhouse for the rest of the day.

He'd never had sex at the helm, but he'd been imagining all kinds of creative ways to give it a try.

Reflexively his arms came around her to pull her in close. The feel of those spectacular breasts crushed against his chest and her hips pressing against the part of him that was stiff and throbbing released a little of the pressure he'd been holding in with a groan.

The sound startled her, cutting off whatever she'd been about to say. Instead her eyes locked on his.

Through the haze of lust he realized something was wrong, but he couldn't seem to see beyond her eyes—they were such an incredible shade of green—her smooth and creamy cocoa-butter skin, and her really soft-looking mouth. A mouth that was red and ripe and gently parted as if waiting to be kissed.

The urge rose inside him, powerful and overwhelming. He didn't think anything could stop him from lowering his head and putting his mouth on hers.

"Capt—" she started. "Dan." The sound of the false name sounded so wrong coming from her it brought him harshly back to reality.

He let her go and stepped back.

Christ, what the hell was that?

"I . . . I . . ." She blinked a few times—as if clearing her head (he knew the feeling), and then seemed to remember what she'd wanted to say. "I need to talk to you."

Furious at himself for how he'd reacted, and how easily he'd jumped to the wrong conclusion about why she was here, he found his response a little harsher than he intended. After he turned down the music, he said, "So talk."

"Adele?"

Yeah, he liked Adele—so shoot him. Despite what most of his friends thought, there were more than two types of music: country and western.

Putting aside her surprise at his musical taste, she launched into what had brought her. "We have to do something. They are planning . . . Oh God, I don't know what they are planning, but it isn't good."

Anger and embarrassment took a backseat when he realized how upset she was, but he was having a hard time following her. "Slow down, take a breath, and tell me what happened."

His voice seemed to calm her. She looked up at him almost gratefully, nodded, and took that deep breath before continuing. "I wasn't completely honest with you about what we were planning to do. It wasn't just a dive or to make a film."

He finished for her. "You are going to try to board the drillship and stage some kind of sit-in."

She didn't seem all that surprised that he'd guessed. "That's what I thought, but then you gave me that look, and I heard Julien and Jean Paul talking about something, and I decided to become a superspy—more like Pandora actually."

She was losing him again. What look? He had no idea what she was talking about, but whatever the hell it was, it was serious. "Just tell me what the problem is, Annie. I assume you aren't just now realizing how out-of-your-mind dangerous it is to board a ship in the middle of the ocean or that you would be arrested."

She gave him a glare that would have curdled milk. "Of course I knew that, but those were risks I was willing to take if it meant someone would finally listen to what we were saying and put an end to the exploratory drilling."

"So your little illegal publicity stunt is okay because you have good intentions? A pirate isn't a pirate as long as he has convictions—is that it?"

"Pirate?" She looked horrified by the comparison. But that was exactly what they would be doing. "We aren't hurting anyone."

"What about all the time and resources that go into getting you off that damned boat safely? Not to mention the men who risk their lives to do so. I hate to break it to you, but causing problems and putting others in danger isn't the way to convince people to see your side."

"I . . . God, why are we arguing about this? That isn't the problem. I went into the storage room where the cases are being stored while the others were eating lunch. In one of them, I found something that looks like explosives."

Dean's demeanor changed in an instant. He got real serious, real quick. He took her arm and drew her closer to him, forcing her to look at him. "What the hell do you mean, it looks like explosives? What did you see?"

She described—a little hesitantly, given the change that had come over him—the plastic-wrapped cylinders that looked like cookie dough, taped together with black-and-yellow cording, which presumably was the det cord to set off the blasting cap.

Dean swore, and let her go. He returned to his instruments and charts, making sure he had their position fixed before turning on the autopilot.

"What are you doing?" Annie asked, her voice anxious. "Didn't you hear what I said?"

Dean turned to her, barely able to contain his rage. It was mostly directed at himself, but she was wrapped up in there as well. "I heard what you said. I'm making sure we don't crash while you take me down and show me what you found."

They took the forward stairs from the deck so they didn't have to go by the sleeping quarters, approaching the storage room from the door that linked the hall to the engine room. His quarters were tucked in between.

"I didn't realize it was all connected down here like this," Annie said.

Dean didn't say anything. He was too furious. But it was far worse a few moments later when he was staring down at enough C4 to blow this ship to fucking kingdom come. He was apoplectic.

He'd known this job was a mistake. He should have listened to his instincts. But his damned hero complex had gotten in the way. He'd suspected that Annie was in some kind of trouble and hadn't been able to walk away. And now what she was telling him could ruin everything and put lives at stake—the least being his own.

Lie low. Keep your head down.

Becoming involved in an ecoterrorist plot was about as far from that as he could have managed. The authorities would be all over this. His cover was good, but not *that* good.

Damn it, why the hell hadn't he followed orders? He'd screwed up big-time. Again. Hadn't he learned his lesson? Brian's face flashed before him, and Dean's self-directed anger only grew worse. He should have listened to the LC, but he had to go rushing in. Forward was the only direction he knew.

"Aren't you going to say something?" Annie asked. "Is it bad?"

Somehow he held on to the last thread long enough before snapping to drag her into the engine room, where they wouldn't be heard. "What the hell do you think? Yes, it's bad. Your little friends have enough explosives in there to blow up a couple ships, killing God knows how many people, and putting all our lives in jeopardy."

And so much more.

"I'm sorry," she said, wringing her hands anxiously. "I didn't know. I didn't have any idea what they planned. I would never have gotten involved with them if I had."

"No, you were too busy running around saving the world to actually stop and think about what you were doing. Do-gooders like you are so damned naive. You sit in your idealistic ivory tower bubble, pontificating and passing judgment with no conception of how the real world operates. Well, this is the real world, Annie. It's full of horrible people like your friends out there who are waiting to take advantage of you. But your heart was too busy bleeding to see what was right in front of you. And then when the shit inevitably hits the fan, you expect someone to be there to come to the rescue and clean up your fucking mess."

She didn't shrink from his anger—or from his tirade. It was almost as if she'd heard it before. "You sound just like my father. But what's the alternative? Not caring? Should I sit aside and let all these beautiful islands be destroyed by corporate greed for something we need to be trying to conserve, not keep drilling for more? Maybe I was naive and got involved with the wrong people, but I won't apologize for standing up for what I believe in whether you think it's worth-while or not." She stopped and suddenly seemed to realize something. Her eyes shot to his. "You have an accent! You aren't Canadian—you're American." Her eyes narrowed accusingly. "Texan if I'm hearing it right. God, that's perfect!"

It obviously wasn't. What did she have against the Lone Star State? The best state in the damned country?

But Dean didn't say anything. Forgetting to cover up his accent was the least of his worries right now.

His biggest was figuring out how to get out of this mess without bringing half of Scotland's police force down on top of him. No one could know he'd survived the blast—no one. Not until he figured out how the Russians knew they were coming, and why they'd been set up—if that was indeed what had happened.

If anyone found out that not all the platoon had perished in that explosion, they—whoever they were—would come after him. He was a loose end.

And if there was one survivor, they might ask if there were others. He didn't need any more deaths on his conscience.

Dean swore, knowing exactly what he had to do. He had to get the hell off this boat.

He started toward his cabin, putting Annie out of his mind—or trying to—until she latched hold of his arm. "Wait. Why did you lie to me? Who are you?"

"No one you want to know. So if I were you, I'd stay the hell out of my way."

Annie dropped his arm, obviously startled by his tone. Later maybe he'd feel guilty for taking his anger out on her, but not right now. Right now he was too pissed. Pandora, all right. She had no fucking idea of the potential shit storm she'd just opened.

He went into his room, threw a few things in a backpack, and looped it over his shoulders before moving back into the engine room. He looked around at the pipes, hoses, and vents stacked around twin diesel engines. On the far wall, he flipped a few safety switches and removed a cover to undo a few thick red wires, before replacing it. That should do it. As soon as he cut the engine, it wouldn't be starting again anytime soon. Not without someone who knew what they were doing—and the Euro trio didn't strike him as the mechanical types.

"Is that the ignition system? Why are you disabling the starter?" Annie asked with all that accusation he'd been trying to avoid.

Apparently she *was* the mechanical type. For some reason that didn't surprise him. First diving, now boats? If she wasn't tossing back all that granola, he might be in love.

He was aware that she'd been shadowing him, but he'd been trying not to notice. Right.

"I'm getting out of here, and I don't want anyone following me."

Ignoring the Bambi "you killed my mother" eyes that were now widening with shock and dawning understanding, he made his way up to the wheelhouse before they could turn accusing. He grabbed the emergency handheld marine radio, a few navigation maps, and a heavy-duty Mag flashlight before cutting the engine and letting the anchor drop. For good measure he flipped the kill switch.

He didn't meet Annie's gaze as he walked past her out the door and back down the ladder, and made his way aft along the deck to the inflatable. He went to work lowering it with the dinghy crane. He could use another set of hands to keep the inflatable steady with the ropes, but he wasn't too worried about scratching the sides of the tug. As long as it didn't flip, he'd be fine.

"Wait," Annie said with all the accusation he hadn't wanted to see. "You can't mean to leave me here with them."

"That's exactly what I mean to do." She'd gotten herself into this mess; she could get herself out. Where was that feminist ideology of hers now?

He made the mistake of looking over his shoulder. He might as well have just shot her puppy. She looked at him as if he were the worst kind of ogre. Guilt began to worm its way into his consciousness.

He wasn't an asshole—not usually, at least. "Look," he

said in a more reassuring voice. "Don't worry. I'll radio the coast guard as soon as I'm clear to explain what's going on."

The inflatable splashed as it hit the water. All he had to do now was climb in and release the rope harness.

But she wasn't letting him go. Her hand on his arm was proving to be a pretty strong tether. "What about the explosives?"

"They won't be able to use them if the ship can't go anywhere. But if it makes you feel better, there's a key to the storage room in the top drawer of the table by my bed. Lock the door and toss the key in the ocean. It's a steel door. They won't break it down before the coast guard arrives."

He tried to tell himself she didn't look panicked. It wasn't working. But he forced himself over the side anyway.

He was halfway down the ladder to the boat when she said the one thing he couldn't ignore. The one thing guaranteed to stop him. The one thing that tapped right into all that can't-look-away shit.

"What if they're dangerous?"

Nine

Annie couldn't believe he was just going to leave her.

Who was this guy, and what was he hiding? Clearly the captain didn't want to risk a run-in with the police. Was he on the run? Some kind of criminal?

She didn't think so, but she wasn't exactly batting a thousand right now when it came to stellar judgment on men.

One thing was for sure: she didn't want to be here alone with only Julien between her and Jean Paul when he learned that she'd found the explosives and the coast guard had been alerted.

No, the better of the two evils was definitely the captain. She'd just have to hope he wasn't some psychopathic murderer. Although psychopathic murderers didn't have a conscience, and he seemed to be struggling with his. Which was good. He should be.

Hoping to push him over the edge, she added, "What if they try to hurt me?"

She knew that it had worked when after a pause, he cursed. "Get in the damned boat, Hanoi Jane." She bristled at that. "But as soon as we hit land, you are on your own. Got it?"

"Aye-aye, Captain," she said with a mock solute. "Anyone ever tell you that you'd make a great drill sergeant?"

She'd meant it as a joke, but his expression suddenly sobered. It would be an improvement over the anger if it wasn't tinged with that grim sadness.

"Maybe once or twice." He held out his hand to her. "If you're coming, make it fast."

"What about my bag?"

He gave her a look. "Good riddance. It's too girlie for you anyway."

Ignoring the fact that she thought the same thing when her mother had given it to her, she said, "What is that supposed to mean?"

"It means that the whole 'pink is for girls, blue is for boys' gender color conventions probably offends your feminist sensibilities."

They did. But the fact that he'd guessed that was mildly annoying. "Let me guess. Your favorite color is blue?"

His mouth quirked into something resembling a smile. "Get in the boat, Bambi."

Bambi? She couldn't decide whether the stripper name was better or worse than the slam at Jane Fonda's regrettable photos on an antiaircraft gun on a visit to Hanoi during the Vietnam War.

To get to the ladder, she had to climb over the gunwale. There was usually a step stool, but she couldn't find it, so she started to lift her leg to roll over only to be grabbed from behind.

She recognized the stench of leather and cigarettes even before he spoke.

It was her turn to swear. Cutting the engine or dropping the anchor must have woken him.

"Going somewhere, *mademoiselle*?" Jean Paul asked, mock laughter in his voice. The single arm wrapped around her waist was surprisingly strong as he swept her around to look down over the side. "Get out of the boat, Captain."

Annie looked at Dan, and oddly it was his expression and not the fact that she was being manhandled and threatened by Jean Paul that made her heart stop.

Maybe she should reconsider the psychopathic-killer thing. The captain looked cold, deadly, dangerous, and utterly in control. That "you don't want to fuck with me" air was back with a vengeance.

"Let her go," he said in a voice as hard as steel. "Annie is coming with me."

"Neither of you is going anywhere." Jean Paul had barely finished when he backed up his words by pulling something from his coat pocket.

Oh God, it was a gun. A SIG Sauer semiautomatic pistol to be specific. Her father had carried a similar weapon—a SIG P226—as his service sidearm as a Ranger and later when he'd been recruited for Delta. The Beretta M9 had been standard issue, but he'd preferred the SIG. Why she thought that was important right now, she didn't know.

Unfortunately, if the way Jean Paul was holding it was any indication, he knew how to use it.

He had the gun aimed at the captain, but when it didn't make him move fast enough he moved it to her head. She'd been struggling to get free, but at the sensation of the cold metal kissing her temple, she stilled. Her heart was thumping like an out-of-control freight train, but her mind seemed to open—as if she could see everything in extraordinary detail.

"Wait!" Annie heard Julien's voice from behind her. He must have just come up from below. "What are you doing? You said she wouldn't get hurt."

"She won't," Jean Paul said. "As long as the captain doesn't do anything stupid." He looked back down at Dan. "What's it going to be, Captain?" He seemed to be reading Dan's mind aloud. "Take your chances in the boat, and the girl is killed either before or after I fire at you. You might get away—you might not. We'll both have to live with her death on our hands. I assure you it will mean nothing to me, but can you say the same?" He smiled smugly. "Maybe I was wrong about what I saw, but I don't think so."

Whatever he meant, Dan didn't argue the point. "What's to stop you from putting a bullet in my head as soon as I'm up there?"

"Nothing," Jean Paul said with an indifferent shrug. "You'll just have to trust me. But until I'm sure that Claude can captain the boat, I do have incentive to keep you around."

"Fair enough," Dan said.

Annie didn't know what was more surreal: that she had a gun pointed to her head or the way that they were calmly talking about murder.

A moment later, Dan was standing by her side. As glad as she was for the company right now, she wished she hadn't gotten him into this.

Jean Paul moved the gun from her head, and she exhaled, not realizing until that moment that she'd been holding her breath. It wasn't quite with relief, however, as the gun was still pointed in her direction. He was eyeing the captain as if he were a dangerous animal that could attack at any time.

"There are some plastic zip ties in my bag," Jean Paul said to Claude, who'd suddenly appeared next to Julien. "Go get them."

Neither man looked happy about the situation, but Julien was the only one staring at her with big puppy dog eyes, pleading for understanding. To keep the analogy going . . . he was barking up the wrong tree.

Claude returned a moment later with the entire bag.

"Secure his hands first," Jean Paul instructed, nodding toward Dan.

The captain didn't protest and held out his hands. He seemed oddly complacent. Maybe too complacent. It didn't seem to go along with what she knew of him. She would have said he was a born fighter.

Obviously she'd watched too many Tom Hardy movies—she was confusing Dan with one of the characters portrayed by the actor.

Or maybe not. Jean Paul must have picked up on it as well. "Use two," he said after Claude finished securing the first. Waving the gun toward the gunwale, Jean Paul ordered Dan to "Get down against the side."

The captain sat as instructed, and a moment later, Claude was securing one of the ties around his ankles. It wasn't easy to do with the captain's boots, but the tie was just long enough.

It was her turn next. Jean Paul finally released her and pushed her toward Claude. Her hands were secured—with only one tie—and she was ordered to sit next to the captain. She was happy to do so and might have sat a little closer to him than was necessary. But she couldn't deny that the heat and press of his powerful body against hers were comforting. Maybe big and muscular did have their time and place. Sadly her education and PhD hadn't prepared her for being taken captive by ecoterrorists. She would allow herself this Tarzan/Jane moment of awareness, but when it was all over, she would go back to independent and strong on her own.

While Claude was securing the tie around her ankles, Dan asked, "You okay?"

She nodded. "I'm fine." She looked at him, her heart suddenly in her throat. "I'm sorry."

He nodded in acknowledgment. "Don't worry. It will be all right."

She wanted to believe him, and oddly enough she did. Maybe it was the certainty in his voice or the utter calmness of his demeanor, but she felt her spirits lift.

"Claude," Jean Paul said. "See if you can get the boat running again."

Claude headed to the wheelhouse while Jean Paul and Julien stood guard. Jean Paul was leaning against the opposite side of the boat, smoking a cigarette while holding the gun on them. He'd given himself plenty of room to react if the captain tried anything. Julien stood a few feet away at the rail, also smoking, looking out to sea with his back to her—almost as if he couldn't bear to meet her gaze.

Weak.

Maybe her father hadn't been all wrong.

The weather had turned since they'd left Stornoway, with the sun disappearing behind a gray cloud of the famous Scottish mist, the temperature dropping by at least twenty degrees, and the wind picking up. She was glad she'd grabbed her featherlight down jacket when she snuck out of the room, but wished she had her Red Sox hat. They were her favorite team, courtesy of their spring training facilities at the time being not too far from where she'd been born in Florida.

"Here," the captain said, lifting his hands in front of him to pull off his hat. "It will keep your head warm."

Annie blinked at him. Did he read minds?

He mistook her hesitation. "It's cleaner than it looks."

She shook her head. "It's not that. What about you?"

"I'm used to it. Besides, my jacket has a hood if I need it."

He had on a Gor-Tex rain shell over a fleece sweatshirt.

She nodded gratefully. "Thank you."

He adjusted it smaller, slipping it on her head. It was still a little loose but so warm she didn't care.

"What are you doing over there?" Jean Paul said, catching the movement.

"She was cold," the captain said. "I just gave her my hat."

"I could get you another jacket from the room," Julien offered eagerly, obviously anxious to do something—anything—to get back on her good side.

It wasn't going to happen. Nothing killed a faltering relationship like a case full of explosives and having a gun pointed at her head.

"No one is going anywhere," Jean Paul said.

He was more correct than he realized, as he discovered a few minutes later when Claude returned.

"I can't get it started," Claude said.

Of Julien's friends, Claude had always been the most friendly toward her. She'd always liked him and was disappointed that he was involved with this. How could seemingly normal people think it was okay to blow up something to prove their point? Was it like some kind of cult? Did they get brainwashed or sucked in and lose their sense of reality?

Jean Paul came over to stand before the captain, the gun pointed right at him. "What did you do?"

"Nothing."

Jean Paul moved the gun to her and repeated the question. "Want to try again, Captain?"

Dan obviously decided not to test him further. "I pulled a few wires. I'll show you if you want."

Jean Paul laughed. "I don't think so. You'll stay here and tell me what to do."

Apparently Claude's boat skills didn't include anything mechanical. She didn't need to guess who had made the explosive devices. Obviously Jean Paul had picked up enough technical knowledge to make him think he could handle it.

Dan described what he'd done to the wires and how to put them back. "When the light comes on, you'll know you did it right."

Annie didn't miss that he hadn't mentioned the kill switch in the wheelhouse.

"You better hope this works."

Dan didn't appear concerned. "It will if you do it right."

Jean Paul handed the gun to Julien, who took it none too happily. "Shoot him if he moves." He turned to Claude. "Help him keep an eye on them, but be ready to try to start it again when I call up."

Annie looked at Dan. His expression didn't give anything away, but she sensed this was exactly what he'd wanted.

Dean was biding his time, waiting for the opportunity to make his move, and this was it.

But he'd have to act fast. He'd given confusing directions, but replacing a few wires wouldn't take too long. He wanted that gun before Jean Paul came back. One look in that bastard's eyes, and Dean knew he wouldn't hesitate to use it.

Julien, on the other hand, looked less certain. Clearly things weren't going the way he'd planned. And just as clearly he hadn't been deceiving Annie about everything—he honestly seemed to care about her. He kept staring at her pleadingly, which Dean was about to use to his advantage.

"Talk to him," he said under his breath.

She didn't hesitate or look at him questioningly, understanding immediately where he was going with this.

Apparently she had a few questions ready for her former boyfriend. "How could you deceive me like this, Julien? I thought you cared about me."

Julien looked so relieved that she was talking to him that Dean almost felt sorry for him. Julien glanced first to Claude, who, unlike Jean Paul, didn't appear to object to him talking to her.

"I do care about you," he said. "I thought you felt the same way as I did. That you were passionate enough to want to see things changed and that this was the only way to get them to listen to us."

"By killing people?" she said incredulously. "You thought I would understand blowing up a ship or think that will get anyone to listen to you? It just makes you a terrorist. You are only turning the oil companies into the victims and alienating anyone who might support you."

Julien had the gall to look offended. But he'd stood up while she was talking and stepped toward her as he talked. "We weren't going to kill anyone, were we, Claude?"

The other man hesitated before shaking his head. *Interesting.*

"Our plan wasn't to blow up the ship, just the moorings," Julien explained to Annie. "When the ship broke free, the drill would be destroyed."

"And what if there was oil in there?" she demanded angrily. "You would be doing exactly what we were fighting to prevent."

"That's a lot of explosives to just blow up a few moorings," Dean interjected dryly.

As he'd hoped, Julien didn't appreciate his butting in. He took a few more steps toward him and waved the gun at him. Unlike Jean Paul, Julien didn't seem to have much experience with firearms—which wasn't necessarily a good thing. He could accidentally shoot.

"Shut up," Julien said to Dean. "And stay out of it. What the hell do you know?"

"Enough to suspect that you are part of OPF"—Dean had been briefed a while back on Ocean Protection Front and wasn't surprised when his stab in the dark elicited surprise from Julien—"and that your fearless leader was lying to you and had no intention of targeting just the moorings." Dean saw something flicker across Claude's face. "Ask your partner over there."

"Is this true?" Julien said, turning to Claude.

It was the opening Dean was waiting for. In one harsh move he lifted his hands above his head and pulled them down and apart, snapping the ties with the force of the movement. His feet were even easier as Julien had become flustered by his boots and ended up threading the zip tie in the wrong direction.

Dean was out of practice, but his two opponents weren't well trained and obviously hadn't had much experience in Close Quarter Battle (CQB) and hand-to-hand combat.

Dean had both.

Before Julien could spin around, Dean had already used his foot to knock him off balance. Keeping an eye on the hand with the gun the whole time—cognizant that Julien could squeeze the trigger in fear—Dean grabbed Julien's wrist, holding it firm before snapping his elbow over his knee. The gun fell harmlessly to the floor, and Dean kicked it away from Claude, who was only now reacting.

Julien was moaning—Dean had probably broken his arm—but he shut him up quickly with a sharp blow to the head. Better.

Claude had initially started toward Dean, but seeing how efficiently Dean had dealt with his partner, he'd reconsidered and started backing off toward the stairs.

Dean was on him in a few seconds and quieted him as well with a couple of well-placed blows, but unfortunately not before Claude had called out a warning.

Dean doubted Jean Paul had heard him, but he wasn't taking any chances. Pulling a multitool from his jeans, he sliced Annie's ties with the knife while pocketing the gun that had come to rest not far from her feet. He hoped he wouldn't have to use it.

He could feel her eyes on him. When he finally met her gaze, he wasn't surprised to see her expression. It was shock tinged with a bit of awe and fear. Unfortunately he didn't have time to reassure her.

Machine. He didn't know why he remembered that now.

"Get some of those ties from the bag and secure them.

They should be out for a while, but I don't want to take any chances." He looked at her again, holding her gaze. "Annie, do you understand?"

She nodded.

"Good, and do a better job than your boyfriend over there. Make sure they are on right."

That snapped her back to attention. Her eyes flashed angrily. "He's not my boyfriend."

Dean smiled. "Good."

He was almost to the door when she stopped him. "Be careful."

He nodded. "Get them tied up, all right?"

He was halfway down the stairs when the lights went out.

He swore. Although it was still daylight, with the storm brewing the skies weren't giving off much light. It wasn't pitch-black, but it was dark belowdecks.

One of two things had just happened. If he was lucky, Jean Paul had crossed a couple of wires, interfering with the electrical system. If he was unlucky, Jean Paul had heard Claude's warning.

Dean wasn't going to count on luck. Retracing his steps, he returned to the deck. Seeing Annie still in the midst of tying them up, he put his finger over his mouth to warn her and continued around to the forward stairs that led directly into the engine room.

Retrieving a couple of flares from one of the seats that held safety equipment, he poised himself over the entrance and tossed them down.

Now he had some light, and from the gasp of shock, he knew where to look before he jumped down. He was ready. Jean Paul had found a piece of wood and attempted to level it at his head, but Dean ducked and retaliated with a hard punch to the kidneys.

The other man crumpled but didn't fall, managing to swing the wood against Dean's jaw. The blow both surprised him and pissed him off.

He tackled Jean Paul to the floor. He was a slippery bastard and almost managed to roll away, but Dean got his arm around

his neck in a choke hold first. A few seconds later Jean Paul
went slack.

Carrying him up in a fireman's hold, Dean deposited him—
none too gently (his jaw was stinging, damn it)—next to his
future cell mates and helped Annie tie him up.

Seeing his face, she gasped and unconsciously reached
over to cradle the side of his face in her incredibly soft hand.
"You're hurt."

He shook his head. It must be as bad as it felt if she could
see it through the beard. "I'm fine," he said, shaking her off,
his voice gruff from the strange knot in his chest. "Let's get
out of here."

With the men incapacitated, there was really no reason to
take her with him, but he could see how traumatized she was
by what had just happened, and he couldn't stomach trying
to leave her behind again. Yep, the guy who didn't shrink from
anything was pussying out. But he'd get rid of her as soon as
he could.

Ten

Colt knew the number by heart, though he'd never dialed it. It rang three times before someone answered. The voice at the other end was not the one Colt expected.

It belonged to a man. "Hello."

Colt knew the name that went with the voice but didn't use it. "Put Kate on the phone."

There was a puzzled pause on the other end. "Who is this?"

Colt wasn't going to get angry, but the very proper English upper-class voice set his teeth on edge—big-time.

Jolly good, motherfucker. Just put her on! That was what he wanted to say. Instead he said, "I'm afraid it's a personal matter."

Lord Percy, as Colt thought of him—his actual name was Sir Percival Edwards (*His Excellency* Sir Percival Edwards)— put his hand over the phone, but Colt could still hear him. "Katherine. There's someone on the phone for you. He won't give me his name. Says it's personal."

A few seconds later the phone was handed over. "This is Katherine."

Three years. That was how long it had been since he'd heard her voice.

"Hello?" she repeated.

It took a moment for something to come out. "It's me."

There was a dead pause. It didn't last long. A moment later, the phone was slammed down, and the call disconnected.

Three years obviously hadn't changed her feelings for him.

He'd known she wouldn't make it easy.

Colt picked up his phone. Not to call her again, which would be a waste of time, but to book the next flight to Arlington.

Eleven

Annie wasn't sure whether it was shock or awe that kept her quiet as the captain piloted the small eight-person inflatable away from the dive boat.

The last few hours had been eventful, to say the least. She'd found explosives, learned that not only was her boyfriend a terrorist but he was also planning to embroil her in his madness, had a gun pulled on her by his mentor—who seemed to have no hesitation about the prospect of putting a bullet in her head—and narrowly escaped it all, thanks to the man beside her.

Although "narrowly" probably wasn't the right word for what she'd just witnessed. Thus the "awe" part.

She'd never seen anything like it—except maybe in movies or on TV. Dan—whoever he was—had eliminated the threat with methodical, cold efficiency. He'd moved so fast. One instant he'd been next to her; the next he'd snapped the plastic ties around his wrists as if they were paper and had his hands on Julien's arm with the gun—she cringed, still hearing that sickening crack in her head as Julien's arm had broken—and with a few more well-aimed blows the two men were out cold.

How long had it taken, thirty seconds? A minute at most? A few minutes more to take out the bigger threat of Jean Paul?

It had looked like the extreme fighting mixed with martial arts that she'd seen on TV, although it was much more scary-looking in real life.

She eyed him from under the brim of his borrowed cap as he stood at the wheel of the inflatable's helm station. She was seated next to him on one of the plastic bench seats. They were headed into the wind, and he was pushing the twenty-horsepower engine as much as he could to put as much distance between them and the boat as possible. The lift and slam of the inflatable going over the waves didn't seem to bother him—nor did the spray beating into his face. He looked utterly in control with the same granite expression on his face. Actually, if she thought he was capable, she would think he was having fun—in his element, so to speak.

She on the other hand was struggling not to fly out of the boat, felt her teeth banging and bones rattling from every slam, and couldn't feel her face.

Who was this guy? He wouldn't hear her now if she asked him, but part of her wasn't sure she wanted to know.

Finally, when they'd gone about thirty minutes and the dive boat had long disappeared behind them, he slowed the engine.

She looked around, hoping to see some kind of identifying landmark, but all around them were darkening skies, thickening mist, and the endless dark grayish blue swells of the ocean.

What were they, maybe fifty miles off the northeast coast of Lewis?

The middle of nowhere. It was ocean and stormy skies for as far as the eye could see. *Alone.*

Her heart skipped a few beats.

She eyed him again, realizing how much trust she'd put in him by just getting in the boat. Out here all alone like this probably wasn't the best time to be hoping that hadn't been a mistake. He could toss her overboard with no one the wiser.

Her skipping heartbeat stuttered to a stop. God, why had she thought that?

The boat stopped—or rather idled as the engine was still on.

Cue the dramatic movie music.

"Wh-why are we stopping?" she asked, hoping she didn't sound as nervous as she felt.

He ignored her question, which in her limited experience wasn't unusual for him. "Do you have anything electronic with you?"

She frowned, not sure what he meant. As he hadn't let her fetch her bag, all she had was what she carried in her pockets— her phone and her watch, which was an old Mickey Mouse one that she'd had since childhood. She felt around in her jeans. Oh yeah, and some lip balm and a few tissues.

She didn't even have her passport. Her mom had bought her one of those waist belts to travel with, but she'd hated it and stuck it in her suitcase as soon as they arrived from the airport.

"Keep it with you at all times." She would happily tell her mother she was right just as soon as she got out of this.

"Just my phone," she said.

"Let me see it."

Figuring he was going to call someone, she pulled it out of her pocket and handed it to him—nearly going overboard after it when he immediately tossed it over the side.

Her attempt to reach for it, however, proved futile, and it disappeared beneath the waves forever.

Outrage made her forget that she should be terrified. She spun around on him. "Why did you do that?"

"I didn't want anyone tracking us."

"You could have just turned it off."

"That isn't a fail-safe."

"I highly doubt Jean Paul and his friends are that sophisticated."

"But the police might be. I'm not taking any chances—and OPF is a powerful organization. Don't underestimate them."

"How do you know so much about them?"

He didn't answer, instead pulling a radio out of his bag.

"What about your cell phone?" she asked. "Is yours going overboard, too?"

"Mine's a burner and untraceable."

Great. That wasn't what she needed to hear. Why did he

have an untraceable cell phone? Weren't those the province of drug dealers and other criminals? What was this guy involved in?

She didn't have a chance to ask him, as he was on the radio—channel 16 was the international distress channel—already giving the "urgent" signal of "Pan-Pan."

Mayday might have been appropriate under the circumstances—the situation was grave and imminent to her mind—but he was obviously taking a more rational, less terrified-out-of-his-mind perspective.

It took a few minutes for a response. The fact that they were in the range of a boat or coast guard station was some small relief. Not that five to twenty miles was going to help her much if he decided to get rid of her.

She'd definitely watched too many movies.

The captain was quick and to the point. He gave the name of the boat, the last known coordinates, that there were three ecoterrorists who'd planned to blow up the drillship waiting for them, and told them "not to miss the explosives in the equipment cases in the storage room."

The long pause made Annie wonder whether the transmission had been lost. But the coast guard operator repeated what Dan had said and asked him to confirm. He did, but as soon as they asked him to identify himself and his position, Dan stopped them. "You better hurry. They're tied up and one of them is injured."

He turned off the radio, which she took to mean that he considered his duty done.

Still upset about her phone—it was new and not cheap—she said, "Doesn't that one magically turn on, too?"

He made a gruff sound that she thought might be of amusement. She was certain of it when one side of his mouth curved. "Nope. No way to track it if it's off. I just brought the old radio—no GPS. I also didn't bring the sat EPIRB."

In other words, no satellite beacon to let someone track them down. Not necessarily what she wanted to hear. What if they got in some kind of . . . predicament?

"I hope you know where you are going."

He laughed for real this time. It was kind of charming. But not as charming as when his steel blue eyes met hers and twinkled. That kind of charming caused her heart to forget to beat.

God, he was good-looking. She almost didn't want him to shave the stupid beard anymore. It might be too much to take.

"Don't worry. I won't get us lost."

"What, are you some kind of expert navigator?"

"Something like that."

She looked up. "I don't see a lot of stars around."

He nodded toward his bag, which he'd pulled out of the dry storage box. "I have a compass and the boat's navigation maps. We'll be fine."

She must not have looked convinced.

"You don't believe me?"

This time it was her turn not to answer. Her eye had caught on something. The plastic handle she'd been holding on to had pulled away from the boat, and one of the seams had started to split. "Look at this," she said.

Dan glanced over and swore. He moved over from the helm to inspect it. "Whoever rented this boat to your friends"— seeing her expression, he corrected—"your former friends didn't inspect it very well. This entire seam wasn't glued correctly."

"Is it leaking?" Annie asked warily.

"Not yet. I have some duct tape, but I'm not sure how long it will hold."

Great. Just what she wanted to hear. "You carry duct tape with you?"

What psychopath didn't have that in his torture bag?

"Not usually, but I had a tear in my bag and needed to improvise." He reached down into the backpack and retrieved the tape, letting her see the patch he'd done on the bottom.

He gave her a sidelong look as he worked. "You don't have to look so nervous. I'm not going to hurt you."

Embarrassed at being caught out, she blushed. "You might be right. But let's just say my judgment in men has taken a beating the past couple of days." Not to mention that he'd lied to her about not being American and clearly didn't want a run-in with the police. But, even though she hadn't forgotten how Mr. No Sugarcoat had torn into her a while ago—some of which was admittedly deserved—and then had tried to abandon her, she owed him her life. "I'm sorry. After all that you've done I should be thanking you. I'm grateful—truly I am."

He nodded, turning back to the repair work as if her gratitude made him uncomfortable. When he was done, he sat back and looked at her. "You don't have anything to worry about, Annie—I'm harmless."

She blurted a nervous laugh. "Right. I saw exactly how harmless you are a little while ago. How did you learn to do that?"

He frowned, all signs of amusement vanishing. "They deserved worse. When he held that gun to your head . . ."

He stopped, and she wondered what he was going to say. Had he been more affected by the strange connection she'd sensed between them than he let on?

Maybe so. She sucked in her breath as he reached across to swipe a few windblown hairs from her cheek, letting his fingers linger on her face.

There was a softness in his eyes she'd never seen before and a huskiness to his voice when he spoke. When they were combined with that sexy drawl, she had to admit it made her feel a little tingly in areas that she shouldn't be thinking about right now. "You are safe as long as you are with me."

She wasn't sure that was true. The way her heart was beating in her throat didn't feel very safe at all. It felt dangerous. It felt intense and a little scary. It felt as if she were on the edge of a precipice about to jump with nothing to catch her.

This man could hurt her, all right, although not in the way she'd been imagining.

Physically, at least, she knew she could believe him: he would keep her safe.

He leaned forward and just for a moment she thought he might kiss her. She was surprised to realize how much she wanted him to, and how disappointed she was when he dropped his hand instead.

It was so sudden that she wondered if maybe the moment had been too much for him as well.

"The tape won't last forever—especially in the rain." He indicated the skies that looked a few minutes away from unleashing. "We need to find somewhere to put in and wait it out."

Opening one of the maps, he studied it for a moment and seemed to be doing a few calculations in his head. "We should be around here." He pointed to an area on the map. "There should be a small archipelago about eight miles to our southwest."

Eight miles was a long way to go in a storm-frenzied ocean in an inflatable. As the waves rose their speed would have to lower, especially as there were just two of them in the boat. On flat water, this boat would probably go twenty to twenty-five miles an hour, but in a storm they would have to be much more careful and be lucky to go a quarter of that.

"Will we make it?"

He grinned. "No problem. Even if I have to swim us there."

He was joking. At least she thought he was joking.

"I'd rather not have to test out this life jacket or ruin what I have left of my wardrobe," Annie said dryly. "I've already lost a phone today."

He chuckled. "Glad to see you haven't lost your sense of humor."

She was, too. And when the first drop of rain landed on her nose a few minutes later, she suspected she was going to need it.

Dean was glad she wasn't looking at him as if he was a serial killer anymore, but the trust in her eyes didn't sit much better.

The leak bothered him more than he wanted to let on, and the storm was going to complicate things. If the clouds and wind were any indication, the weather was coming in a lot faster and heavier than the forecasts predicted. Hardly unusual in Scotland but not great timing for them.

He also didn't have the heart to tell her that he had no idea what they'd find when they reached the archipelago. For all he knew they were a couple of sea stacks with no place to land unless you were a bird.

But he wasn't going to worry about what he couldn't control. One step at a time.

A bad seam. He shook his head. It wasn't common, but it happened. It was shit luck to have the first time it happened to him be in the middle of the North Sea in a storm. They were, however, fortunate that she'd noticed it before it had fully broken apart and the rain had started. Getting the tape to stick when it was wet would have taken a miracle.

These boats were built to stay afloat for a while if one of the tubes lost air, but he wouldn't want to put it to a test in a storm. Water was already sloshing in from the waves, and it was bound to get worse.

He'd been forced to ditch most of his gear in Russia. After the LC had dragged him back from where the explosion had thrown him and rendered him unconscious, they'd tossed all their gear—anything that might enable someone to track or ID them—into the fire. But Dean had replaced many of the items in his E&E (escape and evade) survival kit—SEALs didn't leave home without 'em—including the duct tape that had made Annie so nervous and a compass.

He preferred a full-sized military compass to the button-sized one that was standard issue in his kit. Good thing, as not only was it much more accurate, but it was also water-proof. A fixed marine compass with the lubber's line aligned would have been better, but he would make adjustments. Besides, at this point beggars couldn't be choosers.

Dean was so focused on navigating the boat he didn't realize it had begun to rain until Annie shivered.

He swore, realizing her jacket—although down—wasn't waterproof. Of course, one of the things he hadn't replaced in his kit was the emergency Mylar blanket. "Here," he said, starting to unzip his waterproof shell while holding the wheel with the other. "Take this."

She shook her head and stopped him with her hand on his arm. "I'm not taking your jacket. You need it more than I do.

Besides," she added with a smile, "what kind of card-carrying member of NOW would I be if I let you do that?"

"A dry one," he quipped. She laughed, and he looked at her sideways. "Let me guess. You have all kinds of cards in your wallet."

She was the type to put her money where her mouth was. Or maybe he should say where her heart was.

She grinned—a little too happily to his mind—and started rattling off every bleeding-heart, save-the-whales type of organization he could think of and some he'd never heard of.

But he held up his hand when she got to the political ones. "Stop. I can't take it anymore. You had me at that last one." He gave a dramatic shudder.

"They do a lot of important things—"

"Annie?"

She paused to look up at him. The brim of his hat had kept most of the rain off her face, but one or two drops had caught in her lashes. Her eyes were gorgeous—especially when they were sparkling with amusement. "I'll keep the jacket if you promise to stop."

She smiled as if that had been her intention all along. "Deal." It was her turn to look at him sideways. "Let me guess. . . ."

He grinned. She didn't even need to say it. "Cold, dead hands, baby." He sobered. "'Baby' in the nonmisogynistic sense of the word."

"Obviously," she deadpanned back at him. "Although I'm surprised that they teach that word in caveman school."

He gave a sharp bark of laughter. He'd never met a woman who gave him shit the way she did. "Yeah, it was in the words-over-four-letters class, right between Dragging by the Hair 101 and Patriarchal Society 200."

She threw back her head and laughed, which stopped his jesting cold. It was replaced by a hard bolt of lust. Lust that despite the weather and their precarious situation made him hot and about a half second away from pulling her into his arms and putting his mouth on that very tempting, creamy-looking throat. Which would be a really bad idea.

That he could lose focus in a situation like this, even for a moment, was disconcerting enough to snap him back to attention. Situational awareness on an op was something he'd never lost sight of before.

He didn't like it.

Having no idea of the effect she'd just had on him, she lifted her head to meet his gaze, still smiling. "Let me guess. You excelled in all your subjects?"

"Enough to teach you a few things if you are interested."

"I think I'll pass," she said dryly.

"You don't know what you are missing."

She rolled her eyes. "I can guess."

He wondered if they were talking about the same thing. If they were, she had no fucking idea. "Let me know if you want a rain check."

"I'll do that."

He had to force himself to look away. She was so beautiful he was getting distracted again.

He lasted about a mile. That was the point when the drops of mist turned into full-fledged rain. Sexist pig or not, he wasn't going to sit here with a coat on that was keeping him dry while she got soaked.

He thought about pulling her into his lap and not giving her a chance to argue, but as that might be seen as coming a little too close to the pig part of the equation, he decided to take a more subtle route. There was a first time for everything. "I need you to help me with something."

She sat up. "Of course. Anything."

"I can't keep the compass steady, hold the map, and steer the boat with the waves like this."

"What do you need me to do?"

He scooted back a little on the seat. "Come sit here." Said the spider to the fly. He motioned in front of him. "You can hold the map and the compass where I can see it, while I steer."

She frowned as if wondering whether she should be suspicious.

As MacDonald would say, smart lass.

Dean had to slow the speed, and it took a little jostling, but a few minutes later she was tucked against his chest, and his coat was discreetly pulled around her, shielding her from most of the rain.

There was one big problem—a problem that was getting bigger and bigger by the moment. The plastic seat in front of the helm could be adjusted, but not enough to give their bodies any space between them. Which essentially meant that her back was pressed against his chest, her head was tucked under his chin, and her firm, perfectly curved ass was nestled right into his crotch, and with every bump of the boat, that very incredible bottom was slamming against him. His dick— the brainless, too-long-ignored idiot that it was—was taking notice and standing hard at attention. Emphasis on hard.

There was too much of him and too little between them, namely a couple of layers of denim, for her not to notice.

She tried to sit stiffly for a while, keeping as much distance between them as possible. But as the weather grew worse, and the waves higher, it became impossible. She gave up, sinking into him fully.

It took everything he had not to groan. But she felt good. Really good. Body-on-fire, skin-too-tight, every-instinct-flared good.

For the next half hour, he had to fight to keep them on course while struggling to ignore the havoc the motion and rhythm of the boat were wreaking on his control.

The warmth and softness of her body didn't help. Nor did the fact that she smelled incredible. Perfume? Shampoo? He didn't know, but it was feminine, sweet, and made him want to bury his face in her neck and hair.

He was almost glad when the weather got worse and required his full attention.

Almost.

Twelve

They were getting pummeled by rain that was coming down in proverbial sheets with no intention of stopping, white-topped waves that were climbing higher by the minute, and sharp gusts of wind that blew it all together in great geysers of water leaping and spraying all around them.

Clearly this was the wrong time to think about how good Dan felt behind her or how close his arm was to her breast or that the erection hard against her bottom was every bit as impressive as it had felt in her hand. Yet despite the tumult swirling around her, the flush of desire—all right, *lust*—was hitting her hard. He was turning her on. Big-time.

In the cocoon of his coat and body heat, she was warm and soft and inexplicably relaxed for a castaway at sea in a leaky boat in a monsoon. Well, maybe the storm wasn't quite that bad, but it was definitely not the time to be thinking about sex. Really raunchy sex. Really hot sex. Sex like what she'd only imagined.

But if the sensations turning her liquid every time her bottom rode up against him were any indication, she'd definitely been missing out in the doggy-style category. She could too easily imagine him bending her forward against the wheel, lifting her hips to him, and sinking that thick column inside her. And the thrusts. She could definitely imagine the thrusts. Every time the boat lurched over a wave and came down hard, she felt the slam of him behind her, sending a reverberation of need through her bones. She was hot and achy and more turned on than she'd ever been in her life. Which given their circumstances was pure crazy sauce.

Maybe she was imagining it all a little too well, because as they rode over the next wave, and the motion carried her hips back, she might have arched her back a little and made a sound that was suspiciously like a moan.

He stiffened behind her, growing so taut the muscles in his chest and arms seemed to turn to steel. Hello, Mr. Six-Pack—or Eight-Pack. Unless she wanted to turn around and count them—which she kind of did—the exact number of rigid bands would remain a mystery. Her back felt even hotter—like sitting in front of a furnace that had just been stoked. Which admittedly she might have just done.

What was she doing? Grinding against a guy she barely knew like a teenager when they were in danger of disappearing under the next wave or sinking in a deflated boat?

Cheeks aflame with mortified heat, she tried to pull away, but he caught her with one of those rock-hard arms and pulled her back in tight. "Don't. I want you right here."

His voice so close to her ear sent shivers down her spine. Sure, that was it. It wasn't the sensual promise in his words. He was feeling it, too. He liked it. He wanted her.

Was that what she wanted? Sex with a stranger? Even if he was a really hot stranger?

Suddenly she realized what this must look like. She was acting like a sex-starved porn star in a really bad movie—*Perfect Sex Storm*, maybe? She didn't even know who he was. A half hour ago she thought he could be a serial killer.

No, she'd never thought that. There was something about this guy that she'd trusted from the beginning, and that was making her come up with ridiculous scenarios to try to talk herself out of doing so. Her mind was telling her not to be an idiot again—that she had no reason to trust him—but her gut was telling her something else.

"Listen to your gut," her father had always said. But how could she do that when that gut had just been so wrong?

Naive. Of all the things Dan had said to her earlier in his no-sugarcoat, cut-right-to-the-heart-of-it lambasting, that had probably been the most stinging.

Because it was true. But it was also because naive seemed to be used too often as a synonym for "stupid." Which it shouldn't be. She just didn't think like that. She didn't look for treachery behind every corner. She didn't see bad people; she saw good. Did that sometimes get her in trouble? Yes. But she didn't want to see the world as the dark place that he obviously did.

Maybe she should have asked Julien a few more questions, and certainly gotten to know him a little better before embarking on an adventure like this, but there hadn't been any sign that he'd been involved with a terrorist organization like OPF. He'd been acting strangely, and she hadn't liked Jean Paul, but she hadn't missed something. He'd deceived her plain and simple.

But hard-eyed cynics like Dan—or her father—had a way of making her feel bad for not assuming the worst of people and treating everyone as if they were a suspect.

She didn't see how they could live their lives like that. Or didn't live in her father's case, when the anger, unhappiness, and ugliness got to be too much, even for a superhero.

She didn't want that kind of dark in her life. She'd stayed away from men like Dan her whole life. Why now was she forgetting that?

He must have sensed the change in her. "You all right?"

His voice brought her back from the memories. She nodded.

"Good. I'm going to need your help. The swell is getting worse. I don't want to take my eyes off the waves for too long, so you're going to have to use the compass and keep us headed in the right direction."

Her father had tried to teach her the basics of navigating with a map and compass, but she'd never really gotten the hang of it—and she certainly had never tried on the ocean. But that didn't mean she wouldn't try. If he needed her to do this, she would. "All right."

"Good girl."

She'd get annoyed with him later for that little bit of paternalistic sexism. "Dan?"

He paused a moment before responding. "Yep?"

"Is it really bad?"

If she hadn't been sitting so close to him, she wouldn't have felt the slight hesitation that answered her question. Yes, it was bad.

"You don't need to be scared, Annie. I got this, okay?"

Strangely she believed him. If anyone was capable of getting them out of this, she'd put her money on him. "Okay."

"Just keep us pointed southeast at a hundred and seventy degrees."

The next twenty minutes were perhaps the most harrowing of her life, which was saying a lot, as not all that long before she'd had a gun pointed at her head. The storm whipped around them like a hurricane. At least it felt like a hurricane when she was in an inflatable that was being held together by duct tape in seven- or eight-foot swirling seas.

It felt even worse when the duct tape came off.

Whether it was too much water or the pressure building underneath, Annie didn't know, but one minute the tape was holding the seam and the next it was flapping against the side.

"The tape!"

"Don't worry about it," Dan said.

She turned back to look at him to see if he was as confident as he sounded. There wasn't a crack or a chip of uncertainty in that granite facade.

God, was he even human? How could anyone be that calm?

"'Don't worry about it'?" she repeated incredulously. "It's deflating!"

Blue eyes held hers. Ice-cool and steady. "There's nothing we can do about it right now. It's one air tube. We'll stay afloat, but you might have to bail. Just keep us on course." She must not have responded fast enough. He took her chin. "Annie, I need you to trust me, all right?"

She thought about it for a moment and nodded. It was crazy, but she did. The last thing she should be doing was trusting a stranger. Except this one had saved her life. And what other choice did she have? She had to trust him. She didn't have anyone else.

"That's my girl."

My girl. Why didn't that sound as bad as it should? Before she could process that, he leaned down and put his mouth on hers in a kiss that was so fast and fierce she was too stunned to object or respond. She felt the warmth, the surprising softness of his lips, and the firm pressure in a hard blast of awareness that flooded her senses and instantly engulfed her with heat.

He tasted of wind and rain and the faintest hint of coffee. She felt the tickle of his beard against her skin—it was softer than she realized—and then it was gone, leaving her spinning. Reeling. Dumbfounded.

Wanting more.

But the kiss had served its purpose. Though brief, it had forged a connection between them. They were in this together, and he would keep her safe. He had this.

It had also discombobulated her, which she was pretty sure had been his intention as well. She was too busy thinking about the kiss to be scared. Too busy wondering why he'd done that—and whether he would try to do it again—to panic.

Somehow Annie stayed calm, even when one side of the boat grew so deflated they began to take on water. Even when he told her a few minutes later to start bailing. She didn't panic. The solid strength of the body next to hers was reassuring. Anchoring. A tether in a storm.

He never lost his cool. Never once showed even the barest flicker of worry or anxiety—even when one side of the boat began to sink visibly in the water. He was focused. In command. Poseidon and the other sea gods could throw their worst at him, and he would keep on fighting back.

He seemed to know exactly what to do. How to maneuver the boat over the vicious swells. When to increase and decrease the throttle. How to ensure that the small boat didn't flip or take on too much water from the crashing waves. How to keep them heading steady toward their destination even without her holding the map and compass. She was too busy bailing.

His confidence, determination, and skill told her that she was in good hands.

Still, she'd never been so happy to hear the words "there they are" when the series of small islands finally appeared on the horizon. She was even happier after they circled and found a place to land and her feet touched solid ground.

Dan dragged the inflatable up the rocky beach of the biggest island—although the other four "islands" of the archipelago hardly qualified. They were more like big volcanic rocks shooting out of the sea covered in white guano from the thousands of seabirds that nested on their cliff sides. This was the only island of size—probably a half mile by a quarter mile—and the only one with a bay. She didn't want to think about that for too long. They were safe. What-ifs didn't matter.

The island was shaped like a crescent. Ahead of her, up a little from the shore, was a flat, grassy, relatively sheltered area that looked as though it might have been used for pasture at one time—if, as she suspected, the strange round stone huts that littered the hillsides had served as shelter for animals. Once they were beyond the small flat area, the grassy hills rose steeply to the top of the cliffs that she'd seen on the other side as they came around.

While she looked around, Dan had secured the boat by tying it to a rusty steel post and putting a few heavy-looking boulders in its hull to prevent it from blowing away if the winds reached the bay. But the storm didn't feel as powerful here. The natural shelter had taken the edge off its fury.

"Let's see if we can find someplace dry. If those cleats"—the cleats must be the stone huts—"and this pole mean anything, this place was inhabited once."

Annie gave him a horrified look. Who would want to live way the heck out here?

He smiled at her expression. "They probably wouldn't have lived here year-round. Some of the smaller islands in the

Hebrides are used to graze sheep in the summer. I suspect this one would have also been used for the birds."

Annie's nose wrinkled with distaste. She'd heard of the traditional Lewisian "Gana Hunt" for young gannets. Every year a small group of men traveled to a remote island off the north coast of Lewis to kill thousands of birds for the meat, which was considered a delicacy. It was the method of killing—by blows to the head—that provoked outrage from some groups. She knew it was part of the Lewis history and tradition, but that didn't mean she didn't find it distasteful and wish they would find a new one.

Dan was looking at her with amusement, clearly guessing her thoughts.

"What?" she demanded, hearing the "bleeding-heart" even without him saying anything.

He gave her a "back off, angry woman" hand. "I didn't say anything."

"But you were thinking it."

"You aren't exactly hard to read."

She arched an eyebrow. "Pot. Kettle."

He laughed. She was a little scared how much she was growing to like that sound. "Maybe so. But I for one am hoping there were hunters here who were nice enough to leave some kind of shelter behind. You look frozen."

Secretly she hoped so, too. She hadn't noticed how cold and wet she was on the boat when she was fighting for her life, but now that she was safe—and no longer had his body next to hers—she couldn't stop shivering.

They found the cabin a short while later, tucked against the hillside on the other side of the flat area. It wasn't much to write home about, but she wasn't going to complain. The cabin—or bothy as Dan said the Scots called it—was a one-room stone building with a turf roof. At about ten by fifteen feet, it had a couple of steel bunks in one corner and a "kitchen" on the opposite side. There was a sink, but with no running water; there was also a big wooden bucket on the ground for hauling water from the sea. She hoped there was a freshwater source nearby as well.

The best news was that there was a stove that served the dual purpose of cooking and heating.

Dan quickly went to work loading the few bricks of peat that had been left underneath into the stove and getting it lit, while she did the best she could knocking the dust from the furniture, blankets, and mattresses. She was glad not to see any cobwebs—spiders weren't her favorite.

She was just beginning to feel the first warm tingles of heat coming from the stove when she lifted the bottom mattress from the bunk to shake it out and screamed.

The sound of Annie's scream turned Dean's blood to ice. Considering how desperate their situation had been a few minutes ago—if this island hadn't had a place to land the boat, they would have been in real trouble—his reaction was laughable. Dean knew how to control his emotions. He didn't experience fear or anxiety the way most people did. He buried it. Put it aside. Compartmentalized.

But her scream scared the shit out of him.

He spun around from his position by the stove to see her running toward him. He barely had time to open his arms before she was leaping into them. He could feel the frantic pounding of her heart against his. At least he thought it was hers, but his was freaking slamming against his ribs.

She latched on to him as if she were a terrified kitten who had no intention of letting go. Which was fine, as he had no intention of letting her.

Scanning the area behind her, he didn't see anything out of the ordinary. No dead bodies or bogeymen lurking in the corner. As she didn't seem inclined to offer an explanation, he asked, "What is it?"

She turned her face toward his, and his throat caught. Terror still made her voice tremble. "A r-rat! I saw a rat!"

Dean stilled. Jesus fucking Christ, she had to be shitting him? All that for a rat? Relief ate away at his composure. He couldn't help himself; he started to laugh.

She looked up at him again, no doubt feeling the reverberation in his chest. "Don't you dare laugh. It was terrifying."

He tried to sober. Not very successfully. "I'm sure."

Her eyes narrowed. "Don't say it. Don't even think it."

He feigned innocence. "I don't know what you are talking about."

"'You are such a girl.' Tell me you aren't thinking that right now!" He couldn't do that. "It would have scared anyone. It had teeth! And a tail. It must have been this big." She pulled away from him long enough to show him about a foot. But he still had his arm slung around her waist and had no intention of letting her go.

He peered over behind the bed and didn't see anything. "I'm sure. But I don't see anything."

Tentatively she broached a look. He could feel her relax. "It's gone. But you need to find it."

"I don't know. That sounds a little sexist to me. Why do I have to do the hunting? Because I'm a man? Does that mean you're doing the cooking?"

If looks could kill, he'd be roadkill. "That isn't funny."

He grinned. It was fucking hilarious.

"I don't want you to kill it. Just put it outside. But fine. I'll do it myself."

She pulled away and took a few steps back toward the bed. But a gray blur shot past her feet like a torpedo, and with another ear-piercing scream, she was right back in his arms.

He savored the sensations for a minute before breaking the news. "Annie?" She looked up and he felt something in his chest thump. Damn, she was pretty. Especially in this position. Glued to his chest and tilting her head up to his. Looking at him as if she needed him—as if he were the only man in the world. He could get used to it—maybe a little too easily. "I hate to tell you, but your Remy is a Mickey. And he was about three inches long."

"What difference does it make? It was terrifying." She scowled at him, probably to encourage him to not start laughing again. "And how do you know Disney movies?" Something seemed to occur to her. She pulled away in horror. "Oh my God. You're married with kids. I'm sorry. What a fool you must think—"

He didn't let her finish and pulled her back in his arms. "I'm not married. No kids. But I have friends who do. I never would have kissed you if I was married."

Most SEALs were married by his age, but the men picked for Team Nine had been chosen specifically because they weren't married and didn't have connections—or close ones at least. It made it easier for them to operate without anyone around to ask questions. It also made it easier for them to disappear on highly covert, clandestine deployments. There wasn't anyone to look for them.

But it wasn't foolproof. One of his fallen comrades' estranged sister sure as hell was stirring up trouble with her articles on the "Lost Platoon of SEAL Team Nine." Brittany Blake—the reporter—had been Brandon's sister.

Annie appeared marginally relieved. But the kiss comment had obviously thrown her. "Why did you . . . ?"

Her voice fell off. She didn't need to finish the question. If the heat in his eyes wasn't an explanation, the way his body was reacting to her closeness sure as hell was.

It was way too easy to remember how good she'd felt riding up against him in the boat. How her body had melted into his. How she'd arched her back to press harder against him. How she'd driven him so wild he forgot himself and kissed her.

But nothing more could happen. Annie wasn't fool-around material. Smart, confident women like her always wanted more. He'd wager she'd never had a one-night stand in her life. He'd had more than he'd like to remember, but the deal had always been understood. Sex, but don't look for anything more. The only happy ending would be of the orgasmic type. Even before he had to go dark and play dead, he hadn't wanted anything more.

Machines, Annie had called them. The idea of the heartless, unthinking killer following orders pissed him off, but in some respects she was right. SEALs were a different breed. Most of his fellow SEALs might have married by his age, but they were also likely to be divorced by the time they were forty. SEALs didn't make good husbands—or boyfriends for that matter. He'd tried before Team Nine, but inevitably—go figure—women wanted to know where he went, what he was doing, and when he would be back. Being gone for months at a time with little communication didn't make for long relationships. Short hookups he did fine. But that was all he had to offer.

Now, with what was on the line, he didn't even have that. Until he could find out what had happened out there, he had to be dead.

He had to let her go. But damn, she felt good. Just one more minute . . .

Too late.

Apparently he wasn't the only one remembering the boat. Her hands had been braced against his shoulders, but slowly she rose on her toes to loop them around his neck and leaned into him. She pressed that soft pink tastes-like-cherries mouth on his, and all the pent-up lust that had been building up on the boat came back in a violent rush.

The rest, as they say, was history. His big head checked his honorable intentions at the door, leaving the little head to do the thinking.

Which never ended well.

Thirteen

Dean didn't hold back. The dam had burst open, and he met the tentative press of her lips with a fierce growl. A primitive call of possessiveness. A signal of what was to come. She'd unleashed the desire that he'd been fighting hard to contain. Now that it was loosed, there was no reining it in. And there sure as hell wasn't anything tentative about it.

He dug his hand through the damp strands of her hair to cradle the back of her head and draw her in close, tilting her head at the perfect angle to allow him to taste her deeply.

He found her tongue with his and showed her what he wanted. He wanted to fuck her hard and fast, and then he wanted to do it again slower. Exploring every inch of her body the same way he was her mouth.

But if she kept moaning and swirling her tongue against his like that, it might take a couple of times before he could manage slow.

Dean was in a haze. He hadn't felt like this in too damned long. She was so sweet and responsive; her body was incredible, and the way she moved against him was driving him wild. He'd known that she'd be good—that they'd be good. But not *this* good.

Mind. Fucking. Blown.

His other hand had slid down her back to cup her ass and

lift her to him. That was where he wanted to be. Oh, shit. Right there. Circling. Sliding. Thrusting. Hard and deep.

She was meeting him at every bump and grind. At every thrust of his tongue. Her hands were on his back. On his arms. Squeezing. Pleading.

He'd had a lot of wild sex. He'd had frantic sex. But nothing like this. It was as if someone had lit a match and the whole room had gone up in flames. Zero to sixty in a heartbeat.

His mouth was on her throat. His hand was cupping a breast that was every bit as incredible as he'd imagined. He couldn't get enough of her. He was so ready for this; he could fucking explode.

He nearly did when she touched him. Rubbing her hand up and down the long, rigid length of his shaft. Squeezing through the damp denim. He felt like a thirteen-year-old in his first make-out session. He forgot to keep kissing her for a moment. He literally had to grit his teeth against the urge to surge deep in her hand and give in to the pounding at the base of his spine.

Too many clothes. He wanted her naked. He wanted his mouth on her breast and his hand between her legs. He wanted to feel how wet she was, find out how fast he could make her come.

Pretty damned fast if those urgent little sounds meant anything.

She was so fucking hot; he had to touch her.

Somehow he managed the button and zipper of her jeans, and then his hand was inside her pants, delving under the thin silk of her panties to the tender flesh between her legs.

She cried out at the first touch. He covered her mouth with another hungry kiss, feasting on her lips as his finger slid inside that damp little slit.

He swore. Groaned. Tried to find a thread of control. But she was so tight. So warm and soft—and wet. Deliciously wet. But he wanted her wetter.

He couldn't wait to make her come. It was all he could think about. All he could focus on. It became his only mission. And like any SEAL worth his salt, he approached his mission with single-minded determination that left no option for failure.

He cupped her with his palm, giving her circling hips all the friction and pressure they needed as he thrust and stroked with his finger in a rhythm matched by the thrust of his tongue. When he found that sensitive place, he felt her stiffen. Her breath hitched with anticipation.

Oh, fuck yes, she was going to come.

Dean felt the heady delight of knowing success was at hand. *His* hand. He held her right there. Right in the palm of his hand for a long heartbeat, savoring the moment of primitive masculine satisfaction before finally giving her the caress she needed.

She flew apart instantly—her eyes locking on his. Something jammed in his chest. He couldn't breathe.

He swore he saw what looked like surprise in her eyes as her body pulsed. Contracted. Shattered.

It was the most beautiful thing he'd ever seen.

He wanted to see it again. Right now. When he was deep inside her.

Instead she said something that stopped him cold.

"Dan . . ."

It wasn't the soft plea to finish what they started that Dean heard; it was the name. The *false* name. It was a harsh reminder of everything that was at stake.

What the hell was he doing? He didn't lose control like this. He hadn't meant to kiss her. He'd wanted to kiss her, but that wasn't the same thing. This—them—was a bad idea. A really bad idea. She knew too much about him already. He should be cutting ties, not making them.

Every bone in his body fought against what he was about to do—some more powerfully than others—but with a sharp curse, he pulled away, setting her forcibly away from him, and pretending not to notice as her legs wobbled. He couldn't touch her. Couldn't do this with her sagging in his arms all warm and weak with surrender.

With her looking at him like that.

He turned away so he wouldn't have to see her face as he fought for control, waited for his blood to cool, and his cock to stop aching.

But it hurt like hell. His body was still primed and ready to go, angrily protesting the sudden change of plans.

It was the wrong time for her to touch him.

Annie had never experienced anything like that in her life. She'd had an orgasm before. At least she thought she had, but whatever she'd experienced in the past paled in comparison to the sensations that had just come over her. It had been intense. Fierce. Powerful. All-consuming. Everything she didn't even know she'd been missing.

That was what her friends were talking about. What made Lisa drop their plans to go see a movie in the afternoon—in the afternoon!—when her boyfriend called. What made her former roommate, Mary, stay locked up with her boyfriend—now husband—in their room all weekend. Literally all weekend, barely coming out to grab food or go to the bathroom. It was what made the walls shake.

Hot sex.

Wild, crazy, hot sex.

Except they hadn't quite gotten that far. Why had he stopped?

Dan was turned away from her, but from the way the muscles in his neck were pulled tight and his jaw was clenched, it looked as if he was in pain.

She reached out and put her hand on his arm. "Are you okay?"

He flinched away from her as if he couldn't bear her touch. "I'm fine."

She felt a prick in her chest; a tiny pin had just poked the bubble of euphoria. "Then why did you . . . ?"

Stop.

Suddenly Annie realized what was happening. He didn't want her. Didn't want this. He was stopping it.

She'd been so caught up, so lost in his kiss, that she'd forgotten how it had started. *She'd* kissed *him*.

Mortification mottled her cheeks with heat. She'd thought that was what he'd wanted, but obviously she'd been wrong.

He'd gone along with it—more than gone along with it, he'd taken complete control—but he wouldn't have started it.

He wouldn't have started it. She could see it so humiliatingly clearly now. If a hole in the ground opened up and swallowed her, she would have welcomed it.

The universe wasn't that kind.

She took a few deep breaths, trying to break through the tightness in her chest.

"I'm sorry," she said. "I didn't mean . . . I've never done anything like that." Her first move would be her last. "I don't know what came over me."

Yes, she did. Lust. Good old-fashioned, lose-your-senses-and-act-like-an-idiot lust.

He finally looked at her. All signs of pain—of any emotion—had been wiped from his expression. If she hadn't seen his face a few minutes ago, she would have thought he'd been completely unaffected by the entire thing. Steely silvery blue eyes glinted back at her. Cool, emotionless, impenetrable.

God, had she actually thought she'd seen something in there when she came apart?

Humiliation twisted the knot in her stomach a little tighter.

"Forget about it," he said. "It's no big deal."

Not a pin, there was a knife stabbing in her chest now. Wow. Way to put it into context. No sugarcoating, all right.

He wasn't done. "You were upset—you don't look as tense now."

He hadn't just said that. Was he honestly just claiming to have gotten her off so she wasn't so tense? Could he be that much of a dick?

Her eyes narrowed. Taking in the tiny white lines around his mouth and the rigid set of his shoulders. Maybe he'd wanted it a little, after all. "You're looking a little tense there yourself. I could offer to return the favor . . . unless you'd rather handle it yourself?"

Just in case he didn't know what she was talking about, her gaze slid down to the still sizable but not-quite-as-prominent bulge in his jeans.

His jaw went slack before he caught himself. Clearly the captain wasn't used to anyone firing back at him.

"No favors necessary." His voice sounded a little ragged.

Annie was never provoking—especially about anything sexual. That was about to change. Her eyes flickered to his for only an instant before settling back down on his crotch. She ran her tongue over her bottom lip before catching it with her teeth. "Pity."

The sharp tense of muscle told her that she'd won that round.

She glanced up just in time to see his mouth fall in a hard line before he grumbled something about fixing the fire that had apparently gone out while they were . . . occupied.

Annie continued where she'd left off with the mattresses, stewing and surreptitiously watching him the whole time.

She was glad he'd pulled back. Of course she was. Hadn't she learned her lesson with Julien? Had she really been about to fall in bed with a man she barely knew who was clearly hiding something? Although with Julien at least she'd waited awhile. She wished she'd waited longer. Like never.

Dan bent over, putting his head in the stove to try to look into the flue. She caught herself staring at the tight, perfectly shaped backside that was made for football pants.

Furious at herself when her cheeks started to warm, she forced her gaze away. Physical attraction. That was all it was. That was what had made her dissolve the moment his lips touched hers. What had caused her pulse to leap and her heart to beat like a frantic drum. What had made her bones melt and her blood catch fire—everything catch fire.

Annie had experienced something like this once before, although it had been a long time ago. She recalled the one and only date she'd had with the high school quarterback.

He'd looked good in football pants, too.

Shane Madison had pretty much looked good in everything. Tall, solidly built, with an impressive amount of muscle for a high school boy, he was an all-around super guy: smart, confident, and good-looking. Maybe a little cocky, but he was so charming you didn't really notice.

She (along with most of the other girls in the school) had

been half in love with him for three years in high school before he asked her out their senior year. It wasn't that she didn't think he'd noticed her or only dated cheerleaders; he just didn't seem very interested in dating. He had big plans—the details of which she hadn't been aware of at the time—and was concentrating on football and a heavy slate of AP classes.

That was how everything had changed. They'd been paired off as lab partners in AP Chemistry—which turned out to be appropriate. The chemistry between them had been reactive. Off the charts. Elemental. She'd nearly given up her virginity in the backseat of his car on their first—and only—date.

That wasn't the problem. The problem was when she found out what he wanted to do. Shane was working so hard in school to get into Annapolis. He wanted to go to the United States Naval Academy and have a career in the military. He'd even mentioned—shiver—that if things went well, he was going to try to be a SEAL. She had no doubt he would do it. Shane was the kind of guy who could do anything he put his mind to.

Her dad would have loved him. Or her dad would have loved him before the war destroyed him.

What was it about big, strong guys and wanting to save the world? Alphas, her mom called them. Annie called them wannabe heroes. Either way she had no interest. She wanted someone *she* could count on. Someone who would be there for *her*. Someone who was normal.

She refused to sign up for more of the same pain, which meant it couldn't go any further.

The Monday after their date, she'd asked the chemistry teacher to find her a new partner. Shane had called a few times, but she told him it wasn't going to work out. Eventually he believed her.

Unconsciously, maybe, she'd avoided the type since then. Until now. Dan reminded her a lot of Shane. An older, harder, more dangerous, not as charming and carefree version maybe, but otherwise the same confident, take-charge, "there isn't anything he couldn't do" persona.

Similar builds, too, although Shane had been a boy, and

Dan was definitely a man with the years of added muscle to prove it. The captain was also a couple of inches taller at six-three or -four.

She felt a twinge of awareness she didn't want to remember—exactly how her hands had felt all over his body—and quickly quashed that train of thought. It was physical attraction—extremely strong physical attraction maybe—but nothing to be worried about.

Apparently she had a weakness for a few muscles, so what? She was sure that was a weakness shared by a lot of women. It wasn't a big deal. *He* wasn't a big deal. Just as he said.

She needed to stop imagining feelings that weren't there. This was about her libido, not her heart. Lust, not love.

Love? What was she, a twelve-year-old girl drawing hearts in her journal? Nearly dying—twice—was obviously making her a little crazy.

He'd knocked out whatever had been blocking the flue and was rebuilding the fire by standing the dried turf blocks over a stack of kindling in a pyramid shape. Using a flint and a stone that he must have picked up outside on the way in, he struck it until one of the sparks caught.

"You would have made a good Boy Scout," she said, breaking the silence. Then suddenly realizing that she knew nothing about him, she added, "Were you a Boy Scout?"

"An hour ago you thought I was a serial killer. Now a Boy Scout?"

He hadn't answered the question. Clearly he didn't want her to know anything about him. Which rankled. They were in this together. Didn't she deserve to know what she'd gotten into?

"Weren't you the one telling me not to be so naive? To ask questions? Well, I'm asking them. If the police are chasing you, don't I deserve to know who I'm on the run with?"

"Slow down, Bonnie. You watch too many movies. I didn't say the police are chasing me."

"That's the problem. You didn't say anything. You lied about being American and are clearly hiding something. You had no interest in waiting around for the coast guard, so what else am I supposed to think?"

He shrugged as if what she thought was immaterial. "I have my reasons."

Prying information from him was like squeezing water from a rock—and provoked about the same level of frustration. She felt her temper rising. "Why don't you share a few of them?"

"I can't."

"Can't or won't?"

"It doesn't matter. It's none of your business."

Ouch. Nothing like the slap of cold, hard truth to make the skin sting. Although unfortunately it wasn't just her skin stinging. But she wasn't going to let him get away with it. "No, you just had your hand down my pants. Why would I think you owed me anything?"

She turned away, but he stepped toward her and caught her arm. "Annie, wait. I'm sorry. I didn't mean to hurt your feelings, but I can't tell you what you want to know."

Hurt her feelings? She should thank him. Now she wasn't stinging; she was furious. "You can't tell me anything about yourself?"

He dropped her hand. "It's better that way."

"Better for who?"

He didn't answer. She stared into his eyes, looking for any crack, any sign of weakness. She should have known better. "Just tell me, is it something illegal?"

He couldn't be a drug smuggler . . . please.

He shook his head. "It's not."

"But you are in some kind of trouble?"

Apparently she'd gotten as much out of him as she was going to get. He ignored the questions and went on with the business of getting the place habitable. She watched as he retrieved his backpack and started pulling out items and setting them on the table. Not a Boy Scout, huh? He certainly came prepared.

It took her a moment, but eventually she figured it out. She sucked in a breath through lungs that were suddenly on fire. The back-off attitude and scruffy appearance had prevented her from seeing it sooner. And he didn't have the usual swagger and cockiness, but after seeing him in action today, she *knew*. "Army, navy, air force, or marines?" she asked.

Fourteen

Dean hoped to hell she hadn't seen him flinch. But when he turned around, he could see he hadn't been that lucky.

He cursed under his breath. How the hell had she guessed? He'd taken special care not to walk, talk, or act like military.

She answered his question with a knowing look. "My father was a Ranger—and later Delta. I recognize the signs. Cool under pressure. Capable. Badass. Not to mention that you have obviously been trained in hand-to-hand combat and survival skills."

Dean's instincts had been dead-on. Being with her was a *very* bad idea.

Her father was Delta? What kind of shit luck was that? Dean would have to be way more careful. Guessing that he was military was bad enough—he didn't want her any closer than that.

Realizing that he needed to cut his losses before it got worse, he said, "I was in the navy for a while."

Technically that was correct. Retiarius Platoon didn't exist anymore. And neither did he.

His confirmation seemed to seal something for her. Whatever interest there might have been sparking in her eyes—and other places a little while ago—died.

He still couldn't believe she'd propositioned him like that.

It had been a long time since anyone called him on something—and certainly never with an effort to get him off. Not that he hadn't deserved it. But what the hell could he have done? Those big wounded eyes had been eating away at him. Maleficent was easier to take than Bambi.

But neither prepared him for the cool flatness of indifference. It wasn't hard to guess the reason for her sudden change of heart.

He should be glad. Her not being interested in him made it a lot easier to fight the attraction between them until he could get her someplace safe. But he couldn't stop himself from saying, "Don't worry. You don't need to say anything more. I know exactly how you feel about the military. We're all a bunch of programmed machines, right?"

He didn't quite erase all the bitterness from his voice.

She had the decency to blush. "You heard me?"

"The entire bar heard you."

Her flush of embarrassment deepened. But she didn't shy away from the taunt. She tilted her chin up to look at him. "I have my reasons."

"I'm sure you do." But he didn't need to hear them. He picked up one of the buckets from under the sink and turned toward the door. "I'm going to see about getting us some water." It was almost dark.

"Dan, wait."

He was surprised how much he hated the sound of the false name coming from her lips. It was wrong, but he couldn't make it right.

He stiffened as he felt her hand on his arm. He could feel his heart beating strangely in his chest. It felt out of place. Higher and too close to his ribs.

"I . . ." She stared but seemed to not know what to say. Only when he looked down into her eyes did she blurt, "My father killed himself."

Fuck. Whatever he'd been expecting her to say—maybe some crap about peace talks and nonviolence being the answer—it hadn't been that.

"Christ, Annie, I'm sorry. I didn't mean . . ." He put the

bucket down by the door and raked his fingers through his hair. "I shouldn't have brought it up."

She shook her head. "No. I want you to know. Delta. The war. They changed him. They made him into something I didn't recognize. If you could have known him before . . ." She had a faraway look in her eyes as if she were in another time and place. "He was funny and kindhearted, always smiling and doing nice things for my mother and me. They'd married out of high school, and everyone said they'd never seen two people more in love. He doted on her—adored her—and me. I remember his carrying me around on his shoulders everywhere when I was young, and taking me fishing and to the park. He even tried to take me hunting one time."

Her mouth quirked, and he couldn't help wondering how that had gone. Something occurred to him, and he groaned. "Don't tell me you are a vegetarian?"

"Okay, I won't." She managed a smile. "But I hope you have something other than fillet of Mickey planned for dinner."

"Protein bars?"

"That'll work."

"Did he give you that?" He indicated the watch she was fiddling with. He'd noticed how careful she was to protect it in the rain and suspected it was special.

She nodded. "On a trip to Disney World before he left for Iraq. It is one of my best memories of him."

Dean wasn't sure if she would continue, but she seemed to want to get it off her chest, so he didn't stop her.

"After my dad went to Iraq, he started to change. He was more irritable when he came home. He couldn't sleep. He'd snap at me and my mother a lot. And he drank more—a lot more. Not beer like he used to but Jack Daniel's." She wrinkled her nose. "I still hate the smell of whiskey. But all that was nothing compared to after he was recruited for Delta and went to Afghanistan. He wouldn't talk about it, but whatever he did over there—whatever they changed him into—he came back a different person. It got really bad after he was nearly killed by an IED. He'd lose his temper at the smallest thing, and his anger was terrifying—he'd go into this dark rage. He withdrew from my mother—and from me. He lost track of things and even forgot my birthday. But that wasn't the worst. The worst was when they started fighting." She closed her eyes as if she could block out the sounds. When she opened them again, he could see the horror. "He hit her. My smiling, loving father who never raised a hand to a woman in his life backhanded my mom so hard across the face that she needed stitches."

Dean started to reach for her, wanting to give her comfort, but she shook him off and stepped back. "No, let me finish. I need to say it all. Do you know I've never told anyone this?" She didn't wait for him to respond. "He was drunk, but it wasn't an excuse. He knew it as well as everyone else did when he finally woke from his haze in jail. My mom didn't waste any time. She packed a few things and took us to a hotel, planning to leave the next morning for Florida, where my grandparents live."

Up until this point there had been very little emotion in her voice, but that was about to change.

"I was a teenager. I didn't understand everything that was going on. I didn't like what had happened to my dad, but he was still my dad, and I loved him." She looked up at him, pleading somehow for understanding. He did the only thing he could and nodded. "I snuck out of the hotel to go back to our house to see him before we left. To ask him to work it out with my mom. I didn't want to leave." She drew a deep breath. "I was the one who found him."

Ah, shit.

Dean hadn't said it aloud, but she turned to meet his gaze as if he had. Her eyes were so glassy and full of pain, it felt as if he had a vise around his chest, squeezing out his breath. "He was so ashamed and so filled with self-loathing at what he'd become—at what our military had turned him into—that he put a bullet through his head."

Dean had waited long enough. This time she didn't resist when he drew her into his arms. He wanted to make it all better for her and take away all the hurt. But as that wasn't possible, he did the only thing he could and just held her.

She let him for a few minutes, but then seemed to collect herself and pulled away. She dabbed a single tear from her eye and looked up at him. "So now you know. That's why I said what I did."

It wasn't the first time he'd heard a story like that. A guy in Retiarius had killed himself a few years back after leaving the Teams. You didn't come out of what they did unscathed, but it didn't mean they were all violent volcanoes waiting to erupt, either.

He should just let it go. He had no reason to change her mind. It would be easier when they parted if he didn't. But it somehow became the most important thing to him at that moment that she not see it that way. "Your father needed help, Annie. He should have gotten it. I'm not making excuses, but things have changed since then. There's been more training, and the people in charge know the signs and what to look for. I don't know what your father saw or did or what caused him to do what he did—and PTSD is a serious problem—but there may also have been a physiological explanation for what happened."

"What do you mean?"

"You said he was nearly killed by an IED?" She nodded. "There were probably a half dozen other blasts that you didn't know about—guys fighting over there had to deal with it constantly. The symptoms you describe—forgetting things, not sleeping, depression—are hallmarks of brain injury from explosions that doctors have identified in returning veterans."

She looked stunned. "You mean like the football players?"

"Kind of. I'm not a doc, but as I understand it, it's in a different part of the brain and doesn't look the same under the microscope. CTE—the football concussion problem—is a buildup of a protein over time, but what they see with blasts is more like scarring."

"How come I've never heard about this?"

"It's only come out recently. But the military is taking it very seriously. They now have a written protocol for handling guys exposed to blasts—checklists, test questions, things like that." He didn't mention that guys actually learned the answers to try to avoid being pulled out, so the military had to develop a number of different tests. Not everything had changed. Guys were still resistant to being pulled out, but it was Dean's job to make sure they were. That included himself. He'd seen a doctor as soon as he reached safety. Apparently he had a hard head. "And guys in combat zones wear tiny gauges on their uniforms that show if they've been too close to a blast."

She sat down on the edge of the bed, obviously trying to process all he'd said. "So it might not have been his fault?"

"I'm saying there might have been a reason that had nothing to do with him being a 'machine.'" He paused. "Look, I'm not saying that guys like your dad don't have to deal with some fucked-up shit." He'd seen his share of it. "And that can sometimes mess with their heads and make it difficult to adjust when they get home. But what he did—as a Ranger and with Delta—those guys are some of the best in the world at what they do." Of course, Dean would never say that in front of any of the Delta boys—wouldn't want to confuse them on who was *the* best. "No matter what the liberal pundits want to think, until this world turns into Disneyland, we need people like him to keep everyone else safe. People who make the hard choices and difficult decisions so you don't have to.

"ISIS isn't going to play nice if we put away our guns and go home. There isn't going to be a meeting of the minds no matter how hard we all 'try to get along.' They have one goal and that is to destroy us and our way of life. That's it. And they won't stop until we stop them. That's the ugly reality whether liberals want to acknowledge it or not. So every time you think about whether we need 'machines' like your father, think about the alternative. I sure as hell wouldn't want to be a woman under ISIS rule. Your father made a sacrifice so that you have the freedom to wear those little shorts you had on earlier, get your PhD, and protest a drillship."

Dean didn't realize how passionately he was talking until he stopped, and the resulting silence dragged on for a minute. Her mouth was slightly open and her cheeks looked a little pink—maybe from the shorts comment.

He probably shouldn't have said that. Not because it might be construed as sexist—whatever—but because it gave too much away.

He'd been looking.

Annie shouldn't be surprised by the captain's defense of her father and other men like him. She'd heard many of the arguments before—albeit not so plainly and forcefully put. But the possibility that her father might have had a brain injury still had her reeling.

"You certainly don't mince words, do you?" she said. "Disneyland?" She shook her head. "I'll remember that. But in defense of 'liberals,' we don't all live in Fantasyland—conservatives just don't allow for the possibility that they could be wrong. You make it sound too simple, but good and evil aren't always that black-and-white, and the people making the decisions don't always know what's right. Actually, if you look at recent history, they tend to make plenty of mistakes. Toppling Saddam"—she couldn't resist pronouncing it like the first Bush president— "made room for ISIS to step in. And frankly a lot of political leaders today—on both sides—are not the ones I want making those 'tough' decisions." She paused, taking his silence perhaps as begrudging agreement. "Look, I'm not saying that the military or Special Forces aren't sometimes necessary. I'm saying that they are being overused for questionable purposes when the cost is so great. There are too many families like mine."

He didn't disagree—with that, at least. "If we let everyone make decisions, nothing would ever get done," he said. "Someone has to be in charge. That's why we have elections." He thought for a minute. She liked that about him. He thought before he spoke. And even if that speaking was too blunt, it wasn't hyperbole and inflammatory statements. "The system doesn't always work, but it's the best one we have."

"Which doesn't mean we shouldn't be trying to make it better. And there are other ways to make a difference."

"You mean like your stunt with the drillship? The only difference that was going to make was alienating anyone who might be inclined to agree with you. Inconveniencing people, interfering with their jobs, and making them angry isn't the way to persuade anyone. Didn't anyone ever tell you that you get more bees with honey?"

She felt her temper pricking at his sarcasm. "Don't you think that's a little ironic coming from you? Did you use a lot of honey when you were in the navy?"

He surprised her with his reply. "Sometimes yes. Despite how the media like to portray us 'machines'"—her cheeks heated—"combat is usually the last resort. When I was in Afghanistan, we spent a lot of our time making friends with the locals and training them to defend themselves."

Her heart sank on hearing that he'd been in Afghanistan. What hidden scars did he have?

She forced her mind back to the topic. "But weren't you just saying something about ISIS and justifying the use of our military because diplomacy is never going to work?"

"You aren't equating a drillship looking for oil with fighting ISIS?"

"No, I'm just saying that honey isn't always enough. Of course I didn't want anyone to be inconvenienced or angry, but sometimes agitation isn't just effective—it's also *necessary* to get people to listen. It's a method. Not one I'd want to rely on all the time, but peaceful, orderly, sign-holding protests don't always work. Sometimes you have to do something dramatic—something big—or maybe even something unpleasant to get the job done."

"Said every terrorist everywhere. That's exactly the type of argument that the bad guys use to justify their 'wars.' I bet that's how Julien and his friends were justifying what they were planning to do, too."

Her cheeks heated. "That isn't fair. There's a big difference between a sit-in on a ship and blowing it up."

"Agreed. Just as there is a big difference between what our military is doing to combat threats like ISIS and trying to prevent drilling for oil. Even so, we aren't doing very much blowing up at all. But as much as I'd personally like to hit the reset button, that isn't how our government operates."

"Reset button?" He waited for her to understand. She was incredulous. "You mean wiping them out?"

He shrugged. "These are evil people, Annie, who want to set our civilization back hundreds of years. They aren't messing around. They're fighting a war with us, but we're engaged in some kind of PC bullshit. Our response has turned reactive rather than proactive. George W might have opened the door in Iraq, but it was later administrations that allowed these organizations to flare up again. If we'd taken care of them when we had a chance, we wouldn't be in this position."

She didn't disagree with everything he said, which was surprising. "You might be right, but that is part of the cost of being a civilized nation. We don't go around hitting the reset button just because we don't like someone's beliefs. You conservatives love to hold up the Constitution and wave it around anytime someone mentions guns, but I sometimes wonder whether you've actually read it."

To her surprise he didn't argue with her; he just laughed. "I'm beginning to feel like I'm on CNN."

She smiled back at him. "Minus all the yelling and vitriol."

Which was nice. She liked that they could disagree and still have an intelligent conversation. Maybe they understood each other better now, too.

He was thoughtful, watching her for a moment before speaking. "You really think that climbing on board a drillship in the middle of the ocean is the best way for *you*—a scientist—to make a difference? You sure that your 'big and dramatic' aren't about something else?"

Maybe he understood more than she wanted. "Like what?"

His gaze was cool and steady. "You tell me."

She knew what he thought. That this was about her dad—or rather his memory. But he was wrong. She wasn't trying to prove herself to him or anyone else.

She did want to make a difference, and protesting was a legitimate way to do so. "I think we'll have to agree to disagree about methods. But just because you don't like my way doesn't make it wrong." She eyed him speculatively. "Besides, if you believe in the system so much, what are you doing here hiding?"

From the way his jaw clenched, she could tell he wasn't happy with the question. Nor did he have an answer for her. "It's getting dark. I'm going to see about finding some water. You can get started on one of those protein bars if you want." He gave her a long look. "We should get some sleep. Assuming the storm breaks, I want to leave at first light."

"What about the boat?"

"I'll fix it as best I can, but without the waves and the rain, it should get us there."

Should.

"Where are we going?"

"The closest island is Lewis, but as I don't want to risk that, it's North Uist instead. It's in the same chain, but I don't think they'll be looking for us there."

"And then?"

He held her gaze, giving her nothing. She hadn't thought he would. He would leave her and go on his way. What else was she expecting?

It was for the best anyway. She'd avoided his type for a reason. Even if he wasn't in trouble, she couldn't go *there*. Conservative, former military, and alpha. The trifecta of not going to happen. No matter how attracted she was to him. And how hot that kiss had been. She'd had enough of wannabe superheroes.

"Get some rest, Annie. I'll be back."

When the door closed behind him with a slam, something in her chest seemed to do the same.

They left the small island not long after dawn. Dean hadn't slept well, and he was anxious to be away. The longer he spent with Annie, the greater the risk—and not just from discovery. He knew there was something growing between them, and it had to stop.

He *needed* it to stop. And not just because he'd spent the

better half of the night calling himself a fool for not having her under him. On top of him. In front of . . .

Fuck.

But it wasn't just a hard dick. He wished it were. No, the reason he wanted to get away from her wasn't just that he wanted to fuck her—which he did really badly—it was that he liked being with her.

He'd never talked to a woman the way he did with her. With her it was more like talking to the guys on the team, although with them it was usually preaching to the choir. They all had pretty similar politics. Who knew idealistic left-wingers could be so much fun?

She also wasn't intimidated by his rank and gave it right back to him. And didn't seem intimidated when he challenged her back.

It was oddly freeing. He could say what he wanted and not worry about how she took it or hurt feelings. Had he unconsciously been holding back in previous relationships? Maybe. Although admittedly the women he met at Hula's weren't usually environmental scientists with a PhD.

He might need to change things up when he got back and this was all behind him. Which had better be soon. Dean had never had much patience, but what little he had had been exhausted a long time ago. He couldn't sit back and wait with his hands tied much longer.

As soon as he landed somewhere safe, he was going to make a call. She was right. He did believe in the system, and going dark like this went against every instinct.

"How much farther?" Annie asked.

She'd been unusually quiet all morning—and contemplative. Other than thanking him for another protein bar and for sharing the small travel-sized soap and toothpaste he carried in his bag to freshen up in the morning, she hadn't said much. It was almost as if she was as anxious as he to put this all behind them.

He was glad they were on the same wavelength about not getting involved. He might not like her reasons, but it made things easier. He didn't know whether he'd be able to stop things a second time. Not after a long night of thinking about the first time. He could still taste cherries—from the lip balm he saw her use—and feel the spasms of her body as she came apart, and the firm grip of her hand on his cock.

That most of all.

He didn't know whether to be relieved or disappointed that Mickey hadn't made another appearance.

"Not far," he answered, forcing the memories away. "Probably another ten miles or so. You can try the radio again. We'll have a better signal now."

Dean had turned on the radio this morning to check the weather report before they left. It had stopped raining in the middle of the night, and the skies were clear, but he wasn't taking any chances—not with the inflatable being held together with duct tape.

In the emergency box on board, he'd found a hand pump that enabled him to do a bit of repair work on the boat before leaving the island. Sometimes inflatables of this size also had acetone and tape or a repair kit on board. He wasn't that lucky. The acetone would have given him a better seal on the tape. But so far it seemed to be holding.

The signal earlier hadn't been good enough to hear the full report, but "clearing skies" had sounded promising enough to leave.

The signal was much better this time. They caught the tail end of the weather, but it was what they heard next that changed everything.

Fifteen

Dean's expression was grim as the broadcaster repeated the warning for all sea craft and seaside communities of the Outer Hebrides to be on the lookout for two suspects—a male approximately six feet three inches tall, fifteen stone, thirty years old, light brown hair, heavy beard, and a female approximately twenty-five, five and a half feet tall, nine stone, long, dark hair, and green eyes, both presumed armed and dangerous.

The descriptions were off a little in the particulars—he was six-four, two twenty—more like sixteen stone—and thirty-three—but close enough to identify them.

"What's going on?" Annie said. "They are making it sound as if we are the criminals."

That was exactly what it sounded like, which Dean knew wasn't good. "Try another channel."

It took a few tries, but eventually she found a news broadcast from Lewis. The bulletin came a few minutes later. "The big story this morning is the two men found murdered on a local dive boat, and the hunt for the two suspects responsible. The sole survivor of the horrible ordeal at sea, which took place about fifty miles northwest of Lewis, is telling a harrowing account of robbery and murder carried out by the charter captain and his American accomplice. Islanders are warned not to approach on their own, suspects are armed and dangerous, but to report any sightings to the police immediately."

Dean swore.

Annie looked at him wide-eyed and pale. "Murder? What is he talking about? We didn't murder anyone."

Dean slowed the motor to meet her gaze. "No, but it sounds as if someone did."

She made a sound that was a cry and gasp combined. "Jean Paul?"

He nodded. "That would be my guess."

"But how is that possible? He was tied up."

Dean had checked all the ties and made sure their hands had been behind their backs, where they couldn't get the leverage as he had done to break through them. Jean Paul hadn't gotten loose that way.

But Dean had made a mistake. In the hurry, he hadn't patted him down to check for weapons. "He must have had a knife on him. Somewhere that he or one of the others could reach."

"But what about the explosives? Why didn't they mention anything about that?"

"I assume they are at the bottom of the ocean right now. Jean Paul probably threw them overboard before the coast guard arrived."

It finally set in what that meant. "That means Julien . . ." Anguished, tear-filled eyes locked on his. "And Claude."

"I'm sorry, Annie."

She shook her head as if she didn't believe it, tears streaming down her cheeks.

Dean reached out and swept a few away, but that was all the comfort he could give her right now.

He had to focus on other things. Like how the hell they were going to slip through a net cast for a murderer that was getting wider every minute.

Julien dead? *Murdered* by his former teacher and the man he admired so much? It couldn't be true! But the tears pouring down her cheeks told her she knew it was.

As angry as Annie had been with Julien for involving her in this nightmare—and she'd been furious—she hadn't wanted to see him killed for it. Punished for his crimes certainly, but not like this.

She'd believed him when he said he never intended for anyone to get hurt. Julien had been duped as well.

Oh God, poor Julien. Maybe she'd jumped into a relationship too quickly, but Annie had truly cared for him. She didn't want to think that he would have gone through with blowing up the ship as Jean Paul had planned.

Was that why Jean Paul had killed him? But that didn't explain Claude. He'd been in on the full plan. There had been no reason for Jean Paul to kill him. Unless Jean Paul's only intention had been to turn the scrutiny from himself and put it on them. Had she unwittingly played a hand in Julien's and Claude's deaths?

The thought made her ill.

She couldn't let Jean Paul get away with it. As soon as they reached the island—North Uist—she would find the nearest police station and clear everything up.

The question was whether she could convince Dan to come with her. If he truly wasn't involved in anything illegal, the seriousness of the charges would have to make him want to clear his name . . . right?

"Jean Paul can't get away with this. You have to come with me to the police station when we reach North Uist."

Dan was standing at the wheel, looking out over the helm with his returned cap flipped backward against the wind. His gaze shifted to her for only an instant. "We aren't going there."

It wasn't easy to hear over the loud throttle of the engine, but she knew she'd heard him correctly. "What do you mean we aren't going there? Is there someplace closer? We have to find someone to explain this to right away. They think we are *murderers*! What if Jean Paul gets away?"

"I'm more worried about us getting away. With the storm over, I'm sure they have all the coast guard in the area out looking for us. Unfortunately there is a Maritime Operation Centre in Stornoway. They only have two helicopters on site, but it won't take long to call in a few more. The one good thing we have going for us is that not knowing about the leak in the boat, they'll have assumed that we would be able to travel all night."

How did he know so much about Scottish Coast Guard operations?

"I don't want to get away," Annie said, her voice getting higher as her panic increased. "We didn't do anything wrong!"

"That's not how it looks right now, and I don't have time to sit in jail while they figure it out."

"That's crazy. No one is going to put us in jail. As soon as we tell them what happened, they'll realize Jean Paul is a liar."

"How will they know that? What proof do you have? It's his word against ours. And there is no way in hell I can get caught up in a murder investigation."

"That's what this is about! Whatever trouble you are in, it can't be as serious as this. Please," she begged. "The longer we wait, the worse it will look—and what if they let Jean Paul go?"

His mouth was clenched hard enough for the muscle below his jaw to tic. "That bastard is the least of my worries. You are wrong. It is very serious, and you can't conceive the type of trouble this could bring. I never should have gotten involved. But I—" He stopped suddenly and stared at her. It was almost as if he blamed her. But then the flash of anger cleared, and he shook his head. "I'm sorry, Annie. But I can't risk it. As soon as we are somewhere safe, I will do what I can."

"What is that supposed to mean?" Her frustration was getting the better of her. She couldn't believe he was being so stubborn. Whatever he was involved in must be worse than she realized. First ecoterrorism and murder, and now God knew whatever he was caught up in.

She didn't want to be involved with any of it. "Fine. You don't need to come with me. Just drop me off and go wherever it is you are planning."

He gave her that grim sidelong glance she was getting used to. "I can't take the chance that someone will see us."

Seeing his resolve, Annie felt her panic become desperate. "I thought you were joking about Bonnie and Clyde—I don't want to be on the lam. Running will only make us look guilty."

"I suspect you already do."

She had no idea what he was talking about.

"Think about it," he explained. "This is an experienced, professional terror organization. They usually operate in cells, which makes them even harder to penetrate. My bet is that all three of them were using false identities, and that they covered their trail in the event something went wrong." He paused long enough to give her a pointed look. "The charter rental was in your name, wasn't it?"

Annie paled, having just had the same thought. She nodded. "As was the room. Julien always paid cash. I noticed it but didn't think anything of it."

She knew a number of students who tried to use mostly cash to keep costs down. It was far easier to charge on a card than hand over big wads of cash. She had actually liked that about him. It made him seem responsible, prudent, and careful.

"Did Julien ever use your computer?"

She shook her head. "No. Not that I can think of."

"Did he have access to it when you weren't around?"

She thought a minute. "When I was in the shower or sleeping. A few times I left for class before he did."

"Did he know your password?"

She bit her lip, embarrassed. "I don't have a password. It's my home computer—a desktop. You just have to hit Enter."

Every word she said made her feel more like an idiot. She could practically hear him thinking "naive." But it wasn't as if there were state secrets on her computer. It was mostly just research backed up to a cloud account. She'd never had any . . . *Oh no.*

He read her expression. "What?"

"I had to cancel a credit card a few weeks before I left. There were a bunch of random Internet charges on it that I didn't recognize. I assumed my number had been stolen."

"Does your computer automatically remember your card number?"

She nodded, feeling like such a fool. Such a *naive* fool. "But he would have needed the three-digit code."

"Which would take him a few minutes to find on the back of your card when you left your purse around."

Oh God, he was right.

"I suspect some bomb-making supplies were purchased with your card," Dan said.

She'd reached the same conclusion on her own. "I was the patsy," she said, her voice hollow with humiliation.

"Julien probably hoped it would never come to that."

He was obviously trying to make her feel better. Which only made her feel worse.

Now she didn't just feel sick; she felt like crying again. What a mess. It was bad enough being tangled up with an ecoterrorist plot, but a murder investigation? "What am I going to do?"

She hadn't been expecting Dan to answer, but he did. "Don't worry. We'll get it straightened out. But not from jail."

"How?"

He paused. "I have someone who I think can help. As soon as we get somewhere safe, I'll call. They also may be able to get the police on the right track with Jean Paul."

"Is it a lawyer? My stepfather is an attorney. He doesn't practice law anymore, but he has tons of contacts."

Dan gave one of those rare curves of the mouth that she took to be a smile. "It's not a lawyer. If we need your stepfather, I'll let you know, all right?"

She nodded. "Where are we going?"

He pointed to an island on the map just off the west coast of North Uist. "Here, to wait it out until dark. We are sitting ducks in the daylight like this. We'll look for a cave or someplace else where we can hide the boat. At least it's gray and not orange or red."

"And then?"

"As soon as it's dark we'll make our way around here"— his finger traced a path around an island called Mingulay at the southern end of the Lewis chain of islands—"to one of the islands in the Inner Hebrides as far south as we can go. We should have enough fuel to reach Tiree."

He pointed at a roughly triangular-shaped island due west of the Port of Oban on the mainland. He had great hands. Big and strong with blunted fingertips and enough scars to make her think he probably worked in a shop of some kind. Although a couple of the scars looked like burn marks.

"Won't they search there?"

"Eventually. But there are hundreds of islands in the Hebrides. We could spend months hopping between them, getting lost. It will take a while to check them all, and being this far south should give us some time."

He'd obviously given this some thought. "Sounds like you have it all planned out." She looked down at the bag he had by his feet. "I just hope you have a few more protein bars in there or it's going to be a long day. I get cranky when I'm hungry."

He winced. "I hope you aren't one of those vegetarians who won't eat fish."

"You're in luck." She smiled, which seemed crazy under the circumstances. "I love fish."

"Sushi?"

"My favorite."

"Then I guess I know what I'm doing when we get there."

She lifted an eyebrow. "I guess that means I get to make camp."

He grinned and she felt that bump in her heart getting bigger.

"If it won't offend your feminist sensibilities."

"I think I can manage this once. But if you call me Bambi again, all bets are off."

"I didn't think you heard that," he said with a laugh, and then gave her a nonapologetic shrug. "It's your fault for looking at me that way."

"Like a stripper?"

He thought that was hilarious and laughed. "More like I just killed your mother."

"You were going to leave me!"

He sobered, and their eyes met. "I'm glad I didn't."

She knew he was talking about what might have happened to her, but the intensity of his gaze made her wonder if he meant something more.

"Me, too," she said softly.

From the way her chest tightened, she suspected she did.

Only when his gaze flickered behind her and he swore was the moment lost.

Sixteen

Old habits died hard, Colt thought. Rain or shine, the first thing Sunday morning—before coffee or breakfast—Kate went for a long run. With her multimillion-dollar town house in McLean overlooking the Potomac, it wasn't hard to anticipate her route.

Colt sat on a bench overlooking the river path and waited. He was tired. His red-eye flight from Los Angeles had landed at Reagan National at six, and he'd come straight here so as not to miss her. She was always out the door by eight. On the rare Sunday that he'd been around to sleep in, he'd grumbled about it.

Once or twice he'd made her late.

It was probably best not to remember how. Sex had sure as hell never been their problem.

Two or three runners went by—none younger than seventy (who else liked to be up this early?)—before he saw the familiar slender form approaching, thick blond ponytail swinging with every long stride.

Summer in the DC area was hot and humid, and she was dressed for the weather in a skimpy top and tight spandex capris that left nothing to the imagination. Although he didn't need to imagine. He remembered.

She'd always had an incredible body—lean, athletic, and

toned. It hadn't changed, except that she was thinner than he remembered.

But still sexy as hell.

She was wearing earbuds and not paying as much attention to her surroundings as she should be. Something he'd warned her about countless times. She didn't notice him until he stood.

She stopped so suddenly that she stumbled. Surprise didn't give her time to completely mask her expression. He saw the flash of pain before it was carefully swept away behind the classically patrician facade.

With her blond, blue-eyed, WASPy beauty, she looked more Junior League and Hamptons than CIA.

That had always been part of her appeal. The stuck-up country club facade made him want to dirty her up a little on his side of the tracks.

But it was only a mask—one that had even fooled him at first. Unfortunately there was no hint of the quiet, kind of shy, heart-of-gold girl he'd married when she looked at him. It was all ice. Must be something they taught you at country clubs or cotillions. He'd laughed his head off when he found out she was a debutante. All that fanfare to be introduced into society and she'd ended up with him.

It was still hard to believe that someone who looked so icy on the outside could be such a wildcat in bed.

Her eyes were hard and unfriendly. He studied the flushed face and noticed a few more lines around her eyes and mouth. But she still looked more late twenties than almost thirty-five.

"How did you find me so quickly?" She stopped, answering her own question. "You've been keeping tabs on me."

He didn't deny it. "You made it easy—habit and routine are tricks of the trade."

She flushed angrily. "Your tricks. Not mine. I'm an analyst, remember? I leave the dirty work to the experts."

As the jab was well earned, he didn't object.

"I thought I made it clear when you called that I don't want to talk to you. You and I have nothing to say to each other."

That was true. They'd said it all. More than they should have. Things that could never be unsaid.

Water, bridge, he reminded himself. "I need your help."

She shook her head. "I'm sorry, Colt. Whatever it is, I can't help you. You . . ." She stopped, and straightened, looking him right in the eye so there would be no mistaking. "It took me a long time, but I've moved on. I'm finally getting on with my life, and Hurricane Colt isn't going to blow in and mess that up."

The words she'd uttered a long time ago came back to him. *"You're like a hurricane. You destroy everything around you and leave nothing but misery in your wake."*

She'd been crying then. Bawling. As if he'd ripped her heart out when it had been the other way around. He might have pushed her away, but did it have to be with someone he considered one of his closest friends? He'd said some ugly things to her—things he'd hoped she would deny—but she never did.

Hurricane Colt. Maybe it was true. He'd destroyed their marriage long before she'd turned to Scott. He'd tried to warn her. But she thought she could change him. That her love would be enough to wash away his sins. For a while even he'd believed her. But eventually they both realized the truth.

"I heard about your engagement to 'Her Majesty's Ambassador to the United States.' Congratulations."

She ignored the well-wishes, assuming he hadn't meant them. Had he? He might have. She wasn't the only one to move on. Although his kind of moving on didn't involve an engagement ring. That fucking ship had sailed once. Kind of like the *Titanic*. All those big hopes and dreams . . . crash and burn. Or sink.

"Leave me be, Colt. I'm happy. For the first time in a long while, I'm happy."

She started to walk away.

"Get me in to see the general, and you'll never hear from me again."

She stopped. He thought the temptation would be too great. Not for the first time, he overestimated himself in her eyes. "I stopped caring what you do a long time ago. Do what you want as you always have. I pity anyone who thinks they can have a say in anything you do. But whatever it is you want with my godfather, leave me out of it."

In other words, she didn't care enough to get rid of him.

Had he really expected anything else?

He was nothing to her. Whatever hold on her he'd once had was long gone. She'd cut him out of her heart forever. Just as he'd wanted.

His fists clenched, anger and resentment burning hotter than they should. But he knew how to get to her—how to force her to help—and it pissed him off.

He wanted to grab her arm as she ran past him and break through that ice-princess facade. But he knew better than to touch her. Instead he said the one thing guaranteed to stop her in her tracks. "It's about Scott."

Seventeen

Dean cursed, seeing not one but two large boats on the horizon ahead of them. The dots of orange told him everything he needed to know.

Coast guard.

Which meant two things. The island directly opposite North Uist that he'd been headed for was out, as was taking the longer and less risky route around the chain of islands from Barra to Lewis that made up the Outer Hebrides.

Change of plans. He was going to have to chance cutting through the Sound of Harris, the narrow five-mile-long channel that separated Harris from North Uist, and hope to hell they could take shelter on one of the small islands before anyone saw them.

Because of the size and color of the inflatable, Dean didn't think the coast guard boats had sighted them—assuming no one had been using binoculars.

He cranked the wheel, quickly turning the inflatable around in the direction from which they'd come. After about a half mile, he veered east toward the sound.

He'd been keeping the speed moderate to try to conserve fuel, but that was now secondary to getting the hell out of there.

He opened up the throttle and the inflatable tore across the waves. As he had to keep his focus on the seas in front of him, he shouted at Annie to hold on tight and watch behind them to see if they were being followed.

Even if she couldn't hear everything he said, she'd heard enough to get the gist.

She held on to one of the handles—not the one with the taped seam—and kept her eyes peeled on the seas behind them as the boat thumped across the waves.

"Anything?" he shouted above the roar of the motor.

"Not ye—" She stopped. "Wait. I think I see one."

Dean swore again. He was pushing the boat as hard as he dared—almost full throttle. One bad move on his part and they could easily flip. The inflatable was too light with just the two of them to go this fast in these kinds of waves.

"Keep an eye on it, and let me know if it changes direction or speeds up."

Adrenaline shot through his veins, but he'd been in fucked-up situations too many times to panic.

But getting caught wasn't an option. His fake identity was good, but it wouldn't hold up under the scrutiny of a murder investigation.

Dean didn't even want to think about what the LC would say. If Lieutenant Commander Scott "always-have-an-ace-up-his-sleeve" Taylor didn't already regret pulling Dean from the explosion in Russia, he would if Dean blew their cover.

"Go dark. Do what you've been trained to do and disappear. Keep your head down and wait for my orders."

Disciplined and always under control, Taylor would blow a fucking gasket if he knew about Annie. Rightly so. Dean never should have gotten involved with her. But given what had happened, he couldn't regret it. She would have been forced to go along with Jean Paul's plan, or the bastard probably would have killed her.

Dean doubted that foiling an ecoterrorist plot and possibly saving a young woman's life would impress the LC.

But Dean couldn't just leave her—then or now. He would try to help her before he disappeared again.

Taylor was going to be pissed when he heard what Dean wanted to do. Assuming he got out of this, that is.

Which was a big assumption.

"They're still heading this way," Annie said, fighting the wind that had her hair blowing in thousands of different directions. "But I can hardly see them now."

Dean hoped that was a sign that the coast guard boat was just heading in this direction and hadn't actually caught sight of them. He didn't usually like coincidences, but he would sure as hell welcome one now.

The coast of Harris on the left and North Uist on the right appeared ahead of him. In between he could just make out the dark forms of one or two of the islands that dotted the channel. Boating through the sound could be precarious with its small islands, reefs, and rocks—especially at low tides.

But low tides actually worked in their favor with an inflatable. It had a very shallow draft compared to a coast guard boat.

He slowed the boat as they neared the sound, not wanting the blare of the motor to draw attention. Fortunately it was still early enough and no one seemed to be around. Although this probably wasn't the most populated place even in the middle of the day.

Annie said it at the same time he was thinking it. "Where is everyone?"

He had no idea. The coasts were desolate, and there didn't appear to be a single boat in the water.

All of a sudden it hit him. Finally some good luck! "It's Sunday."

She gave him a look that said, *So?*

He realized she hadn't been in Scotland for a Sunday yet. "Everyone is at church. The Sabbath is serious business in these parts."

Lewis and Harris had been referred to in the paper as the "last bastion of Sabbath observance in the UK."

Her brows drew together. "You mean like how in some parts of the US you can't buy alcohol?"

She was referring to remnants of America's old "blue laws," prohibiting the sale of booze on Sunday. But the staunch Presbyterians of the "wee free," as the Free Church of Scotland was known, put those to shame.

He nodded. "That on steroids. Shops, restaurants, golf courses—you name it—pretty much everything but hotels shuts down. Good luck even trying to find gas—or petrol as they call it here. There's one station in Stornoway open for a few hours, that's it. For years you couldn't catch a ferry on a Sunday. That changed a while back, but it caused a lot of controversy. Even hanging out your laundry on Sundays can cause offense in some places."

"That sounds a little medieval."

He shrugged. He'd thought that way, too, the first time he visited. It was hard for Americans to wrap their heads around it in today's always-connected world.

The prohibitions had been even worse twenty years ago. His mother had been a MacLeod, and he'd been sent to stay with a great-aunt one summer when his mother wanted to get rid of him. He'd made the mistake of riding his bike one Sunday and Aunt Meg—who'd been named after some illustrious ancestor—had given him a hellfire-and-brimstone rant that would have made any preacher he'd ever heard on the TV proud.

Religious aspects aside, he'd come to appreciate the day of rest and the practice of keeping one day of the week special. "It's part of the culture and kind of nice sometimes." He looked over his shoulder. "See anything?"

She shook her head. "No." She bit her lip, worry clouding her windblown features. "The water looks really low."

That was another piece of good luck for them. "The tide is almost all the way out."

"Will they be able to follow us?"

"I don't know, but I'm not going to wait around to find out. We're going to make a run for it."

"Won't that be dangerous?"

Only if he made a mistake. "Don't worry, Annie. I know what I'm doing."

She managed a small smile. "I'm sensing a theme."

He grinned but turned his attention to the mission at hand: getting them through this channel without hitting something or running aground. He scanned the channel, glancing back and forth at the map. He found a path through the rocks and reefs and took it, hoping for the best.

It was slow, tense going. Navigating and maneuvering through the shallow waters required every bit of his concentration and skill, but about a half hour after they entered the channel, they were out.

He exhaled, releasing the tension that had been holding him in its tight grip.

Annie hadn't said a word the entire time. He wasn't sure she'd breathed. Hell, he wasn't sure *he'd* breathed.

"See anything?" he asked her. Annie had been keeping watch behind them.

She shook her head, not hiding her relief. "I think we lost them, but God, that was close. I thought we might have to get out and carry the boat a few times."

He smiled. "You must have Viking ancestors."

She shook her head. "Not that I know of—Dutch, German, and Brazilian." That explained her golden coloring. "Why?"

"Vikings sometimes picked up their boats to cross narrow pieces of land."

"Clever way to make a shortcut."

It was. One he could appreciate right now.

"Now what?" she asked.

He motioned to a barely visible dark shape beyond the much bigger island—the Isle of Skye—ahead of them. "Tiree. And if we are lucky, someplace to get cleaned up and eat."

She gave a heavy sigh of pleasure that reminded him way too much of the moans she'd made when he had his hand . . .

He was trying really hard not to remember that. But it wasn't easy when every time he looked at her his body temperature shot up a good twenty degrees.

It was going to be a long couple of days. He figured it would take at least that long before he could get things straightened out, and he could disappear.

"That sounds divine." Suddenly her expression changed. "I just remembered. I don't have any money."

"Don't worry about it," he said. He had an emergency stash of cash in his bag—he never left home without it—to cover him until he could safely access the various accounts he'd set up with different identities in case one or more were compromised.

Dan Warren was history.

SEAL operators were trained to escape and evade after an op went wrong. But the kind of going dark he'd done after Russia had required much more than navigation tools, water collection, and signaling devices to survive in hostile territory for a few days. Fortunately the operators of Team Nine had been trained to disappear—to ghost and live off the grid.

Access to funds was part of that, so he'd taken precautions, including setting up an account at a bank in Liechtenstein— one of the new places to hide your money *and* your identity, after the recent fall from favor of Switzerland for releasing names of American tax cheats.

Still, it might be a few days before he could access it and arrange for a new identity. He would have to budget accordingly. Their best bet would be a hostel or small guest house that would be happy with cash. Of course, they'd have to find someplace to clean up and get her some extra clothes so they didn't look as if they'd just washed up off the beach—which they had.

He realized she was frowning. "What's wrong?"

Her mouth turned up in a wry smile. "You mean aside from being on the run for the murder of my ex-boyfriend and his friend, without anything beyond the clothes I have on and one cherry lip balm?" she asked, pulling it out of her pocket. "Nothing."

He was tempted to throw that cherry lip balm overboard as he'd done with her phone. It might be the more dangerous of the two.

He wanted to kiss her again. Badly. Not just as a way of telling her it would be okay, but also because she was incredible. He couldn't think of many women he knew who could go through what they'd just had to do and still have a sense of humor.

Instead he held her with his gaze. "Hang in there, Annie. I promise it's going to be okay."

That was one promise he would do everything in his power to keep.

He just hoped to hell it would be enough.

I t took longer to reach the island than Annie expected, but fortunately they only saw a few boats in the distance and none with the distinctive orange paint.

The near run-in with the coast guard had been too close. And although it was still midmorning by the time they pulled the inflatable up onto the beach, she was exhausted. Sitting on the edge of her seat—literally—for a few hours had sapped what little energy she possessed after only three protein bars in about twenty-four hours.

She also felt a little like a drowned rat. Thanks to the fire Dan had made last night, her clothes had dried out by morning, but the sea spray from their high-speed dash across the Western Isles had her damp all over again.

He'd picked a beautiful natural harbor with a white-sand beach and jagged black volcanic rocks below a gentle hillside of green grass, wildflowers, and a handful of the ubiquitous white cottages that seemed to be scattered across most of the islands.

It was incredibly picturesque and not what she imagined when she thought of Scotland. The Caribbean maybe, but definitely not the Western Isles of Scotland.

Compared to some of the others she'd seen on her unexpected tour around the islands, Tiree seemed relatively flat and grassy. It also seemed a little warmer.

"Where are we?"

"A village called Balephetnish, according to the map."

Another one of those Scottish towns that she wouldn't be attempting to spell.

She looked up at the houses overlooking the beach, of which there were precisely six that she could see. "This is a village?"

He grinned. "It is in the Western Isles."

"Is one of those white houses a hotel by any chance?"

He shook his head at her tone, which was between plead-ing and begging. "Could be that one lets out rooms as a small B&B, but we aren't staying here. We'd draw too much notice."

She didn't know whether to be relieved or disappointed. She was exhausted, but the accommodations looked basic to say the least.

"I pulled in here because I saw that." He pointed toward an old wooden shed.

"What is it?"

"I'm not sure—probably a boat shed or a gear hut at some point. But it looks derelict, and it will be a good place to hide the inflatable. This island doesn't seem to have any caves."

"What if someone sees us?"

He shook his head. "That's why I came in the way that I did. That sea stack should have blocked our approach."

The inflatable was definitely heavier than it looked, and even though Dan was shouldering most of the weight, Annie was breathing hard by the time they pulled it up the last stretch of beach to the very shabby—not chic—wooden building.

She was surprised it hadn't blown over; the island was breezy. The shack was a simple square construction with a gable roof. A few of the gray weathered boards were missing or broken, and the door no longer had a lock but was secured instead with a rope.

Dan made an attempt to untie the knot, but time and rain had made the hemp strands about as yielding as steel. After a few minutes, he gave up and took out the multitool he'd used before to cut it.

The rope must have been to deter teenagers from using the place for partying. Once inside, they could see the old beer cans and cigarette butts strewn around the wooden floor. The only boat—an old rowboat—had been turned into a makeshift bed with the addition of a very scary-looking bedroll.

Raging teenage hormones: the mother of invention.

"We could always stay here," Dan said. "I don't see any mice."

Her face dropped, and he burst out laughing.

"That isn't funny," she admonished. "Especially when I've been promised a shower and food."

She could see from his grin that he didn't agree, but he

wisely chose not to argue with her. "Help me bring in the boat, and I'll see about both."

After pulling in the inflatable and securing a new knot on the door with one of the pieces of cut rope, Dan located the walking path that he said should take them into the main village of Scarinish.

The island wasn't that big—probably three miles wide by twelve miles long—but she hoped the village wasn't too far away. She was getting hungrier by the minute, but the last thing she was going to do was complain.

Annie felt that same ridiculous need to prove herself that she'd always felt with her father. With her father, she suspected it was because she somehow didn't want to make him regret not having a boy. But with Dan, it was something else. Maybe she suspected he appreciated toughness?

Why she wanted to impress him, she didn't know. But she would faint from hunger before complaining.

They'd probably walked about two miles before he said, "Almost there." He paused long enough for her to be relieved. "Just another five miles to go."

Five miles? Oh God. She didn't say it, but her expression must have given her misery away.

He burst out laughing again. "Just kidding. It's right over there."

She didn't look where he was pointing but turned on him with a scowl. She had never socked someone in the stomach in her life, but she was dearly tempted. "Boy, you are a barrel of laughs today."

He was still grinning, and if she wasn't struck by how good-looking he was when he smiled, she would have been furious.

"I'm sorry, but if you could have seen your face you would understand." He started walking again, and she fell in beside him. "It's okay to admit you're exhausted."

"I'm not—" She started to deny it, and then muttered, "Why bother?" under her breath. "Has anyone ever told you that you have a cruel streak?"

"All the time." He sounded proud of it. "It's how you separate the men from the boys." He gave her a smirk. "Or girls."

"What? Let someone think they are close to an oasis, and then tell them it's only a mirage?"

"Pretty much."

"Fun games you guys like to play."

"Maybe so, but you can take it."

Why that made her so ridiculously proud she didn't want to know.

As the small village came into view, he told her his plan. They'd find a store, pick up a few things, and then use the public toilet—just about every village or town of this size had one—to clean up a little before finding a hotel.

It wasn't until he told her what else he wanted her to do that she nearly forgot her intention not to complain. "You want me to cut my hair?"

He gave her one of those clueless guy looks—the kind they get when they've said something that got a reaction but they aren't sure why.

He nodded. "The shorter, the better." His brows drew together as he studied her. "Have you ever thought about coloring it? Maybe lightening it a little?"

Slow down, Paul Mitchell. He didn't exactly strike her as the hairstylist type. "You want to give me highlights?"

He frowned. "What are those?"

She shook her head. "Forget it. No, I've never thought of coloring it. It's too dark—it would look silly. Unless you want me to go red?"

She'd been joking, but he didn't seem to notice.

"Na, that would stick out too much. Oh well, we'll just have to work with the haircut. Maybe you could try curlers."

Not a chance. The visions of Little Orphan Annie were going to give her nightmares for weeks.

In the realm of things, of course it was silly to be attached to her hair, but she was. She'd had long hair her entire life, and maybe she'd gotten a little used to the "you have such pretty hair" comments.

Before they went into the store, he had her tuck her soon-to-be-short hair up into his cap. Inside he was the typical male shopper—quick, impatient, and overly efficient. He picked up the bare necessities—toothbrushes, toothpaste, deodorant, razor, shaving cream, liquid detergent (presumably to wash out their clothes)—which she added to with *her* bare necessities of moisturizer, mascara, blush, eyeliner, mousse, and a hairbrush to go with the scissors that he'd tossed in. He frowned at the items before looking at her. "Why do you wear that stuff? You don't need it."

She supposed that was a backhanded compliment, but it didn't matter. "No one does, but I like it."

Especially if he was making her cut her hair.

Annie wasn't normally vain, but looking like a drowned rat—a soon-to-be-shorn drowned rat—was bringing out a rather hefty streak of vanity now.

He gave her a whatever shrug and proceeded to the checkout. They passed by a refrigerated display of ready-made sandwiches, sausage rolls—*yuck*—and salads.

"You hungry?"

This time she knew he was messing with her. She didn't bother responding. Instead she chose enough food to feed a small army: a caprese sandwich, fruit salad, salt and vinegar chips—or crisps as they were called here—and a couple of hard-boiled eggs.

Proving he was human, Dan doubled down on just about everything.

The store was quiet, and when they reached the checkout, the cashier was unusually talkative for an Islander. Most of the Scots Annie had met to this point were friendly but quiet. This woman was the first but not the second.

Reddish brown hair, apple-cheeked, with the windblown ruddy complexion that seemed commonplace, she had the sturdy build of someone who worked hard for a living outside and lived in green Wellies—a farmer or serious gardener. Maybe both.

"It's too early for the ferry, so you must have flown in on the eight fifty from Glasgow."

Dan nodded. "We did."

Annie was too shocked that the small island had an airport to say anything.

The woman nodded toward the items Dan had just finished pulling from the basket. "And by the looks of it, they lost your luggage? They are usually pretty good with keeping track of bags on those small planes."

Clearly she was poking around for more information. Dan didn't disappoint her. "It wasn't them. It was the international flight before."

The woman nodded, pleased. She looked back and forth between them. "I thought so. Where are you from, the States?"

"Originally, but I live in Brazil now with my wife."

"Brazil?" The woman looked at Annie with renewed interest. Annie was still digesting the wife part. "How wonderful."

"She doesn't speak much English," Dan said before the woman could question her.

"You must be here for the windsurfing contest," the woman said, only too happy to turn back to Dan. "You're early. Most people won't start arriving for a couple days."

Dan gave her a killer grin that even made Annie, who was not the recipient, twitter a little. "How'd you guess?"

He might as well have added "dude" or "brah" to that surfer drawl.

If the woman wasn't old enough to be his mother, Annie might be more angry by the clearly flirtatious and cheeky grin she gave him. "I can always pick out the athletes."

Annie was surprised that she didn't reach out and squeeze one of the muscular arms she was ogling. Apparently Annie wasn't the only one in the room with a silly weakness for tall and built like a linebacker.

"Any idea where we can pick up a few things until our bags catch up?" he asked.

Annie wanted to snort. Mr. Hard-Ass was laying the laid-back-surfer—windsurfer—thing on a little thick, to Annie's getting-annoyed mind. But the woman was eating it up.

"There's a small boutique next to the big hotel. It has mostly women's things, but Sara has a small men's section of basics. Tell her Patsy sent you and she'll take care of you. There are also a couple beach shops for T-shirts, sweatshirts, and bathing suits if you need those. And a charity shop further down the road."

"That should be plenty to get us through," Dan said, taking the package that Patsy seemed reluctant to let go of. "Thank you, Patsy."

The woman blushed like the proverbial schoolgirl—of fifty, Annie thought uncharitably.

"My pleasure," Patsy said. "Hope to see you and your wife around during the competition."

Annie thought Patsy had forgotten she existed. Normally Annie was the typical overfriendly American. But since she was now Brazilian, she must have forgotten. Annie also didn't speak a word of Portuguese. It was close to Spanish, which she did speak, but she wasn't going to take a chance on *hasta luego*.

Dan must have noticed. "What's the matter?"

"No hablo inglés."

He laughed. "That's not Portuguese."

"Which is why I didn't say anything." She side-eyed him. "I didn't take you for flirtatious."

He shrugged. "When the situation calls . . ."

"Yeah, well, a little advice. If you ever have a *real* wife, I wouldn't do that in front of her."

He gave her a look as if she were crazy—which was exactly how she was feeling. "You're right. You do get cranky when you are hungry. Let's eat and then get cleaned up."

Annie devoured her brunch in an embarrassingly short time, and then headed into the public bathroom to wash up a little. Dan said they'd go shopping afterward to pick up clothes to change into after showering, but he wanted to change their appearances a little before checking into a hotel and too many people saw them.

The mirror was one of those nonglass safety types found in public restrooms and didn't give off the best reflection, but she managed to dampen her hair, cut a good six inches off in a mostly straight line—her hair was wavy, so it didn't matter as much—to just past chin level, and do a light application of makeup.

She was fine until she started filling the paper bag Dan
have given her for the purpose with her hair. Looking down
at the pile of thick brown waves, she wanted to cry. Maybe it
was good that she couldn't really see in the mirror that well.

It's just hair.

How much difference could it make?

A lot. As she discovered when she left the bathroom and
found Dan waiting for her. She took one look at him, and her
stomach dropped. Or flipped—she couldn't tell. But everything
inside her seemed to be skidding around in all kinds of directions.

Oh, crap.

He'd shaved.

Eighteen

Dean took another sip from his pint, wondering what he'd said this time. The newly dubbed Mrs. Thompson—of the Mr. and Mrs. Thompson who'd registered at the guest house—had been prickly since their trip to the market earlier.

"Thanks," Annie grumbled, barely looking at him before turning back to her food.

Maybe she was cranky because of all those vegetables she ate. He was tempted to offer her some of his steak but figured she might not see the humor right now.

All he'd said was that her hair looked cute. She'd done a good job with the cut. The silky, dark strands fell to just past her chin in those loose, sexy waves that were popular right now, framing her face and emphasizing the delicateness of her features. Except for her eyes, which looked enormous.

She had this vulnerable thing going that if anything made her look even hotter, but he sure as hell wasn't going to tell her that. But definitely Bambi 2.0.

He'd been having a hard enough time keeping his eyes in his head since she walked into their shared room after using the hall bathroom—the guest house didn't have en suites.

He'd never seen her dressed for dinner before, and she looked like a million bucks. Which was all the more impressive since he'd only given her a couple of hundred to buy the clothes she would need for a few days. She'd come back with an impressive stack of garments. And even though like most straight men he didn't know shit about fashion, he knew enough to know that wasn't enough money for anything designer. But somehow she'd turned a slinky black sundress, a black cotton wrap sweater, and thin black flip-flops into a fashion model straight off the pages of a glossy magazine.

He, on the other hand, had bought the first white polo and tan cargos he could find, as well as a few pairs of shorts, T-shirts, board shorts, and surprisingly—given that it was Scotland and not Coronado—a Baja-style sweatshirt.

Windsurfing was big on the island, and the big competition that Patsy had assumed he was participating in—the Tiree Wave Classic—was the longest-running windsurfing contest in the world. Not bad for a small Scottish island most people probably hadn't heard of. But it explained the beach vibe of the place. "The Hawaii of the North" was what they called it. He wasn't sure he'd go that far, but it had been a lucky pick.

Dean wasn't a professional by any means, but he was a decent surfer and windsurfer courtesy of the years spent in Coronado and Hawaii. If the need arose, he would be able to fake it.

As for faking the laid-back surfer dude? For that all he had to do was harness his best Donovan impression. Maybe he should have looked for an ugly Hawaiian shirt in that secondhand store.

He watched Annie pick at her food while enjoying his pint of the local ale. As he'd chosen a small guest house that only served breakfast, the innkeeper had suggested the restaurant down by the harbor for dinner. It wasn't cheap, but Annie deserved a nice meal after what she'd been through. He had a feeling that now that they were out of immediate danger, it was all catching up to her.

"You okay?"

She looked up at him. She had that surprised strange look on her face again before she lowered her eyes and blushed. "I'm fine."

She'd been doing that all day. Ever since he'd walked out of the public bathroom minus the beard and longer hair.

Dean frowned. "Why are you looking at me like that?"

Or maybe not looking was the better question.

She glanced up again. Warily. "Like what?"

"Like I'm some kind of freak from *X-Men*?"

The blush deepened. She lowered her gaze again before forcing it back to his. She'd never seemed shy before, but that was definitely how she was acting.

"I'm just not used to seeing you without the beard and long hair. You look"—she paused for so long Dean started to feel self-conscious, which was an entirely new feeling for him—"different."

Different? What the hell did that mean?

Maybe he was getting the cute issue now.

Dean found himself rubbing his chin, which was definitely self-conscious. Christ. What was he, seventeen? Why did he care if she didn't like it? "It'll grow back soon enough."

"It's not that," she said quickly—maybe a little too quickly. "I like it."

Suddenly he understood the blush and shy looks. Ah, shit. She was attracted to him. Given that he was feeling the same way, it probably wasn't a good idea, but he said it anyway. "I feel the same way about your hair."

He was glad he'd said it when she gave him a smile that reached all the way up to her eyes. He could get really used to making her smile like that.

As he was on a roll, he thought about mentioning the dress—the low-cut, tight dress that showed off a pretty spectacular chest and got even lower every time she leaned forward to take a bite—but he thought that might give too much away. Yeah, he was also a pig and not above taking cheap thrills where he could find them.

This place was too romantic anyway. A small table tucked in a corner, low light, sea view, intimate conversation . . . It wasn't a date, but it felt a hell of a lot like one.

The problem wasn't just that he was hot for her. He was hotter for her than he'd ever been for any woman in his life. So hot that the next few nights sharing a room with her—and not touching her—were going to be fucking torture. The kind of torture that would put last night to shame.

But even *one* cheap room and food were going to deplete his stash of cash quickly. They couldn't do a his and hers.

Better not to think about that right now. "Tell me about your dissertation."

She eyed him warily. "Really? Mr. Anti-Save-the-Whales is interested in my liberal, environmental agenda?"

He was interested in everything about her. Shit. He had to stop thinking things like that. "I wouldn't have asked if I wasn't. And I'm not anti-Shamu or environment."

She arched a very pretty dark eyebrow. "I notice you didn't say anything about the liberal-agenda part."

He smiled, caught.

"I thought so! Well, to pay you back, I'm going to bore you senseless."

She was wrong. She didn't bore him at all. It was fun listening to someone who truly loved what they did.

She told him how she'd switched majors after the Gulf Oil spill, and how she wanted to make sure nothing like it ever happened again.

Dean remembered some of the pictures of the dead wildlife after the disaster—dead birds and dolphins coated in crude oil. They'd been disturbing, but given some of the things he'd seen as a SEAL, they hadn't made much of an impact.

When you'd seen men blown apart by an IED or seen heads explode like watermelons from a gunshot, the loss of a few birds didn't seem that important.

But through her eyes, he realized that wasn't the way to look at it. Valuing human life more highly didn't mean that nothing else had value. Senseless loss was senseless loss. And someone who cared deeply about protecting living things big and small from that should be commended, not dismissed.

She'd been willing to put herself on the line by getting on that ship. He might not have been one hundred percent behind the method, but he could admire the action. Maybe they were more alike than he wanted to think.

"I wasn't just interested in what happened right after the spill," she said. "That was easy to see. I wanted to prove that even when the oil is dissipated and 'cleaned up,' there are lasting effects. I was looking at the levels of different types of PAHs, polycyclic aromatic hydrocarbons," she translated, although he knew what they were, "which are commonly found in crude oil in Gulf fish—particularly tilefish, since they're bottom feeders, where the oil eventually settles—at various distances from shore and morphological changes in heart structure."

In other words, changes to the actual form or structure of the organism. "Did you find any?"

She nodded enthusiastically. "Enough to put in question the current thinking on how far is 'safe' for offshore drilling operations."

"So what's next?" he asked. "More lab research?"

"I thought so. I've been offered a position at a private research lab."

"But."

She smiled, realizing he hadn't missed her hesitation. "I've been gone for eight years. My mom wants me to go back to Florida for a while."

"What do you want?"

"I don't know. I love lab work, but I miss being out in the field. The lab sometimes feels a little detached."

She stopped talking when the waiter interrupted them to take their plates, refill her wineglass, and ask if they wanted dessert.

She shook her head, and he ordered another ale, not ready for the evening to end.

When the waiter left, she looked at him apologetically. "I've been talking all night. What about you? I don't even know where you went to school."

He wasn't surprised by the assumption. It wasn't the first time it had happened. It was the first time, however, that he cared about the reaction.

He wasn't embarrassed. College hadn't been for him, and God knew, he'd learned more as a SEAL than he ever would have in the classroom. But she had a PhD. In his experience, the more educated the person, the more biased about the value of education—whether warranted or not—and the more likely to equate not educated to not intelligent. More than once after telling a date he hadn't gone to college, he'd heard, "Wow, but you seem so smart."

"I went to JC for a few semesters, but it wasn't for me."

If she was surprised, she hid it well. Instead she seemed curious, studying him with an intensity that made him want to squirm a little. "College isn't for everyone. They seem to have a much better grasp of that here," she said, referring to the UK, where it wasn't necessarily assumed that after secondary school you went to university (or "uni" as it was called). "With the exorbitant cost of tuition, I think kids should be weighing that decision a lot more. Your parents must have been happy not to have all that debt."

She'd meant it lightheartedly, and he didn't want to make her feel bad, but he also wanted her to know the truth. At least as much as he could tell her. "My dad wasn't around, and my mom didn't have money."

Nor would she have given it to him if she had.

She seemed to sense that there was more—a lot more. But didn't press, probably because she knew he couldn't tell her. "I'm sorry."

He dismissed the sentiment with a shake of his head. "Don't be. I got over it a long time ago."

"Is that why you went into the navy?"

He nodded. "It was the best thing that ever happened to me." He'd spoken without thinking.

"Then why did you leave?"

"I . . ." The frustration of the situation was eating away at him. He couldn't tell her anything, but he didn't want to out-right lie to her. "I can't talk about it, all right?"

She seemed to understand, although he could see she wanted to ask more. "You never thought about going back to school to become an officer?"

"Hell no!" The words were out before he could stop them. He might be a Senior Chief Special Warfare Operator—a petty officer—but he was still a ground pounder. "Paperwork and politics aren't my thing."

She laughed. "Understatement of the evening. You don't

have a politic bone in your body, which you need to rise up the ranks. You are all about hard truths and saying what's on your mind."

He knew what she was talking about. "I'm sorry, Annie. I shouldn't have spoken to you that way. I was pissed."

She shook her head. "No. You had every right to say what you did. I was naive, and I should have asked more questions. I'm just sorry that I got you messed up in all this."

He wasn't. He should be, but he wasn't. And that scared the shit out of him.

Soap made lousy makeup remover. Annie stared at her reflection in the bathroom mirror, but it wasn't the dark circles she was worried about. What was she going to do?

She liked him. She liked him a lot.

Tonight had been nice. Actually it had been better than nice. It had been pretty close to a perfect first date. Which was all the more ironic because it hadn't been a date at all.

Maybe after what they'd been through, it was understandable that Dan was so easy to talk to and that being with him felt so natural. But that didn't explain the constant hum and buzz of awareness that made her feel as if there was a magnet drawing them closer and closer together.

The magnet was physical attraction, she told herself. Physical attraction that had gotten a hundred times worse after he walked out of that public toilet earlier.

Someone should have prepared her.

She'd felt as if she'd been hit by the proverbial freight train. Her tough, grizzled longshoreman had turned into a clean-cut, all-American tall drink of gorgeousness. He was every bit as good-looking as she'd feared—maybe more so.

He had a great jawline—strong and masculine but not overly Neanderthal square. And with the beard gone, she could really see his mouth. On anyone less masculine looking it might be sensual, but on him it was just . . . sexy.

Pretty much everything about him was sexy. And every time she looked at him, her heart stopped a little and she remembered exactly how it had felt to have him kissing and touching her.

This wasn't good. Not good at all.

Annie splashed her face with cold water from the tap, but it didn't help. She still felt flushed.

She knew better than to blame it on the wine. It was him. Her. The blasted awareness between them.

Realizing she'd dawdled in the no-frills but clean little girls' room long enough to get ready for bed—*bed!*—she gathered up her discarded clothes and limited toiletries and padded barefoot back down the hall toward the room.

Their room.

God, she had to stop thinking like that.

It was a small guest house. Four rooms shared two hall bathrooms—a women's on one end of the long hall and a men's on the other. Annie wasn't sure, but she thought they might be the only people staying here tonight. She hadn't heard any sounds behind the other three doors she passed to get to room number one, which they'd been given.

It was more like being in someone's house than a hotel. Although the bathroom had been white utilitarian—stand-up shower, toilet, towel bar, hamper, and small pedestal sink—the rest of the house was an explosion of Victorian. She hadn't seen so many doilies, flowers, and dark wood since her grandmother died. Even in the hall the decoration was dark maroon carpet and mauve-colored rose wallpaper on the walls.

She stood outside the bedroom door. This was ridiculous. She was being silly. It was the twenty-first century. There was no reason to make such a big deal about this. Two adults could sleep in the same room. She didn't need to get weird about it. They'd slept in the same room last night.

In separate beds.

They would still be in separate beds, she told herself. The large king bed that dominated the room had given her a moment of panic when she saw it. But then she realized it was actually two twins that could be pulled a few inches apart—apparently a typical setup in this part of the world.

There was only one duvet—they were supposed to be married, so they could hardly ask the room to be made up as twins—but it was big enough so that there wouldn't be any touching. Not that touching was a worry anyway. He'd made it pretty clear last time that he wasn't interested in pursuing anything.

God, she was being such a girl! Did she have to overthink everything? He probably hadn't given the sleeping situation more than a passing thought.

Man up, she told herself, and opened the door.

Manning up lasted about as long as it took for him to turn from where he stood at the window and take in her apparel with a glance.

She'd found a three-quarter-sleeve sport-jersey-style night-shirt that went to her knees. It was far more modest than the shorts and tank she'd had on yesterday, but from the way he was looking at her, she felt as if she'd walked in wearing a silk teddy.

Although with the level of heat penetrating from those steely eyes, she probably would have felt naked in one of her grandma's old flannel nightgowns.

Maybe she hadn't been the only one overthinking.

But when he clenched his jaw and hardened his gaze—lifting it from her bare legs and feet—she knew it didn't matter. He wasn't going to act on whatever this was between them.

Suddenly she realized he was still wearing the polo and khakis that he'd worn to dinner. "You didn't change?" she asked, feeling as if she'd just shown up to a party and was the only one dressed in costume.

"I need to go out for a little while. Go ahead and get some rest," he said, all Mr. Business again.

In other words, don't wait up. "Where are you going?"

She was beginning to read the little signs in his expressions, and this one said "curtain is down." Granite curtain, and good luck lifting it.

"There's something I have to take care of. It's nothing for you to worry about, okay?"

What choice did she have? She nodded, feeling unaccountably hurt. She knew that he didn't have any obligation to tell her anything. But that didn't mean she didn't want him to.

If anything it was a harsh reminder that this little escapade didn't mean anything. They might be temporarily stuck together, but in case she'd been under any illusions—which she might have been—as soon as he could be unstuck, he'd be going solo.

He'd made it clear from the beginning that he didn't want her along. He'd promised to help her, but she knew that was all she could count on.

She wasn't a girlfriend. She wasn't a wife. She wasn't anything.

One mind-blowing, never-felt-anything-like-that-in-her-life orgasm didn't mean anything. She certainly didn't have any kind of claim on him. Where he went was none of her business.

Maybe he was tired of her and needed a break. For all she knew he was going to a pub to drink and find someone he did want to pursue something with. He was a man. A very good-looking man, and he'd had more than one or two looks in his direction tonight as they left the restaurant and bar. If he wanted to pick someone up, she was sure it wouldn't be difficult.

"All right," she said in as normal a voice as she could manage. "Good night."

She put her things down in a pile on the dresser and walked over to the bed. Choosing the side that was the farther from the door, she crawled under the duvet, pulled it over her shoulders, and turned on her side to face the wall.

There was a long pause where she was tempted to peek and see if he was looking at her. If he wanted to say something.

But she didn't. A moment later, she heard him walk to the door, flip the light, and lock the door.

Then all she could hear was the sound of her own heart beating.

She lay there for a long time. Alone in the dark with nothing but her thoughts to occupy her, she felt the emotions of the past two days finally catching up with her.

Nineteen

She'd done the Bambi-eyes thing again, and it was eating away at him.

Dean hadn't meant to be gone that long. He'd needed to make a call and hadn't wanted to do it with her around. Taylor hadn't answered, and Dean had instead left the LC a text telling him to call.

The whole thing had taken less than five minutes. But Dean hadn't gone back to the room right away. He didn't trust himself. Not with the thoughts that had been running through his mind when she appeared all freshly scrubbed, barefoot, and in that long T-shirt thing that made him feel as if he were back in high school, and she was wearing his football jersey. He'd always had a weakness for women wearing one of his shirts, but he'd never wanted to rip one off so badly.

He needed to calm the fuck down. Unwind. De-lust. Was that even a word? It didn't matter; he needed to do it.

He was damned close to breaking his rule about drinking. Instead he sat outside for a while, let his body cool down, and then snuck back into the room long enough to retrieve a few things for a shower. The cold water didn't do much, but his hand took the edge off his problem in short—very short—order. All he had to do was think about the night before—or that dress she'd been wearing—and he went off like a rocket.

Considerably less tense, if far from satisfied, Dean dried off and got ready for bed.

It was dark and quiet when he returned to the room. He tried not to make any noise when he put his stuff down and locked the door. Sitting on the edge of the bed, he pulled off his shirt and removed his pants before slipping under the comforter. Unlike her, he hadn't thought to buy something to sleep in. He'd be up before she was, so it wouldn't matter. Besides, he burned hot and the room was stuffy even with the windows cracked.

He lay awake, staring at the ceiling in the darkness, trying not to think about the woman sleeping a couple of feet away from him.

At least he thought she was sleeping. But then he realized she was too quiet. He should have been hearing the steady sounds of her breathing. Instead she seemed to be holding her breath.

When her breath hitched and she let out a muffled sob, he realized that was exactly what she'd been doing.

Ah, hell. She was crying. And Dean was in trouble because he knew he wasn't going to be able to ignore it.

He shouldn't have left her alone. He'd given her time to think and let it catch up to her. Julien had been a douche bag, but he hadn't deserved to die.

She was still turned away from him, but Dean rolled onto his side, leaned over, and reached out to wipe a tear from her cheek with his thumb. Christ, her skin was as soft as a baby's.

Her face nuzzled into his hand at the touch, and his heart took a big, hard thump. "It'll be all right, sweetheart."

Shit? Where the fuck had that come from? He didn't use endearments. Ever.

She turned to him in the darkness. He could see the damp sheen of her eyes reflecting back at him. "No, it won't. They're dead." Her voice broke. "Dead. They didn't deserve that."

He caressed her cheek again with his thumb. He'd never felt anything so soft. Something clenched tight in his chest. "No, they didn't."

"It's my fault."

"How do you figure that?"

"If I hadn't found—"

He stopped her right there. "If you hadn't found that, a lot of innocent people might be dead—including me and you. You aren't to blame for what happened, Annie." His tone left her no room to argue. "All right?"

He could feel her eyes on his face as she nodded.

"Good. Then let's get some rest."

"I'm trying."

Dean debated for all of a split second before doing the one thing he'd told himself he wasn't going to do. He stood up, pushed the mattresses back together, and pulled her against him.

She might have been a child lying here with her cheek on his shoulder, and her palm lying flat on his chest.

But she wasn't. She felt incredible. As if she belonged there. All soft and firm in the right places. The skin-to-skin contact took his attraction to an entirely different level, flooding him with all kinds of impulses.

But he pushed aside his own demons and gave her what she needed—comfort. He held her in his arms, stroking her head gently, until they both fell asleep.

Which was fine until morning came.

Annie woke slowly from a deep, deep sleep. The dreamy fog took a while to dissipate. She was so warm and comfortable, it was almost as if she didn't want to let it go.

Instinctively she snuggled deeper into the body that was holding her from behind.

She sighed, knowing exactly who it was.

God, he felt good. His chest was like a wall of warm steel at her back, and his legs and arms were like a muscular fortress wrapped around her. She felt safe and protected and . . . hot.

Very, very hot. And very, very turned on. Especially when she realized he was awake and hard.

Awareness shot through her like a lightning bolt. The sensation of that big, powerful body behind her—and the sizable column pressing against her bottom—set off all kinds of primitive instincts that she didn't even know she had. The most demanding being hunger. Although that didn't really cover the overwhelming desire she was feeling.

Last night she'd needed comfort, but this morning she needed something else. She needed him inside her. Now.

Rocking back against him, her body told him exactly that. It practically screamed *Fuck me.*

He answered with a groan and a slow, purposeful caress of those big callused hands down her waist and hips as his mouth sank against the warm skin at the nape of her neck.

His kiss electrified her, her skin tingling and tightening. Everything seemed to jump to light speed. There was no hesitation. No thinking to slow them down. It was the continuation of a dream from which neither of them wanted to wake.

Whatever qualms he'd had the other night were forgotten. He was in full command, leaving no doubt of where this was going. Fast.

Just the way she wanted it. Her body responded to the frantic urgency, moving more insistently. Demandingly.

Hurry.

He heard her. Responding in kind. He devoured her neck and shoulder as his hand skimmed her waist to take hold of her hip to pull her firmly against him. Grinding. Thrusting. Giving her a hint of what was to come.

She couldn't wait. She whimpered, almost coming apart. Her body didn't feel like her own. She felt like a stranger. An uninhibited stranger who was giving in to every sensual impulse she'd ever had. The warmth of his mouth on her skin was incredible, but the feel of him behind her was something else entirely. It was indescribable. *Perfect.*

Her nightshirt had risen up to her waist during the night, meaning it didn't have much farther to go before it was pulled over her head. Her thong was hastily slid down over her hips to her feet, where she could kick it off, as his hand dipped between her legs to stroke her.

She started to moan, instantly wet. Like last time, he knew just how to touch her. Where to touch her for maximum pleasure. She didn't open her eyes; she just let herself feel, giving over to the powerful sensations that had taken control of her body.

There was no stopping it. No drawing it out. His breath was coming too hard, his stroke too demanding, the feel of their bodies grinding too familiar.

It was like a freight train of need barreling down on her. She started to cry out as he forced her over the edge.

She'd barely had time to come down before he was lifting her hips and probing her tingly flesh with the thick, blunt tip of his erection.

A new shudder that was like nothing she'd ever experienced before went through her. It was raw. Primal. Pleasure at its most extreme. She wanted him inside her now. She wanted that big body pounding inside her, muscles flared and taut with need for her.

She was warm and wet and ready from her orgasm, and he didn't hesitate. With one hard thrust he surged inside her.

She cried out at the sensation. At the possession. At the feel of him deep inside her. He was big and thick and long, and she could feel every powerful inch as he thrust a little deeper and harder.

When he was touching the deepest part of her, he stopped and held himself there as if savoring the connection. She'd never felt closer to anyone in her life. In the midst of the sexual frenzy, it was a strangely poignant and romantic moment.

But then, as if the brief pause had taken all his reserve, he started to move. Thrusting slow and deep. Hard and possessive. Her body jolting with every stroke.

This was what she'd been craving. Hot, wild, dirty sex. To be fucked by a man who knew exactly what he was doing.

Faster. Harder. Oh God, yes. Just like that. Take me. . . .

Had she spoken aloud? When he swore and tightened his grasp on her hips to quicken his stroke, she thought she might have.

She arched against him, wanting even more. She loved the feel of her bottom against his groin, her back against his chest, and her breasts straining toward . . . his hand. He cupped and squeezed her breast while his fingers plied her nipple to a tight bud.

She could feel the need building in her again. The storm of frenzy waiting to unleash. She knew he'd be good in bed, but she'd never thought it would be like this.

"That's it, sweetheart—come for me again." She could feel the warmth of his breath by her ear, and it only made her shuddering worse. "You are so fucking hot. You're making me wild. I don't think I can hold back much longer."

His hand skimmed down her stomach and he touched her between her legs just as he thrust deep and hard. She went off like a bomb. Sensation shattered in a thousand directions. Her head exploded in an array of blazing light and color.

He shuddered once, and then cursed.

He pulled out so suddenly it took her a minute to realize what had happened. He'd nearly come inside her. Which wouldn't have been such a big deal if he'd been wearing a condom.

No condom. It took a moment for that to sink in, given the other very powerful feelings that were still reverberating through her body. It wasn't just orgasmic bliss—it was something else. Something she didn't want to put words to.

Unfortunately, he did.

Twenty

What the fuck was that? Something had just happened, and whatever it was had left Dean reeling.

It had been . . . Shit, he couldn't even describe it. But it had been an entirely different level. He felt as if he'd been wallowing in the minor leagues and had just gotten called up to the bigs.

He rolled onto his back, staring at the ceiling as the blood pounding through his body—including his heart—returned to normal. His breathing was hard and heavy, not from the length of his exertion—he sure as hell wasn't going to win any marathon awards for that—but from the intensity. Every muscle, every bone, every fiber of his body had been invested and focused on what he was doing to her. What was happening. The feelings, the sensations had taken hold of him completely in a way that he'd never experienced before.

Also never experienced before? Sex without a condom. Christ, he'd been a split second away from coming inside her! He raked his fingers back through his hair, forgetting that it was short again.

What the hell could he have been thinking? He hadn't been thinking; that was the problem. He'd been acting on pure animal instinct.

He'd woken up with that taut, curvy ass pressed against

him, and he'd been in a tunnel of need so dark and deep, nothing could have pulled him out. *Take her. She wants it. You both want it. Don't think. Just fuck. Fuck her until you can't see straight.*

Mission accomplished. Hooyah.

But what a fucking mess. He said the first thing that came to mind as he felt her turn toward him. "That was a mistake."

Annie usually liked Dan's blunt tell-it-like-it-is, no-sugar-coating brusqueness. Now, however, was not one of those times.

She'd been feeling oddly vulnerable and had instinctively sought the warmth and connection of his body by curling against him.

But when he made his pronouncement, she stiffened and started to roll away. He swore and caught her by the arm.

"That isn't what I meant." He must have realized he sounded like an ass. Great. Give him the prize for awareness. Their eyes met for the first time that morning. Her chest squeezed. Whatever she'd hoped to see, it wasn't regret. "I'm sorry. I wasn't thinking. But I've never had sex without a condom—I'm clean."

Annie knew that the mistake he'd been talking about wasn't just about protection. She could see it in every white etched line of his grim expression. *This* was a mistake, was what he meant. The most incredible sexual experience of her life—by far—had been a "mistake."

Ouch. So much for postcoital cuddling and warm reassurances about how amazing that had been. How he'd never felt anything like it. How it had been as earth-shattering for him as it had been for her. How it might have meant something.

All those overwhelming, complicated, *vulnerable* feelings she had twisting and squeezing inside her? Yeah, well, they were one-sided.

She told herself that she had no reason to be disappointed. No reason to be hurt. Hot monkey sex—or, in this case, doggy without the hands and knees—wasn't romantic. It didn't inspire tender moments of postorgasmic bliss. She had no reason to expect more than a wham, bam, thank you, ma'am.

Although technically she hadn't even gotten that.

What was her problem? He'd made it clear that he hadn't wanted this, that he didn't want to get involved. That she chose to ignore it was her fault. If she was feeling hurt, she had no one to blame but herself.

She buried her disappointment and forced a cool, nonchalance to her expression. "We both made a mistake. It was a heat-of-the-moment adrenaline type of thing. I've never had unprotected sex, either, and I'm on the pill, but I am happy to get tested if you want."

"That isn't necessary." His obvious relief that she wasn't going to make a big deal out of this—even though it very much felt like a big deal to her—stung much more than it should.

She was being ridiculous. She needed to act like an adult. Adolescents thought sex meant feelings; she should know better. It didn't mean anything. Hot sex was just hot sex.

Their chemistry was off the charts, so what? That didn't mean it was time to start picking out china patterns. Chemistry didn't equate to soul mate. Good in bed—okay, *fantastic* in bed—didn't make ideal life partner.

She needed to stop imagining feelings and connections and look at the reality. She was attracted to him. Who wouldn't be? Look at him. He was seriously put together. Not just a great face but the body as well. She was painfully aware that he was lying in bed naked beside her with the duvet only partially covering him. But the glimpse she'd caught of his bare chest and arms before she turned away had been enough to turn her to jelly all over again. Big and cut up didn't cover it by half.

It was probably better not to look. Just the feel of that rock-hard body behind her had made her act stupid enough.

But beyond attraction and apparent sexual compatibility, they didn't have anything in common. Even if he wasn't on the run from something and she hadn't just gotten out of a bad relationship, it would never work. They were polar opposites. What had happened to her trifecta of not going to happen?

There was also the former military issue. The cool, confident, hard-as-nails "machine" she had been talking about pretty much summed him up. She had to admit in situations like this his alpha-man skills were welcome—and sexy—but in everyday life? No, thanks. She didn't need another wannabe hero in her life. She had no interest in going there. Ever.

Then why was she so disappointed?

She thought she'd done a good job of hiding it, but she must not have been as good an actor as she thought.

"Look, Annie, I don't want you to get the wrong idea about this."

Now, *that* made her perk up. As in hackles perked way up. "Wrong idea?"

He frowned at her tone, but in typical guy fashion plowed right on through the danger sign. "I like you, and this morning was . . . great." *Great?* "But you and me . . ." He shrugged uncomfortably. "It can't happen."

She tucked the duvet around her chest as she sat up to stare at him. It was a testament to her flaring temper that she didn't gape at her first full view of his chest. But good Lord. Her mouth went dry. There wasn't an ounce of fat on him. *Eyes back up.* "I think it did just happen."

Rather spectacularly as a matter of fact.

His frown turned a little wary, as if he knew he might be stomping through a minefield. "Not that. I meant about anything more."

In other words, don't get your hopes up, it didn't mean anything, and don't read anything into it.

All that confusion she'd been feeling a few minutes ago? It was gone. He'd just cleared it right up for her.

"You think after all that's happened in the past couple of days that I'm looking for something more?"

He put one hand behind his head to look at her, bending his elbow and causing the muscles in his arm to flex.

Holy crap! She forced her gaze away so she wouldn't stare, but the flush in her cheeks got a little hotter.

He gave kind of an amused sigh. "You don't exactly strike me as the one-night-stand type."

She should consider it a compliment, but right now it just annoyed her. He thought he knew her so well, did he? Or was he just used to women falling in love with him after sex? Neither sat well with her. "I'm not," she said with a sugary smile. "Mornings, on the other hand . . ."

It took him a moment to realize what she meant. One-*morning* stands. When he did, his gaze darkened. "What's that supposed to mean?"

She shrugged. "It means that you don't know anything about me or what I like."

"Oh, I think I know what you like well enough."

He gave her a cocky look that made her nipples tighten and her body tingle in places that should be too sore to be doing so. Jerk.

Her cheeks were no doubt bright red, but she ignored the sensual taunt. "You don't have to worry about me getting 'the wrong idea,'" she said. "I knew exactly what I was doing." She gave him a long look, letting her eyes slide over every inch of his well-muscled chest. "It couldn't have escaped your notice that I'm attracted to you. Your body is incredible." She thought about asking him about the scars and tattoo, but didn't want to get off track. The same small scars she'd noticed on his hands were on most of his body except for his chest. "But now that we've gotten it out of our systems." She shrugged. "It's not as if we have a lot in common. You aren't exactly my type."

She wasn't the only one angry now. He sat up and glared back at her. "What . . . not educated enough or not girlie enough?"

She clutched the duvet tighter, her cheeks flaming. Julien hadn't been girlie. Well, maybe compared to *him*, but that wasn't exactly a fair comparison. He oozed testosterone. "Neither. More like too conservative, too good ol' boy Texas, and too macho military."

"Macho? What is this, the eighties?"

"Alpha, whatever you want to call it."

"Machine."

Their eyes met. She didn't say anything, but yes, that about summed it up.

She'd pissed him off, and she could tell he wanted to re-taliate. To do something to prove her wrong. And having a feeling she knew what that might be, she started to scoot away, edging off the bed.

But she was saved by the bell—or, in this case, the buzz.

It took them both a minute to realize where it was coming from. He swore and got out of bed.

She sucked in her breath, her heart beating like a jackhammer. Whether he'd forgotten that he was naked or just didn't care—probably the latter—she got an eyeful of a first-rate backside.

She'd been wrong. He didn't need football pants. He looked pretty damned perfect as is.

He reached for his pants to retrieve his cell phone from one of the pockets, but the buzzing had already stopped.

Taking a look at the number, he muttered something under his breath that rhymed with "duck."

Seeing him reach for his clothes, she did the same.

"I have to make a call." She looked in his direction after pulling her nightshirt over her head. Had he been watching her? She couldn't tell from his expression, but from the way his muscles were clenched she thought he might have.

"I thought you said no one knew your number."

"I said it was a burner and untraceable."

In other words, he wasn't going to tell her who called.

He reached for his shirt and started to put it on, when she caught sight of the tattoo again and frowned. "That tattoo on your arm. What kind of crest is it? It looks familiar."

He froze. At least it seemed that way at first, but when he turned to look at her, his expression was normal. "You probably have many times. It's a popular beer."

She thought for a minute and then it came to her. "You have a Budweiser tattoo?"

He arched an eyebrow. "Not highbrow enough for you?"

"I prefer Coors Light. So yes."

He bit out a sharp laugh and shook his head. "You don't back down, do you?"

It was rhetorical, so she didn't answer. Instead she said, "How did you get the scars?"

She was learning to read him better. His expression gave nothing away on first glance, but the slight tensing of his jaw and whitening of his lips told her the question was not a welcome one.

"Car accident," he said so indifferently that she knew it was a lie. "I'll be back in a little bit. If you're hungry you can go down to breakfast without me."

"All right."

"Annie?"

She looked up.

"We're not done here."

She wasn't so sure. It felt as if they were very done.

Twenty-one

Colt got the meeting he'd wanted, although the old bastard made him wait over an hour first in the "drawing room."

Who the hell had a drawing room anymore? Relics like General Thomas Murray, that's who. The entire place stank of old money, old family, and old America. A Murray had called "Blairhaven" (named after the family's ancestral castle in Scotland) home since the time of the Revolution.

Colt had been uncomfortable the first time Kate brought him here, and it had never changed. The old plantation house in Alexandria, Virginia, harked back to a time of Jeffersonian pastoral America that felt not only out of touch, but repressive, given the unavoidable connection with its slave past. It represented an idealized vision of a bucolic world that had never really existed.

The rooms themselves felt like a museum, filled with antiques and oversized paintings of illustrious long-dead relatives. The family's old and distinguished military service figured in many of them.

Colt sat on one of the sturdier-looking carved mahogany chairs, hoping it would hold his weight. It had a cushion made out of that fabric Kate had loved. Toile, he thought it was called. He'd never been a fan. Probably because it reminded him of this place, and that she'd come from somewhere where people were rich enough to have names for fabric.

He fiddled with the hands of the brass clock on the side table beside him. It was one of three in the room, which made sense, as two didn't seem to be working.

He'd declined tea from the disapproving maid, having never acquired the taste for it and recalling how he'd broken an "irreplaceable" cup the first time he was here.

Ah, the fond memories.

Finally the butler—yep, the butler—showed him into the general's study.

The bastard didn't even look up when he entered the room and was "announced." The general finished reading some document before slowly lifting his head.

Colt barely hid his shock. General Thomas Murray, vice chairman of the Joint Chiefs of Staff, had aged in the three years since Colt last saw him in person. He was in his late fifties, but he looked a good decade older. Whether it was the stress of the job or the loss of his son, Colt didn't know, but the intervening years had not been kind to him. His once distinguished graying-at-the-temples dark hair had thinned and gone almost completely white, and his skin now sagged with deep lines like a basset hound's. But it was his eyes that had changed the most. Once sharp with intelligence and suffer-no-fools harshness, they now seemed glassy and weary behind the thick wire-rimmed glasses.

The room smelled of leather, smoke, and whiskey. The latter, Colt suspected, was coming from the man behind the desk. It might be five o'clock somewhere, but here it was only noon.

"What do you want?" the old man snapped impatiently.

So much for pleasantries. The general had never liked him, and after the breakup of Colt's marriage—which the general probably blamed him for—he had no reason to hide it.

"Information."

"And why the hell would I tell you anything? You may have fooled my goddaughter for a while, but the best thing she ever did was toss your sorry ass out."

Colt didn't bother correcting him, but that wasn't exactly how it had gone down. He'd done the walking away in the end, although Kate might have said he'd done so from the beginning.

"If you think I'll let you worm your way back into her life, just when she's found someone worthy of her—"

Colt ignored the implication and didn't rise to the bait. Whether he'd been worthy of her had ceased to matter a long time ago. "This has nothing to do with Kate."

The general's eyes narrowed. "Bullshit. It would be just like you to take advantage of a tragedy to prey on her kind nature."

"So you know why I'm here. I want information about Retiarius. And I'll tell you exactly what I told Kate. Give it to me, and I'll never bother her—or you—again."

"Why would I believe the word of a hoodlum?"

"Haven't you heard?" Colt said sarcastically. "I'm one of the good guys now. All those hoodlum skills have been sanctioned and paid for by the United States of America. Hooyah."

The general ignored the taunt. They both knew what Colt did, but as with many higher-ups, the general preferred not to acknowledge the part Colt played in implementing their "foreign policy." Colt did the dirty work so that men like the general could keep their hands clean. The kind of black ops he was sent on gave politicians plausible deniability that couldn't come back to bite them later. Like, for example, if they were thinking about running for office, as he'd heard the general was considering.

General Murray had the sympathy vote after losing his son—that was for sure. Colt hadn't liked Thomas Junior (known as TJ) any better than he did the senior. And it wasn't just because he'd been in the "chair force," although that didn't hurt. Naw, Junior was a selfish, entitled prick who had a silver spoon so far up his ass he probably shit quarters.

He'd hated Colt on sight and done everything he could think of to discredit him in Kate's eyes. Admittedly it hadn't taken much effort, but Colt always wondered what TJ's real motivation had been. Had there been more than just god-brotherly love on Junior's part? They weren't related by blood. Kate's mother and the general's wife had been sorority sisters. Kappa Kappa something or other.

"Just say what you want and get out of here," the general said.

"I want to know what happened out there, and I need you to help me."

"How the hell am I supposed to do that? No one knows what happened out there."

"By telling me everything you know and getting me the clearance I need to see the feeds, files, and anything else that might be relevant."

"What purpose would that serve? Better minds than yours have gone over those things backward and forward. It isn't going to tell you anything we don't already know."

"Which is jack shit."

The general didn't argue.

"How many of those better minds went to Russia afterward to investigate?" Colt asked.

For the first time since he'd entered the room, something sparked in the general's eyes. "The president has forbidden sending in a team."

"I'm not talking about a team."

The spark dimmed. The old man gave him a dismissive laugh. "Go in by yourself? You're mad. Besides, POTUS would never approve."

"What's that old saying?" Colt asked. "It's better to ask for forgiveness than ask for permission? Besides, I'm on vacation, and I've always had a hankering to visit Siberia."

The general sat back in his big leather swivel chair and stared at him, an appraising look on his face. "It would be a suicide mission, and if anyone discovered you, it could cause problems."

"Maybe for me, but it won't for you. I won't be taken alive, and I'll make sure none of this ever leads back to you. It's not as if I haven't done missions like this before."

The general seemed to be considering it for a moment, but then he shook his head. "As appealing as the prospect of you not being taken alive makes it, I can't take that chance. Not now."

Colt squeezed his fists, unable to prevent the bitterness

from seeping out. But God, he hated politics. They were talking about men here. Fourteen men who'd given their lives for this fucking nation. They deserved more—a hell of a lot more—than this. "When you intend to run for office, you mean?"

"Nothing has been decided."

"But you won't take the chance—is that it?"

The general sat there, stone-faced.

Colt leaned forward. "That is bullshit, and you know it. You can't let them get away with this. I would think you more than anyone would want to stick it to the Russians." Colt got his first real reaction. The old man flinched, and Colt pressed on. He'd always been good at finding weak spots. Cracks. Ways to hurt. "If I find proof that the Russians took them out, then maybe the president will finally listen to you and your hawk friends about the need to do something about it."

"She'll never make the first move," the general said, but there was a gleam in his eye anyway. He paused, clearly deliberating. After a moment, he looked back at Colt. "Tell me what you need."

Twenty-two

Dean was still fuming when he went outside to the "car park" to return the call he'd missed from the LC.

He didn't know what he was so angry about. He should be glad that Annie understood that nothing more could come of their morning, too-hot-to-think-about lapse into the steamy and pornographic. He wasn't exactly in a position to get involved with anyone. He couldn't even tell her his real name, for fuck's sake.

So why was he pissed that she saw it the same way?

"Your body is incredible. . . . You aren't exactly my type."

So it had been purely physical for her—so what? How many times had he had sex with someone for the same reason? That was what it had been about for him, too, hadn't it?

Of course it had. There wasn't any other option, and he never wasted time worrying about things he couldn't change. He dealt in hard truths all the time. Accept and move on.

He punched in the numbers on the keypad and waited. It didn't take long. The LC answered on the second ring.

Taylor waited for Dean to speak first. It was part of the code they'd worked out to ensure that nothing had been compromised.

"Johnson's plumbing?"

The dick euphemism had lost its humor quickly, but a code was a code.

"This better be fucking good, Tex," the LC said. "And not be another one of your damned calls about how this is all a waste of time—"

"It isn't." Although anticipating Taylor's reaction, Dean wished it were. "I've run into some trouble."

"What kind of trouble?"

The brown-haired, green-eyed, drop-dead-gorgeous, "just made me see stars" kind.

Already hearing the suspicion in the LC's voice and knowing he was about to get an ass-chewing, Dean knew he had to just bite the bullet. It wasn't like him to prevaricate anyway. But he and the LC had never really gotten along—even before the mess with Colt Wesson and his wife. Had the LC really messed around with Kate? It didn't seem to fit with Taylor's by-the-book, aboveboard personality, but who the hell knew?

Dean and the LC were like two bulls in the same china shop, and they often went head-to-head on things. The difference was that Dean was usually confident that he was in the right. But he'd fucked up, and he knew it. He'd compromised their cover, and for someone who prided himself on being a professional—always—that was hard to take.

"The involved-in-an-ecoterrorist-plot-and-murder-charge kind of trouble," Dean said.

Dead silence followed for a good thirty seconds. It was a little bit like waiting for a punch in the face.

"You've got to be fucking kidding me. Tell me you are fucking kidding me."

"I wish I were." Dean explained about the charter to the drillship, about finding the explosives, and how the terrorists had pulled a gun on him when he was trying to leave.

"So you killed them?"

"No. They were alive when I left the ship. I suspect the leader was able to free himself and killed the others to cover up the crime and blame it on us before the coast guard arrived."

Us. Shit. He'd slipped, and it was too much to hope that the LC wouldn't pick up on it.

"Don't tell me you are still with the girl?"

Dean could practically hear the LC's blood boiling over the phone.

"Let me guess. She's blond with blue eyes and a nice-sized rack?"

Dean would object if that didn't pretty much size up his normal hookups to a tee. But there wasn't anything about Annie that was normal. Well, maybe one out of the three, but he would use the word "exceptional."

"She's attractive"—understatement—"but that doesn't have anything to do with it."

"You can't be that effing stupid—or hard up. You know what's at stake."

"I couldn't leave her there. She could have been killed."

"Fine. So why didn't you drop her off at the first place you could when it was safe?"

Good question. That was exactly what Dean should have done. But then she'd looked at him with those big eyes and the steel in his resolve had turned to fucking putty. "They set her up and made it look like she was in on it. I told her I'd help her clear it up with the police."

"And how the hell do you plan to do that? You can't let anyone know you survived that blast."

Taylor didn't think they could trust anyone. Whatever the warning message the LC had received before the missile exploded had said, it had spooked him and made him certain that they'd been set up. But when Dean pressed him, he'd refused to say anything more. He was protecting someone.

Dean listened to the LC tear him a new one for a good two minutes, before he finally told him what he wanted. "I want you to call Kate."

The dead silence this time wasn't as long, but it was a hell of a lot more ominous. The LC's fury was almost palpable. As was the one-word response. "No."

"If you don't, I will," Dean said.

They'd all been friends at one time, although Dean and the LC had never been particularly close. Dean didn't know the exact details of what had gone down in the breakup of the Wesson marriage—nor did he want to—but it had been bad. Dean had sided with Colt in the whole fiasco. Whether they'd slept together, Dean didn't know, but clearly they'd gotten too close. And wives were off-limits. Period. But he had to work with Taylor. By unwritten rule he and the LC hadn't mentioned Kate or Colt since Colt left. An unwritten rule that Dean had just broken.

But he'd been patient too long. Although he wasn't as ready to see conspiracy theories as the LC, he'd given Taylor time to see what he could discover. But it had become patently clear that they weren't going to be able to figure it out themselves. They needed someone on the inside. Someone in a position to help them. Kate was CIA but didn't have anything to do with the navy or Special Operations. She was perfect.

"The hell you will," Taylor spat out. "You aren't contacting anyone. That's a fucking order, Baylor."

That the LC had violated his own rule about saying their names over phone lines spoke to the level of his anger.

"Right now you aren't in any position to be issuing orders," Dean said bluntly. "We're pretty far off the reservation with all this."

Annie would probably object to . . . *Fuck*. Now she was making him think about how he talked. It was just a phrase, damn it. Whatever the original context, it was part of the vernacular. Not everything had to be overanalyzed.

Which was exactly what he was doing.

Shit.

"This is still my operation, and I'm still your fucking commander."

Dean didn't say anything, but they both knew there was nothing regulation about what they'd done. Operation White Night had ended the moment they ditched their gear in that fire. They were on their own. AWOL.

But he wasn't going to press. Dean had been a SEAL for too long not to have a healthy respect for authority and the command structure, and AWOL or not, they were still a team. They needed to work together if they were going to get out of this. But the LC was intent on doing it on his own. He didn't want to risk any more lives when too many had been lost already.

"Look," Dean said, trying to strike a "let's be reasonable" tone, which admittedly was a stretch for him. "This is too big. You can't do this on your own. We aren't any closer to finding out what happened than we were two months ago. We need someone on the inside."

The LC took too long to respond.

Dean guessed why. "What aren't you telling me?"

"I don't know if it's anything yet."

"I've been sitting with my thumb up my ass, looking for nonexistent subs, for weeks, and you've been fucking holding back on me?"

"I wanted to be sure."

Dean could hear the LC's defensiveness. For good reason. The lone-wolf shit had to stop. That wasn't how SEALs operated. "Sure of what?"

"I've been looking for motive. If someone betrayed us—"

"If," Dean reminded him. He still didn't want to believe someone would do that. But he couldn't ignore the fact that the Russians had known they were coming, and that someone on the inside had been able to warn Taylor. That ruled out a mistake on the platoon's part and made the Russians having figured it out on their own unlikely. Possible, but unlikely. The easiest explanation was that someone on their side had betrayed them. But that was hard to accept. But the inescapable truth was that someone had wanted them dead, and they had to find out who and why before they surfaced. Not only because of the danger they might still be in, but also because it was easier to find out information when no one thought they were looking.

"If," the LC acknowledged. "There had to be a reason. And for something like this, the reason would have to be pretty damned big."

Dean agreed. Big enough to sacrifice an entire fucking platoon of Navy SEALs.

"I came up with four possibilities," Taylor continued. "We saw something we shouldn't have on a previous mission, revenge for something we've done—God knows we've pissed a lot of people off—espionage or money."

"You think someone sold us out?"

"It's one possibility. I've been researching everyone who knew where we were to see if I could find anything in their backgrounds that might be relevant."

"No undercover Russian nationals?"

The LC gave a dry laugh. "Not so easy, I'm afraid. But did you know that Admiral Morrison's wife filed for divorce recently? Apparently the rear admiral has an Internet gambling problem."

"How did you find that out?"

"Social media. People really need to get a clue about privacy settings. The missus used her maiden name, but it wasn't hard to track down her posts on various gambling anonymous sites. Apparently it's bad, and they were in enormous debt. But around two months ago her posts stopped."

Dean didn't believe it. He'd known Ronald Morrison for too long. He'd been in charge of Group One when Dean joined. "Selling out an entire platoon of SEALs to Russia to cover gambling debts? That's a huge stretch, and you know it."

"I didn't say otherwise. But it's something."

"And even more reason to contact Kate. She can help. She has resources and contacts that you and I don't. She can clear up this mess in Scotland, and help find out whether there is something to what you've found out." Dean paused. "Don't you trust her?"

"Of course I trust her. But I don't want her involved."

Dean understood. He was trying to protect her. "Kate can take care of herself. She was married to Colt, for Christ's sake." He was beginning to recognize the silence. "What aren't you telling me?"

Was Kate his person on the inside? Taylor had sworn she wasn't.

"She's dead."

"Who's dead?"

"The person who sent me the text."

Dean's stomach sank. Fuck. "When? How?"

"A few days after the missile."

"And you didn't fucking say anything? How could you keep something like that to yourself?"

Silence for a moment. Then, "It's complicated."

Dean was furious. It sure as hell was. This put an entirely new spin on everything; he finally understood why the LC was so certain that they'd been betrayed. "What the hell else are you holding back?"

"Nothing."

"You going to tell me who this woman was?"

Pause. "It isn't important now."

There was something in his voice that stopped Dean from pressing. For now. "We need help, Scott. Someone we can trust. If there's someone you trust more than Kate—"

"There isn't. Fine. You win. I'll call her. You happy now?"

Dean didn't say anything. This time it was his silence that gave the LC time to think.

"What is this girl to you, Tex?"

"Nothing."

It was harsh, but true. It couldn't be any other way.

Besides, the LC was right. Anyone connected to them could be at risk. Kate could take care of herself; she was CIA. But Annie . . . she was smart and sassy, but she was an idealistic environmental scientist. She wasn't cut out for this kind of ugly. And Dean had no doubt that before this was all over, it was going to get very ugly.

When Dan found her in the breakfast room and told her he was going to see about finding a windsurf board to "train" with, Annie thought he was taking their cover story a little too far but didn't try to stop him.

Maybe he needed some time away to clear his thoughts. God knew, she did.

He reminded her about not speaking English and left her some money for lunch in case he wasn't back.

Too bad she didn't have her phone. She could use one of those translate apps for Portuguese. At least she would be able to converse with people.

Wait . . . Was that it? Had he told people she was foreign so she wouldn't be able to talk to anyone and unwittingly give something away? It sounded like him. Untrusting. Suspicious. Anticipating. Prepared.

Mr. Boy Scout, all right. The perfect soldier. *Sailor,* she corrected herself, remembering the conversation she'd had at the bar with Julien.

Suddenly she remembered the rest of the conversation, and it clicked. *Special Forces.* If she were a betting woman, she would wager her entire savings (which weren't insignificant) that Dan had been Special Forces.

It fit. Though he'd done everything he could to hide it, the signs were all there. Big. Badass. Tough as nails. Secretive. Extreme fighting skills. Invincible, can-do-anything, "I got this" attitude. That unshakable code of duty, honor, "and the American way."

The only thing he was missing was the swagger, which she was sure was there but temporarily out of commission.

She'd seen enough of them to know. She'd been surrounded by the type through most of her childhood with her dad and his friends. At times their living room had felt more like a locker room or frat house than a family home. But her mom had said they acted that way—always teasing, making jokes, screwing around—to release the pressure.

The tattoo.

Of course! Rangers had tattoos, and other Special Forces units probably did as well. Was that what it was? Some kind of Special Forces insignia?

Her heart started to pound. She had to find out.

But perhaps she could kill two birds with one stone. . . .

After finishing her breakfast, she thanked the innkeeper in broken English, and then opened and closed her hands— pantomiming a book—to ask about a "biblioteca." She hoped the word for library in Spanish was close to the one in Portuguese. Although the chances of the innkeeper knowing the difference were pretty slim, as it took her quite a while to figure out what Annie wanted.

"A library!" the woman finally guessed. "We have a wee one near the ferry terminal. Is that what you're looking for? Ah, you poor wee thing. You must be bored out of your mind. I'm not sure they'll have many books there for you to read, but they'll have a computer."

Bingo.

Annie nodded gratefully, and the woman was off to find her a map. She came back with a tourist booklet and marked the route, although it wasn't far.

Annie didn't waste any time. It was a sunny start to what promised to be a warm day as she walked along the seashore to the port.

The library was right where it was supposed to be. The long white portable with a flat green roof was on the far side of a complex that housed the primary school and a preschool or day care.

The innkeeper had written her a note to hand to the librarian, saving Annie from having to act out some more. The woman welcomed Annie and told her to look around all she wanted. If she wanted to borrow anything, she could just leave it with Mrs. Collins—the innkeeper—when she left.

Annie was no longer surprised by the informality and trusting nature of the locals. It was like that on Tiree—unlocked doors, kids playing out on the street, borrowing a library book even without a card.

An older man was using the computer terminal, so Annie wrote her name down on the clipboard and headed for the reference section.

She hit the jackpot. There wasn't just one—there were two Portuguese dictionaries. One was hardback and definitely more comprehensive, but the other was a beaten-up paperback "for travelers," containing English to Portuguese in the front half, and Portuguese to English in the back.

Her English was about to get a lot better.

She smiled, already anticipating the look on Dan's face. He wouldn't like being outplayed, but Annie had to admit it was fun trying to do so. *Mrs.* Thompson wasn't the quiet, barefoot, and pregnant-in-the-kitchen type. *Mr.* Thompson needed to figure that out.

Annie poked around a little more, picking up a paperback mystery that took place on the Isle of Lewis that looked interesting, until the older man finished and her name was up.

It was an ancient PC, something she was used to in university research and with many of the nonprofits she'd worked with. Making sure no one could see the screen while she browsed, she went to work.

It took her a few tries. "Special Forces tattoo" and "Navy Special Forces tattoo" didn't come up with much, but when she added the word "Budweiser," that did it. A nickname for the Navy SEALs trident insignia was "the Budweiser."

A little more poking around, though, and she realized that Dan had probably been telling her the truth—it was a Budweiser tattoo. SEALs didn't get tattoos that would identify them by branch or unit. They were more subtle. One article mentioned tattooing frogs (a reference to the frogmen that had predated SEALs) with numbers or things like that. The Budweiser was no doubt Dan's tongue-in-cheek play on the insignia.

It made horrible sense, given his knowledge about diving and his skill with boats.

Being right didn't soften the disappointment. He'd gone from not a good idea to no way in hell.

His defense of her father suddenly took on a new light. A personal light. He'd been defending himself also.

She was tempted to run to the beach to confront him, but what would that do? It wouldn't change anything. She already knew he wasn't for her; now she was only more certain of it. She knew only too well the kind of baggage and scars those guys came with—visible or not—and she had no desire to wade in that cesspool ever again. The memories of finding her father had haunted her for years; she wouldn't resurrect them. Nor would she take the chance of coming home again one day to find someone she loved with a bullet through the head.

She should stick to her type: intellectual, cultured, and not so brutally masculine. A little more passive. Beta with a capital *B*. If a little voice pointed out that that hadn't exactly worked out for her lately, she pushed it aside.

She wasn't going to throw the baby out with the bathwater, as her stepfather liked to say. Just because Julien had turned out to be a dud didn't mean the next guy would be. She wasn't going to change what she knew was best for herself because she'd had great sex.

Discovering Dan's Special Forces past had only solidified things in her mind. Their attraction had been off the charts, but now that they'd given in to it, they could move on. She could stop thinking about it.

Which was easier said than done. *Knowing* what it was like was much worse than speculating about what it would be like.

A SEAL . . . She shook her head. Just perfect.

She had a little more time—the computer terminal slots were for fifteen minutes—so she searched for news of the murders. Most of the stories were versions of a short Reuters article, but there was a longer, more detailed one from the local paper on Lewis.

She gasped, seeing a picture of herself staring back at her from the screen—she definitely needed a new passport picture—along with pictures of Jean Paul, Julien, and Claude. Even though she'd known it was Jean Paul who'd killed the others, seeing the picture of him in the hospital room in Stornoway made her sad all over again. Poor Julien and Claude.

She read through the story quickly, seeing there wasn't much new information but distressed to read that they'd tried to contact her mother. She logged in to her e-mail and thought about sending her a message, but something held her back. Or rather, some*one*.

Whatever Dan was involved with, it was serious, and she didn't want to do anything that would put him in jeopardy after everything he'd done for her. He'd been adamant about the need for secrecy. She would explain everything to her mom in a few days when this was all over. She hoped.

She scrolled down over four days' worth of e-mail—she

hadn't been checking regularly on Lewis—and stopped when she saw the header from her bank.

After the credit card problem, she'd put a Fraud Alert on her credit file. Opening the e-mail, she realized it didn't have anything to do with that. Apparently someone had tried to access her bank account from a different computer. It was dated a couple of days ago. Could it have been Julien?

She didn't know, but she felt the stab of betrayal all over again.

God, how had she not seen it?

Just in case it had been someone else, she went ahead and changed the password after verifying the library computer with her security questions.

Her time was up and someone was waiting, so she quickly cleared her browsing history and logged off.

Thanking the librarian for the dictionary and the book, Annie walked back to the guest house. Now that she had her answers, she was more anxious than ever for this nightmare to be over. She wanted to go home and put it all behind her: Julien; Jean Paul; ecoterrorist plots to blow up drillships; murder charges; and too-sexy, Navy SEAL, Texan ship captains who spoke in hard truths and made her weak. While she still could.

Twenty-three

Dean spent the morning in the water, doing his best to put what had happened earlier out of his mind.

It was easy to see why Tiree was such a popular place for windsurfers. The combination of white sand beaches, temperate weather, consistent waves, and prevailing westerlies made it ideal. He and his rented board had cut across the waves for hours.

It was exhilarating, exhausting, and exactly what he needed. He felt a shitload better dragging the board out of the water than he had going in.

Shaking the water from his hair, he thanked the kid working at the rental hut and retrieved the towel he'd borrowed from the guest house to dry off his chest and back as he walked up the beach.

He was about halfway up when he stopped dead in his tracks.

Ah, hell. The blood drained from his body, and whatever clarity of mind the time on the water had brought him was gone in the instant it had taken him to see Annie standing there in a bikini. As there wasn't much of it, it didn't take long.

He gritted his teeth, trying not to look—stare—but Christ Almighty, it wasn't fair. The small triangles of silky fabric that covered her breasts didn't leave much to the imagination, revealing the perfectly round shape of the youthful flesh underneath. She was long and lean with the lithe muscles of a dancer and legs that went on—and on.

Shit, stop staring. But a flat stomach, gently curved hips, and all that cocoa-buttery tanned skin were impossible to turn away from.

He hadn't exactly been in the best position to get a full look at her this morning, but all the details had just been filled in perfectly.

He'd been right. She had a killer body. More swimsuit magazine than PhD scientist, but damn . . .

"Is there anything you can't do?"

Her question snapped him out of his lust-induced daze. But his synapses weren't firing all that quickly, and it took him a moment to realize what she meant.

She'd been watching him windsurfing.

He shrugged, oddly embarrassed. He didn't believe in false modesty, but her obvious admiration made him uncomfortable. Maybe because he liked it. Usually he didn't care.

When he didn't answer, she added, "I thought you were going to wipe out on that big wave at the end. You must have been five feet in the air."

More like ten, but who was counting?

She was shielding her eyes against the sun with her hand, but for some reason he didn't think he was the only one staring. She was looking at his chest. He could feel her eyes on him, and it was making him crazy. And hot.

As his low-hung board shorts weren't going to leave much to the imagination, either, he tore his eyes away.

He noticed a couple of twentysomething surfers sitting nearby and obviously checking her out. His muscles flared a little as he gave them a stare that suggested—rather forcefully—that they think again. They didn't quite run away, but they weren't staring any longer.

The unwelcome (and uncharacteristic) possessiveness made his reply come off a little sharper than he intended. "What are you doing here, Annie?"

She dropped her hand and pointed to the spread-out towel that he hadn't noticed a few feet away. "I was reading. I didn't know this was the same beach you'd gone to until I realized the rainbow sail guy was you." She lifted an eyebrow. "I thought real men didn't do pink."

He smiled and shook his head. "I figured one stripe wouldn't do too much lasting damage." He gave her a long look. "And I'm reconsidering. I think pink might be my new favorite color."

The drawl was natural; the flirtatiousness was not. But she brought out all kinds of weird shit in him.

She blushed adorably, obviously embarrassed by his appreciation for her bathing suit, but pleased as well.

Remembering that this—them—wasn't a good idea, he glanced over at the open book resting cover side up on the towel. "That's a good book. Where did you find it?"

"The library." She reached down to pick up another one that had been tucked under a bag that must have held her lunch. "I also picked up this."

It was a Portuguese-to-English dictionary. There was a triumphant grin on her face that told him she'd guessed his motive. He wouldn't apologize, though. He was just trying to be careful. He didn't want her to slip. "Annie . . ."

She waved off his concern. "Don't worry. I'm not going to blow our cover. It still won't be easy to talk to people, and it forces me to think before I speak. But you can't expect me not to talk to anyone for days. Speaking of . . . did you get ahold of the person who might be able to help us?"

"Tired of me already?"

She bit her lip. "I didn't mean it like that."

"I know. I was teasing. And yes, it's in the works."

"So what do we do now?"

"Sit back and wait. You can read your book and enjoy the beach."

She might be able to finish the entire trilogy.

"What are you going to do?"

"Didn't you hear? I have a competition to get ready for."

She gave him a look that told him he wasn't fooling her with the laid-back routine; apparently she already knew him too well. "Sit back" wasn't in his vernacular. He was going to do a little research on his own on the Ocean Protection Front and North Sea Offshore Drilling. There was something about the whole thing that bugged him. Why kill Julien and Claude? Why not just toss the explosives overboard and go with the robbery angle alone? Murdering one's compatriots seemed extreme even for an ecoterrorist group. Was there another reason? Something they were missing?

He also wanted to check out what Taylor had found on the rear admiral. It wasn't that he didn't believe him; he just had the feeling the LC was still holding back about something.

"There are a few things I need to take care of this afternoon." He eyed the two surfers who'd been watching her earlier, but they were clearly avoiding looking in their direction. "You okay here by yourself?"

"You don't need to worry about me, Tex. I'm a big girl. I can take care of myself."

He tried not to jelly at the name, but damn . . . how had she guessed? Although admittedly it wasn't the most original nickname in the world. But . . . *shit.*

Oh well, he supposed it was better than Dan.

"Besides," she said with a wry smile and a nod in the direction of the two guys who were now three. "I think you scared them off. Those guys won't come near me with a ten-foot pole. I doubt any guy who saw me talking to you will."

He frowned. He couldn't tell from her voice whether she was disappointed or not. She wasn't interested in those bozos, was she? And why did that thought make him feel like cracking a few heads? "I didn't like the way they were looking at you."

She waved off his concern. "They're harmless."

He wasn't so sure. She was hot enough to make men stupid. He should know. "I'm not."

"I think they figured that out. But you don't need to go to all the trouble; I'm not planning on talking to anyone."

If that was why she thought he'd done it, he wasn't going to put her straight. "No trouble," he said. "But I'm going to make sure they got the message. Come here."

She might have taken a step back. "Why?"

"I think you know why."

She eyed him warily. "I thought you said that was a mistake."

"It was. But I'm about to make another one."

He closed the distance between them in a long stride and pulled her into his arms. One palm slid over the warm smooth skin of her waist before coming to rest on the silky pink bottoms of the bathing suit he'd admired a few minutes ago. God, that ass. He couldn't resist squeezing and lifting a little. It was taut and firm and fit perfectly in his hand.

Her hands had looped around his neck almost instinctively. He liked that. But what he really liked was the feel of all that warm, bare skin plastered to his.

She was looking at him with a bemused smile on her face. "You don't strike me as the PDA type."

"You do strange things to me."

"You don't need to do this."

"Yes, I do." He was fucking dying to do this. The next time when he made love to her, he was going to be doing it just like this—facing her.

There wasn't going to be a next time, he reminded himself.

Right. He was fucking crazy if he thought he could stay away from this . . . from her.

The next moment his mouth was on hers, and he was kissing her. He groaned at the contact—at the taste of cherries.

She was killing him. But what a fucking way to go. He threaded his fingers through her hair to clasp the back of her head and bring her mouth more fully against his. He filled it with his tongue, taking long, deep strokes until the fire in his blood started to pound in his ears.

For a moment he forgot where he was. All he could see was stars. But his cock was thickening by the instant. If he didn't want everyone on the beach to know exactly how much he wanted her—although that was probably pretty damned obvious from the kiss—he'd better pull away.

He released her. She stood staring up at him, gasping for a moment before looking around sheepishly. Apparently he wasn't the only one who'd forgotten where they were for the moment.

The huskiness in her voice nearly did him in again. "I think they got the message that time."

He hoped so. Because he sure as hell did.

After that strange episode on the beach, Annie wasn't sure what to expect. But when Dan met her in the room later, it wasn't nearly as awkward as she feared. They went to dinner and talked the same way they had the night before.

He told her a little more about his past. It sounded pretty messed up. His alcoholic mother and abusive deadbeat father certainly weren't going to win Mom and Dad of the Year. Reading between the lines, she realized that the military had been a stabilizing force in his life, taking the place of the family who had left him to fend for himself. She asked a little about his time in the navy, but it was clear the subject was off-limits. Not wanting to ruin the night, she didn't voice her suspicions about his being a SEAL.

Maybe she didn't want confirmation.

It wasn't until they'd finished getting ready for bed that the air in the room grew thick with tension.

She was already under the covers when he came back from the bathroom. He was wearing gym shorts and a T-shirt, which she suspected were for her benefit.

"I can sleep on the floor," he said, holding her gaze, his jaw tight.

In other words, he was leaving the decision up to her. They both knew what would happen if he got into bed next to her again.

The air practically crackled with heated anticipation as he waited for her to make up her mind. It should have taken much longer than it did. But she wanted to be with him again. This morning had been amazing, but it had just been a taste. A wicked, delicious taste, perhaps, but she knew there was much more.

Just because she'd never done casual didn't mean she couldn't do it.

Was it a good idea? Probably not. She already liked him too much and had become strangely attached. But she took that to be largely due to their circumstances, and she wasn't going to waste the chance to experience what she expected was going to be phenomenal, mind-blowing, no-holds-barred sex.

She met his gaze unhesitatingly. "I don't want you to sleep on the floor."

The clear invitation didn't lessen the tautness in his body any; he seemed to be holding himself by a very tight rope.

Did he have any idea how attractive he was right now? She couldn't take her eyes off the dark, chiseled lines of his face, the hard line of his jaw, and the silvery blue of his eyes.

Tough guy. Hard as nails. Too blunt. But hot. Really, really hot.

"I don't want there to be any misunderstandings," he said. "I can't offer you anything more."

"I'm not asking for anything more."

He put one knee on the bed and pulled off his shirt.

Holy shit, that wasn't fair. His body was . . . built, incredible, insane. Pick your extraordinary adjective. She wanted to run her finger down all those lines and ridges.

Or maybe her tongue.

Unaware that he'd just turned her body into a pool of liquid heat, he still seemed hesitant. "Casual, right?"

"Very casual."

All-night-long casual, she hoped.

"You sure?"

She shook her head. "Do you always give a girl this many times to change her mind?"

He smiled—that not-quite-half smile that she loved. "Maybe not. But this feels"—he shrugged—"I don't know—different."

She told her heart not to catch at that.

It didn't listen.

"I don't want to hurt you." He leaned down and smoothed a lock of hair back from her cheek, but his hand stayed and he caressed the curve with his thumb.

The gesture was so gentle and sweet—so opposite everything she thought of him—her already caught heart tightened a little more.

Don't flip. Please don't flip.

Too late.

She didn't want him to hurt her, either. But she wanted him on the floor even less. No tenderness, she reminded herself. *Physical. Make it physical.*

"You won't." She pulled him down on top of her. "But I want you to make me very, very sore."

He muffled a curse and groan as his mouth covered hers, his good-guy efforts finally giving way. All the hesitation was gone as he came down hard on top of her.

The weight of all those muscles should be crushing, but it wasn't. It just turned her on even more. She loved the solid feel of him. The hardness of his body on top of hers. It made her feel vulnerable and small, but protected at the same time.

She was a strong woman. Confident. Independent. Capable and happy to take care of herself. She'd told herself she'd never need a man to protect her. But there was some tiny primitive instinct buried deep inside her that responded to his strength. To his sheer physicality and blatant masculinity. And it was weeping with pleasure right now.

She would have muffled a protest when he rolled slightly off her, but her mouth was too busy sliding against his tongue—she would never taste cinnamon again without thinking of him, thanks to that toothpaste—and then she realized he'd only done it so that his hand could have free roam over her body.

No protest necessary. His touch set her aflame. She was on fire. Hotter for him than she'd ever been in her life.

She didn't understand this kind of attraction. How her body seemed to shoot from zero to light speed in an instant. How her skin felt hot and too tight. How her nerve endings were tingling and on edge. How every inch, every muscle, every fiber of her body was tuned to him. She just went with it. Let the fierceness of the attraction take over.

And God, was it fierce!

She arched in his hand when he covered her breast. Wrapped her leg around him to hold him tighter when he notched himself between her legs.

Her entire body went liquid.

She responded to his kiss as she'd never responded to another man. Savoring every stroke of his tongue. The roughness of his just-shaved jaw on hers. The feel of those big callused hands claiming her body. Her hands on his body.

She wanted everything he had to give . . . and more.

Physical, she reminded herself. *Keep it casual.* But there was nothing casual about this. It was fierce. Intense. Powerful. Overwhelming.

It was need at its most primitive. It was two people who wanted each other with every fiber of their being. Two people who couldn't wait to have sex again because they knew how good it had been the first time. It was pleasure and sensation at its most erotic.

He pulled back long enough to remove her nightshirt. He stared at her breasts for so long her cheeks warmed and her nipples tightened. She started to lift the sheet that he'd tossed off her back up, but he stopped her.

"Don't. God, do you know how badly I wanted to strip that damned bathing suit top off you today?"

He rubbed the back of his finger over one nipple, and she sucked in her breath. It wasn't just from the touch, but from the heat in his eyes when he looked at her.

"I wished you were in a burka with the way those assholes were looking at you, but I was imagining you naked. I could see the pebble of your nipple, but I didn't know they'd be this pink." His accent got deeper when he was turned on, and it was heavier than she'd ever heard it. He lowered his face to her breasts. "Yes, definitely my new favorite color." He licked one, circling his tongue around the taut tip in a delicious swirl of heat.

She moaned as her body melted. Dampness and heat spread between her legs. The throb of need intensified.

"I'm going to suck you now, sweetheart." His breath blew over the damp and throbbing skin. "Do you want me to do that?"

"Yes," she breathed—gasped. "Oh God, please yes."

He covered her with his lips, sucking her into his mouth. A tight vacuum that pulled the pleasure from deep inside her in a sharp needle of sensation. His tongue swirled the tip, making it tighten some more. She arched into his mouth as the pleasure wound tighter and tighter into a spiral of need.

"Do you like that, Annie?" he whispered. "Will you come if I touch you?"

She whimpered at how good that sounded. She wanted him to touch her. Her body was primed for it. She wanted to come.

"As good as that sounds, I think I want to taste you first."

His mouth was already sliding down her stomach, licking a gentle, warm trail along the way. She felt his hand on her hips as he quickly worked her underwear down her legs.

"So fucking beautiful," he said.

His mouth was so close to her crotch she was practically shaking.

Did she say she didn't like foreplay? She was wrong. She liked it a lot. She liked *this* a lot.

He moved her legs over his shoulders and then his face was between her legs. She nearly shot off the bed at the first stroke of his tongue.

The sound of his groan nearly made her come right there. It was warm and sweet and filled with pleasure. It was the groan of a man who liked to give a woman pleasure. "God, you taste good. So fucking sweet."

And then she lost the ability to think as he nuzzled his mouth against her and went to town. Feasting on her as if he couldn't get enough. Swirling his tongue. Sucking. Rubbing his face and jaw against the soft insides of her thighs. Her legs tightened. Her heels pressed into his back. Her hips pressed and lifted against his mouth.

More. Pressure. *Oh God, yes. That feels so good.*

She split apart. Coming in a burst of white-hot pleasure that shot through her like a bolt of lightning.

He let her ride it out against his mouth. Drawing every spasm of her climax out.

When it was over, she was drained. Completely wrung out. She should have just collapsed.

But that wouldn't be right. Turnabout was only fair play.

Twenty-four

Dean couldn't wait another minute to be inside her. But he had to take precautions. He reached over on the bedside table for his wallet to retrieve a condom. He intended to come inside her this time.

Her body was still limp and flush from her climax, so he was surprised when she sat up and grabbed his wrist.

"Not yet."

She took the wallet and condom from his hand and set them down on the table.

Oh God, please tell him she wasn't having second thoughts....

"On your back, sailor boy."

She wasn't. He had an inkling of exactly where this was going, and his nerve endings buzzed with anticipation and something resembling fear. His instincts were flaring like a fire alarm. His body was fighting what he knew was coming: complete and utter helplessness.

But he did as she asked. Did she have any idea how sexy it was to be ordered around like this? Probably. She looked really, really pleased with herself when she moved over him. Her fingers trailed absently over his stomach, but he was aware of every movement. His skin went off like a firecracker every place she touched.

"I don't have a lot of experience with this, so you'll have

to let me know if I'm doing it right." Her fingers were already skimming under the band of his shorts, and his cock was doing its best to meet them, straining hard toward her hand. But when she made her little confession, he popped right through. She noticed, smoothing her thumb over the plump head. "I don't know. You're kind of big."

There was no "kind of" about it. And if he wasn't gritting his teeth, fighting to fucking breathe while she knelt over him naked and played with his cock, he'd tell her so.

She traced her finger down the long length of him.

"Not sure how deep I'll be able to take you down my throat."

He swore. He'd never taken her for a dirty talker, but he was happy to be mistaken. Fuck, this was good.

"You feel a little warm in there. Should I take your shorts off?"

She didn't seem to expect him to answer. Probably the straining of his body and the muscles standing out in his neck gave her the heads-up that he was in no condition to talk.

She slid his shorts past his hips, and his erection bobbed free. The cool air wasn't much relief.

Her naughtiness faltered a little bit. Their eyes met, and he could see her hesitation.

As he said, no "kind of" about it.

"Um. Wow." She wrapped her hand around him, getting a feel for his girth.

He gave her an encouraging lift of his hips. Or maybe it was a begging lift. Semantics were past him right now.

She started to stroke him. Long and slow. Just enough to settle him down a little and bring a drop of come to his tip. She smoothed it over the fat head before lowering her body over him.

Those little kisses along his stomach made the already tight bands of muscle turn rigid. He was struggling for control.

When her mouth was poised an inch from the tip, his muscles started to shake with restraint. He wanted to push himself into her open mouth so badly. The pressure at the base of his spine was so intense . . .

Oh, shit. He didn't know if he could handle this. But he wanted it more than he'd ever wanted anything in his life.

Finally that little pink tongue flicked out to lick him. The feel of her tongue circling the blunt head nearly made him come. He pulsed once or twice and fought to pull back.

"Poor baby," she cooed. "It looks like you want to come real badly, but you're going to have to wait until I get you in my mouth. And that might take some time. I want to suck every inch of you."

The pounding intensified. *Oh God, yes. Please.* He was about to start begging.

But he didn't need to. She ran her tongue down the bulging vein, before bringing her mouth over him and covering him. She sucked and swirled. Flicking her tongue in the sensitive slit as the drops seeped out. The sounds she was making were driving him crazy. She started to pump the base with her hand as the suction and milking increased with her mouth.

She'd lied. She had plenty of experience because this was fucking perfect. His hands were in her hair as her head bobbed over him, sucking faster and harder and taking him deep in her throat.

He didn't have a chance. She forced him over the edge, and he went off like a pipe bomb.

He had no idea what he said as he cried out his pleasure. But it involved swearing and God, and how good she was. His mind went black—or red. Whatever color the pinnacle of pleasure was when you hit it. That was what it was.

But it wasn't the pinnacle. Not even close. As he was about to find out.

He should be dead. He should be tapped out. Done for the night. But the night was young, and she made him feel like he was fourteen.

When she lifted her head and slid her tongue over her upper lip like a well-satisfied cat, Dean reached for the condom.

Annie was feeling pretty proud of herself. It was a heady feeling holding a man like him in the palm of her hand— or, rather, her mouth. She didn't need to ask whether he'd liked it. It was obvious. He'd loved it.

And so had she. She'd never been all that into it before. It usually felt more like quid pro quo. You go down on me, I'll go down on you. Not this time. She'd been into it. *Really* into it.

It had her hot all over again.

She wasn't the only one. She was surprised to see him still half-hard and reaching for the condom.

She took it from him, and by the time she'd finished putting it on, there was no half about it.

She didn't usually get worked up about dick size, but man . . .

Straddling him again, she reached down to take him in her hand. She could barely wrap her fingers around him. "Anyone ever tell you that you'd have a hell of a career in porn?"

He lifted an eyebrow with a surprisingly boyish smile. He was always so serious; it made her heart squeeze to see him so relaxed. "I wouldn't think you would approve of the industry."

"I don't," she said with a cheeky grin. "It denigrates women. I was thinking gay guys."

He laughed. "Men can't be denigrated? Not very PC of you. But I'll keep it in mind. I'm temporarily out of a job, you know."

She assumed he was referring to the charter business. But she liked that he could joke and go along with it rather than say something derogatory. She had no doubt he was as straight as an arrow, but he was confident enough in who he was not to need to "prove it" by objecting to her premise.

Every time she tried to fit him in a neat little package— conservatives and the military weren't exactly known for their enlightened opinions about homosexuality—he did something to surprise her.

"Forget I said anything," she said, still holding him in her hand and stroking him. "It would be too big a loss for womankind."

At least an eight-inch loss, but who was counting?

The time for teasing had passed. His jaw was clenched and his body was straining as if he was fighting for control again.

She could feel the pulse of pounding blood in her hand.

His gaze was heavy and hot as it met hers. "Ride me, sweetheart. I want to watch you as you fuck me."

Surprisingly Annie wanted that, too. She wouldn't describe herself as adventuresome in bed—missionary usually fit the bill—but he was proving otherwise.

Or maybe it was the casual factor. Maybe it was the no-strings-attached part that was oddly freeing?

Whatever the case, she used her hand to guide him into her as she lowered her body on top of him. Slowly. Savoring the tightness. The stretch. The heat. The inch-by-inch filling.

Until finally she was fully impaled.

Or so she thought. But then he took her by the hips and lifted his own at the same time with a little hitch that made her body twinge. She gasped at the feeling—the rawness of sensation.

It was magical. There was no other word for the closeness, the sense of being connected with another person so intimately and perfectly.

He held her like that for a moment, looking into her eyes with an intensity and emotion that she dared not try to name. But it burned and pounded in her chest.

If she didn't know better . . .

Stop. Don't get confused. It doesn't mean anything. It's just attraction.

She closed her eyes, breaking the connection, and started to move. Lifting up and down, slowly at first, trying to get the most out of every stroke.

He let her set the pace. His hands moved from her hips to her breasts. He was squeezing, kneading, plying the turgid tips with his big callused fingers.

She wanted to go faster, harder. The slow strokes grew more frantic as the gentle ride became a wild gallop. She had to hold on to him, her fingers digging into the solid ball of muscle in his arms and shoulders.

He was talking to her. Telling her how good she felt. Telling her how hot she was. Telling her how much he wanted her to come. How much he couldn't wait to come inside her.

He was leading her to him. Lulling her to completion in a dreamlike fantasy. Wrapping a sensual web around them both.

His stomach muscles tightened as his hips lifted to meet

hers. He held her hips again to bring her down harder. Deeper. She could feel him big and thick and hard inside her. Pulsing.

She was almost . . .

Right when she'd reached the peak of sensation, he brought her down hard against him and ground himself against her. She cried out her climax just as he did. The timing couldn't have been more perfect.

Nothing could have been more perfect.

Their eyes met and there was no mistaking the connection or the emotion. It was right there between them. So palpable she could almost touch it.

And there was nothing casual about it.

Twenty-five

Dean tried to keep his mind on what he was doing. He'd found an Internet café and had been clicking through articles on previous targets of OPF, some of which were more high profile than others. OPF had started out small or rather more localized in their attacks, but gradually their targets had shifted to large conglomerates. North Sea Offshore Drilling was actually a subsidiary of a huge oil company. When there was more than one company involved in something they were "protesting," they seemed to target the bigger one.

The strategy didn't make a lot of sense to him. If the object was economic sabotage—to destroy these companies—why hit the one who could absorb it better? Was there something more than ideology at work?

He needed to try to "follow the money." The popular refrain from the Watergate movie attributed to Deep Throat . . .

Fuck. Deep throat. Not what he should be thinking about. His mind instantly shifted—as it had been doing all morning—to last night.

"Epic" was an understatement. Dean didn't know what to think. He probably shouldn't try; he might not like what he came up with.

What the hell had he been thinking? It had seemed like a good idea at the time. They were obviously attracted to each other, they both knew the situation, they were stuck here for a few days—they might as well make the best of it. Why not?

At least that was what he had told himself, but it didn't seem quite so straightforward now. He'd been inside her half the night, and the other half he'd kept her cuddled so tightly against him a good old-fashioned Gulf hurricane couldn't have ripped them apart.

He was an idiot. He should have stuck to the original plan and not given in. He had a "type," as the LC had pointed out, for a reason. Even in the best of circumstances—which this sure as hell was not—his job didn't allow for anything more than casual hookups of the mess-around, nothing-serious variety. To be part of Team Nine, it was a mandate: no close family, no wives, no girlfriends. There were exceptions made like Blake with his supposedly estranged sister, and Colt's marriage to Kate (being CIA, she knew how to keep secrets), but they all knew what they were getting into when they joined. It was part of the deal. You want the most important, dangerous, highly covert ops? No ties.

So yeah, he had a type. Women who were fun to hang out with, maybe go to dinner with and see a few movies with in between hot and heavy sessions in the bedroom, but no one he'd be tempted to want something deeper or more serious with. He kept it simple. Light. Casual.

Fitting Annie in that box, however, wasn't working. There was nothing simple, light, or casual about her, or how she made him feel.

He should have stayed away from her from the beginning and every stupid step along the way. Listened to his head and not his gut—or other parts of his body.

Frustrated with himself and the situation, Dean cursed and returned to his electronic surfing. The wind-and-board variety would come after lunch.

His attempts to delve into the financial history of OPF, specifically who might be funding them, however, hit dead end after dead end. After an hour of banging his head against the proverbial cyber wall, he gave up.

What the fuck was he doing anyway? He wasn't a back-room guy. He wasn't a computer hacker, a forensic accountant, or an analyst.

He was a SEAL. A fighter. The guy running into a firefight or the guy you sent behind enemy lines. He was the person who knew how to run an operation and get the job done.

He could look at a situation, assess, analyze, and make a decision before most people formulated the question. Knowing how to act and being able to trust that those actions were right was almost instinctive. It was probably his biggest strength.

But after what had happened with the kid in Russia and now Annie . . .

His gut seemed to be letting him down.

He needed to get back to what he was good at. Solving problems and getting the job done. In this case, clearing Annie's name and making sure she was safe before he disappeared again.

With that in mind, he left the café and started back to the guest house, making a call along the way to the LC to pass on what information he'd gathered about OPF. Maybe Kate could do something with it.

He'd told Annie he would meet her for lunch on the beach, so he was surprised when she came bursting into the room not long after he'd returned to the guest house.

One look at her face, and he knew something was wrong. She was as white as a sheet.

He felt that strange thud in his chest and didn't hesitate to draw her against him when she raced into his arms.

The frantic beat of her heart seemed to echo his own.

He had to stop this shit. The man known for his cool under pressure went to fucking pieces whenever she jumped.

He drew her back, holding her away from him, where presumably she wouldn't do as much harm. "What's wrong?"

"There were two men at the beach—"

Dean wasn't sure he'd ever lost it before, but that had done it. He went ballistic. Out of control with rage. "If those two assholes touched you, I'll kill them."

Something in his voice seemed to clear some of her panic. She looked at him in surprise. "What? Oh, you mean those guys from yesterday?" She shook her head. "I wasn't talking about them. This was two different guys. They were walking up and down the beach, talking to people, showing them something. It looked like a flyer. I'd just come back from the bathroom when I noticed them. I don't know why I didn't return to my things, but there was something about them. . . . They didn't look like they were from around here."

Dean had calmed down enough to ask, "Why?"

"They were a little too polished. I don't know the right word. . . . Slick, maybe? The fancy-European-designer-suit kind of look. But tough guys. It was just wrong."

"What was the flyer?"

"I didn't stick around to find out. But it has to be my picture."

"You think they were police?"

She shook her head. "No. Don't you see? I think it's Jean Paul's men, and they are looking for us."

He tried to calm her down. "Jean Paul isn't looking for us. He's too busy covering his ass. Anyway, he couldn't have mobilized that kind of manpower in a couple days to check every island. There are hundreds of places we could have gone; there is no reason to think he would have gotten that lucky to pick this one so fast. He couldn't have followed us. It's probably just a coincidence."

He didn't believe in coincidences, but it seemed a stretch that Jean Paul would try to track her down with that kind of intensity. He had to know his story wouldn't hold up. He should be more concerned with getting the hell out of there.

Dean supposed it could be the police or MI6 if they'd given any credence to his terrorism report. But again, mobilizing that kind of manpower that quickly didn't seem likely.

"Wait here," he said, setting her aside. "I'll find out what's going on."

"No." She caught his arm, her slender fingers pressing like a vise. "You can't go down there. What if they see you? What if something happens to you?"

"I'll be careful." He wanted to dismiss her concerns out of hand, but he couldn't. If she was right, this was bigger than he'd thought.

He pulled the phone from his pocket and handed it to her.

"You hang on to this. If I'm not back in an hour, hit nine. It's speed dial. The man who answers will know what to do."

Dean understood the significance of what he was doing. He was handing her his secret. Maybe not in so many words, but if she used that phone she was a part of this.

"Who's on the other end?"

"Someone you can trust."

Someone *he* trusted, he realized. To put Annie's well-being in Taylor's hands, he must. So why hadn't he trusted him in Russia? Good fucking question.

Dean retrieved the gun he'd taken from Jean Paul and stuck it in the back of his jeans.

He could tell she didn't like seeing that, but she didn't say anything. Worry and anxiousness clouded every one of her delicate features.

"What should I do?"

"Sit tight" obviously wasn't going to cut it. She'd go crazy staring out the window, waiting for him to return.

"Change in case we have to get out of here." She was still wearing her suit and shorts from the beach. "Get our things together, and see if you can get Mrs. Collins to make us a couple of sandwiches."

She nodded, obviously relieved to have something to do.

He knew too well the trouble you could get into when you were idle. Like getting messed up in an ecoterrorist plot/murder investigation.

Dean grabbed a few more things and went to the door. "I'll be back soon."

"You better be."

He grinned at her fierce expression and pulled her into his arms again for long enough to press an equally fierce kiss on her mouth until it was yielding and soft again.

"Remember, Annie. One hour."

It took him half that. The guest house was only a couple of blocks from town. The beach where Annie had seen the men was a short distance beyond, but Dean didn't make it that far.

He'd just turned onto the main drag when he saw the two men walking out of the post office and headed toward Patsy's supermarket.

One look at them, and Dean knew Annie's instincts had been dead-on. He could recognize professionals when he saw them. He had no doubt that these guys were hired killers.

His blood turned to ice at the thought of the danger Annie could have been in.

What the fuck was going on here?

He ducked into the post office, happy to see a young kid behind the desk. He looked fresh out of high school—or whatever the Scottish equivalent was.

Dean put on his best beach bum look and looked anxiously over his shoulder. "Who were those two?"

The kid responded to the "sheesh" tone. "They said private investigators. Handed me some kind of badge, but I didn't look at it too closely."

"What did they want?"

"Said they were looking for a woman who may have been kidnapped by her boyfriend."

Fuck.

"But they were lying," the kid said.

"How do you know?"

"It was the same picture of the woman in the paper yesterday for that murder up in Lewis."

The kid was obviously pleased with his detective work.

"Really? You must have a good memory."

The kid blushed. With his cropped strawberry blond hair and transparent complexion, that basically meant he turned beet red.

"It wasn't hard," the kid said. "She's hot. Hard to believe she'd be involved in something like what they are saying."

Dean nodded, not having to feign understanding. "I bet there's more to it."

"Was there something you wanted?" the kid asked, finally remembering his job.

"Yeah, a stamp for a postcard. But I just remembered I forgot my wallet back at the hotel. I'll be back."

Dean had all the information he needed, and he didn't want to waste any more time. If those guys had gone into the market to talk to Patsy, there was a good chance she'd recognize the picture. It wouldn't take them long to track them down to the guest house from there.

He wanted nothing more than to go after the bastards and put them out of their misery, but protecting Annie came first. He didn't know if there were others involved, and he wanted to get her the hell out of here.

None of this made any sense. He'd expected the police to be looking for them, but why was Jean Paul? Was it a loose end to cover up the murders or something else? Whatever it was, Jean Paul obviously meant business. Dean had no doubt those guys had been sent to kill her.

He felt a burst of rage again but forced himself to focus. Annie. He had to get her somewhere safe.

Twenty-six

Kate looked at the screen of the vibrating phone on her desk and felt her heart drop into a dark void of dread and nearly forgotten pain. "Out of area."

Not again, damn him. He'd promised to leave her alone if she did as he asked. She'd done her part. But since when had Colt Wesson ever kept a promise?

"I promise to love, honor, and cherish you, till death us do part . . ."

An icy wall slammed down hard in her head. She wouldn't go there. Never again. Whatever love she'd once had for her ex-husband was long gone. That had been easy to forget. What had lingered was the anger and bitterness. She'd buried them beneath layers of time and perspective, and by building a new life for herself, but his sudden appearance in her life again after so many years had exposed some cracks.

She was tempted to ignore the call. But her therapist had told her she would have to face her past at some point, and Kate knew he was right. Or partially right. What he'd actually said was "forgiveness," but that had about a snowball's chance in hell. Kate wasn't that much of a saint. But neither was she a coward, and she wouldn't let him make her run away.

He was the one who'd done that.

Stay frosty. Wasn't that what he used to say in the Teams?

She would follow his advice. "Hello." Her voice sounded appropriately sharp and brittle.

"Kate? It's me."

Her heart, her breath, everything inside her turned to ice. It was as if she'd just walked over a grave. Literally. The voice belonged to a ghost.

Was this someone's idea of a joke?

"Who is this?" she demanded angrily.

"You know who it is."

She sank back in her chair, nearly dropping the phone. It was Scott. She knew his voice too well. It had been a ray of light through the darkest days of her life.

Tears gathered around her eyes. Her throat went hot, her voice dry. He was alive! Happiness burst through her. "My God, where are you? They told me you were dead."

"Is anyone there with you?"

He sounded so normal, when she felt as if she'd just come out of a dark fog. She shook her head, and then realizing how stupid that was said, "No. I'm in my office at home."

"Is the ambassador there?"

"He left for work. God, Scott, what is going on?"

"It's better if you don't use names."

Kate didn't question him. Scott wasn't paranoid, and whatever this was about, it had to be serious. "All right."

"I need your help."

"Of course."

She could hear the faint sound of amusement on the other side. "Don't you want to know what I'm getting you into before you say yes?"

"It won't make a difference."

There was a long pause. "You always were too good for him."

She didn't need to ask whom he meant. Once she would have argued with him, but she just let it go. He was right. "Tell me what you need."

"Tex is messed up in a murder investigation in Scotland—the Isle of Lewis to be specific. I need you to make it go away."

Kate was so happy to hear that Dean was alive as well that it took her a moment to catch up with everything Scott was saying. He filled her in a little more on the details. Dean had apparently come to the rescue of a woman who unknowingly had become involved with OPF—an organization she was very familiar with—and they both had ended up being framed for murder when one of the terrorists killed the other two.

"That sounds like him," Kate said.

"Not following orders?"

Kate laughed. "He's still giving you a hard time, huh? No, I meant Superman always coming to the rescue and not being able to look the other way. It should sound familiar."

There was a long pause while they both remembered how he'd come to her rescue—and what it had cost them both.

"He's a pain in the ass," Scott said gruffly, "but see what you can find out."

Scott passed on the information about the woman's credit card presumably being used to purchase the UNDEX—underwater explosive—materials, and what Dean had found out about OPF and their targets.

"He thinks there's more to it?" she asked.

"He isn't sure. But I agree—it seems like overkill."

She agreed. "I'll see what I can find out and point the police in the right direction." It would be easy enough to tell them the CIA had been watching OPF—which they had—and assure them that "Dan" and Annie weren't involved. "What else?"

Scott hesitated. "I've already put you in enough danger as it is."

She could hear the worry in his voice. He was trying to protect her. But she wasn't going to let him do that. Whatever had forced him into hiding, he needed her help. She would finally have the chance to pay him back for all he'd done for her. "Then tell me what happened out there so I know what I'm up against."

He sighed. "You don't fight fair, do you?"

She'd learned from the best.

"How much do you know?"

"Not much," she said. "Only what my ex told me, and what my godfather was able to fill in."

She could hear the shock through the handset. "You talked to him?"

She told him about Colt's surprise visit. "He said the platoon had been sent on a mission and was KIA, but that he wanted to go to Russia to make sure. He asked me to put him in touch with my godfather."

She'd been devastated when Colt told her Scott was presumed dead but had tried not to show it. Being careful of Colt's feelings? She was assuming he had them.

Scott swore. "That is all we fucking need. It's bad enough with the reporter and her damned 'Lost Platoon' articles. You have to stop him. If he finds anything or figures anything out, he could put us all in danger."

"From who?"

"I don't know. That's what I'm trying to find out."

He filled her in on what he knew. The lost communications. The warning he'd received. The missile that had taken out over half the platoon. How the rest of them had barely escaped. How he'd ordered the survivors to scatter and go dark until he could find out what had happened. And about the death of the woman who'd warned him. Kate could tell there was more there, but she didn't press. He also told her what he'd been able to dig up so far, and his suspicions on where the leak had come from.

When he was done, Kate knew he was right to be worried. The implications were huge. Whoever had set them up would have a vested interest in making sure the truth stayed buried in Russia.

"You need to call him off, Kate."

"Are you sure?" She paused, knowing how this could go over. "Maybe he could help?"

Colt had no allegiance to anyone and access to resources she didn't even want to know about.

"His hatred of me outweighs everything else. Three years ago, he told me he'd kill me if he ever had the chance. I believed him."

Kate wanted to put her head in her hands and weep. Not

just for the lost friendship between the two men, but because she knew Colt had meant it. "God, I'm so sorry."

His voice softened. "I'm not. But I need you to do this for me."

"I'll try." She had no idea how to get Colt off the trail, but she'd think of something.

Twenty-seven

Annie was relieved to see him, but Dan's grim expression told her that she hadn't overreacted to the two men on the beach.

"We need to get out of here," he said.

She didn't waste time questioning him. They gathered their belongings, left money in the room to cover the cost of lodging, and slipped out the back door that led to the car park.

He moved between the cars as if looking for something. He must have found it, because he stopped in front of a compact silver car, which seemed to be the only car size they did on the islands. It was odd not to see SUVs around. The high cost of "petrol" apparently discouraged gas guzzling. When he opened the driver's-side door on the right, she realized he'd been looking for an unlocked car.

He reached across the seat to open the passenger door, but stopped her before she could climb in. "You need to get in the backseat and lie down. I don't want anyone to see you."

It was tiny back there, but she didn't argue.

He popped the plastic steering wheel casing off and an impressively few minutes later the car came to a rumbling start.

They hadn't taught him that in the navy. "Grand theft auto on your résumé?" she said dryly.

She hadn't really been serious, but he was. "Fortunately for me juvenile records are sealed."

"You aren't a juvenile now."

He grinned. "I'm just borrowing it. I don't want to take the chance of those guys seeing us on foot."

He started to pull out of the stall. A few turns later and Annie guessed they were on the main road. "Where are we going?"

She could see the flash of white of his teeth when he smiled. "I don't want to ruin the surprise."

"Under the circumstances, I don't think you need to worry about keeping the excitement level up."

He laughed and shot her a glance. "You're funny."

"And you're stalling."

He sighed. "Back to the inflatable."

She groaned. "I thought you might say that."

"They could be watching the airport and ferry."

"You think there were more than those two?"

"I don't know."

"Who were they?" He shrugged, which she was beginning to recognize as a sign that he didn't want to tell her. "The police?"

"I don't think so."

She sucked in her breath. "So I was right? They were Jean Paul's men?"

"It's a possibility," he hedged.

"You think they want to shut me up?"

"I think they want something." He glanced at her again, this time sharper. "Is there anything you aren't telling me?"

She tried not to take the question defensively. But it hurt that he thought she could be hiding something from him. "Unlike you, I've told you the truth about everything."

She could see his hands tighten on the steering wheel. "Annie . . ."

It sounded like some kind of warning. "Don't worry. I don't expect parity in the two sides of this equation."

He must not have liked that, either, because his jaw clamped down hard.

"Will you tell me one thing?" she asked after a minute. Taking no no for a yes, she asked, "Is Dan your real name?"

She'd lifted up her head a little, and he held her gaze in the rearview mirror for a moment before answering, "No."

She hadn't thought so, but she still hated to hear confirmation. Wow, she was experiencing all kinds of firsts with him. First casual hookup and first casual hookup where she didn't even know the guy's name.

She couldn't quite cover up all the hurt in her voice. "So what do I call you?"

"Dan is fine. I'm sorry, Annie. If it was just me, I would tell you. But it's not. Okay?"

"All right." What else could she say?

A few minutes later, the car came to a stop. "We're here."

She sat up and saw that he'd parked along the side of the road not far from the beach and the hut where they'd stored the boat.

"I was hoping I'd seen this place for the last time," she said glumly, not looking forward to getting back in that leaky boat.

"It won't be so bad. I checked on the inflatable yesterday and did a little repair work. I'd hoped we wouldn't need it again, but . . ." He shrugged.

"Always have a backup plan. My dad used to say the same thing."

He quickly changed the subject, almost as if he didn't want her thinking about that connection for too long. The Special Forces connection.

Too late.

"We'll head for the Isle of Coll. It's close, and we can catch the ferry from there to Oban. From Oban we'll take a bus or train to Glasgow. It will be easier to get lost in a big city."

"And then?"

He met her gaze. He knew what she was really asking, but he chose to take her question literally instead. "We'll see when we get there. Hopefully my contact will have something by then."

In other words, sayonara.

Got it.

Annie was quiet as they sped across the water the short distance to Coll. The two islands were less than a mile apart, but it would take about forty minutes to reach the port, which was located on the eastern side of the island.

Dean didn't delude himself that she was trying not to distract him so he could concentrate on making sure they weren't being watched or followed.

No, she was pissed and probably—even worse—hurt. That was what was making his chest burn and his jaw hurt from clenching his teeth every time he looked at her huddled in the seat beside him.

But what could he do? He couldn't tell her what she wanted to hear. Not his name, not anything. He sure as hell couldn't tell her that he wasn't going to stick around any longer than necessary. As soon as she was all clear with the police, he was gone. What other choice did he have?

The LC was already ready to kill him—for good reason. Dean had involved her enough as it was. Not only was she a danger to him and the other five men who'd survived if she said the wrong thing to the right person, but he could be a danger to her if the LC was right and someone had wanted them dead.

So why was he in the unfamiliar place of wishing otherwise? He didn't deal in what-ifs. He prided himself on his clear-eyed perspective, his ability to strip away everything but the facts. Seeing things as they were and not how he wanted them to be. So what was his problem?

Big green eyes and the woman who went with them, that was his problem.

Fuck.

But whatever they'd had back there, whatever short stop they'd had on fantasy island, it was over. The arrival of those two thugs had seen to that. It was time to face reality. And the sooner he did that, the better.

Dean let up on the throttle as they turned into the deep V-shaped bay of Arinagour. No one paid them much attention as they tied up the inflatable beside the dock, but he was watchful all the same.

He couldn't shake the black cloud that had been following him since they left Tiree. But maybe that cloud had something more to do with the woman by his side than with the men looking for her. He knew he would have to leave soon.

He looked at his watch. They had plenty of time. The ferry didn't leave for another couple of hours. He'd memorized the timetables in case of something like this. "Why don't you go get us a table in the café over there?"

He pointed to the building overlooking the water opposite the ferry building. They would be able to see the ship coming in from there. As it was coming from Tiree, it would also enable him to get a look at the passengers before anyone saw them. It wasn't inconceivable that the two guys would guess their direction.

"Where are you going?"

"To see about the tickets."

And he had a call to make. He hadn't had a chance to get in touch with Taylor before they'd left, but he wanted to fill the LC in on the latest development.

She looked as though she wanted to argue, but probably guessed his reasons. She was smart and seemed to know him too well. He wasn't sure whether that was good or bad. Probably both.

Dean returned a short while later with tickets, but without having reached the LC. He'd left a message, but the connection had been so crappy he wasn't sure it had gone through.

"We all set?" she asked.

He nodded.

"I ordered you some tea." She nodded toward the pot in front of him. "I'm assuming you don't like herbal, so it's black."

He wasn't much on tea in general, but when in Rome . . .

He poured a cup and reached for the milk and sugar.

He was more relieved than he wanted to admit to see her smile as she watched him.

"What?" he asked.

"Are you twelve?"

Sugar cube number four plopped in the dark liquid. "I'm a growing lad."

She laughed, and just like that some of the cloud dissipated.

"You still mad at me?" he asked.

She eyed him from over the rim of her cup. "I wasn't mad—" Seeing his expression, she stopped. "Okay, maybe I was a little mad, but I know I don't have a right to be. You've done more than I had any right to expect. I should be thanking you for helping me get away. I don't know why those two men were looking for me, but I can't imagine it was for anything good." She looked in his eyes. "I was scared."

For good reason. But he wasn't going to tell her his suspicions. He didn't want to make her any more freaked out than she already was.

Uncomfortable with her gratitude, he shrugged it off and then shook his head thoughtfully. "What I don't understand is how they found us so fast."

"Luck?"

"I don't believe in luck. Luck is—"

"What happens when preparation meets opportunity," she interrupted. At his look of surprise, she gave him a wry smile. "I've heard it before."

He wasn't going to ask, assuming it was her father.

Surprisingly the tea was relaxing; it helped him clear his head a little. "The easiest way to track someone is through the phone, but I took care of that."

She shot him a glare. "You sure did. Do you know how weird it is not to be able to text or check . . ."

Her voice let off, and he saw something in her face. "What?"

She bit her bottom lip, looking at him uncertainly. "I checked my e-mail at the library."

He didn't say anything. He didn't need to. Annie stared at him pleadingly. "I'm so sorry. I didn't think . . ."

It never occurred to her (a) that someone would be monitoring her e-mail account, and (b) that they would be able to track her location from it. This wasn't her world. She was a scientist, not law enforcement—or on the other side of the law, for that matter.

"You think that is how they found us so quickly?" she asked.

"Yep."

One-word answers and granite-hard expressions weren't good signs. She held out an olive branch. "I guess you were right about my cell phone."

Pause. Hard look. Another "Yep."

This really wasn't good. She knew he was furious and doing his best not to lash out at her. He had to be. But he was controlling himself. She should be glad, but she wasn't. It was discombobulating.

"Go ahead," she said. "Give it to me. Tell me I'm an idiot. I deserve it."

She could tell from the anger in his eyes that he wanted to. "What else did you do other than check e-mail?"

"Nothing. There was something I wanted to look up on the Internet, but I was only on for a few minutes." All of a sudden she remembered something. "I had a message from my bank that someone had tried to access my account, so I changed the password. I thought it might be Julien, but I guess that doesn't matter anymore."

"You didn't contact anyone?"

She shook her head. "I was going to send my mom an e-mail, but I remembered what you'd said."

He was biting his tongue. She knew he must have a sarcastic reply to that. But nothing. What was wrong with him? "I know you're pissed. You don't need to hold back. Your no-sugarcoating special way with words is one of the things I love—"

She stopped with a sudden gasp, realizing what she'd been about to say. Love. One of the things I love about you. Which wouldn't have been a big deal if she just hadn't made it a big deal. Now the half-spoken word just sat there between them like a pink elephant—huge, awkward, and impossible to ignore.

His expression hadn't changed, but she wasn't as good as he was at hiding his emotions. She could feel the heat burning in her cheeks.

The silent pause that followed extended the cringe-worthy

moment. She rushed to cover up the gaffe, but only made it worse. "You know what I meant," she babbled. "It's an expression. Of course I'm not . . ."

She stopped again, gazing up at him helplessly.

Ground. Hole. Swallow. Now. *Please* . . .

The steadiness of his gaze as he stared at her only seemed to make it worse. "I know what you meant, Annie."

Did he? She wasn't sure. *She* wasn't sure what she meant. Her feelings for him were unsorted. But strong. Far stronger than they should be, given what she knew—and didn't know—about him.

"What were you looking up on the Internet?"

She would have been relieved by the change of subject, but she suspected he wasn't going to like this any better than the e-mail. "Your tattoo."

He was good at the stone-faced no reaction, but she was watching him close enough to see the slight tic and whitening of his mouth. "Why?"

"I thought it might be some kind of Special Forces insignia."

He looked around to make sure no one in the café had heard her. But she'd picked a table in the corner overlooking the window for that reason. "Why in the hell would you do that? I told you what it was."

"You did. But you know what's interesting? The SEAL trident is referred to as a Budweiser. Apparently they look alike."

If she thought he was mad and controlling it before, it was nothing like now. He was positively apoplectic. She was glad they were in a public place.

But far worse than the anger was the iron curtain that dropped down to replace it. The wintry blue of his eyes made her feel as if she'd just landed in Siberia. Brr. Whatever connection she'd felt between them was cut in two. He couldn't have cut her off any more clearly than if he'd walked away and never looked back. She had a feeling that was exactly what he wanted to do.

He stood, and her heart shot to her throat.

"Wait. I'm sorry. Don't—"

"We should get going."

She heaved a heavy sigh of relief. He wasn't leaving her. At least for now. But it was clear she'd stepped over some kind of invisible line, and he wasn't in any kind of mood to talk about it.

Not that now was the right time for talking. She sensed the change that came over him as soon as they left the café. Watchful didn't quite cover it. He was on guard. Highly tuned. Ready.

If she hadn't guessed he was military or Special Forces before, she would have known it then. He moved just like all those guys on TV and the movies—as if around every corner was a bad guy waiting to take them out.

Even once they were on the ferry—the various-sized blue-and-white ships were a familiar sight moving throughout the islands—he didn't let down. There was a large inside room with tables and seats where passengers could enjoy the crossing in relative comfort, including the requisite cup of tea and snack bar, but after checking it thoroughly, and positioning her in a seat near the exit door, he stood watch outside in the wind and cold. For three hours.

It was evening by the time they docked in Oban. Other than issuing her instructions on sticking close to him as they left the ferry, "Dan" wasn't any more talkative on the short walk to the train station than he had been on board. They stuck with the group of about thirty passengers who were doing the same. Annie didn't see anything unusual, but admittedly, she didn't know what she was looking for.

Dan was in his hypervigilant Special Ops mode and didn't look as though he was going to relax anytime soon. She was surprised he didn't insist on coming inside the ladies' room with her, but after three cups of tea, no, she couldn't wait any longer.

She sensed the change the moment she emerged; she could see it in the darkness of his expression even before he spoke.

"We have a problem."

Twenty-eight

The train station in Oban consisted of a single building with a ticket window, a small waiting room, and two platforms, one accessed by an underground walkway. Dean could tell something was wrong by the long line and commotion at the window. While waiting for Annie to finish up in the restroom, he asked the first person who walked by and learned the bad news.

"What's wrong?" Annie asked after he'd told her they had a problem.

"There's an issue with the signal lights. Apparently it isn't uncommon. The train to Glasgow tonight has been canceled. We'll have to catch the one first thing in the morning."

"Oh," she sighed with relief. "For a minute I thought they'd followed us."

He didn't think so. But the delay could give them time to catch up. There weren't many ways off the island, and once they figured out they were no longer there . . .

"We'll have to find someplace to spend the night," he said. "The guy I talked to said there is plenty of accommodations in town."

They'd walked about fifteen minutes away from the picturesque harbor town where the ferry had docked to get to the station and would have to retrace their steps. Oban was a good-sized town in the Highlands and a popular destination for tourists embarking on cruises around the islands. Under different circumstances he wouldn't mind a night's stay—it was the biggest town he'd been in for months—but he wanted this over with as soon as possible.

She'd fucking guessed that he was a SEAL. He couldn't believe she'd figured it out. She was too curious and too smart for her own good. Or maybe, more accurately, for his own good. He couldn't risk her seeing another one of those damned articles and putting two and two together. She'd gotten too close as it was.

He'd gotten too close. He had to put an end to this, and one more night wasn't going to make it any easier.

"... *one of the things I love—*"

She couldn't be falling in love with him. They'd known each other a week. Admittedly part of that week had been pretty intense, high-adrenaline, get-to-know-someone-fast bonding time, but they wouldn't seem so perfect together when it was all over. Their differences would start to grate and eventually draw them apart.

She clearly had issues with the military—understandably— and he'd seen too much to have a very high tolerance for dewy-eyed idealists. Besides, he liked his guns. And hunting. For meat.

He could hear Donovan giving him shit about that for years. A vegetarian? An activist? A Democrat (aka "the Party of Santa Claus" as Dean referred to it) with Mr. Bootstraps and "everyone should keep their eyes on their own paper and not worry about what everyone else has"?

That should be all the discouragement Dean needed. So why was he pretty sure that he wouldn't give a shit? That he could hear the endless razzing and not mind?

Because she was worth it. She was incredible. And even if a bleeding heart led her down the wrong path every now and then, he respected her passion and drive to change things. It was the other side of what he did.

Crap.

But it was all theoretical. Even if he wasn't in hiding, a relationship with her would mean giving up the team. He wasn't ready to do that. He wasn't sure he'd ever be ready to do that.

With the station emptying quickly, Dean escorted her out of the building behind a couple who from their backpacks, poles, and boots he assumed must have been trekking on the islands. He wanted to stick with the crowd. He was pretty sure they hadn't been followed, but he wasn't about to relax his guard.

"I'm sorry," she said after they'd been walking for a few minutes. "I know you're furious with me, but I didn't mean any harm." When he didn't say anything, she grabbed his arm and pulled him around to face her. "Can you blame me for being curious? We are sleeping together, for God's sake, and you've barely told me anything about you." She stopped and even before he heard the emotion in her voice, he could see the tears in her eyes. "I don't even know your name."

Dean felt about as big as one of those annoying biting midges. He didn't want to hurt her, and yet that was exactly what he was doing. But what choice did he have? He couldn't tell her what she wanted to know.

But if she started crying, he didn't know what the fuck he was going to do. Just seeing the glimmer of tears in her eyes was twisting him up inside something fierce. It was making his chest pound in an odd way, and making him antsy and uncomfortable—as if he were walking across hot coals. Hell, he'd rather walk across hot coals than see her cry.

He did the only thing he could do. He pulled her into his arms. "Aw, shit, Annie, I'm sorry. I know you don't understand, but you'll just have to trust me that I don't have a choice. If I could tell you, I would."

As he was wearing the backpack, she'd slid her arms around his waist. He still had the gun tucked in his jeans at the small of his back for safekeeping and easy access. Her cheek had been resting on his chest—which felt pretty damned amazing—but she tilted it back to look up at him. "If you told me, you'd have to kill me?"

He smiled, and lifted his hand to stroke a finger down her cheek. "Something like that." But he quickly sobered. "But it's serious, Annie. I know you are curious, but it's dangerous—

and not just to me. I'm asking you to stop. To put whatever it is you think you've learned aside and forget it."

Forget me.

She knew what he was asking. "I'll try, but I'm not sure I can."

Unfortunately that made two of them.

She looked so gorgeous staring up at him with all those emotions he didn't want to see in her eyes, he would have kissed her.

If he hadn't sensed the movement behind him.

Without realizing it, Annie had stopped them in the perfect place for an ambush. It was a dark curve in the road where they couldn't be seen from town or by their fellow passengers, who were now ahead of them. Were there any stragglers behind them? Dean would guess not or their attackers—he was assuming there was more than one—wouldn't have made their move.

They must have been watching from the station and followed, waiting for an opportunity. Were they the source of the signal failure?

Shit.

Sensing the movement behind him, Dean reacted. As he couldn't both reach for his gun and get Annie out of the way, he chose the latter. He pushed her away from him and spun, instinctively using his hand to knock aside the weapon that he was pretty sure had been coming toward the back of his head.

He connected with enough force to do some damage, but the guy was well trained. He grunted with pain but didn't release the weapon—an HK USP Tactical with Swiss-made suppressor, from the looks of it.

Dean was ready with his next move before the attacker could bring the gun back around. He wasn't going to mess around, not wanting to take any chances. He didn't know how many or how skilled they were. It was kill or be killed. He went for a blow to the throat, targeting the trachea with the side of his forearm and swinging his leg around his ankle at the same time to knock him off balance.

There was a sickly crunch and gasp as the guy's throat collapsed. He crumpled and started to fall back but had enough presence of mind while he was asphyxiating to swing the muzzle back around. Dean stomped on his gut and tried to knock the gun away again, but at the same time he sensed the second guy out of the corner of his eye to the right, taking aim.

Fuck, he wasn't going to have time to do both. He went for the gun that was in his reach. He swore he could see down the barrel as he reached for the choking man's hands and tried to point the muzzle in the direction of his compatriot.

He didn't make it before the shot went off. It went wide of Dean, but not wide enough to come close to the second attacker.

The guy was going to shoot him.

Dean heard the muffled sound of a gun being fired, and in the split second of awareness, he steeled himself for impact.

It didn't come.

Shit. The sound had come from behind him. He watched in disbelief as the second attacker who'd been standing about ten feet away fell—or dropped—backward as the bullet struck him right between the eyes.

Holy shit.

Dean turned slowly around, already guessing what he was going to see. Annie stood there frozen, still holding the gun in the firing position.

It had happened so fast. Annie didn't know what had possessed her to grab the gun as "Dan" pushed her away. It was there tucked in the back of his jeans, and her hand just kind of clenched the grip on instinct, and as he pushed her back, the gun came with her.

Neither did she consciously think about shooting the second attacker. Dan was locked in battle with the first guy. Out of the corner of her eye, she saw the second guy approaching with a raised arm and a gun on the end of it pointed in Dan's direction. She didn't think. She just lifted her hands and fired.

Instinct again. Although it was the first time she'd shot anything other than a piece of paper at a shooting range.

Oh God, she'd just killed someone.

Slowly awareness dawned, creeping over her in a mottled flush of shock. She couldn't seem to move. She was still holding the gun; her finger was still pulling the trigger. She wanted to let it go, but she couldn't release the death grip.

Dan came toward her and wrapped his hand around her wrist, forcing her arm down at the same time as he released the gun from her hand.

She looked at him wordlessly. What just happened?

She didn't think she'd spoken aloud, but she couldn't be sure. The noise in her head was too loud. "You just saved my life. You didn't have any other choice. He would have killed me." He shook his head in amazement. "Shit, how the hell did you learn to shoot like that? I thought you didn't like guns."

"I don't. I hate them."

He laughed. "You could have fooled me. You shoot like a pro."

She frowned. "I haven't touched a gun since my father died."

"But he trained you?"

She nodded. He'd insisted she learn how to defend herself. He'd said she was a natural. She'd almost been able to hear the "if only you'd been a boy."

"He did a hell of a job," Dan said. "That was a perfect shot."

She shook her head. It had been horrible. "I was aiming for his heart."

"Well, that was a hell of a miss." He paused, giving her a long look. "You look a little pale. You aren't going to throw up or anything, are you? It's all right if you need to. Lots of guys do their first time."

She shook her head. She felt something. Numb, maybe? A little cold? But not ill. "I don't think so."

"Good. Give me a minute. I want to get rid of them in case someone is behind us."

The path along the harbor that would take them back to the village had the sea on one side and a two-lane road, houses, and a hill on the other. The men had obviously been waiting in the shadows of one of the houses.

After quickly patting them down and pocketing the guy's wallet and phone, Dan dragged the guy who had attacked him across the path and pushed him under the railing of the concrete walkway onto the rocks and beach below. He did the same with the man she'd shot, and Annie had to admit, she was glad when the prone body disappeared over the side where she didn't have to look at it anymore.

"The tide will be coming in soon," he said. "With luck they'll wash out to sea."

"Without luck?"

He shrugged, apparently not worried. "They won't be seen until morning, and it will take them time to determine identities and time of death. We should be well on our way to Glasgow by then."

"They were the same guys from the beach," she said.

He nodded. "They must have come straight here, figuring we'd head to the closest major port." He thought for a minute. "They either had someone watching at the airport or were able to tap in to the computers and realized we hadn't flown. Have you seen either of them before today?"

She shook her head.

He took out the wallets and flipped to the identities. "Hans Richer from Germany and Jonas Meier from Switzerland. Mean anything to you?"

"No."

"I didn't think so. I assume they are aliases." He pulled out the phones, which were cheap disposables, and started to toggle through the mailboxes. "No recent calls or texts on this. I'm sure they've been careful, but I'll check the trash just to be sure." He finished the first phone, and went on to the second. A moment later he swore, and his expression darkened.

"What's wrong?"

"This one has a text. It was sent about fifteen minutes ago. He must not have had a chance to delete it."

"What does it say?"

"Nothing. It was a picture." He paused, and she could see the self-recrimination burning in his gaze. "Of me."

Twenty-nine

Annie knew Dan was furious. What she didn't know was whether he was angry with her. Did he blame her for the man getting a picture of him? She didn't know why it was so horrible that he had done so; she just knew that it was. Actually, from the look on his face, it wasn't just horrible; it was catastrophic. And they both knew that if he hadn't come to her aid, none of this would have happened. Whatever had forced him into hiding had obviously been serious, and by helping her, he'd revealed himself.

"I'm sorry," she said.

He shook his head, seeming to take away some of the anger with the movement. "It's not your fault." He reached out to take her hand. "Come on. We should get out of here, and I think we could both use a drink."

That might be the biggest understatement of the week—which was saying something.

They walked quickly back into town. As he didn't seem the hand-holding type, she was surprised when he didn't release hers. Instead he wrapped it in his big palm and tucked it in his Baja sweatshirt pocket as if he wanted to keep her close.

Which was fine by her.

Though small by American standards, Oban was a decent-

sized town in the Highlands. The harbor was at the center,
and most of the businesses hugged a half mile or so semi-
circle of coastline with the ferry terminal to one side. There
were a number of restaurants and hotels right along the waterfront, including the fancy-looking one that they went into.

"I thought we were on a budget," she said after they walked
by the imposing-looking doorman into a large reception hall
that seemed to be wall-to-wall marble. Not the new and shiny
kind, but the old and stately.

One corner of his mouth lifted. "I figured we could both
use a few creature comforts, and I'll have access to more
funds in Glasgow."

She would have asked about that, but the attractive woman
behind the desk asked Dan if they were checking in. He
smiled, obviously going into his charming mode again, which
he was definitely better at than Annie would have anticipated.
Although when a guy was that built and good-looking, he
could pretty much smile and that would be enough.

He explained that he and his girlfriend—as she'd been
downgraded from a wife, Annie guessed they must not be as
traditional in Oban as they were on Tiree—had been caught
unexpectedly in town and didn't have a reservation.

"You must have been booked on the train to Glasgow," the
woman said with a smile. "You aren't the first unexpected
guests we've had tonight. It's not a problem. We aren't fully
booked. One or two rooms?"

She looked at Dan as she asked, but her gaze slid over to
Annie for a second—or maybe passed over Annie for a second
was more accurate. Clearly she wasn't impressed and thought
he could do better—i.e., herself.

The woman was in her early twenties, but doing everything
she could to look older with thick foundation, heavy eye
makeup, and bright red lipstick. Her long hair was pulled back
in a bun, but very heavy, long, dark bangs contrasted dramatically with her pale Scottish skin and light blue eyes.

Compared to how done up the woman was, Annie looked
as if she'd been camping for a week. All right, she wasn't

exactly looking her best, but what part of "girlfriend" did the woman not understand?

"One room will be fine," Annie said maybe a tad snippily, before Dan could respond.

He gave her a questioning look, which she didn't answer. But he wasn't that slow on the uptake. He figured it out and grinned. If the woman hadn't been watching, Annie would have elbowed him in the gut.

He made it a little better by sliding his arm around her waist, tugging her in tight against him, and pressing a kiss on her head. The feel of his body against hers was still too new not to cause all kinds of tingly reactions.

The woman quoted a price that seemed outrageous for one night, but he paid in twenty-pound notes and she handed over the key—an actual key, not a key card—with a big wooden placard attached that Annie suspected made it difficult to walk off with. The room was on the second floor, which in Brit-speak Annie knew meant the third.

The elevator barely fit the both of them. Clearly these places hadn't been built with guys sized like him in mind. His shoulders almost spanned the width. He took advantage of the closeness to drag her in against him again. "You don't have any reason to be jealous."

The tinge of amusement in his voice made her feel again like elbowing him.

She might have if he hadn't added, "I haven't looked at another woman since you landed in my lap."

Okay, maybe she'd melt instead. She looked up at him, and their eyes met. "Really?"

He shook his head. "Have you taken a look in the mirror lately, Doc? You're pretty hot."

Usually a superficial comment like that would be an instant turnoff, but instead it made her obnoxiously happy. He was bringing out all kinds of weird reactions in her. She couldn't ever recall being jealous before or needing reassurance about her looks. She'd arrived in Scotland a confident, self-possessed, newly minted PhD (admittedly with horrible taste in men), and he'd time-warped her back to high school as a moody teenager in constant need of reassurance. She'd lived through *Mean Girls* once; she didn't need to do it again.

"Yeah, well, you're a little *too* hot, so you can probably ease up on the smiles and go back to Mr. Stern and No Bullshit. Or grow back the mountain man beard."

They'd arrived at the door by then, and he just looked at her and laughed. "I'll remember that. But some women like the beard."

There was something a little too wicked twinkling in his eye, and she decided she'd better not follow up on that one. It might make her angry—or curious. She couldn't decide which was worse.

He flipped on the lights, and she sighed so deeply it sounded almost like a moan. The bathroom was enormous and fitted with a huge jetted tub. On rare occasions she enjoyed baths, and this was definitely going to be one of them. She might never get out.

But then she wouldn't be able to put on the plush robe and slippers. Or use the fancy British Molton Brown toiletries.

"It's all yours," he said, obviously noticing her reaction. "I have to make a call." He paused, giving her a long look. "You doing okay? I won't go if you don't want to be alone right now."

She shook her head. "I'm fine." Surprisingly she was. The numbness and coldness had faded to be replaced by . . . nothing. She actually felt a little guilty for not feeling horrible and falling to pieces. Wasn't that what most people—especially women—did in books and movies?

She wasn't making a feminist statement—although that did drive her nuts—nor was it that she didn't value human life. She just valued his more. There had been a threat, and she took care of it. There was nothing else she could have done. If she hadn't acted, he would have been killed. It was as simple as that.

Maybe she had more of her father in her than she wanted to acknowledge. For the first time in a long while, that thought didn't make her sad. She had him to thank for that.

"Make your call, Tex." She couldn't call him Dan anymore.

It felt too weird now that she knew that wasn't his real name. "And you can bring me back that drink you promised. But no whiskey—with or without the *e*."

He nodded, smiling at the reference to the Scot spelling of whiskey without the *e* that they were very particular about. "I remember." He grimaced. "I have a feeling after this call that I'm going to need it more than you."

The phone only rang one time before it was answered. No passwords this time. "Where the fuck have you been? I've been trying to call you for hours."

"Busy," Dean said. The LC might be his commander, but he'd been doing this too long to let him tear him a new asshole—even when it might be deserved. "I had to leave Tiree unexpectedly."

He could almost hear Taylor narrowing his eyes and giving him the scowl of death through the cell towers. "What do you mean, 'unexpectedly'?"

Dean filled him in on the two professionals on the beach, the boat ride to Coll, the ferry to Oban, and the attack near the train station. He didn't get halfway through before the LC started letting off a string of curses that would do Miggy, who swore every other word, proud. As Taylor didn't usually curse, it was even more impressive.

Dean wondered what the hell Ruiz was up to. But the LC had insisted that none of the guys know where the other survivors had gone. Taylor was the only one who could reach them. Dean understood operational security, but he didn't always like it. They were used to working in teams; this solo bullshit sucked. It felt as if he'd lost the entire platoon. Dealing with eight deaths was bad enough. All seven of Lieutenant White's squad and the kid. Brian. The death that was on him.

Although Annie had filled in well enough earlier. He still couldn't believe that shot she'd made—or how cool and calm she'd been afterward. Weren't women supposed to fall apart at things like that?

Okay, so maybe that was a little sexist.

Shit, she was already getting to him. Pretty soon, he'd be quoting Gloria Steinem and buying his future daughters GI Joes and Power Rangers rather than Barbies. Or maybe he'd buy them both and let them choose.

Fuck. He was losing his damned mind. Most little girls liked pink and Barbies, and most little boys liked trains and trucks. What was wrong with that?

Nothing. He could almost hear her voice. *But what about the kids who don't?*

Shit, shit, double shit. He didn't want to be evolved. He was fine primordial. He liked primordial. Liberals were too serious and uptight—they couldn't joke about anything. Everyone had to be "the same." But no matter how much you leveled the playing field, equal opportunity wasn't going to bring equal results. Some people were smarter, some people worked harder, and some people were just fucking luckier. Dean hadn't gotten a hall pass. He'd pulled himself out of a shit hole; why couldn't other people be expected to do the same?

Life wasn't fair, and you couldn't make it so. Kids died of cancer. One kid is born in Africa to a life of starvation while another is born in England a prince. He didn't understand why so many people fought against that incontrovertible fact. You had to play the hand life dealt you.

The LC paused his litany of swearing long enough for Dean to tell him the worst of it. "That isn't all."

"What? Do you have more dead bodies to tell me about? Five this week isn't enough?"

"Five?"

"I'll tell you in a minute. First you tell me what else I need to worry about."

"They got a picture of me."

The silence that followed was worse than he had anticipated. Dean had been a SEAL for twelve years, chief for three—senior the last year of that—and had been downrange on some of the most high-risk, no-fail missions in the world since 9/11, and he still felt like squirming. He'd blown it. Bigtime.

"It wasn't very good," he added. "The cell phone was crap and it was taken from a distance, but if they hack into the right database, good facial recognition might be able to make a match."

Finding pictures of active SEALs wasn't easy, but Dean didn't fool himself that someone who was determined—or lucky—might not be able to find something. He was careful about photos, but they existed.

"You got to be fucking kidding me."

As that was rhetorical, Dean didn't respond other than to apologize.

"It's a little fucking late for that now. I can't believe you fucked up like this. Dynomite, Miggy, Dolph, Jim Bob—especially Jim Bob," he said, referring to Travis Hart. "I can see one of them doing this but not you. You don't act stupid over women."

Well, apparently he did. Annie was different, and Dean suspected he could act plenty stupid when it came to her.

"I hope to hell she was worth it, because you just put all of us on the clock," the LC finished angrily.

"She was," Dean said without hesitation. "Is."

He'd finally succeeded in shutting the LC up. He didn't say anything for a long minute. "I'm sorry to hear that," the LC said.

"Why?"

"Because you have to cut her loose and get the hell out of there. Now."

Dean's reaction was visceral. He rejected it with every bone in his body. The hand holding the phone tightened to stone. "I told you I wouldn't do that until she's safe."

"She's safe."

"How can you say that after what I just told you? There were two guys after her—two professionals. Jean Paul must have hired them to shut her up."

"Well, he won't be hiring any more men. That's what I was calling to tell you. I heard from Kate. You and your girlfriend are in the clear. The Stornoway police still want to talk to her, but she isn't a suspect. Kate gave them enough information to point them in the right direction and away from you. They think you are CIA working covertly over here, which they aren't happy about, but Kate got it all worked out. They were suspicious of Jean Paul already. His story started to fall apart as soon as they started questioning him, and the doctors were able to examine his 'injuries,' which appeared to be mostly self-inflicted. He fled the hospital before they could arrest him."

Dean hoped the LC hadn't heard his sigh of relief. "Then Annie is still in danger if he's out there."

"She might have been, but in a spark of divine intervention, Jean Paul was hit by a car a couple blocks from the hospital. A tourist got confused, turned onto the wrong side of the road, and plowed into him as he crossed the street. The officer said the woman was beside herself with guilt until they told her he was wanted for murder."

In other words she'd done them a favor.

"Oh," Dean said. What else could he say? "That's great."

Of course it was. He and Annie could go their own ways. That was what he wanted, wasn't it?

"So you see, she's safe and doesn't need a protector anymore. You can cut her loose with a clear conscience." When Dean didn't respond, he added, "And if it makes it any easier, that's an order."

It didn't. Maybe it should, but it didn't.

"Maybe if we get really lucky," Scott continued, "Jean Paul's phone was destroyed in the accident and the text with your picture never arrived. Give me the number, and I'll have Kate check it out."

Dean repeated the number he'd memorized. He'd pull out the SIM cards, destroy the phones, and toss everything in different trash bins before going back to the room to say . . . what? Good-bye? Nice knowing you?

Fuck.

"Where are you going?" the LC asked.

"I have someone in Glasgow who can get me a new ID." They all had contacts. People who didn't ask questions and didn't care what his name was as long as he could pay. "Then fuck if I know. But Russian subs in the North Sea is a dead end."

"I'm beginning to agree with you. Hang tight when you get to Glasgow, and we'll figure something out."

"You better figure *all* of this out soon, Ace," Dean said, with a rare use of his code name. "I'm not going to live a secret life forever."

Dean could hear the surprise in the LC's voice. "Damn, this girl really got to you, didn't she?"

She did. But there wasn't a damned thing Dean could do about it. Annie was the first woman he'd ever wanted a relationship with, but he was going to have to let her go.

Annie was lounging on the bed in her comfy robe and slippers when "Dan" came back into the room. Her hair was still damp, and her skin had been rubbed with almost the entire bottle of lotion.

Right away, she could tell that something was wrong. He hadn't brought her back that drink he'd promised, and his expression was grim—even for him. He'd stopped at the end of the short hall that led from the door and stood there just staring at her.

"Who died?" she said half jestingly, getting up from the edge of the bed where she'd been sitting.

"Jean Paul."

Her eyes widened with shock. A moment later the relief came. "What? How? That's wonderful. I probably shouldn't say that, but after what he did to Julien and Claude, I'm not going to pretend otherwise." She stopped, tilting her head to look at him. "Why aren't you happier?" Suddenly an explanation occurred to her and she blanched. "Oh God, did they find them already?"

Were there police swirling all over the beach trying to find out who had killed the two men and then tried to dispose of them in the ocean?

He shook his head. "No, no, it's nothing like that." He explained what had happened to Jean Paul and how Dan's contact had cleared everything up with the police.

"This must be a pretty powerful contact."

He shrugged, not taking the bait. "I think the police were already figuring it out on their own. They'll want to talk to you, but you are in the clear. You are safe."

He held her gaze as if trying to tell her something. She drew in a breath that singed her lungs. She knew what this was about. "You're leaving," she said softly.

He nodded.

She shouldn't be surprised. She'd known this was coming. He'd been clear with her from the beginning that he was going to leave, but there was still a small part of her that thought— hoped—it wouldn't come to this. That maybe he would change his mind. That maybe this didn't have to be the end.

All she could do was stare at him, silently begging him not to do this.

But it was like looking into a wall of granite. Eventually she lowered her gaze. "All right."

But it wasn't all right at all.

He must have heard the disappointment in her voice and reacted. "What the fuck else do you want from me, Annie? I told you how it had to be."

She suspected it was defensiveness rather than anger, but that didn't make his crude retort sting any less. He had told her, but that was before this . . . before *them*. Didn't he feel what was happening here?

"I know what you said, but are you so sure that is how it has to be? I know you are hiding from something, and I know it's serious, but there must be a way to help. My stepfather is an important man with all kinds of connections—maybe he can do something. If you just tell me what kind of trouble you are in—"

He didn't let her finish. He took her by the arm and forced her to meet his angry gaze. "There is nothing you can do, and there is nothing your stepfather can do—no matter who he is or who he knows."

"You don't know that. I know you aren't a criminal. The best I can figure is that you are either CIA or—" She stopped and looked at him. "You aren't former military, are you?" Her heart fell. Oh God. He was still in the military. "That's it, isn't it? You are on some kind of covert op and I got in the middle of it, didn't I?"

His expression was almost too still. He released her arm. "You read too many spy novels. You are way off base."

"No, I suspect you are the one off base—*the* base."

She knew enough about Special Operations to know that men didn't typically work on their own. Was he some kind of black ops?

It didn't feel right with what she knew of him. But despite his stoic facade and refusal to address her suspicions, she suspected she was on the right track.

"Think what you want," he said with too much indifference. "It doesn't change the fact that I have to go, and you have to forget about me."

If what she suspected was true, and he was still a SEAL, he was right. She should be the one running for the door.

But she couldn't do that. Instead she took a few steps toward him. He might be everything she thought she didn't want, but apparently her heart hadn't gotten the message. Somewhere along the line Mr. Not Going to Happen had become Mr. Feels Really Right. She couldn't lose him—not without a fight.

He was still standing only partially in the room, almost as if he didn't want to come too close. She could see his muscles draw tight and rigid as she neared. His hands were balled into fists at his side; his nostrils flared as he probably caught a whiff of the lotion she'd doused herself with. His eyes burned hot as he watched her. With anger, but with something else also.

Lust. Desire. Electricity. Whatever that powerful connection was burning between them, it was flaring in full force.

He was trying to fight it, trying to ignore what was between them, but she wasn't going to let him off that easily. If he was going to walk away, she was going to make damned sure he understood exactly what he was walking away from.

"What if I can't do that?" she asked softly. She took a deep, nervous breath, her heart beating tightly in her chest. "What if I think I'm falling in love with you?"

There. She'd said it. She'd put words to the feelings that neither of them wanted to acknowledge.

The silence was deafening, his utter lack of reaction stinging.

Her cheeks were on fire, but she wouldn't let herself feel humiliated. She wasn't going to let him walk away and wonder "what if?" She was going to put it out there. Put herself out there.

"What happened to casual?" he snapped angrily.

Her heart flinched. But anger was good, right? If he didn't care, he wouldn't be mad. He'd be uncomfortable. Embarrassed. Feel sorry for her. But not angry.

She was standing under him now. Close enough to put her hand on the flat of his chest and look up at the day-old gold-flecked dark stubble on his chin. Would she ever get used to the power and size of him? "It has never been casual for me. From the first time you touched me, I knew you were different. And I don't think it's ever been casual for you, either. Can you honestly say that you don't feel anything for me?" His lack of response coupled with the frantic beat of his heart under her hand emboldened her. "I think you care about me, too. I think you want this just as much as I do."

He gritted his teeth, wrapped his hand around her wrist, and pulled it from his chest to her side. It was harsh but not hurtful. He knew his strength. He was in control even when furious. Even when she was forcing him to acknowledge something he didn't want to acknowledge. Something he might not be able to walk away from so easily.

"I think you've confused good sex with something else. We barely know each other. You're a nice girl, Annie, but . . ."

Ouch. She stepped back. If he was trying to push her away, he was doing a fantastic job. She felt skewered. Her already shaky confidence faltered.

But he was lying—purposefully downplaying his feelings—to make a clean break of it . . . wasn't he? Or had she been wrong? Had she imbued him with feelings that were only one-sided?

She lifted her chin to meet his gaze. She would know from looking into his eyes, right? "So that's it? After everything we've been through, you are just going to walk away? Leave and never look back? It was nice knowing you—is that it?"

She'd never seen his face look so dark. He was almost shaking as he yelled at her. "Yes, that's exactly what I'm going to do, damn it."

He meant it. She could see the truth in his gaze, and she felt a stab of finality plunge through her heart.

Her eyes were hot, her throat burning and tight as she turned around. "Okay. If that's what you have to do, go—" Her voice broke. "Please just go."

She'd done everything she could do, but she couldn't fight for them both. He had to want to make it work, too. She'd told him her feelings, and it hadn't changed anything. He was determined to go through with this, whether he cared for her or not.

She hoped it wasn't not, but it certainly felt that way right now.

What had she expected? Him to pull her in his arms, and tell her he was falling in love with her, too, and they would find a way to work it out together?

She bit her lip. Maybe a little.

Okay, maybe a lot. No matter how unrealistic that might have been.

She'd tried, but he'd shot her down.

She just wished it didn't have to hurt so much.

She steeled herself for the slam of the door that would bring an end to it. Whatever "it" might have been.

Thirty

Dean knew it was wrong. He should just leave.

But he couldn't.

He'd never felt so helpless in his life. She had him all twisted up in knots and unable to think straight.

The subtle taunt of her body pressed against his had been hard enough to resist. Did she have any idea how sexy she looked in that damned robe and how much he wanted to rip it open and see if she was as naked as he suspected she was? She smelled incredible. All clean and girlie. He wanted to bury his face in her damp hair and breathe in every inch of her.

It had been fucking torture not to take her up on the "take me" look in her eyes. He wanted her something fierce, and it had only grown worse since he'd had her. Now he knew exactly what he was missing.

And then she'd had to make it even worse with that little confession. *"What if I think I'm falling in love with you?"*

Christ, that was the last thing he wanted to hear. Except for one long heartbeat it hadn't been. It had been about the best thing he'd ever heard, and he'd wanted to put his arms around her, cradle her against his chest, and kiss her until she was damned sure.

But he'd pulled his head out of his ass and would have left, if the shimmer of tears in her eyes as she told him to go to hell hadn't cut him to the quick. All the pretense, all the bull-shit, was stripped away. Gone. He couldn't lie to her or to himself.

She wasn't wrong. It wasn't casual. It never had been. From the first the connection between them had been different. It had only grown stronger as they'd gotten to know each other. A week, a month, a year, it wouldn't make a damned bit of difference. It was there, and he couldn't let her think other-wise.

He reached for her, and then it was too late. He couldn't change his mind if he'd wanted to. She was in his arms, his mouth was on hers, she was under him, and he was inside her again. Thrusting. Pounding. Loving.

Over and over. All night long. Telling her with his body what he could not with his words.

I want you.

I need you.

And then sometime near dawn when her legs were wrapped around his neck and he was pinned deep inside her making her come for the last time, *I . . .*

Shit.

I can't.

Annie thought she'd won. Somewhere in the middle of the night, the lovemaking turned from fierce to gentle. The hard, powerful thrusts grew longer. Slower. More rhythmic. His hands caressed . . . cradled . . . lingered. The heat in his eyes softened, his gaze never leaving her face.

He cared about her. He couldn't make love to her like this and not care about her. It was in every gentle touch, every tender kiss, every deep stroke as he laid claim to more and more of her heart.

The swell of emotion in her chest was too powerful to deny. Too clear not to recognize. She *was* falling in love with him. And he was falling in love with her, too. He couldn't turn his back on this now.

Her fingers gripped. Clenched. Dug into the unyielding

muscle of his shoulders, his arms, his back. Pleading—no, demanding with every stroke.

Don't go.

His body was pressing down on her, solid and heavy. And hot. So incredibly hot. She arched. Pressed. Her body needing to absorb every thrust.

Stay here . . . right here.

It was so perfect. If she could just hold on . . .

He was inside her. Stretching her. Filling her. Each thrust touching a deeper and deeper part of her until she couldn't hold on any longer. Until the sensations were too much. The pleasure too intense. The feelings too powerful.

She felt his final thrust. This one deeper. More forceful.

Mine.

Yours.

She couldn't hold on any longer and let go. He gave her what she wanted. Everything. Holding nothing back. The guttural cry that tore from his lungs was so acute, so overwhelming and all-encompassing, it almost sounded of pain. But it wasn't. She could feel the force of his pleasure, the raw power of his climax, as it reverberated through them both. She let it fill her, join with her own as the shuddering spasms intensified.

When it was all over, there was nothing left to be said. Nothing that needed to be said. It was all right there in the sated collapse of naked bodies and entwined limbs.

She hadn't been wrong. She knew it with every fiber of her being. This meant something. *They* meant something. He'd told her in every way that mattered except for words.

She just hadn't heard what else he was telling her.

A nnie woke to emptiness.

She knew even before her hand reached to the side and landed not on a warm, naked chest, but on the cool, crisp cotton of a sheet that hadn't been lain on for a long time.

He was gone.

She opened her eyes, shying from the light as much as from

confirmation. But the evidence was as plain as day: she was alone. Her things—what she had of them—had been removed from his backpack and were stacked neatly on the dresser next to the TV.

She sucked in her breath. Cold and sharp, the air pricked her chest like needles in a pincushion. The pain was oddly welcome. She was surprised that she could feel at all. The rest of her was numb.

So this was it? This was how it ended? Waking up alone in bed after the most amazing night of her life?

The cruelty of reality overwhelmed her. All she could do was lie there, the sheet pulled up to her chin as if she could hide from the truth, blink back the pain, and fight the tears that rose up the back of her throat in a fist of tightness and heat.

Last night had been so perfect she'd thought . . .

God, she was such an idiot. She'd completely misread what he'd been trying to tell her. He hadn't been making her promises; he'd been telling her good-bye. It had been there in every lingering touch, every sweet stroke, every poignant kiss—she just hadn't been listening. She'd only heard what she wanted to hear.

She thought that if she forced him to confront his feelings, he wouldn't be able to walk away. But real life wasn't a romance novel. He might care for her—and might have given in to their passion temporarily—but it hadn't changed anything. Whatever he was involved with, it was bigger than her. Bigger than them.

He was right. Maybe she did live in Fantasyland. At her core, Annie was an idealist. She thought that if two people cared about each other, they could find a way. That there were no problems too big to be overcome. That if he cared about her—maybe even loved her—he wouldn't be able to walk away, no matter what kind of trouble he was in or mission he was on.

But that wasn't the way the world worked. He'd been telling her that from the start. Mr. Tell-it-like-it-is, not how she wanted it to be. She just hadn't wanted to believe him.

She believed him now.

She wiped angry tears from her cheeks. She was angrier with herself than with him. She had no right to be hurt. No right to be disappointed. He'd never made her any promises—the opposite actually. He'd told her exactly how it was going to be.

She was the one who'd let herself get carried away. She'd tried to keep her distance. Tried to keep it casual. Tried to keep her feelings under control. But just because she'd done a horrible job of it didn't mean he owed her anything.

Not even a good-bye.

She lay back down and curled up in a ball on the bed. If she didn't get up, maybe it would just be a bad dream.

But the dampness on her pillow told her the tears were real.

God, how had she let this happen? How had she let herself think it could work? She *knew* better. The mission always came first with men like him. But she'd convinced herself it would be different—that *he* would be different. She'd relaxed her guard. Made herself vulnerable. Let herself need someone. She'd let herself rely on him—something she hadn't let herself do since she was a child.

Which was fine when they were in danger. But it wasn't so great when they weren't.

For the second time in her life, a bigger-than-life, I-can-do-anything man she thought she could count on had left her. Ironically for opposite reasons. Her father because he'd turned out to be only too human, and "Dan" because he'd turned out to be too strong. Too much the cold, hard professional "machine" she'd accused him of being. The operator who could turn off his emotions for the sake of the mission. He might care for her, but he wouldn't let that interfere with what he had to do.

She wanted to hate him for it, but how could she hate the very qualities that made him the man he was?

She'd been right about him in the beginning. Guys like him were good at coming to the rescue. They were who you'd want by your side when the shit hit the fan. But when it was over, they moved on to the next one just like superheroes. There was a reason it took Superman sixty years to finally marry Lois Lane. Batman was still single.

So now what?

Annie wiped the tears from her cheeks and sat up. This puddle-of-tears, abandoned girl wasn't her. She was devastated, but she wouldn't lie here in misery.

She had to pull on her big-girl panties and suck it up. Face reality. He was gone and not coming back.

She might feel weak and helpless at the moment, but she wasn't. She was a strong, capable, grown woman who knew how to be happy on her own. She might have *wanted* a life with him, but she didn't *need* it.

But the "girl power" pep talk wasn't helping right now. Right now she was too raw. Too fragile. Too hurt. But tomorrow she would hone her inner Scarlett and maybe feel a little better, the next day a little more, and so on.

She hoped.

She needed to talk to the one person in the world who would understand. She picked up the phone and put the collect call through.

"Hi, Mom. It's me." Even before the last two words were out, tears were choking her throat. She was that heartbroken, disillusioned teenage girl again who'd had the rug pulled out from under her feet.

Ten minutes she would allow herself. Then she would be an adult again. But there was nothing like a mother's love and understanding to make it feel safe to be a kid again.

Thirty-one

It took an hour. But when Annie finally ended the phone call with her mother, she was feeling considerably better and lucid enough to make a few decisions.

The first was a shower. When she was done, she would begin making preparations to return to the scene of the crime, so to speak.

After bursting into tears and choking through a truncated version of the past few days—and assuring her mother a hundred times that she was physically unharmed and safe—Annie had spent the last half of the conversation talking her mother out of hopping on her stepfather's private plane to come get her.

Annie loved her stepfather, but his kind of wealth embarrassed her. It embarrassed her mother, too, except—apparently—when it came to her daughter. Annie wasn't surprised to hear that a private search team had already been mobilized. Her mother agreed to call that off, but stopping her from jumping on the plane was like pulling a meaty bone from a pit bull.

When pointing out the number of wasted and unnecessary carbon emissions from taking a private plane across the ocean didn't get through to her, Annie had to risk hurting her feelings. She loved her mother and promised to come home soon, but she needed some time on her own, and she wanted to finish what she'd started. She'd come to Scotland to protest exploratory drilling in the Western Hebrides, and she wasn't going to leave without doing that. She promised no more Lucy Lawless, but she could join the protests and marches that were being planned for the next week.

Besides, she needed to pick up her stuff and talk to the police. There was a stack of twenties—about two hundred dollars— and a ferry timetable on the bureau beside her clothes, presumably for her to do that.

He'd thought of everything.

Annie had kept her comments about "Dan" brief, not telling her mother any of her suspicions, only that he was in hiding and in some kind of trouble. Her mother had as many questions as she had—none of which she could answer. Annie did tell her that she was almost certain that it didn't involve anything illegal.

Then had come the one question that Annie was still thinking about. "Do you want me to have Steve try to find him, sweetheart?"

Steve was Annie's stepfather. As she'd told "Dan," he was a powerful man with lots of connections.

Annie had hesitated, but only for a minute. "No," she'd told her mother. She'd already held her heart out on a platter once. She wasn't going to let it be chopped in pieces again. He'd left. She wouldn't go chasing after him. Besides her pride, she didn't want to cause him any more problems. She owed him that for helping her.

Annie was putting the finishing touches on her eye makeup— a salvage effort—when the phone rang. Her mother had said she would call back to check on her. Annie wasn't surprised to hear "that everything had been arranged."

She groaned. "Oh, Mom, what did you do?"

"Don't use that exasperated tone with me, missy. If you aren't going to let me fly out there, I'm going to make sure you are taken care of any way I can. All I did was call the concierge. You have the room paid for as long as you need it, food will be on its way as soon as you are ready, since I know you forget to eat when you are upset, and I'm having money wired to a local bank. The concierge has already agreed to arrange to have it brought to you. There is a plane ticket waiting for you at the airport to Lewis for this afternoon's flight. It must be a small plane because there weren't any first-class or business seats. By the time you show up, Steve should have the passport issue taken care of."

Annie stopped, feeling the tears welling up again. "You are a force of nature, Alice."

"Thank you."

Annie hadn't necessarily meant it as a compliment. But they both knew that.

"You are my only child," her mother said softly.

Annie sighed. "I know. But first class? Jeez, I would have looked like a bag lady—literally—showing up with all my things in a plastic hotel dry-cleaning bag." She paused. "I had to leave the new duffel you got me on the ship. I'm sure the police have it in evidence now."

The reminder of the pink bag brought back unwelcome memories. Painful reminders of "real men" and "girlie" colors. She'd loved how they could disagree and still find ways to tease each other. She'd never had that before.

She still didn't have it.

"Annie?"

She could hear the worry in her mother's voice.

"You still there?"

"I'm here," she assured her quickly and brightly, not wanting to have to talk her off the private plane again. "Thank you, Mom. I appreciate it. Really I do."

Her mother harrumphed. "You are welcome. Call me when you are leaving. And if you change your mind, I can be there—"

"I know," she said, cutting her off. A knock on the door startled her. For one foolish heartbeat she thought . . . But then she realized whom she was talking to and sighed. "Your room service is here," she told her mom.

"I didn't order room service. I said you would call when you wanted it sent up."

The foolish heartbeat was back. Stronger this time. Oh God, what if it was . . .

"I'll call you back," Annie said, and hung up, not giving her mother time to argue.

She practically ran to the door, heart in her throat, her entire body fluttery and jumpy. Did he reconsider? Had he come back to tell her he'd made a mistake?

She looked through the peephole, and her heart sank. It wasn't him, although she had no doubt that the man standing there had been sent by him.

Resolved, heart hardened, Annie opened the door.

The LC was going to be pissed. Dean shouldn't be hanging around, but he couldn't leave without making sure Annie was taken care of.

He sat on one of the benches along the waterfront, facing toward the harbor while keeping his head turned just enough to watch the entrance to the hotel where the man he'd sent had gone through about thirty minutes ago.

He wasn't hungry, but every now and then he broke off a piece of a Styrofoam-like bagel to chew on and took a swig of lukewarm coffee to wash it down. He didn't want anyone to wonder what he was doing. But there were enough people about enjoying the clear morning to not make him too conspicuous.

Still it was a risk. An unnecessary risk, the LC would definitely say, but not to his mind. He needed to do this. He couldn't just walk away. He had to make sure she was all right. Taken care of. Protected.

Leaving her like that, all naked and trusting and curled in his arms, had been one of the hardest things he'd ever had to do. Especially knowing that she was going to hate him when she woke up. He'd abandoned her just as surely as her father had. He told himself he didn't have a choice, but that wouldn't matter to her. He was gone whatever the excuse.

With her too-accurate suspicions of what he did, Dean knew how hard it must have been for her to put her faith in a man like him after what she'd been through. He'd kept his word, but he'd abandoned her all the same.

Because he'd fucked up and not followed orders, because he couldn't keep his head down and had to get involved, someone else had been hurt. He wouldn't regret it in Annie's case—if he hadn't been there she could have been in real trouble—but he should have had better control. He should have kept their relationship at a distance.

Right. He would have had more luck trying to sell Texans jerseys at a Cowboys game.

He looked at his watch again. Forty minutes. What the fuck was going on in there? He was anxious and doing his best to contain it, but he felt like a time bomb about to explode.

Guilt was not a small part of it.

But what else could he have done? It would never have worked out. He was supposed to be dead and he and his surviving teammates—as well as anyone close to him—could be in danger if the people who'd tried to kill them found out they weren't all dead.

He could have asked her to wait for him, but that wouldn't be fair to her. Who knew when this would all be over, and wait for what? Was he ready to leave Nine? The team was the only family he'd ever known.

No, it was better this way. Annie would go back home and forget about him just as he was going to do. It might hurt like a motherfucker now, but it would go away. Eventually.

At least that was what he kept telling himself.

He looked at his watch again—0835 hours. Forty-five minutes.

Fuck it. He'd had enough. He pulled out his phone, intending to call the room, when the door opened and she walked out.

The pain was visceral. It reminded him of the fiery blast in Russia that had blown him back at least ten feet. He would have staggered if he'd been standing.

She was wearing that black dress and sweater again. It looked just as stunning as it had the night they went out to dinner, but this time it made him think of mourning.

Her dark hair was slicked back and twisted into a knot at the back of her head, but the short strands were fighting confinement and a few had broken free to catch the morning sunshine around her head. She was too far away to see her face, but he swore he could see the red rims around the brilliant green.

His gaze was too fixed on Annie to pay more than cursory attention to the uniformed officer that he'd had Kate arrange by her side.

It was also too fixed to notice the woman who'd come up to stand in front of him. "Hey, you're up early. I hope there weren't any problems last night?" It took him a moment to recognize the receptionist from check-in. "With your room?" she added helpfully.

"No, it was fine." He tried to brush her off brusquely, but the girl wasn't noticing.

He glanced toward Annie. Fuck, the officer was opening the door for her. She was about to get in the car and drive off. Forever. And he felt as if he was watching the best thing that had ever happened to him get away.

The officer said something, and Annie looked up in his direction, which also happened to be Dean's direction.

Her gaze flickered on the woman and then . . .

Oh fuck. To him.

He was too far away to read her expression, but her body's reaction said it all. She seemed to gasp and visibly stiffen.

He felt as if he'd slapped her.

What would she do? Would she call out to him? Come running toward him? Would she cry, bang on his chest, and demand to know why he'd made love to her like that and walked out after?

Would she unintentionally blow his cover and give him away to the policeman?

She did none of those things. She turned away as if he weren't there. Telling him what he already knew: it was over.

Thirty-two

He'd sent a babysitter.

Annie had known as soon as she saw the uniformed officer through the peephole that Dan was responsible. He might not be able to see her safely back to Lewis, but he had sent someone who would.

He thought of everything, all right, and covered all his bases. The quintessential operator, always watching his "six," even when he was walking away.

That he'd stayed to make sure his babysitter found her only made it worse. Seeing him had sent a fresh whipcord of pain shooting through her all over again. But she didn't delude herself that it meant anything. He was just finishing the mission like a good operator. She didn't want his guilt.

Annie's babysitter was a thirtyish sergeant from Police Scotland's Oban office, which was part of the Argyll and West Dunbartonshire division. Sergeant Brooks had been conscripted into service early this morning by the assistant chief constable and told very little other than that she was an important witness to the double murder and now international terrorist plot whom he was to escort to Lewis, where he would be met by Ministry of Defense Police (MDP) and other local officers.

Reading between the lines, Annie figured Sergeant Brooks

had the misfortune of being close, qualified (he was authorized to carry a firearm), and available.

If he'd recognized her face from the papers, he didn't let on—nor did he treat her as a recent suspect. He was polite, professional, and apparently not much on small talk—which suited her fine in her present mood.

Over the long hours they sat waiting in the small regional airport for their flight to Lewis, they probably exchanged no more than a dozen words. It wasn't until right before they landed when he mentioned his two young daughters that his dour, nondescript face brightened with a smile. He was positively beaming with pride at her genuine admiration as he showed her the phone pictures of the two redheaded and adorable twins. She hadn't noticed until then that he had quite a bit of red in his brown hair. The girls were about six—five and a half, he later told her—and were about to start school in the fall. She took it that the girls' mother was more excited about that than he was.

"Lots of trouble out there for young lassies," he said somberly.

Annie could hardly argue with that.

Admiring someone's children had a way of breaking the ice, and the sergeant was considerably more animated for the rest of their journey. He told her a little about the organization of the police force in Scotland and gave her an idea of what she could expect when they arrived.

Annie wanted to be angry with Dan for his guilt-motivated protective services, but she had to admit the presence of the sergeant wasn't entirely unwelcome. She knew Jean Paul was dead, but the armed officer did provide some comfort after all she'd been through in the past week.

It was with genuine gratitude that she thanked the sergeant for his safe escort when they arrived at Lewis and were met by local police and MDP officers.

From Sergeant Brooks, she'd learned that the MDP was a separate civilian—not military—special police force tasked with, among other things, policing high-security sites from nuclear facilities to military facilities and oil and gas terminals around the UK. They were involved because of the oil drilling operations. Unlike most police officers in Scotland, the MDP were heavily armed and reported to the UK government rather than to the Scottish government—neither of which played well to the local population.

She was introduced to a few others (two men and one woman) when they reached the station. They weren't identified by the local chief inspector, but Annie marked them as "spooks," aka MI5. Or would it be MI6, which like the US CIA dealt with matters outside domestic boundaries?

She didn't know, and it didn't really matter. For the next three hours she answered all their questions about Jean Paul, Claude, and Julien as best she could. Unfortunately, as she'd been kept completely out of the loop—or cell, in this case—she didn't know much. Julien had never told her about his family or background. Now she understood why.

The MI agents also asked quite a few questions about the man who'd helped her. There wasn't much she could tell them other than he'd saved her life. What she'd guessed, she kept to herself. She wasn't going to be the one to blow his cover. Whatever he was mixed up with, it was obviously serious and dangerous.

She hated that he'd left her, but she didn't want to see him killed.

Maybe he wasn't the only one acting protectively.

The men questioning her seemed to know more than they were letting on as well, but they didn't press her too hard. Dan's contact must have a very long and strong reach.

It probably didn't hurt that they'd learned who her stepfather was as well. Well-known billionaires had a way of making people overly ingratiating, which was one of the reasons she rarely mentioned him.

It was close to eight when the authorities finally finished questioning her. They were happy to hear that she didn't intend to leave right away and said they might have some questions for her over the next few days as the investigation progressed.

Her pink bag was returned—along with her things from the guest house, which had been seized when she was a murder suspect—and a young constable offered to take her to a hotel.

She was glad he didn't suggest the Harbour Bar & Guest House, which had too many memories. He took her to the Stornoway Hotel, where a room was waiting for her.

Her mother had been busy.

Annie had had very little to eat over the past twenty-four hours and didn't object when the very effusive manager told her a late dinner was being prepared for her.

After forcing a few bites of the vegetarian pasta dish down, she collapsed on the bed and fell asleep moments after her head hit the pillow.

It had been a long and difficult day. Tomorrow would be better.

But God, how long would it take for her to stop looking over her shoulder, wondering if he would ever show up again?

And when would she stop missing him?

Dean didn't know what was wrong with him. After getting rid of the receptionist in Oban, he'd caught the train to Glasgow, found a cheap hotel to sleep in, and made contact with the guy who was going to take care of getting him new docs. His passport would be ready in a couple of hours.

Everything was proceeding smoothly. He'd gotten away with minimal damage—and if that picture turned out not to have gone beyond Jean Paul's phone, no damage. So why the hell couldn't he relax? Why was he going over every detail of the past few days, feeling as if he'd missed something?

He couldn't let go of the feeling that he'd made a mistake.

What had happened to his hard truths? He didn't waste time by dwelling on things he couldn't change. He'd always been able to accept and move on. It was one of his greatest strengths, enabling him to mentally adjust quickly to changing circumstances. On an op, those changing circumstances almost always meant when things went to shit.

But this with Annie . . . ? His mind wasn't adjusting, and it definitely wasn't moving on twenty-four hours later. It was dwelling, big-time.

Frustrated, he decided to walk the forty minutes to the

East End, where he was meeting his contact, rather than take a local train or cab. It was raining, or rather that drizzly mist-like rain that Scotland was famous for, but wet and uncomfortable were something he barely noticed anymore. He'd had it beaten out of him in BUD/S thirteen years ago.

They were meeting at a pub near Celtic Park Stadium, the legendary home of the Celtic Football (aka soccer) Club. Though it wasn't game day, Dean had been cautioned against wearing Ranger blue and red. The fierce rivalry between the two Glaswegian clubs was serious business with a sectarian component that he hadn't been aware of. He thought Protestant and Catholic crap like that only existed in Northern Ireland, but apparently Glasgow had its share.

The East End wasn't the best part of Glasgow, but despite recent proof to the contrary, Dean did know how to keep his head down, and he was a bigger target than most "Neds" (a derogatory term for Scottish hooligans who had a penchant for track suits) wanted to fuck with.

The sites along London Road covered the gamut of residential, business, and industrial, but like with many parts of Glasgow, the main theme was red brick. Lots of it.

Like Liverpool in the south, Glasgow had made its mark as one of the great industrial cities, and it still retained some of its grit. Most people preferred the "nicer" Edinburgh, but Dean liked the working-class vibe of Glasgow. It was a long way from east Texas, but he could relate to the values, toughness, and underdog fighting spirit.

Dean arrived at the appointed time, found a booth, and ordered a pint of ale while he waited. The reason for choosing this place was clear. It was packed with men—women were a rarity at these kinds of working-class pubs—who didn't give a shit and were too drunk to remember even if they did.

His contact was a few minutes late, but the transaction was completed before his glass was empty. The kid—these guys seemed to be getting younger every time—made his living by not asking questions, and once Dean had assured himself of the quality, there was no reason to stick around.

Now that he had what he needed, there was no reason for *him* to stick around. He could set up his new bank account online. He recalled Annie's mention of the e-mail from her bank. He'd been too pissed about the tattoo and her accessing her e-mail to think about it. It didn't seem significant, but he texted the LC to have Kate check it out anyway. He wasn't going to leave any stone unturned.

He was almost back at his hotel when his phone vibrated with a return text. He pulled it out and looked at the one-word response: Belfast.

Shit. Dean had his marching orders. He knew what he had to do. Even if every instinct in his body fought against it.

He went inside and loaded up.

Annie had become a minor celebrity among the Stornoway activist community, as she found out when she arrived at camp and was immediately surrounded.

It wasn't the kind of attention she wanted, but her fellow protesters were so genuinely horrified by everything she'd gone through and supportive that she patiently answered their questions and retold the story a couple of times.

The biggest welcome—and biggest surprise—was the hug from Marie. As part of the graduate student group that had traveled with Julien from America, she and Sergio had been questioned by the police extensively. But like Annie, the two Italian grad students had both been completely in the dark about what Julien, Jean Paul, and Claude really intended. Marie's connection to the group had been a short-lived romance with Claude that had fizzled into friendship and a shared interest in the environment. She and her cousin Sergio—a fellow grad student—had been completely shocked by Julien's and Claude's connection to OPF.

It was oddly comforting to know that Annie hadn't been the only one duped, and the two women bonded as they joined the group making signs for the big event that was taking place that weekend. According to Marie, she'd heard they hoped to have nearly five hundred people in town by then. The camp had already doubled in size since she left last Saturday.

God, had it only been five days?

So much had changed.

Martin, the director of a big marine conservation group here in the UK who was kind of serving as head honcho of the camp, asked her if she would be willing to give a few TV interviews to help get publicity for the event.

The aging English hippie bore an uncanny resemblance to the ice-cream guru Ben—or was it Jerry?—with his beard and curly brown hair that receded in a wide path to the back of his head.

He must have read her hesitation. "I know you probably don't want to talk about it, but I think it could really help raise awareness. The media are trying to portray us as a bunch of crazy terrorists, but when people see you . . ." He shrugged. "I think it will put a positive spin on the story. We don't want to do anything illegal—we just want to get our message across. I know a little about your research. Maybe you could try to slip that in as well."

He was right. Talking about it was the last thing she wanted to do—especially on TV. Nothing like telling the whole world you were an idiot.

"Could I think about it?" she asked.

"Sure. Take all the time you need as long as it's by tomorrow—and I'm going to keep trying to convince you in the interim."

She smiled. "Deal."

He started to walk away, but then turned back. "Hey, do you dive?"

She nodded.

"A few of us are headed to the *Stassa* wreck on Harris later this afternoon. We have room for one more if you are interested. Marie is going."

"I'm a novice," Marie said. "Julien told me you were some kind of expert."

Her thoughts immediately went to her Texan SEAL. "I'm not a professional—more of an enthusiast."

Again she hesitated. She wasn't exactly in a social mood.

But the lure of a wreck dive was tempting—especially the *Stassa*. It was one of the "must do" dives she'd hoped to find time to do while she was here.

"Come on," Marie said. "It will be fun."

Annie hadn't had a lot of that. The stay on Tiree had been painfully brief. Besides, she could use the distraction.

She nodded, and both Marie and Martin looked pleased.

Thirty-three

The hairs at the back of Dean's neck were buzzing as he made his way through the terminal. *There's nothing to worry about,* he told himself. He'd done everything he could. Jean Paul was dead. Annie wasn't in danger.

Move on. Focus. He had a job to do—which included watching his own skin. He needed to calm down and stop looking like a meth addict crawling the walls for a fix or he was going to draw attention to himself.

An airport in the twenty-first century was not the place to act suspicious. Normally Dean avoided them because of the heightened security, preferring softer border checkpoints—or no border checkpoints. But as he didn't have access to a boat anymore, and it wasn't an international flight (Northern Ireland being part of the UK), he decided to take his chances rather than traveling three hours to the south of Scotland to catch a ferry that would take another few hours.

He got himself under control, and his new British passport passed the ID check without comment.

Everything was fine until he got in line to board the budget airline for the 1345 to Belfast and the buzzing intensified. His spidey senses weren't just flaring; they were going crazy, telling him to turn back. That something wasn't right.

He'd stayed alive for almost fourteen years by knowing

when to listen to his instincts, and he wasn't going to start ignoring them now.

He stepped out of line and found an empty gate where he could make the call.

"That was fast," the LC said after they'd exchanged the code.

Dean paused. "I'm still in Glasgow."

There was a return pause, where Dean was pretty sure Taylor was fighting to stay calm. "What's the holdup?"

In other words, he'd sent him the text a few hours ago, and he should be on his way to Belfast by now. They might operate on a four-hour string in Honolulu, but the LC had expected him to be wheels up in more like one.

"I can't go."

That apparently exhausted the limits of the LC's stay-calm reserves. "What the hell do you mean, you can't go? Blake's damned not-so-estranged sister just published another story, and I need someone to shut her up."

"Donovan will have to take care of it." Dynomite and Blake had been BUD/S buddies. If anyone could take care of Blake's sister, it should be him.

"He's occupied."

"So am I." He bit back some of his anger and tried to explain. "I can't stand down on this, Ace. Something's wrong— or it feels like something is wrong—and I can't go until I'm sure Annie is okay. Hasn't anyone ever . . . ?" *Gotten under your skin? Made you lose your head?* "Fuck, I don't expect you to understand, but I can't let this go."

He couldn't let *her* go.

There was a long enough silence where Dean wondered whether maybe the LC did understand. Was it Kate? Or maybe this other woman who'd warned them?

Eventually Taylor responded, "You can't stand down on a lot of things."

His tone was more wry than sarcastic, but Dean immediately stiffened. "Go ahead and say it."

"What?"

"What you've been wanting to say for over two months. It

was my fault the kid was killed. If I'd followed your orders, Brian would still be alive, and you and the others wouldn't have been almost killed pulling me out of there."

"The kid wasn't a kid—he was a twenty-four-year-old highly trained, elite operative. He made his own decision to follow you. His death isn't on you." The LC's voice was so tight and angry that it sounded as if he was gritting his teeth. "I'm only going to say this once, so put down that whip for a few minutes and listen up. You didn't do anything that I didn't want to do or wouldn't have done if I were in your position. Damn it, do you think I wanted to leave them there? I wanted to try to warn White's squad every bit as badly as you did, but as the officer in charge I was responsible for the mission and saving the lives of the men I could. But you go with your gut. You act when most people are still sitting around, trying to figure out what to do. That's what makes you so good."

Dean was shocked. He didn't know what to say.

But a whip? Was that what he'd been doing?

"No one blames you for Murphy's death," Taylor continued. "If you hadn't stopped in the yard, we would all have been in that building and died. Think about that."

Dean did.

"If you want to keep beating yourself up about it, that's up to you. But if it starts making you second-guess your decisions and affecting your performance, then it becomes my problem. But, Tex?" Dean waited. "Disobey another direct order from me like that again, and I'll see your ass in the brig. Understood?"

Dean knew he was getting off lightly. They both knew if they got out of this, Taylor could have his ass. "Roger that, sir."

"Don't fucking start with the 'sir.' You'll make me self-conscious."

"Does that mean you are all right with me going back to Lewis?"

"No, I'm sure as hell not all right with it. But you gotta do what you gotta do, and I'm not going to try to stop you."

And he trusted him. That was what he wasn't saying. But Dean heard it, and it meant more than he'd thought it would. He and the LC would never be best buddies, and undoubtedly they would lock horns again, but they trusted and respected each other. That was what mattered.

"I'll call you if Kate has anything. And, Tex?" Taylor paused. "In answer to your question, yes, someone has."

The LC had already hung up when Dean realized what he meant. He'd asked him "if anyone had ever . . . ?"

So the LC wasn't immune, either. Someone had gotten to him.

It was nice to know Taylor was human. He was so buttoned up and by the book, sometimes Dean wondered. Distance from the men was part of being an officer, but except for Colt, the LC kept himself apart more than usual.

Dean had changed his ticket and was waiting at the gate for his 1400 flight to Lewis to board.

It was thirty minutes delayed, which was why he was in cell range and not thirty thousand feet up when the call came through that confirmed what his gut had been telling him. It wasn't over.

This was a mistake.

Annie had spent most of the ninety-minute drive from Stornoway to the small fishing village of Rodel in South Harris trying to have a good time. The seven other protesters in the rented minibus certainly were. But she didn't feel like humming songs until someone guessed the tune or laughing along with the others at the range of vocal abilities. She just wanted to be alone to think. To gaze at the coastline and the crashing waves from the beach or the privacy of her hotel window, not watching it blow by in a blur from a car window.

She wasn't ready for company, she realized. She was still in the licking-wounds stage.

"You're very quiet, Dr. Henderson."

It took Annie a moment to realize the woman was addressing her. She wasn't used to her new title. But as proud as she was of all the work that had gone into her PhD, she was going to be the type who only used "doctor" in formal academic or research situations.

"Annie, please," she said. "I guess I'm more tired than I realized."

"Not surprising," the woman said, turning from her place in the passenger seat to give Annie a smile. "After all that you've been through. But I'm glad that Martin invited you to come along."

"Me, too," Annie lied, returning the older woman's smile. She'd been surprised to see that Julien and Jean Paul's friend Sofie was part of the dive group. Annie hadn't seen her since that night and had assumed she'd left. But apparently Sofie had a thing going with Martin. They seemed an odd pairing, but it was none of her business.

Annie wondered whether Sofie had been questioned by the police, too, but no one had mentioned it.

"As the only American in the group, you'll have to tell us what you think about the latest story," Sofie said.

Annie didn't understand. "What story?"

"You must not have seen the news today," Martin said. "It's all over the papers."

"There's another article about your lost legion," Marie explained, clearly amused. "What do you think? Is it true?"

"I have no idea," Annie said.

"They even posted a picture of the reporter's missing brother with a few other men she claims not to be able to locate," Sofie added.

Annie tried to act interested when her mind was other places. "Really?"

Sofie passed the paper back to her. "It isn't very good quality. You can't really see their faces."

"Who needs to see their faces?" another woman in the van said with a wag of her eyebrows. Annie hadn't caught her name, but she sounded English. Or Scottish. Or Irish. Annie hadn't really gotten the accent distinctions down, and she'd learned not to ask. If she guessed wrong—no matter what it was—people tended to get offended.

Annie understood what the woman meant immediately. The photo was of four men on a beach. They were dragging a sailboat from the water and all wore board shorts, baseball hats, and sunglasses. And nothing else. All four were exceptionally well built. Um. *Exceptionally* well built.

She scanned the photo quickly and then slowed as something processed. Her heart stopped and she sucked in her breath as her eyes went back to the second man from the right.

Oh . . . my . . . God.

She felt the blood drain from her face as she took in the familiar physique—minus the scars and burn marks. She would know those broad shoulders, muscular arms, and six-pack abs even if she didn't also recognize the bearded jaw, broad smile, and blue hat. Although this hat was new and still had the Dallas Cowboys star patch on it. She wrinkled her nose with distaste. That explained the beaten-up, old-school-uniform powder blue cap with the missing logo.

She noted the names below the picture from left to right: Brandon Blake, John Donovan, Dean Baylor, and Michael Ruiz.

Dean Baylor. Dan was Dean. Her heart squeezed. Finally she at least knew his name.

Suddenly the rest hit her, and everything fell into place. He was one of the SEALs who'd supposedly vanished. That was why he was hiding. That was why he'd walked away from her.

It all made sense. He didn't want her mixed up in whatever had caused him and the other survivors to go into hiding.

"Is something wrong?" Sofie asked. "You look as if you've seen a ghost."

Annie shook her head, forcing herself out of the daze although her mind was still reeling. "I was just reading the article. It's interesting, but I'm afraid I have no more insight than anyone else on whether it's true." She forced a light-hearted laugh from a chest that was beating like a war drum. "But it certainly makes a good story."

"It certainly does," Martin agreed as a big gray building—from the sign, apparently a hotel—appeared on the road in front of them. He turned into a small parking lot overlooking the water. There were a few other cars around, but the hotel itself appeared to be permanently closed. "We're here."

Annie was glad for the interruption. As they climbed out of the minibus, she tried to process what she'd learned. Did this explain why Dean had left or was she just trying to make excuses for him and deluding herself again? What if the truth was that he really didn't care about her?

Now that she knew who he was, did that really make a difference?

The group unpacked their gear and made their way down the grassy path from the parking lot to the pier where the chartered boat was already waiting for them in the small harbor.

In her short stay in the Western Isles, Annie had grown used to the stunning vistas, but Rodel, with its dark sea loch, stone shoreline, and grassy green rolling hills, seemed quintessentially Scotland. Beautiful, but eerily desolate and remote. It wasn't hard to imagine things like sea monsters lurking in the deep black waters. If Loch Ness looked anything like this, she could see why the Nessie legend had persisted for so long.

The shuttered hotel seemed to be the only building for miles, although from her dive research she knew there was a medieval church nearby.

In no other place to which she'd traveled had she ever felt so completely removed from civilization as she had in some parts of Scotland, and Rodel topped all others. She felt as if she were standing at the edge of the world. It was a strange feeling. She felt at once small and alone, yet also closer than she'd ever imagined to the natural world around her.

"Beautiful, isn't it?" Sofie said.

Absorbed in the vista, Annie hadn't heard the other woman come up behind her. They were standing at the edge of the pier while Martin spoke with the captain. Annie hoped he was qualified. He looked about eighteen.

"It is," Annie agreed.

"Pretty to look at," Marie said, joining them. "But I'd go crazy if I had to live in a place like this. I can't imagine they have very good Internet connections—I can't even get a cell signal."

Like any millennial, Annie probably would have said the

same thing a few days ago. But she actually kind of liked not having a cell phone—for a few days at least. It was oddly freeing. Although she'd have to get another one soon, if nothing else for emergencies and so her mom could reach her. She was surprised Alice hadn't had one waiting for her at the hotel with her number already speed-dialed in.

Some of the group had brought their own wet suits and gear, but Annie and the others were relying on the charter company's rental equipment. They'd given them their general sizes ahead of time, and after a thorough inspection, Annie began the process of gearing up. As much time as she'd spent in a wet suit, you would think she would like them better. But they were a necessary pain in the ass. Actually a dry suit would be better for this type of cold water, but most companies didn't rent them.

Although the day was blustery and gray, they wouldn't have far to go even if the weather turned. The wreck of the 1950s steamship SS *Stassa*, which had run aground in 1966, was at the head of the loch and not that far from shore. It was still mostly intact, and lying on its side in about twenty-five meters of water.

They boarded the blue-and-white converted fishing trawler called the *Gaelic Princess*, and Captain Niall—who was indeed eighteen but assured them that he'd been doing this for "years"—ferried them the two-thirds of a mile or so out to the dive site.

After an inauspicious start, Annie found herself getting a little excited. She wasn't a wreck bagger—she'd just made that term up—but she found them fascinating. She probably had James Cameron and the movie *Titanic* to thank for that. She'd been a child when she first saw those eerie images of the rusticle-laden ship materializing out of the deep blue water.

Up close, shipwrecks were even more moving. There was something both incredible and haunting about seeing an enormous steel machine lying in a watery grave.

Annie was the last diver in the water. She was sitting on the edge of the boat about to drop back when she was pulled into the water from behind.

———————

"**D**on't do anything stupid."

That had been the last thing the LC said to him before he hung up, and Dean hoped to hell he could keep his shit together. But sitting on the tarmac waiting for the flight to take off was like playing an agonizing game of trying not to lose his mind.

God, how much fucking longer were they going to be sitting here?

The police were being notified, but until Dean got there—until he saw her—he wasn't going to be able to relax or "calm the fuck down" as the LC had so eloquently put it.

But this thing was a hell of a lot bigger than any of them had guessed.

Dean's tip to Kate about OPF targeting large companies—large *public* companies—had paid off. It hadn't been just about a failed ecoterrorist attack on the drillship. Jean Paul had murdered his two compatriots and gone after Annie not because of the environment or a protest. He'd gone after them because of money. OPF was a front for something much bigger than ecoterrorism—and a hell of a lot more profitable: shorting stock.

Basically, as the LC explained it, shorting stock was betting against the market with borrowed shares of stock. If the stock went up, you could lose your shirt, but if the stock went down, you could rake it in. It was more complicated than that, with things like margin and calls, but the basic idea was that you could win big when the stock went down and lose big if it went up.

Dean's observation about the group targeting progressively bigger and bigger companies had led Kate to look deeper into the companies' finances and stock. She'd found a pattern in the short interest chart. Immediately before OPF hit a target company, she'd noticed a spike in the percentage of shares of that company being shorted. It was as if someone knew what was going to happen.

Someone obviously did. OPF. The investors behind OPF shorted the stock of the company they were planning to sabotage, and then afterward when the stock price dipped, they covered the stock they'd borrowed at a higher price, pocketing the profit.

They made out like bandits—literally—every time they bombed one of these publicly traded companies. Kate estimated they'd made millions.

It was fucking brilliant—assuming the blast went off and the stock dipped.

The problem was that this time the ship hadn't been destroyed or damaged, and the stock hadn't dipped. It had gone up. And when the margin calls went out, those investors were going to lose a lot of money. They were the types of investors—probably an organized crime syndicate—that didn't like losing money and would be looking for someone to pay.

Someone like Jean Paul. That had been the second alarming piece of information. It was beginning to look as though Jean Paul's death had not been an accident, and that he might have been killed intentionally. A witness had come forward and said that the tourist's car had sped up as she made the turn, "almost as if she'd been targeting the guy." And not only had the woman disappeared; she'd been using a name and a passport that appeared to be fake.

If Jean Paul had been killed, it was because he'd cost lots of bad people lots of money. And if they knew about Annie, would they blame her and go after her, too? She was no one. There was no reason to think . . .

But Dean couldn't take the chance. Nor could he escape the knowledge that if something happened to her, it would be his fault. By sending her back to Lewis, he might have put her right in the bastards' hands.

Fuck.

Finally the captain's voice sounded over the intercom. They were ready for takeoff. Dean sat back in his seat and prayed as he'd never prayed that his gut was wrong.

———

It was the longest forty-five-minute flight of Dean's life. He'd turned his phone on as soon as they hit the ground, and the text waiting for him made his stomach sink like a ball of lead.

Kate had connected the dots. The two guys who'd attacked them in Oban had washed up and been identified. They were part of a crime syndicate in Germany and had been on Interpol's and the CIA's watch list for a long time. Unfortunately no one had thought to share the information with officials in Scotland, and they'd gone through immigration without a problem. They had been photographed after clearing customs, however, with a woman. The text from the LC included a grainy airport picture of a woman of indeterminate age with long blond hair.

Police in Inverness, where Jean Paul had been taken and killed, confirmed her identity as their missing tourist. Not surprisingly, the woman Interpol knew as Greta Johansson, a Swedish national, was part of the same syndicate. With the Swiss Meier and German Richer, a Belgian, and two Frenchmen, it was a regular United Nations.

Dean couldn't get off that plane fast enough. Fifteen minutes later he was in a cab and found out the rest in a quick phone call to the LC. Jean Paul's cell phone number didn't match the one that Dean had pulled from the hit man's phone, which meant that not only was his picture still out there, but the two guys hadn't been reporting to Jean Paul as they'd thought. It probably belonged to the woman, but she still hadn't been located.

Neither had Annie. The police had gone to the protester camp, but apparently they hadn't made a lot of friends after the attempted bombing and no one was talking.

Dean had the cab make a beeline for the camp, and five minutes later he was running down the dock.

It might have taken longer if he hadn't recognized one of the guys from the table the first night he'd seen Annie and her so-called friends in the pub. Sergio had tried to slink away, but Dean intercepted him. The hand around his throat probably convinced him that Dean wasn't in any mood to fuck around, and Sergio told him what he wanted to know faster than he could piss himself—which he did.

Annie had gone to Harris to dive an old wreck "about an hour ago." Dean knew it. The *Stassa* was the first dive he'd done when he signed on with Old MacDonald. But Dean knew his worst fears had been realized when he showed Sergio the picture of the woman and he confirmed that she was part of the group.

Figuring it could cut a good half hour off the travel time to go by boat, Dean looked around the harbor for something fast. He wished to hell he had access to one of the Special Boat Teams' CCM Mk1 stealth speedboats, but there was a company that did speedboat rides around the harbor, and one of those would have to do. He hoped to hell it would be enough.

The kid manning the booth recognized him. "Hey, people have been looking for you."

Dean ignored him, grabbed the key that was hanging from the board nicely marked, and hopped into the boat.

"Hey, what are you doing? You can't take that."

"Call the police," Dean said. "Tell them that the woman they are looking for is on Harris diving the *Stassa* wreck. Tell them to get a chopper if they can."

Dean had already texted the information to the LC, but it wouldn't hurt to tell the police twice.

He knew the risk he was taking by getting the police involved, but it couldn't be helped.

What if he didn't reach her—

He stopped the thought from forming. He would get there in time. He wouldn't consider any other possibility.

Thirty-four

When Annie surfaced after being pulled in, Martin was already motioning the riot act to Marie to never do that again. As a newbie, she apparently didn't realize it was an unwritten rule that you should never touch another person's dive equipment or pull someone in the water when that person wasn't ready.

Annie was glad she was partnered with Sofie and a university student from England named Joe. From the "hey, man" lazy smile and distinctive smell of Joe's clothes, he enjoyed smoking quite a bit of pot. In Annie's book, marijuana—like alcohol—and diving didn't mix. She wouldn't have gone down with just him to rely on as a dive partner, but with Sofie there, she let it go.

The twenty-five-meter dive of the *Stassa* wreck was not considered difficult, but going inside to explore the wreck should only be undertaken by experienced divers—and even then it was dangerous. They were the only three in the group who qualified.

They descended the buoy line with the rest of the group. The visibility was outstanding. The enormous ship was lying on its starboard side, and as advertised, it was virtually intact. Annie could see the funnel, masts, winch, railings, and catwalks. A small break in the hull in the middle of the ship was the only evidence of damage.

The rusticles called to her. She couldn't wait to go explore. She'd read about a rumor that the IRA had a secret shipment of illegal weapons on board, hidden under the cargo of timber. Maybe she'd be the lucky one to find it.

When everyone was down, Sofie motioned to Martin that the three advanced divers were going to separate to start their exploration inside.

Before they could, however, Joe motioned that he had a problem. Something was wrong with one of his air tubes. Sofie and Martin tried to help him, but eventually he just made the sign that he was going to head up.

Annie couldn't say she was sorry to see him go.

She and Sofie broke off from the rest of the group and headed aft toward a few broken windows, which were one of the ways inside. Because of the clear conditions and multiple entry points, they weren't planning to use a dive reel, but Annie had a finger spool just in case.

Sofie motioned for her to go first, and Annie headed inside. They'd planned their general route on the boat ride over, and for the next twenty minutes they carefully explored the cavernous insides of the ship from the engine room, to the funnels, to the holds (where unfortunately she didn't find any weapons), and eventually to the wheelhouse. They used a flashlight—or torch as they called it here—in the deeper sections and were careful to avoid anything that could shift or that they might get tangled on.

The wheelhouse was a tight space with a danger of silting, so Annie set the finger spool and started to let out line.

That was when the banging started. It was the faint sound of metal on metal.

She and Sofie looked at each other. Annie checked her watch and her tank and realized she hadn't lost track of time—they still had another twenty minutes or so before they had to start up. But it was clear, someone wanted their attention.

Annie motioned to the other woman that they should head

up. She started toward the doorway that led to the broken windows where they'd come in, but something pulled her back.

At first she thought her tank or line had gotten caught on something. But when she turned her head and saw the knife coming toward her, Annie realized her mistake.

Dean cut the throttle as he approached the loch. He didn't know what he would find, and he didn't want to spook the woman into doing anything rash. He suspected she was planning to kill Annie and make it look like an accident—presumably to not draw any more attention to OPF—but he couldn't count on it.

He cautiously inched the boat into the mouth of the loch until he could see the dive boat. It was empty except for a slender-built male who he assumed was the charter captain.

Dean swore. It would be too much to hope with their hour lead that he would have caught up with them, but he'd hoped.

He tried to control his rising panic, but at the thought of everything that could go wrong down there, a cold sweat spread over his skin.

Stay cool.

He couldn't recall ever having to tell himself that before.

He glanced to the harbor and pier. There were a few docked boats, but no chopper and no blue-and-yellow police cars. If and when they showed up, they weren't going to be much use, though—not out here and not unless they requisitioned a boat.

He carefully steered the boat around the buoyed dive site and called out to the captain as he approached. The figure didn't budge from his seat at the wheel until Dean was practically next to him.

From the tapping foot on the rail, Dean figured out why.

The kid broke out into a smile and pulled the headphones from his ears. "Hey, man. I didn't hear you. What's up?"

Dean cut the engine. "How long have they been down there?"

The kid was startled by his tone, and had probably gotten a look at Dean's expression. "What's wrong?"

"How long?" Dean repeated.

"Thirty minutes. What's going on?" he repeated.

Dean didn't have time to explain. "Do you have an acoustic diver-recall system?"

"A what?"

That was a no. Dean wasn't surprised, given the cost. "Find me a wrench."

Dean reached over to grab one of the dive boat lines and used it to draw his boat close enough to jump on board.

The kid had hustled to do his bidding and was back in a minute with the wrench.

"Start banging on the side," Dean said. He took a sniper position, kneeling behind the port-side rail, and pulled out his gun. He didn't want any of the divers to see him first.

The banging stopped. "What the fuck?" the kid said, his voice shaky. "Who are you? What are you going to do?"

"Stop someone from being murdered. The police will fill you in when they arrive, but until then bang like your life depends on it."

Dean wasn't sure whether it was his words or the gun that convinced him, but the kid banged. And banged. One by one the divers surfaced. He counted six. It was hard to identify anyone with only mask- and hood-covered heads popping out of the water like seals—the animal kind—but Dean knew Annie wasn't one of them.

An older guy had swum over to the ladder and pulled off his mask as he came on board. "What's going on?" he said to the kid.

The kid turned to Dean, who stood and walked into the man's view while sticking his gun in the waist of his jeans. He addressed the older guy. "Where is Annie?"

The older guy turned and scanned the water. "She and Sofie must still be in the wreck. Why?"

Dean wasn't answering. "I need a tank," he said to the kid.

"They're all being used."

"You don't have a backup?"

"We had one, but one of the divers had to use it. His hose got cut somehow."

Dean swore. The panic was starting to claw. He strode over to where the older man had just climbed aboard the boat. "Give me your tank."

"Not until you tell me—"

He stopped when Dean pulled out the gun. Dean was out of patience. "Give me your tank now."

The old guy was defiant. "I'm not going to let you hurt one of those women."

Dean cursed. Of course, he had to be the English hippie who decided to play brave knight. "I'm trying to save one of them. The police will explain everything when they arrive, but you need to give me that tank."

Dean didn't know whether it was him or the approaching sound of sirens, but the old guy shrugged off the tanks and handed them over.

Dean checked the gauge, saw that there was still a half tank, put on the vest, and didn't even take time to adjust the waist belt before grabbing the guy's mask and jumping in.

The shock of cold water was something you never got used to—no matter how many times he experienced it, it still sucked. It was pretty much like jumping into an ice bath. Although that might have been warmer. Fuck, it was cold. He knew he wouldn't last long and his movements and reflexes were going to be shit, but there was nothing he could do.

He spat in the mask, wiped it around, fitted the regulator in his mouth, and dove.

Hold on, Annie. Just hold on.

Thirty-five

Thank God for physics, Annie thought. The resistance of the water gave her the time she needed to evade the knife blow that was meant for her neck.

Sofie reached for her, swiping with the knife again, but Annie pushed off against her, sending them both backward in opposite directions. Annie felt one of the metal walls behind her and knew she had to think of something fast. Sofie had dropped the knife in the struggle, but she was reaching for something.

Oh God, a gun. They were about ten feet apart. Annie had watched a *MythBusters* episode where they'd shot a couple of different-sized bullets underwater. One had died in three feet and one in eight feet. She wasn't going to count on the right equation of distance, depth, and caliber.

She'd lost hold of the finger spool in the struggle, but located it quickly. Swallowing the fear, she reached for the line with one hand while diving to the debris on the bottom to stir it up.

An instant later, the water filled with silt, cutting off visibility completely. It was like being in a pool of mud.

This was how people died, she thought to herself. A silt-out could create terror and panic in even the most experienced divers. Even with the line in her hand, Annie felt fear crawling up her throat, and her heart racing to escape.

But she forced it back and slowly used the line to guide herself out of the wreck.

Every second, she half expected Sofie to come lurching out of the murky water toward her.

She really needed to stop watching scary movies.

She thought she could sense someone flailing around near her, but she couldn't be sure.

She reached the end of the line and knew the broken windows were above her. The visibility was better, and she was able to feel around to find the opening.

She started to go through but quickly realized she'd made a mistake. It was the wrong opening—a smaller one—and now she was stuck.

But that wasn't the only disaster. What she'd thought was panic whistling in her head was actually the sound of escaping air. She lifted her air pressure gauge to see the needle dropping way too fast. Her air tube had been cut or damaged. Sofie must have nicked it with the knife.

She kicked again, trying to untangle herself or force her way through. But she could only move a few inches in either direction. Her tank was hooked on something.

Don't panic. Don't think about how much air you have left. But the "stay calm" reminders weren't working. She tried to reach around to untangle herself, but her efforts only seemed to make it worse.

How long would the silt take to settle? Would it matter or would she already be out of air? Bullet or suffocation, in the end it didn't matter.

She fought against the urge to take deeper and deeper breaths of air, but she knew she was running out of time.

She was going to die.

The panic was harder to keep at bay, which was why at first she thought she imagined the person swimming toward her.

She had to be imagining it because the person wasn't wearing a wet suit.

It was only when he was close enough for her to look into his mask that she realized she wasn't imagining anything.

It was Dan.

Dean, she corrected. He was here. He'd come back. He'd found her.

If she had any air left, she would have exhaled with relief. But she was literally sucking on fumes.

He was trying to ask her what was wrong, but she was too panicked to remember any hand signals. Fortunately he grabbed her pressure gauge and figured out what was going on.

Pulling the regulator from his mouth, he handed it to her. In her haste she almost took in a mouthful of water along with the air that she greedily sucked in. She tried to hand it back to him, but he shook her off and went to work on her tangled equipment.

He unbuckled the waist belt and helped her shrug off the vest, eventually slipping the tank off her shoulders.

Why hadn't she thought of that? Panic had prevented her from thinking straight.

He pulled her through the opening, and she was free. The relief was overwhelming. A million questions were racing through her mind, but the only thing she could think was that he was here, and she'd never been so glad to see anyone in her life.

She handed him the regulator again. He took a quick breath this time, shaking his head when she tried to force him to keep it for longer. He looked *totally* calm. Totally in control. As if he could hold his breath and go without air indefinitely. Maybe he could.

SEALs, she thought ruefully. They were inhuman. And maybe that wasn't always a bad thing. The world needed men like him. *She* needed him. Without him she'd be dead. Maybe there was something to be said for superheroes after all.

The water was his territory. She knew SEALs were trained to be just as comfortable underwater as they were on the surface, and she was seeing proof positive of that.

He made a few signals with his hand, and her head had cleared enough to know what he was asking. He wanted to know where the other woman was. Annie pointed down in the ship and put her hand in front of her mask, hoping to indicate a silt-out.

He nodded, and they started to swim away from the wreck toward the surface. Dean was at her side, holding her arm as if he wasn't ever going to let go of her—which was pretty much fine by her.

He'd made her feel like that before, but somehow she knew this was different.

He'd come for her.

She felt a swell of happiness rise inside her before it was harshly jerked back. Someone had her by the fin.

Dean didn't need to tell himself scary stories—he lived through enough real ones—but he couldn't stop thinking what would have happened had he been a few minutes later.

He could have lost her. He hadn't. But knowing how close he'd been . . .

He had a sick feeling in his chest that moved between panic and wanting to throw up. He was surprised to feel anything through the bone-numbing cold. He needed to get out of this water soon. His hands were already like clubs.

The unbearable cold coupled with the overwhelming sense of relief at finding her turned his operational awareness to shit. That was how one minute Annie was at his side, and the next she was yanked from his hold.

He looked down to see the wild-eyed face through the mask of the woman from the photo. She was clearly in a rage and dragging Annie down with one hand while waving a gun through the water with the other.

Oh, fuck. She's going to shoot.

That was the only thought he had as he dove between them, putting his body between the gun and Annie.

He heard the shot and then felt the impact. But he didn't feel pain, and realized from a pinging sound that the bullet had hit his tank. As the tank didn't shoot off like a missile— or explode if you believed *Jaws*—the bullet must not have penetrated the metal.

He pushed Annie out of the way as the woman waved the

gun around wildly toward him again. But he'd already reached for the gun he'd tucked in his pants.

It wouldn't have been a contest if he wasn't so fucking cold, but his icy fingers and frozen brain made it closer than he would have liked. His bullet hit her right between the eyes a split second before she fired. She might have hit him, if Annie hadn't distracted her. Annie had lunged toward the woman with her dive knife, but it was too late. The last signs of life were already fading from the woman's frozen-forever-in-surprise eyes.

Dean quickly located the regulator and held it out to Annie. She took a few breaths before pushing it back toward him. He'd been without air for a couple of minutes and didn't argue.

He forced himself to breathe normally. Having been here too many times before was the only thing that prevented him from sucking it in. He handed it back to her and slowly they ascended, stopping once to trade breaths.

When they finally broke through the surface, Dean half expected them to be surrounded by police. He was relieved to see that they were alone. His "borrowed" transportation had floated toward a small islet, but the dive boat and Annie's fellow divers had returned to shore. He could see why. The police chopper had finally arrived and must have radioed the kid to come get them to bring them out.

But Dean didn't give a shit about the police. He yanked off his mask, tossed it in the water next to him, and pulled her into his arms.

She was alive. That was all that mattered.

Thank God, he'd arrived in time. But it would be some time before the image of her gasping for breath and trying not to panic faded from his memory. He was too torn up to say anything—emotion stuck in his throat like a logjam.

He was glad that she'd lifted off her mask, because it made it easier when he kissed her—kissed the hell out of her. It was as if all the emotion, all the bundled-up tension, all the panic and fear gave loose in a fierce—savage—explosion of need. He'd almost lost her, and he wasn't ever going to let that happen again.

She was kissing him back with the same ferocity. A tangle of lips, tongues, and salt water. *Frigid* salt water.

He wanted to go on kissing her forever, but he had to get out of this water. He pulled back and looked into her eyes. "Hit pause until we get on the boat."

Her eyes flew open. "Oh my God, you must be freezing. I wasn't thinking . . ." Her voice cracked. "How did you know I was in trouble?"

"I'll tell you everything when we get on that boat."

Normally he could swim the distance of a football field in just under a minute. But the fifteen minutes or so that he'd been in the icy water had sapped his strength and turned his limbs to bricks. The increasingly choppy waters didn't help, either. It was a good five minutes before he was climbing the ladder onto his borrowed speedboat and reaching down to help Annie up.

But her head was turned toward the pier. The dive boat had just left the harbor and was making its way toward them, presumably with the police on board.

She turned back to him and shook her head, refusing to climb aboard. "You have to go, Dean. You can't let them find you."

"I'm not going to leave you—" Suddenly he stopped, staring down at her in shock. "How do you know my name?"

"I guess you haven't seen the paper today. The reporter doing those lost platoon stories posted a photo of her brother and a few of his friends. It was hard to make out your faces, but you weren't wearing a shirt, and I . . . uh . . ." How the hell was she blushing in ice-cold water? "I knew it was you."

He wasn't going to ask her how. Not right now at least. Not while he wasn't naked and she couldn't show him.

"That's why you're hiding," she said. "You're part of the SEAL platoon that she said disappeared."

"Aren't you going to ask me why?"

"I assume you have a good reason, and you'll tell me what you can when it's safe." She stared up at him, her expression suddenly uncertain. "I'll wait for you—if you want me to."

He reached down the ladder and pulled her on board. She'd

probably be pissed off later at his high-handedness, but he'd make it up to her. He thought of all kinds of ways he was going to make it up to her, and he felt a spark of warmth pulsing through his frigid veins.

"Want you to? Fuck yes, I want you to." He pulled her in tight against his body to emphasize his point. He'd give everything he had right now to strip off his wet jeans and her wet suit. But she was right. He had to go.

For now.

"I wasn't sure," she admitted. "I didn't know why you came back. How did you know I'd be in danger?"

He gave her a twenty-second recap of what they'd found out about OPF and Jean Paul's death. She was clearly shocked.

"Short-selling? Blowing up the drillship was about money?"

He nodded. "When I learned that the woman who'd killed Jean Paul had gone diving with you . . ." He shivered—and not from the cold, though it wasn't much warmer on this damned boat. "I've never been so scared in my life."

She smiled. "I thought big, badass SEALs didn't get scared."

"Sweetheart, you scare the livin' shit out of me."

The confession seemed to please her enormously. She looked like a kid in the proverbial candy store—him being the candy store. "I do?"

He wasn't going to elaborate on how much. He'd do that the next time they were alone, preferably in bed. "If anything had happened to you, it would have been my fault. I shouldn't have left you."

"I understand why you did now."

"Yeah, well, I still shouldn't have left the way I did." His fingers caressed the side of her cheek along the edge of the neoprene hood as she gazed up at him. His voice was suddenly husky. "I should have told you something first."

She was scanning his gaze so intently that he felt his chest squeeze. She seemed scared to ask, "What?"

They were words he'd never said to any woman before, but he didn't hesitate. The last few hours had made him damned sure. He would figure out how to make it work. That was what he did for a living. Found solutions for the impossible. "That I love you."

She blinked, tears suddenly filling her eyes. "You do?"

He nodded and kissed her again. This time far more gently, and unfortunately far too briefly. He hated this. But there would be time. Lots of time. He'd make damned sure of it.

"I love you, too," she said when he released her.

"Good," he said with a smile. "You can tell me how much next time I see you."

He could tell she wanted to ask, but bit her lip to stop herself. That she understood how it worked—that he wouldn't be able to tell her about what he did—was going to make things a hell of a lot easier.

He answered the unspoken question as much as he could. "Soon, sweetheart. As soon as I can."

"How will you find me?"

He grinned. "Trade secrets."

He reached for his backpack, glad that it was waterproof. The short swim to shore was going to be mostly underwater. The dive boat and police would be able to see them soon.

"You can't get back in that water. Just take the boat. I can handle the cold with this wet suit."

He shook his head. "There will be police all over the area soon. I would never be able to get away in the boat. But there are a bunch of sea caves along the shore. I'll find one and stay there until they stop looking. Tell them I died—and be convincing. It will slow them down."

She nodded, tears streaming down her cheeks. "Be careful. You must be close to hypothermia already."

He was, but she didn't need to know that. A fire would be too risky, even in one of those caves, but getting out of these wet clothes would help.

"I have to go," he said.

"I know."

He leaned down and gave her a quick kiss before diving in the water. He wanted to surface and tell her he loved her again, but he'd already stayed too long. He couldn't risk the police seeing him.

But he intended to tell her again very soon. He wasn't going to take any chances that she might reconsider waiting for him. For however long that might be.

God knew it wasn't great timing—and he was going to do everything he could to help the LC figure out what the hell had happened so they could come out of hiding—but he'd met the woman he wanted to spend the rest of his life with. For the first time since the missile had exploded in front of him, Dean felt hope for the future.

Thirty-six

It had been a long day of travel. Annie was exhausted as she walked down the stairs of the small regional plane—she didn't think she would ever get used to flying in a bathtub—and crossed the tarmac to the terminal. She was surprised by how good it felt to be back in Scotland.

It didn't feel like Oz anymore. Actually she'd begun to think that it might feel like home. For a while anyway.

She tried not to worry about Dean, and wonder where he was and whether he was all right. He would find her when he could.

She had to get on with her own life, and she was beginning to think that might be here.

Her mother hadn't been happy when Annie told her that she was returning to Scotland, but her stepfather's reminder that she could take the plane anytime she wanted had calmed her down a bit.

"No more boarding ships out at sea," Alice had made her promise.

After everything that had happened, that would be an easy promise to keep. But Annie's goal had not changed, and she'd taken up Martin's offer to return to Lewis after her visit home to continue the pressure on the oil company not to proceed with drilling in the fields so close to the Isles.

After everything that had gone down with Sofie/Greta at the *Stassa* wreck, Annie knew that Martin felt bad—he'd been just as taken in by her as the rest of them—but she knew it wasn't just guilt that motivated him. The TV interviews Annie had done had helped raise public consciousness enough for the Islanders to start asking questions. Lots of questions. Martin thought they had a real chance of getting the oil company to delay drilling. It would be a huge victory—even if just a temporary one.

So for the next few weeks she'd agreed to participate in the discussions. And after that?

She'd been in touch with a local university here in the Isles that had some interesting marine research projects going on in Orkney and Shetland, including one with mussels that seemed right up her alley. It wasn't flashy, but it would enable her to continue her work and ensure that oil companies operated safely and responsibly. She would be doing something important and making a difference, just as she'd wanted to. The fact that the islands were remote and secluded—where people wouldn't be looking for a missing SEAL—made them all the more appealing.

Annie stood at the luggage turnstile, waiting for her bag to come off. The first glimpse of that horrible bright pink made her heart squeeze.

She missed him.

Soon, he'd promised. She had to be patient. But it wasn't easy. They had so much to talk about.

Of course, talking wasn't all she was thinking about. There might be a few other things she'd like to do first.

Slinging the duffel over her shoulder, Annie left the terminal and started to cross the street to the taxi stand.

That was when she saw him.

Her heart practically flew out of her chest. Dean was leaning against a white car with his arms crossed over his chest as if his being there was the most commonplace thing in the world.

As if she hadn't been worried about him every minute of the last two weeks. As if the last time they'd seen each other he hadn't been nearly frozen to death, and she hadn't nearly been shot. As if she hadn't been longing for this moment for every minute since he jumped off that boat. As if she didn't want to race across the street, throw herself into his arms, and stay there forever. As if he wasn't about the best thing she'd ever seen in jeans, a T-shirt that showed off his tanned arms, and that seen-better-days de-logoed Cowboys hat.

It was only when she saw his eyes—or felt them—that she knew he wasn't as casual as he appeared.

No, "casual" was definitely not the word for the searing intensity of those steely blue eyes as they locked on hers. "Mine" and "I can't wait to strip you naked and screw your brains out" summed it up better.

Her heart was pounding and fluttering in her chest as she calmly crossed the street to stand before him.

He stared at her, and she stared right back. It was amazing how silence could say so much. How silence could say everything.

But he hadn't moved. Maybe he didn't trust himself. Maybe he felt like her: that if he started touching her he wouldn't ever be able to stop.

Finally she spoke. "Aren't you going to get my bag?"

"And make you feel weak and inferior? No, ma'am. You see, I've been doing lots of reading the past couple weeks."

The deep drawl and "ma'am" were getting to her a little, but she managed not to smile as he rattled off a bunch of names she hadn't heard since the women's studies class she'd taken as an undergrad. She wasn't foolish enough to think she'd converted him. No, it was him getting prepared for their next argument. "Know your enemy?" she said to him.

He grinned. "Something like that."

She might not be able to bring him over to the dark side, but that didn't mean she wasn't going to try. And she was sure he was thinking the same thing. If occasionally—very occasionally—she might be a little naive, she was sure he would point it out. And if he started acting like a cynical machine, she'd make sure he had a little more compassion.

Maybe they'd even each other out a little. Or maybe not. But he would keep her on her toes—that was for sure.

She tossed him the bag, which he caught against his stomach with an oof. "Don't believe everything you read, Tex, and you need to put all those pretty muscles to use."

"I can think of a few other uses."

She felt a flutter low in her belly. "So can I."

"Get in the car, Annie."

"Where are we going?"

He gave her a sidelong glance. "It's a surprise."

"It better have running water and heat."

He laughed and opened the door for her. "It's not as fancy as that hotel you were registered at—which I canceled, by the way—but I promise to keep you warm."

He slid in behind the wheel and she gave him a look. "I'll bet. But one rodent, and we're going to the hotel."

He shook his head. "I knew rich girls were high maintenance." He looked over at her as he pulled onto the road. "You've been holding out on me, Doc."

She assumed he was talking about her stepfather. But he wasn't. "You have over a million dollars in your bank account."

He actually sounded pissed, which wasn't the reaction she was used to. It was her cash reserves. She had about five million in investments, but now was probably not the time to tell him that. Her stepfather had helped her invest the money she'd received after her father's death.

"Why would that be important? It's savings. I don't live off it."

He rolled his eyes. "Only a rich person could be that delusional. Money always matters. Did Julien know about it?"

"I didn't tell him, but he probably found out about it when he was on my computer."

He nodded. "That's what I figured as well. He must have seen your balance at some point and tried to give Jean Paul a reason to keep him alive by passing on your password and account info."

"It didn't work."

"No, it didn't." He didn't say anything for a minute. "You all right?"

Though the question was asked softly, it packed a surprising amount of intensity. She hadn't been the only one worried. It had been as hard for him as it had been for her not to be with him after the attack. But maybe it had proved what she already knew. She was strong enough to handle life with a SEAL. Though his job would take him away from her far more than she wanted, she knew he would come back.

She nodded. "A lot better now." She paused. "I missed you."

He gave her a wry smile. "I missed you, too. A lot."

"How long can you stay?"

She didn't know if she wanted to hear the answer, fearing he would say a couple of hours or tomorrow.

"A few days at least."

She nodded, relieved. Although she knew it wouldn't be enough.

It only took about fifteen minutes for them to reach their destination. Dean had let a cottage overlooking the beach not far from town. It sat by itself on a hilltop, not quite secluded— there were a handful of other cottages nearby—but it should afford them plenty of privacy.

Anticipation was racing through her veins as he got their bags out of the trunk (aka "boot") and led her up to the pretty robin's-egg blue front door.

She was pretty sure he was thinking the same thing as she was, and she wondered whether they'd make it to the bedroom the first time.

They didn't.

No sooner had the door closed behind her than his body was pressing her up against it. His lips were on hers, and he was devouring her with his mouth and hands.

And she was devouring him right back. She couldn't get enough of his heat, of his tongue, of that delicious taste of cinnamon.

She'd missed this. God, how she'd missed this. The heat. The fierceness. The intensity. How one minute she was herself and the next she was dissolving into a puddle of desperate need.

His body was so big and hard against her. The warmth and solidness of him never ceased to amaze her. Holding him. Touching him. Letting her hands roam over the heavy slabs of muscle.

He lifted her up a little against the door to notch himself between her legs and she moaned, her body drenching.

He lifted his mouth and unbuttoned his jeans and lowered hers. "This isn't going to be pretty."

"I don't want it pretty."

"Good. I need to be inside you."

And with a hard thrust he was.

She jarred at the contact. At the thoroughness of the possession. It was always like that with him. When he was inside her, she felt consumed—claimed—in a way that she never anticipated she would like.

He hooked one of her legs over his arm to wrap around his waist and kissed her again, swallowing her moans and cries as their bodies slammed together with every deep thrust.

It took her breath away.

He was right. It wasn't pretty. It was raw and fierce and primal. He was out of control, and she loved it.

He was so big and hard inside her, and his body was so hot he seemed to be on fire. All it took was a few thrusts of that powerful body surging into hers, and she was breaking apart.

He didn't last much longer. With one last deep thrust he cried out, and she felt that powerful shudder as he came inside her.

He collapsed against her when he was done, the weight of his body holding them both up against the door.

After a few heavy breaths he regained strength enough to pull back and look into her eyes. She still couldn't believe that he was here. That he was hers.

But guessing what he was about to say, she stopped him before he could speak. "I'm fine, but if you apologize or say anything about a condom, I'm not going to be."

He gave her an apologetic grin. "That didn't go exactly as I'd planned."

She understood what he meant when she looked over his shoulder and saw the bottle of champagne and roses on the kitchen counter.

She arched an eyebrow. "I didn't take you for the romantic type."

"I'm not," he admitted, pulling back enough to lower her down gently. He raked his fingers through his hair and redid his jeans.

Her legs were wobbly as she pulled hers up and did the same. "But as I said before, you bring out all kinds of weird shit in me, and I wanted this to be special."

"It already is," she said softly, staring into his eyes.

His gaze softened as he wiped a strand of hair from her lashes. "You're right about that."

"Although you did kind of ruin my surprise." She'd been looking for a way to pay him back for leaving her at the hotel and had the perfect thing. She knew how to hit him where it would hurt.

"What surprise?"

"You'll see."

He did—a bottle of champagne and two more times in the living room later—as she was coming out of the bathroom after getting ready for bed.

He'd already stripped down to his boxer briefs and was stretched out waiting for her with his head propped up under a bent elbow.

He took one look at her and shot up, every muscle in that impressive body taut. His eyes were slitted, his gaze deadly. "I can tolerate NOW and maybe even a few whale groups, but that? No fucking way. Take it off, Doc."

She crossed her arms in front of the jersey, but didn't block the "Texans" across the top. "No. It's my favorite team. And don't try to order me around like one of your men, *Senior Chief*, or I'll make you regret it."

He stood up and walked toward her in full battle mode. All six feet four inches of ripped, powerfully muscled male.

Her mouth might have been watering a little and her uterus might have contracted, but she stood her ground.

"Bigger, stronger. Do I need to spell it out for you?"

In case she didn't get it, he was looming over her threateningly, his fists flexing at his side as if he couldn't wait to rip the damned thing off her.

Unfazed, she didn't budge or cower. Instead she lifted her chin and met the furious glare. "If you do anything to this jersey, I will make it my life's mission to ensure that every one of our children—especially the boys, since I know Mr. Misogynist wouldn't dream that his daughters with their little girlie heads so full of Barbies could be football fans as well—is a dyed-in-the-wool Texans fan."

He thought she was bluffing and called it. That cocky SEAL thing that she knew was lurking came out in full force—with just a touch of smugness. She was going to enjoy wiping that off his too-good-looking face. Yes, revenge was sweet.

"Good luck. My sons *and* daughters are all going to be Cowboys fans."

He started to reach for the neck of the jersey, probably planning on ripping it down the front. But she put a quick stop to that. Holding his wrists, she said, "It won't be hard to do when they get to know all the Texans players personally from hanging out in the locker room."

He laughed with utter confidence. "Right. Take it off, Bambi, or I'll do it."

Now he wasn't the only one angry. She glared back at him. He was about to have a nickname he'd like even less than she liked Bambi. "Sugar?" As in no sugar. He frowned. "Have I shown you a picture of my mother and stepfather?" She reached down to grab her purse, retrieving her phone—her new phone—and the recent photo she'd taken of them while she was in Florida.

He was clearly confused by what he thought was the change of topic. He glanced down at the picture. "Your mom is pretty. She looks like you. Your stepfather . . ." He frowned. "He looks familiar. I've seen him before."

She hit the screen to go to the next picture—in his office at the stadium—and had the extreme pleasure of watching the blood drain from Dean's face.

She grinned as he figured it out. Nope, she hadn't been bluffing.

"What the fuck? Why didn't you tell me your stepfather was Steve Marino?"

Among the other business interests he had, Steve was one of the owners of the Texans football team.

She shrugged. "You never asked. Actually I think you told me not to call him."

"You said he was a lawyer!"

"Actually I said he used to be a lawyer. By the way, I didn't tell him about you, but if you need help—or an army—let me know. I would trust him with my life."

This time he knew she was serious. She also knew he was probably considering it. Her stepfather headed one of the biggest defense contractors in the world. He had dozens of former operatives working for him. If Dean needed an army, she could get him one.

Dean sat—sagged—on the bed, just staring at her. "Shit."

She smiled.

His expression darkened. He knew he'd lost, but he would go down fighting. "My daughters aren't hanging out in any locker rooms with football players." He thought a minute, and pulled her down on his lap. "And neither is my wife. I'm not asking right now, but when this is all over, that is what I want."

Her throat tightened, and she felt the tears shimmering in her eyes as she wrapped her hands around his neck. She'd suspected as much the moment she saw him swimming toward her near that wreck. He wouldn't have come back otherwise. But it was still nice to hear it. "I want that, too."

"Then I'll make it happen."

Annie didn't doubt him for a minute. He was a guy she could count on to get things done—always.

Keep reading for a special preview
of the next novel in the Lost Platoon series,

OFF THE GRID

Coming from Berkley Jove in summer 2018!

Prologue

"Travel the world," they'd said. "Have an exciting career while doing what you love."

The navy recruiters who'd come knocking on John Donovan's frat house door eight years ago when he was an all-American water polo player at the University of Southern California had promised both. John had been thinking more along the lines of Bora-Bora or Tahiti—not Siberian Russia—but they'd sure as hell undersold the excitement part of the job.

It was hard to get more exciting than a no-footprint, fail-and-you-die recon mission to a supposedly abandoned gulag in Russia looking for proof of a doomsday weapon, with not only their lives but also war at stake if they were discovered.

Yeah, definitely undersold. But that was why he was here. Retiarius Platoon, one of the two platoons that made up the

top secret SEAL Team Nine, didn't do vanilla. They did exciting and impossible, and this op sure as shit qualified.

But so far they'd been giving Murphy's Law a workout in
the "if it can go wrong, it will go wrong" category. They'd lost
their unblinking eye in the sky—nicknamed Sauron from the
Lord of the Rings—lost all comms, aka gone blind, and now
that they were finally at the camp and ready to start looking
around, something else was going down.

They should have been inside the gulag's command building by now, but they'd stopped in the yard for some reason.
From his position at point, John took in the other six members
of the squad through the green filter of his NVGs: Miggy, Jim
Bob, the senior chief, Dolph, the new kid, and the LC.

Whatever it was, it wasn't good. Dean Baylor, the senior
chief, had broken the go-dark-on-comms order and was arguing with the officer in charge, Lieutenant Commander Scott
Taylor.

Heck, John didn't like this. He shifted back and forth, scanning the ghostly Soviet-era labor camp through the scope of
his AR-15. Stalin had sure as shit known how to do grim.
This place was bleak with a big-assed *B*. But that wasn't what
was making him twitchy. It was being out here in the open
like this, exposed for so long.

John getting twitchy didn't happen very often. It was one
of the reasons he usually ended up on point. It was the most
dangerous position, and it took a lot to rattle him. Unflappable,
cool, laid-back, pick your California-surfer-boy adjective—he
didn't let shit get to him.

Usually.

He shot a glance across the camp to the second building—
the wooden barracks where the other half of the platoon was
reconnoitering. He didn't expect to see anything—those guys
were too good and knew how to be invisible—but they were
like brothers to him, and if there was something wrong . . .

Fuck. Something was *definitely* wrong. The senior chief
ran past him, heading not to the command building, but toward the barracks. The kid—Brian Murphy—followed. The
senior chief broke off to the left toward the front of the build-

ing, and the kid broke right toward the rear. But the LC was shouting at them—and John—to fall back and get the hell out of there. In other words, it was a Dodge City.

John understood why a moment later.

He heard the whiz an instant before seeing the blinding flash of white light as the night detonated in front of him. The hot pressure of the shock wave made him rear back, his ears thundering with the powerful boom. The first time John had gone surfing, he'd been struck unexpectedly by a large wave and dragged under—the blast felt like that but with fire.

The debris that pummeled his body like bullets and the rock that struck him in the forehead and took him to the ground were secondary. All he could think about was the heat and the feeling as if his lungs had been filled with fuel-fired air.

When the blast of overwhelming heat finally receded, he choked in a few acrid breaths and looked around him in a daze. He couldn't see. A stab of panic penetrated the haze. Only when he tried to wipe his eyes did he remember the NVGs, which were now shattered.

After jerking the goggles off and tossing them to the ground, he blinked as the world came into view. Dust, ash, and smoke were everywhere. It was like every doomsday movie he'd ever seen.

Suddenly he was aware of men around him, pulling at him and mouthing words to him. The world seemed to be moving in slow motion, and it took his brain a moment to catch up. The two men were Miggy and Jim Bob—aka Michael Ruiz and Travis Hart.

"Are you all right?" John thought Ruiz was saying, but his ears were ringing too loud to hear anything.

He nodded, remembering that Miggy, Jim Bob, and Dolph— Steve Spivak—had been well behind him when the missile hit the barracks in front of them. John had been a couple hundred feet away. Had he been any closer . . .

He swore, remembering the kid and the senior chief running past him. They'd been closer. And the LC?

A moment later his silent question was answered as the LC appeared out of the smoke with Dolph, both dragging the unconscious senior chief. It was hard to see what state Baylor was in the dark, but if he was half as bad as John felt, it couldn't be good.

Miggy dropped down to look Baylor over and administer first aid as necessary. Jim Bob was doing the same to him. Their medic had been with the other squad, but they all had medical training. SEALs might have specialties, but what made them distinct was that they were trained to do any job. If someone went down, any one of them could step up and fill his shoes.

John finally found his voice. "The kid?"

The LC met his gaze and shook his head. "Murphy was too close to the rear of the building, where the first missile hit."

Shit, there'd been more than one?

Suddenly, the full impact and ramifications of what the LC said struck. If Murphy had been too close . . .

The other squad, the other seven men of Retiarius, including his best friend and BUD/S brother, Brandon Blake, had been *inside* the barracks building.

The senior chief and Murphy must have been trying to warn them.

John had to do something. He pushed Jim Bob away, told him that he was fine, and struggled to his feet, swaying as he tried to find his equilibrium. Christ, his head hurt. The ground was spinning. He started to run—stumble—toward the orange inferno.

But the LC had guessed his intent and grabbed his arm to hold him back. "It's too late," he yelled, his voice sounding like it was at the far end of a tunnel. "They're gone."

Gone. The finality of that one word penetrated John's shell-shocked brain.

John wanted to argue. With every bone in his body, he wanted to deny the LC's words. But the truth was right in front of his face. The gulag was gone. Both the command and barracks buildings had been flattened. What was left was incinerating before his eyes.

He'd never been so close to one before, but he suspected what he was seeing: a thermobaric explosion. It was also known as a vacuum bomb, although this one had been attached to missiles. They were nasty shit, frowned upon by the international community for humanitarian reasons. Russia had been accused of using them in Syria, and the US had used them to target the caves in Afghanistan, including one nicknamed the "Mother of All Bombs." The bombs used more fuel than conventional weapons, producing a much hotter, more sustained, and pressurized blast that was far more destructive—and deadly—when used in buildings, bunkers, and caves.

He knew what it meant. Just like that, his best friend, half the platoon, and half the family he had in the world were gone.

It was too horrible. Too hideous to think about.

He couldn't think about it. John had been there once before, and it wasn't a place he ever wanted to go to again. Utter devastation. Feeling as if the entire world had just gone black and he was lost.

He forced himself to look away. To move on and shift gears. Putting the bad shit behind him was what made him so good at his job.

But his eyes glanced back to the fire, the instinct to run toward it still strong. SEALs didn't leave their brothers behind. Ever.

"Donovan . . . Dynomite," the LC said, shaking him as if it wasn't the first time he'd said his name. That was him. *Good Times.* As in Kid Dyn-o-mite from the old seventies show. "I need you to focus. We don't have much time. They'll be here soon, looking for survivors. They can't find us."

John's head cleared. The heavy weight in his chest was still there, but he was back. The op . . . He had to focus on the op. "What do you need me to do?"

The LC looked relieved. "Get rid of anything electronic. Anything that might let them detect that we weren't in one of those buildings like we were supposed to be." Taylor looked at the other three men around him. "That goes for all of us—and the senior chief as well."

Baylor was still unconscious. He didn't rouse until they went into the river. That was after they'd thrown their electronics into the fire. But fearing that the Russian soldiers—

probably their special forces, Spetsnaz—might also be using thermal imaging, they needed to mask their body heat as well.

So into the icy river they went, taking turns keeping the senior chief afloat. Baylor had come around, but he was still out of it, and every time they had to go under and hold their breath as the Russian soldiers drew near, they feared he might not surface.

But he made it. They all did. Although those hours in the cold river weren't anything John ever wanted to go through again. He'd thought BUD/S had prepared him for cold and uncomfortable. But the Pacific Ocean in San Diego didn't have anything on a river in Siberian Russia.

It seemed as if the bastards would never leave. They were having too much fun. John didn't need to understand Russian like Spivak did to know they were gloating.

Spivak could only catch a word or two of what they were saying in between breaths, but other than making some kind of joke that John took to be the Russian equivalent of "shooting fish in a barrel" and having what they needed to make the American "cowboys" pay, they weren't thoughtful enough to mention how they had known the SEALs were coming. If it hadn't been for the LC receiving a last-minute warning—that was what he and the senior chief had been arguing about—they would all be dead.

By time the Russian soldiers had satisfied themselves that there were no survivors, John wasn't the only one battling hypothermia.

But he pushed it aside just like everything else. He never looked back, only forward.

And forward in this case meant getting the hell out of Dodge—or, in SEAL terminology, exfil.

SEALs had contingencies for contingencies, and this op was no exception. They'd all been well briefed and knew the mission plan backward and forward, but they didn't use their original exfil plan or the backup one. They were going to hump a good seventy miles across the Siberian countryside to the nearest city—or what passed for a city in this Arctic wasteland—the old coal-mining town of Vorkuta.

The LC suspected that someone in their own government

had set them up, and until he found out who it was, they were going to stay dead. That meant going dark, staying off the grid, and scattering in different directions as soon as they could.

It also meant getting rid of anything that could identify them as American or military. Due to the nature of their mission, most of their gear was unattributable, but even having it could be suspicious, so into the fires it went. They'd even have to ditch their weapons once they got closer to Vorkuta. Fortunately, they'd been trained in how to blend in—low-vis, as they called it. No buzz cuts or clean-shaven jaws for them. Relaxed grooming standards were common in the Teams. Once they had street clothes, they would be good to go.

The only thing they saved was food—they would need what little they had.

No one argued with the LC. Not even the senior chief, who had a few burns and was cut up pretty bad but was managing to stand up by himself. Of course, the senior chief could have had two broken legs and would likely have found a way to stand up by himself. He was one of the toughest sons of bitches John knew, and given that John hung out with Navy SEALs all day, that was saying something.

Senior Chief Baylor was the link—and sometimes shield—between the men and command. If there were problems, the men went to the senior chief. He was their leader, their teacher, their advocate, their confessor, and their punisher all rolled into one. To a man, they would have died for him. There was no one in this world John admired more.

Officers like the LC were part of the team, but their rank kept them apart.

John had mixed feelings about officers. Some were good. Some were bad. But as long as they didn't get in the way or do something to fuck up one of their missions when it needed to be run up the flagpole for approval, he didn't give them too much thought.

He'd known the LC for years and respected the man as much as he did the rank, which wasn't always the case, but he couldn't say he really *knew* him. Officers had to keep themselves apart. They couldn't let personal relationships interfere with or influence their decisions. Taylor could BS along with them, but he always kept himself slightly aloof.

But it wasn't until that moment that John truly understood the weight of the duty and responsibility that fell on an officer's shoulders. Here they were, all half-frozen, in shock, mourning the loss of their brothers, six thousand miles away from their base in Honolulu in a hostile country where, if they were discovered, they would hope to be killed quickly, with no one they could trust to help them, and it was on the LC to get them out of there.

John had no idea whether the LC's plan would work, but he had to give Taylor credit—he didn't miss a beat. He didn't show any hesitation or uncertainty in issuing his orders. They might have been on a training exercise in Alaska rather than in Arctic Siberia.

The LC knew his role, and he was doing it.

John knew his, too.

As just six of the fourteen men who'd entered the prison camp four short hours before had walked out, John took one last look back and forced down the heaviness that rose in his chest. *Good-bye, brother,* he said to himself, and then aloud, "Hey, LC, I hear they have Starbucks all over Moscow now. Think there's one in Vorkuta? I'd fucking kill for a latte."

There was a long pause before the LC picked up the ball and ran with it. "I thought your discerning palate was too refined for chains?"

John grinned. "You know about the choices of beggars, LC."

"You and your fucking girlie drinks," Baylor grumbled. "If you try to order it with nonfat milk, I may have to fucking shoot you myself."

"Good thing for me the LC is making you toss your gun." John patted his rock-hard abs. "You don't get this incredible body without a little sacrifice, Senior. I have a certain standard to uphold. Just because you don't care what the ladies at Hula's—"

"Dynomite," the senior chief cut him off, "shut the fuck up. My head hurts enough as it is. I don't need to hear about your Barbie brigade right now."

But that was exactly what he did need to hear about—what

they all needed to hear about. And they did. For two of the most miserable days he'd ever spent, John drew upon every story he could think of to keep their minds off the brothers they'd left behind.

Good thing he had plenty to draw on. But even he was tired of hearing his own voice by the time they reached Vorkuta. He wasn't sure what he expected of a coal-mining town in Siberia, but it looked pretty much like any medium-sized formerly industrial American city that had reached its height of modernity in the seventies.

They let Spivak, who with his Slavic languages and looks would be the most low-vis, go in first and do a little recon.

When he came back, he turned to John. "Didn't find a Starbucks, Dynomite, but I did see sushi."

"You gotta be shitting me?" It was his second favorite behind Mexican. "Think it would blow cover if I asked for a California roll? Although they probably use that fake crab shit, and avocado in Siberia this time of year might be a little suspect. I know those brown spots are supposed to be safe to eat but . . ."

This time the senior chief wasn't the only one who was telling him to shut the fuck up. And that was as much normal as John could hope for for a while.

One

TEN WEEKS LATER

Brittany Blake tapped the steering wheel with her thumbs and glanced down at the clock in the dashboard. She had the key partially turned in the ignition so it was lit up, and the bright green LED was about the only light on this deserted stretch of road.

Zero dark thirty. That was what they said for twelve thirty a.m. in the military, right? It sounded much more ominous in the movies, which was probably why she'd thought about it. This felt like a movie. A really scary movie where the heroine was doing something supremely stupid, and the entire audience was yelling at the screen for her not to do it.

In other words, every horror movie ever.

Why, yes, waiting for a "drop" in a not-so-great part of town after midnight on a moonless night under a highway overpass in an old warehouse area in a spot much loved by drug dealers and other not-so-law-abiding folks all by her lonesome sounded like a fabulous idea. Nothing could go wrong there.

Geez, she'd have been yelling at the screen herself.

On cue, a loud crashing sound made her—just like a horror movie audience would—jump. Heart now pounding in her throat, she peered into the darkness but didn't see anything. It had sounded like breaking glass. A bottle dropped by a wino nearby maybe?

She hoped that was it, and it hadn't been some serial killer roaming the streets and breaking the windows of stupid reporters sitting in their cars, asking for trouble.

Slowly Brittany relaxed back down into the cloth bucket seat, but her grip on the wheel didn't lighten any.

Sigh. So this definitely wasn't her most brilliant moment, but neither was it the first time she'd been in a sketchy situation. It went along with the job. It was the "investigative" part of the reporting bit.

But if this new source delivered on what they promised, the danger would be worth it—and then some. She had to find out the truth of what had happened to her brother, Brandon.

Tap, tap, tap. The sound of her thumbs hitting the plastic steering wheel mixed with the gentle whirl of the AC, which the longer she sat here was gradually becoming less and less effective, combating the horrible humidity of a warm summer night. She was starting to sweat, literally and figuratively.

Her source was—she glanced down at the clock again—thirty-*two* minutes late.

It can't be a hoax. Please, don't let it be a hoax.

The caller had sounded so insistent, so knowledgeable, so official. She'd give them another ten minutes, and then—

Who was she kidding? She'd wait all night if she had to. She needed this. She hated to use the word "desperate," but if the proverbial shoe fit . . .

She *was* desperate. She needed something concrete to prove that her suspicions were correct: that her brother, Brandon, was part of a top secret Navy SEAL Team (along the lines of the now not-so-secret-anymore SEAL Team Six) who had gone on a mission and not come back.

"The Lost Platoon," she had dubbed them in her articles, after the famous Lost Legion of Rome. Coincidentally—and eerily—they'd both been numbered nine.

She'd thought the title was catchy, and it had certainly cap-
tured the public's attention. The two articles she'd written so far
had proved wildly popular, after being picked up by the Associ-
ated Press, Reuters, and other news organizations worldwide.

Which had turned out to be a double-edged sword. It was
great in that it got her the attention she wanted and put pressure on the government and military to explain what had happened, but it also increased the pressure on her to come up with
something more than a solid hunch from witness interviews.
Preferably a few facts that could be substantiated. Editors liked
those. Go figure.

The fact that her brother hadn't called two months ago on
the anniversary of their parents' deaths when he'd done so
every year for eleven years might have convinced her that
something had happened to him, but her boss wanted more.

That she and Brandon hadn't been close didn't matter. Her
brother wouldn't have let that day go unacknowledged. No
matter what clandestine operation he'd been deployed on that
the government didn't want anyone to know about, he would
have called or contacted her in some way.

She was so certain of it that she'd flown to Hawaii, where
she knew he was stationed, to demand answers.

Of course, at first the navy refused to talk to her. When it
became obvious she wasn't going to give up, they'd taken the
ignorance route: "You must be mistaken. Your brother is not
stationed here," and her personal favorite, "SEAL Team Nine?
We don't have a team with that number."

Right. And yet they had every other number between one
and ten?

She had found some people who were willing to talk to her.
Most were off the record, which only made her more certain
she was onto something.

But when she'd presented proof of her brother's being stationed there in the form of a handful of very attractive blondes
she found at a dive bar called Hula's who recognized Brandon
and the three other men with him in the single recentish photo
she had of him—she hadn't seen her brother in five years, but
some things apparently never changed—the stony-faced-looking

officers who'd been denying they'd ever seen him before suddenly made an abrupt about-face and claimed that the information was "classified."

Which was pretty much like holding up a bright red cape in front of an angry bull—Brittany being the angry bull—making her even more determined to find out the truth.

She'd done enough research into America's secret soldiers—although SEALs weren't technically soldiers but sailors—to know that they could be embedded for months on training ops or deployments.

But that wasn't what was going on here. She *knew* that something had happened to Brandon and his team—something bad—and the military was trying to cover it up. And she wasn't the only one at the base who thought that. *Proving* it, however, was something else.

The wall of secrecy had gone up, and she'd returned home to DC to try to topple it from a different direction. But so far the navy and the government had ignored her articles. She had to come up with something they couldn't ignore.

She wanted answers. If her brother had died—and every bone in her body told her he had—she wanted to know why. She wasn't going to let them sweep his sacrifice under the rug and cover up whatever mess they'd made. Not this time. She wanted the truth, and she was going to find it. She owed Brandon that at least.

Even if it meant sitting in her car for half the night in a not-so-wonderful part of town, waiting for information that sounded too good to be true. But the handwritten note that had been dropped in her apartment mail slot had promised "proof of what had happened to her brother's platoon."

She started to glance down at the clock again when the beam of approaching headlights reflected in her rearview mirror sent her pulse shooting through her chest again. Temporarily blinded, she looked around over her shoulder, but her entire car was filled with light as the car slowly came right up behind her.

At the last minute, the car pulled alongside her. It was a black town car. The kind favored by government officials and airport transport companies everywhere.

Her heart was thumping hard now. This was it. This had to be it.

When the back passenger door was even with her driver's door, the car came to a stop. Slowly, just like in the movies, the back heavily tinted window started to lower. Fortunately, unlike in the movies, the barrel of a gun aimed in her direction didn't appear.

She lowered her window as well.

It was too dark to see inside the other car, but she could barely contain her excitement when a large manila envelope was passed to her. She caught sight of a medium-sized gloved hand—which, as it was about eight hundred degrees, must have been to hide anything identifying—and a dark wool-clad arm with the telltale gold stripe around the sleeve edge of a military uniform before the window started back up.

"Wait!" Brittany said.

The window stopped with a few-inch gap at the top.

"How can I contact you?" she asked.

There was a long pause. Brittany thought they weren't going to answer, but just as the window started to climb again, someone said in a low voice, "You can't. I'll contact you."

The car pulled away before the window even had a chance to fully close. Despite the effort to conceal their identity, Brittany was fairly certain it had been a woman.

She tried to make out the plates as the car drove off, but it was too dark. She flipped on her headlights just in time to see the government plates with *D* and a few numbers with either a 25 or 26 at the end. She was pretty sure *D* stood for Department of Defense.

Jackpot! This had to be legit. She pressed the overhead button for the interior light and practically ripped open the envelope.

It was a thin stack—only about four or five pages—but any initial disappointment about size slipped away as she started to flip through the pages.

Oh my God, oh my God, oh my God kept running through her head as she saw the satellite images, heavily redacted deployment order, and news article about a large explosion in Siberia picked up by our satellites last May that the Russians had claimed was a missile test. She recalled seeing the story, but as Russians testing weapons these days was not exactly unusual, she hadn't paid it much mind.

She was looking at the redacted deployment order for something called "Naval Warfare Special Deployment Group" (was that a covert name for Team Nine?) when the sound of a very loud muffler reminded her where she was.

She had that horrible moment when she turned the key and the car didn't start right away. Oh God, please tell her she hadn't killed the battery with the AC! But fortunately on the second try, the engine roared to life, and she whipped a U-ey to retrace her steps out of here.

Anxious to study the docs in more detail, she headed downtown to her office rather than to the hovel that she called an apartment across town. Her office was actually more of a cubicle, and the fact that it was less depressing than her home spoke volumes about their relative importance in her life.

She was so excited and trying to order the thoughts racing through her mind that it took her a while to realize someone was following her.

Brittany noticed the car behind her when she exited the interstate onto Massachusetts Avenue, heading toward the downtown headquarters of the DC News Organization (DCNO), which, among other media holdings, included her present employer, the *DC Chronicle*.

There weren't many cars on the road, which was why she noticed the headlights pulling off behind her. But it wasn't until she squeaked through the yellow light at Seventh by the Carnegie Library, and the car sped through behind her, that she felt the distinctive prickle at her neck.

Her heart took an extra beat or two as her eyes darted between the road and her rearview mirror. She couldn't make out the make and model of the car, but she guessed an American sedan similar to those used by the police.

Could it be an undercover cop? But why would they be following her. *Was* anyone following her or was she just being paranoid?

Telling herself to calm down, she switched lanes and flipped on her signal, indicating that she was going to take a left at the next block.

The car behind her did the same.

A spike of adrenaline shot through her. She waited for a car approaching in the opposite direction to pass and made her turn. She was about to take an immediate left again into the circular driveway of a big hotel, when the car behind her suddenly moved out of the turn lane and continued straight.

She let out a long breath, not realizing she'd been holding it. Good God, the meeting earlier tonight must have gotten to her more than she realized. She was now officially imagining things.

The heavy pounding of her heart came back down as she continued down the street a few blocks, turned right, and then took another right into the parking lot underneath the nondescript seventies office building.

In the old days, a paper like the *Chronicle* would have been housed in an old stately building. But with the advent of the Internet and online news, those days were long gone. As many papers in this country were, the *Chronicle* was fighting to hang on.

They were alike in that regard.

It might not have been the most prestigious paper in DC, or the most widely circulated, but it was respected, and coming from where she'd been, that was enough.

Brittany found a space near one of the stairwells on the lower level of the garage and pulled in to park. The elevators in the building took forever, but she liked to take the stairs for the exercise.

She'd been slacking off in the workout arena since she'd moved back to DC and started at the *Chronicle* in January. At five foot three-ish—and what had her friend called it? "Athletically curvy?"—with not a lot of time to cook and taste buds that belonged to a teenage boy, she didn't have a lot of room to mess around and needed all the staircases she could get.

After sliding the manila envelope into the nylon messenger bag that she used as a briefcase and purse—she'd had it since college (thus the Georgetown Tigers black and orange), and it was not only low-profile but basically indestructible—she slung the bag over her shoulder as she got out of the car. There were only a few cars left in the garage at this time of night, and the door closed with a slam that echoed in the cement cavern.

She fumbled with the key fob to lock the doors and swore. Crap, she'd left her phone inside. After opening the door, she reached back inside to grab the phone. Before shutting the door again, she decided to toss the lightweight sweater she wore over her sleeveless top into the backseat.

DCNO was cheap, and it cut any flow of cool air into the building at six p.m. sharp, meaning that even after midnight it was hot and humid even in an underground cement garage.

That was one of the problems with the South and the East Coast in the summer—cold rooms inside and hot and humid outside. It seemed like she was always taking clothes off and putting them back on a few minutes later.

She might have made a dirty joke about that statement if her love life wasn't so pathetic. Weather was the only reason her clothes came off lately. A few minutes or not.

But maybe that would change tomorrow. She'd bitten the bullet and set up her first date using the app her friends told her about. The guy was superhot in his picture, which made her think he must be too good to be true.

She'd just gotten herself all settled and was about to lock the doors when she saw a shadow move behind her in the reflection of the car window.

A spike of adrenaline shot through her again. Fear took her pulse along with it. She could practically hear the pounding of her heart as the figure came toward her.

Oh God. She *had* been followed.

Maybe it was because it was the second time she was experiencing panic that night, but her head was clearer, and she knew immediately what to do.

Thank God, she still had her keys in her hand. What was the range? Ten feet? Five? She slid off the safety lock, put her finger on the nozzle, and spun around.

Ready to find
your next great read?

Let us help.

Visit prh.com/nextread

Penguin
Random
House